For Ian

THE BLUE MEN

With very best wishes

[illegible]

HOTEL ST KILDA

THE BLUE MEN

MICHAEL KNAGGS

Matador
9 Priory Business Park,
Wistow Road, Kibworth Beauchamp,
Leicestershire. LE8 0RX
Tel: 0116 279 2299
Email: books@troubador.co.uk
Web: www.troubador.co.uk/matador
Twitter: @matadorbooks

ISBN 978 1800462 816

British Library Cataloguing in Publication Data.
A catalogue record for this book is available from the British Library.

Printed and bound in the UK by TJ Books Limited, Padstow, Cornwall
Typeset in 11pt Aldine401 BT by Troubador Publishing Ltd, Leicester, UK

Matador is an imprint of Troubador Publishing Ltd

For Carol

Also by Michael Knaggs

Catalyst
Heaven's Door
Lost Souls

For a list of characters featuring in the four books of the *Hotel St Kilda* series, see the author's website:

www.michaelknaggs.co.uk

If I had to choose between betraying my country and betraying my friend, I hope I should have the guts to betray my country.

E. M. Forster

PROLOGUE

January

The two men approached the darkened building, their feet crunching across the gravel driveway. A solitary light shone in the curtained window to the right of the entrance. The single-storey property, a legacy of the 1960s with its rendered walls and metal-framed windows, looked bland and functional except for an open, rustic-brick porchway sheltering a carved wooden door that hinted at the possibility of grandeur within.

The older of the two men pressed the bell on the wall next to the doorway. A shadow passed across the window curtain and footsteps sounded inside. The door was pulled open by a tall, slim man in his thirties, wearing a white work-coat over a pale-blue shirt, grey trousers and black tie, who waved them inside with a sweep of his arm. He clicked a switch on the wall and two chandeliers lit up a long, high and ornate entrance area that had one oak-panelled door off to the right, two to the left and another directly ahead of them. The one on the right, leading to the room where the light had been visible from outside, had the word 'OFFICE' painted on it in gold, inset lettering. 'RECEPTION' and 'KITCHEN' announced the functions of the two rooms on the left. The walls were panelled in dark wood up to a dado rail, with textured wallpaper above it in pale green. A patterned rug edged with gold tassels covered almost the whole of the polished floor, leaving just a few centimetres visible around the perimeter. Except for the absence of a wide, curving staircase leading off from it, the room had the appearance of the entrance hall of a stately home.

The man introduced himself as Sergeant Glen Crompton and the two visitors showed their ID badges.

"This way, please," he said, and led them through the untitled door in the end wall. Another light switch revealed a small area with a pair of full-length, heavy curtains pulled across wall-to-wall in front of them. A deep-pile carpet felt soft under their feet and the walls were draped in dusky-pink velvet fabric. Sergeant Crompton pressed a button near the switch and the curtains drew apart to reveal a glass partition separating them from the rest of the room.

"This is where we would normally conduct the viewing, sir," he said, addressing the older man. "And we can arrange that, if you wish, or..."

"Lead on, Sergeant, we're big boys, y'know?"

"Yes, sir." The sergeant smiled. He closed the curtains and led them out through another panelled door to the left. A strip light came on automatically, illuminating a square windowless room, devoid of furniture, with bare walls and a tiled floor. Its starkness was accentuated by comparison with the rooms they had just passed through.

"This way, please."

Through another door, the descent from opulence to functionality was complete, and with it a distinct drop in temperature. The brightly lit room they entered was a large working area, approximately ten metres square with a terrazzo floor and a pair of exterior double doors at the far end. To the right a metal-and-glass partition wall, with a single door half-way along, ran the full length of the room, screening off a separate area, currently in darkness. To the left was a line of ten two-metre-high stainless-steel refrigerators. The sergeant took an electric scissor-jack trolley from a line of four, then led them to the far end of the room to the fridge closest to the outer wall.

"All the fridges are kept at a temperature of two degrees Celsius, except this end one," he said, as if he were addressing a group of trainees. "This is maintained at a couple of degrees lower, around freezing, and used in cases where we might need to keep them longer or where there is advanced decomposition."

He pulled open the fridge door, releasing a gentle flow of colder air into the room and revealing five shelves, each holding a metal tray on rollers. He adjusted the height of the trolley to align with the second lowest shelf and guided its tray onto it. He walked around to the far side and pulled the white sheet down to the cadaver's waist.

"Male, mid-forties, ninety kilos, one metre eighty-five – that's half an inch short of six foot – B-negative."

"Tattoo?"

"This side." The sergeant pointed to the right shoulder and the two visitors leaned over to see the image of an upward-pointing sword with the words 'BY STRENGTH AND GUILE' on a banner around its hilt. The older man nodded towards the white sheet.

"Please, if you wouldn't mind." The sergeant removed the sheet. "Thank you, could you give us a few minutes?"

"Certainly, sir."

The sergeant left the room and the two men stood in silence, their eyes fixed on the body, their breath condensing above it in the dropping temperature.

The older of the two men was in his mid-sixties, tall and barrel-chested, with a huge moustache and mottled red highlights to his cheeks. He wore a mustard-coloured tweed jacket with a matching waistcoat, and a yellow-and-blue striped tie over a cream shirt. His trousers were light brown with razor-sharp creases and rested neatly on gleaming tan brogues. He looked altogether too bright and flamboyant for this place of death. His companion was twenty years his junior, the same height but slim and broad-shouldered. He wore a long, black leather jacket over a dark polo shirt and jeans and clutched in both hands the black baseball cap he had removed as he entered the building.

They studied the body for a long time before the older man spoke.

"So, what do you think?"

"I think yes."

"Right, let's go."

Five minutes later, they stepped outside into the moonlit night and crunched again over the gravel to the Range Rover in its camouflage livery. They climbed into the back.

"Take us home, Corporal," said the man in tweed.

"Yes, sir." The young woman in the driver's seat started the engine and pulled onto the narrow country road. "I take it you don't mean all the way, sir."

He snorted a laugh. "Perhaps not, Vicky. I think we'd better stick with Plan A."

She drove a few kilometres to where a collection of temporary floodlights lit up the corner of a field. They entered through a farm gate and stopped beside a silver-grey Cessna Citation passenger jet. The two men and the woman got out of the Range Rover and climbed the four steps up into the cabin, where the co-pilot awaited them.

"A success, sir?" he asked.

"I think so, yes."

The co-pilot pulled up the steps, sealing the cabin door, and tightened the locking wheel before joining his colleague in the cockpit. They taxied towards another lighted area a few hundred metres away across the field before turning through 180 degrees.

"Seatbelts, please, lady and gentlemen."

The Cessna sprang forward and made a smooth take-off over the lights around the Range Rover.

CHAPTER ONE

Sunday, 9 July

The two women peered up at the skyline high above and behind the cottage, both shading their eyes with a raised hand from the low sun over to their right.

"How did you manage to see something that far away?"

The speaker was the older of the two; tall, slender, in her early forties and beautiful, with golden-blonde hair.

"I was watching a group of red deer through the bins just below the ridge, and they suddenly scattered, shot off in all directions." The younger woman was similar in height and build to her companion but more than twenty years younger and with hair that was white-blonde and straight, hanging loose behind to the middle of her back. "When I looked where they'd been without the bins, I just spotted two heads – silhouettes – right on the skyline, sort of bobbing up and down as they dropped out of sight."

"So, they were walking away from us, that's why they dropped out of sight. Right?"

"But where would they be walking *from*? This is the only place for miles. We'd have seen them climbing the hillside. They must be on this side of the ridge heading towards us." She raised the binoculars again. "We just can't see them against the rocks and heather."

"So, who...?"

"Hold it," the younger woman interrupted. "I've got them. Dropping down along the edge of the burn."

She passed the binoculars to her companion, pointing to where a rough track ran parallel to the course of the waterway.

"Yes, I see them. Two people, can't make out any detail. Could just be walkers, of course."

"Unlikely. There are no trails around here that I know of. Do you?"

"Well, no, but freedom of access and all that… and they're as likely to be walkers as anything else." She lowered the glasses and frowned. "Aren't they? I mean, what else could they be?"

"I don't know, but I don't feel good about this at all after what's happened. Perhaps we're next and someone's come to finish the job."

The older woman gave a little shiver. "Don't even joke about that."

"What have we got, a shotgun and a hunting rifle, right? Are they loaded?"

"Just what exactly do you have in mind?" The other was wide-eyed with horror.

"We're not going to make this easy for them if I'm right."

A baby cried and they looked towards the cottage.

"I'll go," a voice from inside shouted.

CHAPTER TWO

Six weeks earlier

Friday, 26 May

Even at 5.30 in the morning, the public areas at Gardermoen Airport to the north of Oslo were thronged with people. Holidaymakers getting an early start for Mediterranean resorts, and others boarding connecting flights to further destinations, mingled with business people on day trips to European capitals and other major cities.

A group of seven men was occupying a seating area close to the moving walkways as they waited for their flight to be called. The six who were travelling had already checked in and had their luggage routed through to their final destination. They were all in their twenties, olive-skinned and wearing business suits, shirts and ties. Each carried a laptop case and small shoulder bag. The seventh man was in his forties, tall and striking-looking, and dressed casually in jeans and a white linen jacket. He was the focus of the others' attention.

"One last time," he spoke quietly in Arabic. "Your scheduled arrival time at Schiphol is 8.15 and you have a layover there of four hours and twenty minutes. Do not go through passport control but stay air-side for that period before boarding the onward flight. You are in Amsterdam to attend a meeting and will go to the business reception desk to be escorted to the meeting room.

"There, you will be joined by Amir and Fawaz, who will provide you with documents you may need. These comprise detailed agendas, reports and sets of data for the separate meetings you are supposed to be attending in and around Chicago. Hopefully you won't need these, but if you get the wrong officials on Passport Control at O'Hare, the papers will help you explain your visit. Any calls to verify your stories made to contact numbers which appear on the documents will be answered by our people posing as representatives of the fake companies. You already have the booking details for the separate hotels where you will stay the first night if they want to check them.

"Your flight to O'Hare leaves Amsterdam at 12.35 and arrives at ten past two in the afternoon, Chicago time. That gives you nearly nine hours on the flight, which I suggest you use to make yourselves familiar with the documents then get as much sleep as possible. You are travelling business class, but not together so as not to attract attention from other passengers." He looked around the group and smiled. "Six handsome studs all sitting together would be just too memorable." The others relaxed into smiles and laughter. He turned to his left. "Ahmed, take us through what happens next."

The young man leaned forward in his seat, speaking without hesitation.

"When we disembark at O'Hare, we stay separated for the rest of the day. After we get through immigration and customs, we take the monorail out of Terminal 1, three of us to Terminal 3 and three to Terminal 5. At these terminals we will each be met by different drivers, who will display our names, hand-written on a board which will also show the name of the company we are supposed to be visiting. They will drive us to the separate hotels and provide us with details of where we will be meeting up the following day."

He stopped at the sound of the announcement requesting passengers for their flight to go to the boarding gate.

"Excellent – word perfect, Ahmed," said the older man, holding up his hands for them to remain seated. "You will each dine in your hotel and get an early night. You will need it; remember, Chicago is seven hours behind us, so it will already be after nine in the evening, Oslo time, when you land." He stood up and his six companions collected their bags and got to their feet, reaching into their jacket pockets for their boarding passes. "Any questions before you leave?"

The six young men exchanged glances. Ahmed smiled. "Just one, please. We would like to know why they call you 'The Shadow'."

The others shuffled their feet with some muted chuckles of embarrassment. The man smiled.

"It's the name they gave me in Turkey after the attack in Istanbul. There's an ancient Turkish belief that, if a man is evil enough, his shadow alone can bring death and disaster. It doesn't make any sense, of course, because for the shadow to be present the person casting it has got to be there as well, but the world seems to like the title, so I'm stuck with it. Although we are not evil, are we? We are soldiers."

He shook hands with them, looking from one to the other, his eyes resting on each.

"You cannot fail, my young friends. You are the best."

He watched them walk away for their short flight before the long haul to their final destination. He shook his head, knowing that, if things went to plan, it really would be their final destination.

CHAPTER THREE

Sunday, 28 May

The couple stood together on the edge of the pebbled shore, hand in hand, looking out across the water. The man was of average height and build, with a youthful, smiling face, which belied his thirty-two years. He was dressed in a lightweight, dark-blue fleece, jeans and trainers. The girl, a couple of years younger, was of a similar height, slim and pretty with a light-brown ponytail pouring out through the gap at the back of her baseball cap. She was wearing the same outfit as her companion except that her fleece was purple.

She let go of his hand and reached down to pick up a pebble, choosing a round flat one and taking a step away from him to the side.

"God, we're not going to start chucking stones into the water, are we?" he said. "We're supposed to be on a cultural journey of discovery, not messing about on a beach."

"Skimming not 'chucking'," she replied, crouching low and hurling the stone across the surface. "Pretty good, eh… I reckon six or seven."

"I counted two, maybe three at the most."

"Oh, come *on*."

"Alright, four, then."

They laughed as she grabbed his arm and pulled him towards the water. "Right, let's see if you bounce when I try it with you."

"Okay, okay, I surrender. Anyway, let's walk… and discover. There's a great little craft shop with a café round the back."

"Photograph first," she said as they walked the few metres back up to the road which ran along the shore in front of the line of clean, white buildings. "Stand against the rail so I can get the buildings and the water in the same shot and look at me, no dramatic gazing out to sea." He leaned on the rail and beamed at the camera, eyes wide and staring. "And try not to look too simple."

"Make sure you get the shop in," he said. "That way we'll know where it was taken."

She lowered the camera and screwed up her eyes. "Look, who's the photographer here? Just know your place, will you? I didn't come all this way to get involved in a demarcation dispute."

"Point taken." The man raised his hands to acknowledge defeat. "Just as long as I get to write the caption."

"We'll see," she said, raising the camera again. It clicked several times. She turned a complete circle, taking several shots of the street and across the water before putting it back in its case, which was clipped to the belt of her jeans. "Okay, let's go."

She reached for his hand again.

*

The barman turned up the volume on the small television tucked in amongst the line of single malts.

"That okay?" He called across to the group in the corner.

"That's fine, thanks." A hush fell over the room as attention focussed on the news item.

"Earlier today, President John Weston arrived at Heathrow in Air Force One for a meeting with the Prime Minister and a number of senior defence officials before flying on to Oslo tomorrow en route to Berlin for the G20 meeting. This is the first time the President has visited the UK since the tragic death of his wife, Marsha, following a terrorist incident eighteen months ago. He is expected to attend a private dinner this evening with a small number of his own invited guests. It is thought they will include, among others, the Home Secretary, Jackie Hewlett, the Justice Minister, Jonathan Latiffe, and the Ministerial Director of Justice, Grace Goody.

"Senior Fire Service officials say they are concerned that the hot weather across the country may lead to a repeat of the moorland fires..."

"Thanks, Archie, you can turn it down now," one of the corner group called over. The barman obliged and conversations resumed spontaneously as if the same knob on the TV was controlling the voices of the people in the bar.

"Right." The young man turned back to his girlfriend. "Where were we up to?"

They were seated, side by side, in the cosy little bar of the hotel where they were staying. The bar itself stretched the full length of the room and tables and chairs covered most of the floor area, allowing just enough room for customers to move between them. Every table was occupied, many with rucksacks stashed under them. Several pairs of walking poles had been leaned against the walls round the room. The couple had been checking through the photographs the girl had taken.

"I thought I said, 'try not to look simple'."

"You said, 'try not to look *too* simple'. I think I got it just about right."

"At least the others are okay," she said. "You can only be as good as your subject matter."

"I reckon they're right up to your usual standard," he said. "No praise can be higher than that."

She laughed and slipped her arm through his. "Go on, you're just saying that." She felt him tense. "What's wrong?"

"Just go back to the ones with me on," he said.

"Okay." She flicked back through to the start of the half-dozen pictures with him leaning on the rail. "They won't get any better just by looking at them," she said.

His brow furrowed in concentration.

"I want to check something." He took the camera from her. "Wait here, I'll just be a few minutes."

"Why, what…?"

"Just a few minutes, honestly."

He rushed from the bar, leaving her looking, wide-eyed, after him and took the narrow stairs two at a time up to the first floor, bursting into their room and leaving the door open and swinging on its hinges. He pulled his laptop from the top drawer in the small chest by the window and connected it up to the camera, downloading the images into a new folder. Once completed, he disconnected the camera and went to an existing file on the laptop, bringing up a familiar picture onto the screen. He copied the picture and pasted it onto a blank page in Word, before opening the new folder and selecting a photo from the ones that featured him holding the rail. He then copied that and pasted it next to the first one on the same page.

He let out a gasp. The pictures were almost identical except for the person in the foreground. He leaned back and shook his head. An amazing coincidence, he thought, with a wry smile. He saved the new Word document and went to close down the laptop. Then he froze again, the frown returning.

Something was wrong.

He studied the two images again. What was it? What was different, apart from the man in the picture? He went back to the original photographs and clicked on to Picture Manager, then traced round the outlines and deleted the person in each so he could study the background without distraction. He then copied them again, placing them side by side as before.

There was a noise behind him.

"What's going on?" the girl said. "I could have scored three times down there if…"

"Wait." He raised his hand to stop her, because now he knew.

There *wasn't* a difference between the two pictures.

They were exactly the same.

That's what was wrong.

⋆

Monday, 29 May

Immediately after breakfast, the couple set off walking together, heading north along the road leading out of the town, hand in hand at first until the girl took out her camera to capture some of the late spring flora along the roadside. After about a kilometre, just past the golf club, they turned left down a rough track towards the side of the loch. The track finished 200 metres or so from the narrow beach and they picked their way through the rough grass to the water's edge. They turned right and headed north again along the shoreline.

Four small boats had been pulled up above the beach onto the low bank, their oars laid lengthways along the bottom of each. An elderly man in faded blue overalls and a woollen hat pulled down low over his white hair was sitting on the bank about twenty metres away beside the furthest one, repairing a lobster creel. In a circle around the nearest boat, a number of metre-long plastic stakes had been stuck in the ground with the remains of blue-and-white tape still attached to them and flapping gently in the breeze. The young man grabbed one of the pieces of tape and read the words on it – "Police Crime Scene – Keep Out".

The girl's camera clicked away.

He called across to the man with the creel. "Excuse me. Is this the boat?"

"Aye, that's the one. But I canna believe anyone would ha' taken it that far. Not at that time o' year. You wouldna get me out there in that wee thing. They had to tow it back wi' a bigger boat, and that was wi' the wind and tide in favour."

The young man looked down at the boat. It was completely open, no more than three and a half metres long, with a single wooden seat across the middle and rowlocks for one pair of oars.

"I see what you mean."

"Aye, the man must ha' been brilliant or mad, that's all I can say. 'Tis nae wonder the blue men got him."

The girl took a few more pictures before putting her camera away in its case. Then they joined hands and continued along the shoreline.

"Thank you. Bye," she called over her shoulder as they left.

They walked in silence for a full minute before the girl spoke again.

"It doesn't make any sense."

Her companion sighed and shook his head. "None at all.

"And who are the blue men?"

"No idea."

CHAPTER FOUR

Monday, 5 June

The Dog and Duck public house was over 250 years old, dating back to when Meadow Village was first established. The double-doors at the front opened directly into the main bar, which was the extent of the original hostelry. Since then it had been tastefully and seamlessly extended, with the addition of a smaller bar at the rear and a large dining room off the main bar to the right. There were open fireplaces in both bars and the dining room, and the place retained its late-eighteenth-century feel throughout.

The young couple entered at just a few minutes after eight o'clock and looked around the crowded main bar. They were both dressed in jeans and tee shirts; the man was carrying a laptop case.

"Tony!"

He turned to where the shout had come from. The man behind the bar who smiled across at him, was tall, broad-shouldered, slim-waisted and with short-cropped fair hair. He was wearing a tee shirt which did nothing to disguise the definition of the muscular torso it struggled to contain.

"Hi, Jed. I'm looking for George."

"He's waiting through there. I've reserved the Corporate Hospitality Suite for you."

"The what?" the girl asked.

"A.k.a. the snug," Tony said. "Great for meetings, it can take up to six people."

"Less than six today. You'll know what I mean in a minute. Go through and I'll come to get your order for drinks."

"Thanks, Jed. This is Rebecca, by the way." He turned to the girl. "Jed Smithers, landlord. And to save you asking me later, yes, he does work out."

Rebecca smiled. "I can see that." She took Jed's offered hand to shake. Jed leaned forward across the bar and gently kissed her fingers. Rebecca giggled. "Are you sure you need me at this meeting?"

"Yes, definitely."

The Dog and Duck's Corporate Hospitality Suite was a small alcove, about two and a half metres square. It had a narrow table down the centre, with two chairs at either side of it and one at each end. The two men who got to their feet to greet Tony and Rebecca could not have been more different.

George Holland was around five and a half feet tall, in his late sixties and almost bald. The impact of this last feature was mitigated to some extent by having the band of hair which circled the back of his head clipped very short. His handshake was firm and friendly.

"Hello, Tony. Great to see you again."

"And you, George. How are you keeping?"

"Not at all bad," George said. "And you must be Rebecca." He shook the girl's hand but without the landlord's embellishment. "Very pleased to meet you."

"You too," she said.

The couple turned in near wonder to George's companion. The man was in his mid-fifties, two metres tall, broad and muscular with a trim waist and slightly greying hair. The smallness of the snug and George's own modest stature made him seem impossibly large.

"And my little friend here is Chief Detective Inspector David Gerrard, retired. As you can see, he's really let himself go since he gave up work. And this," George said, turning to David, "is the famous Tony Dobson, although he would be nothing without me – he made his name reporting on my UK tour a few years ago."

Tony and Rebecca smiled.

"Well if George has finished insulting us," David said, shaking hands with them, "perhaps we should start. He usually falls asleep about half past eight."

They laughed and sat down. Jed appeared and took their order for drinks.

"Right," Tony said with a conspiratorial smile. "I suppose you're all wondering why I've called you here tonight? I think that's how I'm supposed to start." He turned to David. "First, thank you for coming, David. George told me about you moving into Meadow Village and it was too good a connection to miss."

"You're very welcome; I can't wait to hear what you've got. George tells me you've been doing some detective work yourself."

"Just by accident, initially. I'm sure you know that Tom Brown and I were good friends. That wasn't always the case, as George will tell you, but we became very close during his campaign for the NJR. So, I took more than a passing interest when he went missing last November, now presumed drowned. In fact, I kept a record on here…" he tapped the laptop "… of everything that was reported from the moment he became a suspect in the deaths of the drug users right up to when they drew a line under the search at the end of last year. I was planning to write his biography, but I may think again about the theme of the book based on what we've got and depending on what *you* think about what we've got.

"Last month Becca and I had a three-week sailing holiday, exploring the west coast of Scotland, starting at Greenock and following the coast – including circuits of Mull and Skye – and finishing at Scrabster, not far from John o' Groats on the north coast. We left the boat there and flew back home a few days ago. One of the places we stayed over was Ullapool, which is on its own miles from anywhere, well up towards the north-west tip of the country. And Becca took some photos while we were there."

He slid the laptop out of its case and switched it on. When the menu appeared, he opened a few files then diminished all but one before placing it at the end of the table so they could all see the screen. The picture showed Tony leaning against a rail which separated the road from the beach.

"This is me, trying not to look too simple…"

"And failing miserably," Rebecca put in, making them laugh.

"Well, I tried. Anyway, that was taken on the twenty-eighth of May, a few days before the end of the holiday. It's looking south from the Edinburgh Wool Shop near the north end of the town with Loch Broom on the right. Now look at this one."

He opened another picture, taken from the same place showing the same scene. There was also a man in the new picture, looking slumped and dishevelled, leaning on the same rail, but in a different position, looking across the loch.

"Recognise anybody?" Tony asked.

"Tom Brown," George said. "That's an amazing coincidence."

"Isn't it? That photo appeared on news channels and in the press at the end of November last year. It was taken – allegedly – on the twenty-eighth of October by a tourist who didn't realise the man in the picture was Tom Brown until nearly a month later, hence the delay in it coming to light. And I say *allegedly* because, when I looked at the two pictures, something didn't seem quite right." He reached across and opened another image. "So, I copied the two pictures and put them side by side. Then…"

David held up his hand. "Wait," he said. "Let me see." He studied the two images for about fifteen seconds before pointing to the photo of Tom Brown. "I would say that's a fake. Or at least it's not what it's supposed to be."

"Bingo!" Tony said, sitting back in his chair.

George was screwing up his eyes and frowning in concentration. "Go on," he said. "I give in."

"Look at the trees," Tony said. "There are plenty of Scotch pine and other evergreen, but most of them are deciduous. These were supposedly taken seven months apart, but in both photographs the trees look exactly the same. So, that one of Tom can't have been taken in October. Now, at first, I thought it could *just possibly* have been a genuine mistake and whoever took it might have got their dates mixed up. I know Tom was up in Scotland earlier last year. I'm not aware that he went to Ullapool, but I guess he could have done. Even so, assuming it's a digital image, the date would be on the caption under the thumbnail. But look at this." He opened another picture. "This photo of Tom Brown appeared in the press shortly after his son's death. It was taken after a day-long drinking session somewhere in Woking,"

The picture showed Tom leaning unsteadily on the bonnet of a car. Tony diminished it to half size and opened the picture of Tom in Ullapool next to it. His image was exactly the same in both pictures.

"So, you were right the first time, David. It's a deliberate fake. The picture of Tom in Woking superimposed on one taken in Ullapool. The big question is – why?"

"Here's another question," George said. "Well done to you, Tony, for spotting it, but this is schoolboy detective stuff, isn't it? It took David a few seconds to spot the discrepancy; wouldn't the police be expected to see it at the time? When that appeared in the press, the investigation was still open, as I understand; the hunt for Tom was still on."

David shook his head. "I agree, George. I can only put it down to the fact that it fitted exactly with what the police already had. Tom's car was found abandoned in Ullapool, minus a bag that we know he took with him. The bag and most of its contents were found in a boat taken from a village just north of Ullapool. So, there would be no reason to disbelieve the authenticity of a photograph showing he was up there. Not an *excuse* for missing it, just a possible explanation. Do we know where the photo came from, Tony?"

"No. I've checked with the press and various TV channels but no-one has a record of who submitted it. I wondered if the police had released it, although looking at the editorials at the time there was no reference to that. But you mentioned the boat, David, and I give you…" he changed the image on the screen "…Exhibit B."

Rebecca leaned forward.

"This is the boat," she said, "the one found grounded on the Shiants with Mr Brown's stuff in it. It's back where it was taken from now, a little hamlet called Morefield just a couple of kilometres north of Ullapool. You can see it's still got crime-scene tape around it. We assume it must have been examined again once it had been towed back to the mainland and just left there since then. What seems really strange is that someone wanting to get across to… wherever, should leave a town that's full of boats on the off chance of finding one along the shoreline. I mean there's no reason for a stranger to the area to *expect* to find a boat up there."

"But it's an undisputed fact that the boat *was* stolen from there, isn't it?" George asked.

"That's right," David said. "Go on, Rebecca."

"Well, we spoke to an old guy there who was mending crab pots…"

"Lobster creels," Tony put in.

"Thank you, Dobson," Rebecca rolled her eyes, "that makes *all* the difference. Anyway, this guy looked like he'd been around the sea and boats all his life and he said he couldn't believe anyone could have made it to the Shiants in that thing. Not in those exact words, but that was the gist." She looked at Tony, who nodded.

"So, where does that take us?" George asked. They all looked at David, who drew in a long breath before speaking.

"Well, it seems the lobster man was right in that the evidence points to Tom Brown *not* making it to the Shiants. The boat did, but as far as we know he was not on the island so we must assume he fell or was washed overboard on the way. If he'd have *reached* the Shiants and then been picked up from there, he'd have taken his bag with him,"

"But look at the boat, David," Tony said. "I think the man's point was – in fact, he actually said – Tom would have had to be either mad or brilliant to even try. And Tom knew a bit about boats and what they would be capable of."

"So," David said, "what you're saying is it's more than likely – if we believe the old man of the sea – that Tom *didn't* steal the boat and set off across The Minch."

"That's right – well, possible, at least," Tony said. "So, out of three bits of evidence pointing to Tom being up there, there's now some doubt about two of them – the photo and the boat. That still leaves the car, of course. But, if someone was trying to plant evidence that he was in Ullapool, driving his car up there would be an obvious – and easy – thing to do."

They were all quiet for a long time, absorbed in their own thoughts. Then David placed his two hands palm downwards on the table.

"Right," he said. "Here's one scenario. Tom Brown *did* drive his car up to Ullapool. We know, from the incident outside Guildford Magistrates' Court when he confronted Mickey Kadawe, that his mind must have been very disturbed and that was, what, four weeks before he disappeared? And in the meantime, things had got a hell of a lot worse, night after night of drinking himself into oblivion. That's if we can believe what we read in the press."

He raised his eyebrows and looked at Tony, who gave a little laugh.

"So, staying with the same scenario, we don't know *why* he went up there and it's possible he didn't know either. There was nowhere obvious for him to go so anywhere was as good as anywhere else. He wasn't someone who could just disappear in a crowd. He may well have been the best-known person in the UK at that time. But it's unlikely he was heading for the Shiants. There's nothing there for him to live on. If he *did* take the boat, he must have been going to, say, Harris. And in the SBS he must have taken some wild rides in his time. He would most likely have been confident he could make it that far even in that boat. Lobster man was probably right on both counts: he was mad *and* brilliant.

"So that takes care of the car and the boat. And as for the photograph, that's probably the easiest of all to explain. Someone who hears about the links to Ullapool who was there earlier that year – or a previous year – copies a photograph of Tom Brown off the Internet and adds it to one they took on holiday. Simple as that. Just for a laugh or possibly a bit of fame. And we know how easy it is these days to combine digital images to produce something authentic-looking which is almost undetectable. Right, Rebecca?"

"I guess so."

They were silent again for a while before Tony laughed.

"God, I thought I was heading for the scoop of the century and you've just ripped it up. You've just explained everything away."

David smiled. "I've had a lot of practice addressing conspiracy theories with an ex-colleague of mine. But I said that was *one* scenario. I always try to find the most straightforward explanation first and decide how satisfied I am with that before I start dipping into the realms of mystery and imagination."

They all looked at him, waiting for more.

"Come on, David," George said. "Don't keep us hanging. What do you think?"

"Gut feel?" he said. "I think there's more to it. I suggest we get another round of drinks and decide where we look next."

*

"The US President, John Weston, left Paris early this morning, cutting short his tour of European capitals in the wake of the terrorist attack on the Willis Tower in Chicago. Air Force One took off from Charles de Gaulle airport at 4.00 a.m. local time – 3.00 a.m. UK time – and is expected to land at Chicago O'Hare in around two and a half hours at 11.30 a.m. BST. Homeland Security have not yet released any figures as to the number of casualties resulting from the attack, but it is believed that the part of the building damaged by the explosion was largely used for training events and conferences and was occupied by relatively few people at the time. We will, of course, let you know as soon as we have more information."

The twinkling sound of Chopin's *Minute Waltz* jerked David's mind away from the news item on the television and he juggled with his iPhone as he fumbled to accept the call whilst pressing the mute button on the remote.

"Hello, Detective Inspector."

"Hi there," the caller said. "Sorry to phone so early. I hope I didn't wake you up."

"No, not at all. Eight o'clock's not early for me. Just got in after jogging back from the gym. Well, I say jogging, what I really mean is running… but what a pleasant surprise."

"Pleasant, I hope," DI Joannita Cottrell said, "but hardly a surprise. I got your email, so you must have been expecting a call. It sounds very exciting. And this all started with a photograph?"

"A couple of photographs, actually, which should have been very different but were virtually the same."

"And prove Tom Brown was never in Ullapool when he was supposed to be. Right?"

"Wrong. The picture that appeared in the press last year which seemed to prove he *was* there was a fake, but that doesn't mean he *wasn't* there. You're getting ahead of yourself again, girl. The least sniff of a conspiracy and you're straight in."

"But you must feel the same or you wouldn't have emailed me."

"You're right, as it happens. We have a new detective on the block – Mr Tony Dobson, the journalist – and he's come up with a few good points. The photographs in particular, and also some questions about the boat which, supposedly, was used for Brown to make his escape, or whatever he was doing in it."

"And which couldn't possibly have got him that far at that time of year. Right?"

"There you go again, simplifying to the point of inaccuracy. A local fisherman was of the *opinion* that someone taking that particular boat across The Minch would have to be, quote, mad or brilliant, unquote. That wouldn't exclude our man from trying it in what we assume was a precarious state of mind."

"But, added to the dubious photograph, questions arise."

"That's the point; the two things together started Tony thinking and he brought it to me through George Holland. We met at the Dog last night. He's writing a book about Tom Brown – you know they were virtually best friends – but he's thinking he might change the theme in order to ask a few questions. You know, rather than a biography, an investigation into the circumstances of his death, and he said he was hoping to interview your mate DI Waters. I thought you might be able to put in a word and smooth his way. He wouldn't tell Harry he was looking into the case, as such, but would position it as a means of getting the truth from the police – as much as can be publicly shared – and cut through all the rumour and conjecture which flooded the media at the time."

"But Dobson *is* the media. Wouldn't he be able to filter the crap out of the system?"

"Remember Tom Brown's disappearance was front page news for about three months once the statement went out about his involvement in the murders…"

"*Alleged* involvement."

"Alleged involvement – and each new theory contradicted what had gone before – even in the same newspapers. What Tony will say is that he wants to understand just how much is actually *known* about what happened to Brown, bearing in mind that nobody knows everything. And remember, this is just a means of getting Tony a meeting with the CIO on the case."

"A ruse, you mean. You're asking me – a serving police officer – to lie to another serving police officer? I'm surprised at you, DCI Gerrard. That's not how you brought me up."

"That's true, but how I brought you up and how you turned out are two different things. However, I take your point and Tony is experienced enough to get his interview without any smoothing of the way. Incidentally, he has no idea that I'm having this conversation with you, but I know how you have never wavered in your belief in Tom and how close you are to his wife, so I thought you might *want* to be involved."

Jo did not reply for a long time. David waited out the silence.

"Truth is, David, I *do*. I'm tempted to offer to speak to Tony myself – I probably know enough about the case to provide him with what he wants – but it will get messy when people want to know the source of the information. And Tony may want to reveal the source, so people do know it's the truth and not more rumour and hype. I'm wondering whether John Mackay might be the best man for Tony to see. Now that he's retired, he might be more relaxed about sharing information, as much as he can. Can you give me a few days to think about it?"

"Of course, and I'm sure I don't have to say this, but please don't mention it to anyone else. Okay?"

"My lips are sealed."

"Thank you. Anyway, to more important things – how's the incredibly lucky Mr Carter?"

Jo laughed. "Seb's fine, thank you, and *still* looking forward to meeting you. I really can't believe I've failed to get my two favourite men together for so long. Perhaps I'm not sure I can deal with all that masculinity in one place at the same time."

"But it's working out okay still? Not seeing too much of each other, like you thought might be a problem…"

"Until you stepped in and put me right."

"Well I didn't like to say."

"No, it's fine, thanks. Helps a lot working on different cases. Some days we don't meet at all until we get home. And how's your lady friend?"

"She's not exactly my lady friend."

"Which one isn't she, then, a lady or a friend?"

"Well okay, she *is* my lady friend and she is very well, thank you. Really pretty, excellent company and we are very fond of each other. There, now you know."

"I only enquired after her health. If you're telling me all that other stuff to make me jealous, then you just succeeded. Go on, tell me what she's got that I haven't got?"

"It's more about what she *hasn't* got that you *have*."

"Do explain."

"Well, a boyfriend who's exceptionally good-looking, has a body like a Greek god – allegedly – and who's half my age. How's that for a start?"

"Point taken. What else?"

"A job that's a hundred and fifty miles away."

"Well okay, then. I guess I just assumed that I'd always be the sole female focus of your affection – daughter Linny excepted, of course."

David laughed. "And so you are, DI Cottrell. Listen, you and Marie should get on really well. You never stop talking and she hardly says a word. I put that down to her being constantly in awe of me."

"Well I'm dying to meet her. Perhaps the four of us should have a meal at the Ye Olde London. It would be really good to go back there."

"Indeed, it would. Anyway, Jo, I'll let you go and await your call. Take care."

"You too, David. Bye."

CHAPTER FIVE

Thursday, 8 June

The woman turned onto her side, reached for her glasses and peered at the clock on her bedside table. The display said 05:45. Perhaps he would still call, she thought; she had told him any time, day or night, would be okay. They were six hours behind London, so there was time yet. She rolled onto her back and stretched her arms and legs. She was naked. That wasn't how she usually slept but that's how she wanted to be if he did call.

Swinging her legs out of bed, she went through to the ensuite, turned on the shower and looked at herself in the full-length mirror on the back of the door. Pretty good for forty-two years, she decided. Breasts high, full and firm, waist perhaps a little too thick for perfection, but curvaceous hips and long shapely legs. About time it was all properly appreciated. Perhaps that was the wrong word. She knew it *was* appreciated by just about every straight male at Westminster along with a significant number of women. "Used to good effect" was probably a better way of putting it.

Her thoughts went to Tom Brown. The physical side of their relationship had never developed into anything satisfactory, but she owed him a debt of gratitude for unlocking feelings that had laid dormant inside her for nearly two decades. She felt a pang of sadness and guilt as she thought of how it had ended.

She stepped into the shower and immediately out again. Wrapping a towel loosely around her, she ran, dripping water along the way, to where her iPhone lay trilling on the bedside table. She picked it up, glancing at the number before pressing the answer key.

"Hi, it's me. Did I wake you?"

The woman sighed with pleasure at the sound of the familiar deep and gentle voice. She sat down on the bed. "No, I was in the shower."

"Gee, that was quick; getting dry and to the phone in three seconds."

"I think it was longer than three seconds and I'm anything but dry. Which phone is this? I didn't recognise the number. It's a different one every time."

"This one is my daughter's. I'm pretty sure they don't listen to her calls – well, not yet. And anyway, I don't see why we should worry; this is a private conversation between friends – right?"

She hesitated. "Yes… I guess so. I feel guilty about your phoning me at all under the circumstances, and grateful, of course. I mean given what's going on…"

"Hey, listen, I'm the one who's grateful. I really need someone like you to talk to right now; to keep me sane." He paused. "Just rewind that, what I mean is I need *you* to talk to, *anytime*."

The woman was silent for a few moments before speaking. "Like a special friend, you mean?"

"I'd like to think we're a little more than friends."

"I'd like to think so, too." She paused. "I bet it's desperate there, isn't it? Poor you – I've been watching it all unfold on the news – and we've got an open line to Homeland Security, of course. It's, what…" she looked at her clock again "… just after midnight there, isn't it? You must be shattered."

"Just after one o'clock, actually, so I guess I should be even more shattered."

"That's *five* hours different. Aren't you in Chicago?"

"No, far too dangerous for me, apparently. What they really mean is, I'd be in the way. So, I'm at home in my lonely bedroom in the big house." She heard him sigh. "Wishing you were here with me."

She smiled and swung her legs up onto the bed, lying back and letting her head sink into the pillow.

"Well, say something," he said, "or I'll think I've said the wrong thing."

"Oh, no, that's the rightest thing you've said so far. Are you sure no-one can hear us?"

"As sure as I can be. Look, it's been eighteen months now. Marsha would have wanted me to be happy again – and said so, in fact, just before she died. So, let them all hear us. This is my private life, and I can deal with any concerns about conflicts of interest. And if I can't, then I'll do what your King Edward did when he had his thing with our Mrs Simpson. I'll abdicate; it would be like redressing the historical balance."

She laughed. "You'd have to marry me afterwards to do it exactly right."

There was silence for a few moments before she spoke again. "Now I feel really bad, laughing after all that's happened over there. Have you found out how it was done yet?"

"A massive car bomb – in fact, more than one. Just before the explosion a number of people saw three police vehicles screaming down Wacker Drive underneath Willis, lights and sirens full on. Turns out the vehicles had been stolen from a service yard. People will jump on security for not stopping them but instinct would say let them through; they must be *responding* to an emergency, not about to create one. There was a bomb in each. Pretty clever using emergency vehicles – I wish our intelligence agencies were as good at their job as these guys."

"No links to last time; that was way back, I guess?"

"Twelve years ago. But at the time the FBI said that particular plot was – I quote – 'more aspirational then operational'. Meaning there wasn't a lot of detailed planning or real expectation of success. And the leader of the group's still inside. So, no links to back then. But in the meantime, we've taken our eye off the ball. I blame the last administration. Well, I guess I would, wouldn't I? And, of course, the fear was the next attack would be bio, not bombs or planes. So, where we did show any sort of diligence and application, we were looking for potential threats in the wrong place."

"I'm amazed that more people weren't killed. In fact, from most angles the building looks pretty well untouched."

"That's right. Forty-six dead so far and about twice that number with serious injuries. And as for the building surviving as well as it has, we've got a certain Mr Khan to thank for that."

"I don't think I know the gentleman..."

"Fazlur Rahman Khan was the tower's structural engineer and he used – for the first time, I'm told – what was called a bundled tube design. The Willis – or Sears Tower, as it was called when it was built – is actually nine square-section, vertical tubes, each one essentially a separate building, clustered together in a three-by-three formation. All the tubes rise as far as the fiftieth floor, seven carry on to the sixty-sixth, then five go on higher to the ninetieth level, and just two go all the way to the top. That's what gives it its stepped appearance from outside. Impressed?"

"Fascinating…"

"And very important. The bombs went off at the base of the south-east tube – one of the fifty-floor ones – and the blast followed the route of least resistance; straight up through the tube. It took out five floors completely and parts of three more, but most of the office space was up for let and mainly deserted except for four seminars using the vacant areas. A different building design would have enabled the blast to spread out horizontally, which could have destabilised the whole building. I keep thinking about 9/11 and picturing the towers coming down."

"So perhaps your terrorists weren't as good at their job as you say. You'd think they'd have worked that one out and gone for the Hancock or something, if Chicago had to be the target."

"NSA think it wasn't so much an attempt to kill as many people as possible, but more of a reminder that they're still around."

"Do you believe that? It means they've gone to a whole lot of trouble just to put people on their guard. Seems a bit counter-productive, don't you think?"

"I guess so. As I said, I don't have a great deal of faith in our intelligence agencies right now. Whatever the terrorists' intentions, what they've achieved is to panic the whole country again. It seems like everyone is imagining the Willis coming down like the World Trade Center. The so-called experts are using their TV air-time to postulate on the number of likely dead if the building *had* collapsed."

"Anyone claimed responsibility yet?"

"Everyone but the Mormons so far, but Islamic State is the one we're taking seriously. We all celebrated it as a victory when they were driven out of their stronghold in Syria, but they haven't stop fighting. As you know better than most, they spread through

Turkey, Ukraine, across to Germany and into Scandinavia. And they're now so thin on the ground that they're virtually invisible to the military. It's down to individuals, though, when it comes to this sort of attack, and Abu el Taqha's been mentioned."

"The Shadow? He was al Qaeda, wasn't he? Bin Laden's right hand – 'the hand that rocked the world'. I didn't know he was still active."

"Well, as I say, when it comes down to staging something like this, it's as much about individuals as about causes. Getting the right person for the job and for the right price and there's a limited amount of expertise around to call on when it comes to attacks on this scale."

"So, your guys believe he's still out there but working as a sort of mercenary?"

"Something like that. And when his name hits the press, wait for the surge of national bloodlust. He was almost certainly one of the brains behind 9/11 and the media will be quick to remind everybody. And it was rumoured – though never proven – that he masterminded the attack at the Thanksgiving ceremony where Marsha..." His voice tailed off and there was silence for a few moments, as he gathered his composure. "You know what's really frustrating? Just how quickly and effectively the CIA have been able to work *backwards* from the attack to fill in the events leading up to it and ID the likely perpetrators. If they'd been doing their job properly, they should have been monitoring the *same* sequence of events as it unfolded. And forty-six people would still be alive and filling in feedback forms about the seminars they attended. It's just so..."

His voice tailed off again as he searched for words.

"At least they've responded to the wake-up call." The woman broke the silence. "Perhaps it needed something like this and now we're all on our guard and a bit safer for it."

He gave a little laugh. "My silver-lining girl. You are *definitely* the person I need to talk to... For all sorts of reasons," he added.

They were silent again for a few moments.

"Well," the man said. "I guess I'll go to bed. How quickly can you get here?"

"I'll get Scotty to beam me over."

"I wish." He sighed. "Someday soon, please God."

"I hope so."

"Good morning, Miss Goody."

"Goodnight, Mr President."

★

Grace Goody's joy at the exchange with President Weston was short-lived. As she leaned back in the taxi a couple of hours later on her way to Downing Street, all the barriers to their relationship raised themselves in her mind to block any sense of optimism. It was not just the fact that being in the company of the President of the United States without another fifty people being present in the same room was nigh on impossible; it was what he didn't know about her that was the main problem. What she had done could never be *un*done, and if it ever came to light, anyone associated with her – in *any* capacity, political or personal – would feel the fallout. For someone in such an exalted role as John Weston, it would be disastrous.

She raised a hand to acknowledge the ever-present group of reporters, photographers and tourists at the entrance to Downing Street, who seemed to spend their lives peering through the railings hoping for a glimpse of someone recognisable entering the famous address. As she stepped under the ornate lantern in front of the black panelled door, her iPhone trilled. The uniformed policemen guarding the entrance took a few polite steps away so she could take the call in private.

When she entered, she was met by an aide who led her to where Andrew Donald was waiting for her.

The Study in 10 Downing Street is a light and airy room with pale pastel-coloured walls above a dado rail and white wood panelling below it. The tall white cabinets around the walls and between the three large windows are packed with books behind glass-fronted doors, each with a metal diamond-pattern lattice. Lighting for the room is provided by a number of table and floor lamps and a single ornate gold chandelier with seventeen shaded candle bulbs. At one end of the room is a circular meeting table with eight chairs. At the end closest to the door where Grace entered, Andrew was sitting in one of the four wing chairs positioned round a small rectangular table in polished walnut. Just to the left of the door the portrait of Britain's first woman prime minister looked down on him from above the white marble fireplace.

The Prime Minister was a tall man who carried a lot of excess weight but carried it well, distributed evenly around his large frame. He was dressed fashionably, as always, in an expensive Italian suit, white shirt and deep-pink silk tie. His round face could be described as boyish when it was not creased in a scowl, which it was now, and most of the time. As usual, he did not greet her or invite her to be seated. She eased herself into one of the wing chairs at the low table as he stared at the screen of his iPad.

"The bloody American security services are all over the place, aren't they? They've got half a dozen organisations all doing more or less the same thing and when something goes wrong each one blames the other five. Your boyfriend must be tearing his hair out."

Grace said nothing, refusing to rise to the jibe.

"They've apparently tracked the group back to the Nordics somewhere, that is, those who didn't blow themselves up for Allah. There's a growing number of active cells there. Good place to hide, the region's virtually empty. It seems the name of Abu el Taqha's about to hit the headlines and..."

"Yes, I know. I believe the US are planning a nuclear strike on Norway."

Andrew smiled. "Sorry, am I boring you, Miss Goody? Only I thought that this meeting was to discuss a suitably gushing national response to the latest terror attack on our *special* friends in the US, before I discuss it further with the Cabinet. But, if it's outside your sphere of interest, then I apologise for wasting..."

"Yes, it is – our meeting *is*, I mean, to discuss – what you said. And we should and will... But I've just had a phone call, a few minutes ago..." She paused, gathering her thoughts.

"Don't tell me Beta is going to be even later than the new *even later* deadline?"

"No, as far as I'm aware it's almost ready to be..."

"Well, go on, then. It must be quite important to upstage this. Weston's not dumped you already, has he? I mean, you haven't even..."

"Our tenacious little terrier bitch is chewing on her favourite bone again."

Andrew stood up quickly, taking Grace by surprise. He glared down at her, his eyes wide and angry. When he spoke, his voice was soft and menacing.

"And how and when did this come to light?"

"How? – I think you know. And when? – just now. Well just now to *me*. They called me just as I arrived here. In fact, it isn't her so such, but someone else who has suddenly started asking questions, and it reached her through David Gerrard. He was her DCI..."

"I know who David Gerrard is, thank you. A loose end which we should have removed, along with his side-kick, long ago."

"Well we didn't, and if you remember we decided at the time it was one thing clearing a bunch of anonymous losers off the streets but eliminating police officers – active *or* retired – would be unthinkable. You know how they look after their own and how they react if something happens to one of them."

"You didn't think that about Cottrell on the steps of Guildford Magistrates' Court."

"That was a one-off opportunity to stage an accident, as you know."

"Look, just tell me the story. Who's this someone else?"

"A guy called Tony Dobson..."

"Oh, Christ, the fucking press! And Brown's best buddy." He started pacing the room, barely containing his fury. Grace watched him, waiting for the explosion. It never came; he sat down again and spoke calmly.

"Go on, tell me what's happened."

"It seems Dobson and his girlfriend were up in Ullapool and took some photographs which, somehow – not sure how – proved the one of Tom that appeared in the press in November was a fake. Also, some local had told them that the boat Tom was supposed to have used wouldn't have been fit for the task. That's all, but through George Holland he set up a meeting with Gerrard, who passed the info to Cottrell by email. We haven't seen the email, but the guys picked up a call from Cottrell to Gerrard yesterday morning. Dobson wants a meeting with Harry Waters – the CIO who was on the case – to get as much info as he can under the guise of writing Tom's biography. Gerrard thought Cottrell might be able to help set it up, but it seems she didn't like the idea."

"Well, I guess that's something..."

"*However*, she suggested Dobson might talk to Mackay. And she *did* say she would be interested in getting involved. That's all."

"It's enough. We need to get Dobson wired right away. Get Walcott on it. He is still alive, I assume. You haven't erased him, like you were planning to before you discovered his insurance policy?"

Grace glowered at him, saying nothing.

"No? Good, let's get him onto this now... this morning," Andrew went on. "I thought this had all gone away. I just wish we had a body then, at least... I thought the drop was supposed to be timed so the body would turn up."

"Look, Tom is dead. I as good as watched him die." Her voice broke a little as she spoke. "The guys saw him dropped, their co-ordinates checked with the NTS, and within less than a minute his life indicators flatlined and the signal died. Whether he turns up or not, he's not going to be in a state to demand to see a lawyer or ask for his old job back, if that's what you're worried about."

"And our handsome little Kenyan – he's not likely to turn up instead?"

"I can absolutely guarantee he won't be washed up anywhere."

CHAPTER SIX

Thursday, 15 June

The NAFC Marine Centre in the small town of Scalloway on Shetland is one of thirteen colleges and research institutions which comprise the University of the Highlands and Islands of Scotland. The cluster of colourful buildings in sky-blue and green is situated at the head of a natural bay on the west side of the island. Tony entered the reception area through the main doors.

"I guess you must be Linda." Tony smiled at the friendly-looking woman with the mass of red hair behind the desk and reached forward to shake her hand. "Tony Dobson, I'm here to see Professor…"

"Mark Fellows."

Tony turned towards the person who had spoken, seated at a coffee table in the corner of the reception area.

"At your service," the man said. He was of average height, slim, with a wide, boyish smile and twinkling eyes set in a lineless, tanned face. His movements were smooth and athletic as he rose and approached him, bowing slightly as they shook hands. Tony tried to hide his surprise, but his wide-eyed expression gave him away.

"Let me guess," Professor Fellows said. "You checked me out on Google – Wikipedia or something – looked at my photograph and my age and thought to yourself, 'that must be an old photograph, he can't possibly be seventy-one years old'. If I'm wrong, of course, that will make me sound very conceited."

"No, you're right. That is exactly what I was thinking – and I guess what other people must think – and say. Although your voice on the phone did sort of match the photo."

Mark Fellows laughed. He nodded towards the receptionist. "Linda believes there's a portrait of me in my loft which is changing to reflect my hideous deterioration. I've not been up there for years, just in case she's right."

"I'm *sure* I'm right," Linda said. "But just as long as we can have this sanitised version... You'll need to sign in, Mr Dobson." She pushed a pad across the desk towards Tony. "Then we'll give you a plastic medallion to wear while you're here with us."

"Okay and, please, it's Tony."

He printed then signed his name. Linda tore off the strip and folded it into a plastic badge holder on a blue ribbon.

"There you go, and welcome to Scalloway."

*

They settled themselves in the two wing chairs at the low table in front of the floor-to-ceiling window in his office overlooking the harbour. A narrow worktop – no more than a wide shelf – ran along the full length of one wall and was home to a computer, printer and a single stack of three filing trays, all empty. Tony noticed a largescale map of the area around The Minch on the wall above the PC. Against the opposite wall was a bookcase neatly filled with books and folded charts. Tony's impression was of a man totally at one with his circumstances and well in control of his timetable.

"I still feel a bit of a fraud," Mark said.

"Why do you say that?"

"Well, dragging you all this way just so we could look at some charts together."

Tony laughed. "As I said on the phone, this was the excuse I was looking for to visit this part of the world. I've read all Ann Cleeves' novels set in the place, and watched every episode of every series of *Shetland*. So, I've read the book, seen the movie, now for the tee shirt. I'm sure you've got some souvenir shops up here. Anyway, you explained on the call that you could send me the information, so no need to feel a fraud. Just me exploiting the opportunity."

"Well, I appreciate you're coming in this afternoon at such short notice instead of tomorrow. I have to attend an emergency meeting in the morning to discuss funding for next year. As a department head, it would look bad if I wasn't there fighting for our share. I only found out first thing this morning and wasn't sure whether I'd get you on your mobile. That's why I left a note with the receptionist at your hotel. I hope you didn't have anything planned for today."

"I was planning to go exploring, so I might do that tomorrow instead. Perhaps do a bit of birdwatching."

"There's plenty to see, although it's not the best time of year for the birds. You've missed all the migrants and the early nesting season, but the weather forecast is good, so I'm sure you'll enjoy the day."

The door was pushed open by Linda backing into the room with a tray of coffee and "Shetland shortbreads," she said, putting it down and then leaving.

They sipped their drinks and munched the biscuits in silence for a few minutes, looking out at the view across the water.

"What a wonderful place to work," Tony said. "Not the sort of place I expect you'd ever take for granted."

"Certainly not me," the Professor said, "a boy from the dark side of Dundee. I'm semi-retired now, of course. I don't feel my age – or look it, apparently – but birth certificates don't lie and I'm way past my 'use by' date. But a senior lecturer and researcher from a prestigious university like St Andrews and with honorary professorships in three different countries, including the US, has a good chance of landing a decent role in the autumn of his life. That's probably the winter of his life, come to think of it, in my case."

"So semi-retired means you work only part-time?"

"That's right, a couple of lectures and a few tutorials each week and some research projects. I only started studying the marine sciences around ten years ago and got my post-doctorate last year. The advantage of being such a late starter means I'm more up to date than most working lecturers. But I'm here more for the fresh air and birds than anything – and the spectacular scenery, of course. Oh, and I almost forgot, this is where my wife *told* me we were going to live."

Tony laughed. "Well, if you want a second opinion..." he gestured to the window "... I think it was a good decision. I bet you never leave the place, do you?"

"Oh, yes. I'm an executive officer of the British Oceanographic Society, which sounds pretty grand but all it means is they get another 'professor' to add to their management list and I get a small gratuity for doing not much more than lending them my name and providing them with stuff for their database. But it means I have to attend their annual financial review and their AGM, so I go down to Southampton twice a year on what I believe is the longest trip possible within the UK. But I'm always glad to get back here, away from civilisation."

"I can believe that."

They sipped their coffee again for a few moments before Tony leaned forward in his chair.

"I must have left you guessing a bit as to why I wanted to meet with you. I didn't give Linda many details and, to be honest, I was surprised you agreed to see me without asking a few more questions."

"Well at first I assumed it must be a follow-up to the other meeting. But then I realised you'd given a name, and one which sounded sort of familiar. So, I googled you and realised this was different." He paused and chuckled at Tony's expression of surprise. "Now I guess I've got *you* wondering what's going on."

"You certainly have. Follow-up to what meeting? And what do you mean about me giving a name?"

"Towards the end of last year – between Christmas and Hogmanay, in fact – I had a visit, unannounced, from a couple of men in suits enquiring about tidal systems in The Minch. It was a bit annoying because the Centre was closed for the holidays and they turned up at my house. I brought them here, to my office, and showed them what I'm going to show you. So, I thought when Linda told me about your call that you were following up that meeting."

"Not at all. I had no idea you'd already been approached. Who were they? What did they want?"

"I can only answer one of those questions, Tony, but why don't you tell me what *you* want first. Just in case it's something completely unconnected."

Tony turned and gazed out of the window for a long time deep in thought before turning back to the Professor. He relaxed again and smiled. “Right,” he said, “I’m going to tell you *everything* about why I’m here, including stuff I’d decided I didn’t really need to tell you.”

There was a gentle knock at the door and Linda leaned into the room.

“I’m leaving soon. More coffee before I go?”

“Yes, please,” Mark said.

A few minutes later, fortified by the fresh coffee, Tony continued.

“You may not be aware of this, but Tom Brown is… *was* a very close friend of mine. Actually, there’s no reason at all why you should know that…”

“Except I do,” Mark interrupted. “It was mentioned on Google – how your professional liaison brought you closer – something like that.”

“It brought us *very* close, and, as you can imagine, his disappearance hit me really hard. I’ve only just recently fully come to terms with it, in fact. But what I’ve never come to terms with – and never will – is the alleged circumstances which led to his disappearing. I’m aware that the weight of evidence, albeit mostly circumstantial, is compelling in drawing what are now the accepted conclusions, that he killed up to eight people and then fled to his death in The Minch. But I simply can’t believe he could do that to the defenceless, hopeless people who were mostly the victims. He could kill – I have no doubt about that – but not that type of person and not in the way these people were murdered. I don’t expect you to believe that, Mark, by the way, just because I say so and, shame on me, even I’d got to the stage where I’d put the whole thing behind me.” He took his laptop out of its case and opened it on the low table between them. “Then, last month, I took a holiday sailing around Scotland.”

⋆

The girl behind the desk in the reception area of the Scalloway Hotel felt her stomach give a little flutter as she looked up at the man approaching her. A male model, she thought, or a film actor. He was tall and slim with classically handsome features and short, dark hair combed in an old-fashioned style which, on him, appeared ultra-modern. Even the stubble around his chin and jawline looked as if it had been applied by an image consultant rather than grown naturally. His smile was wide and genuine, displaying perfectly even, dazzlingly white teeth. He wore faded blue jeans and a white polo shirt with a Lacoste motif.

"Yes, sir?" she said, returning his smile, which became instantly wider.

"Well, if that's your definite answer, I might just change the question."

"Please, ask away," she said, before she could stop herself, and felt a flush warming her cheeks.

The man laughed and unfolded a printed sheet of A4, smoothing it out on the desk.

"Joshua Baines," he said. "I have a reservation for three nights. Booked through Tripadvisor; this is the confirmation email."

The girl checked a list on the desk. "Oh, yes, Mr Baines. Could you sign in for me, please?" She handed him a pen and pointed to the hotel register in front of her. "You're on the second floor with a harbour view."

"Perfect. Thank you..." he peered at her name badge "... Emma."

"You're very welcome. Will you be eating in the hotel this evening?"

"After seeing all those wonderful pictures of the food on your website – and now I've met you – how could I consider eating anywhere else?"

Emma gave a little giggle. "How indeed? When would you prefer? We're full, but if you're dining alone, I'm sure we could fit you in any time at short notice."

"I *will* be dining alone and it would suit me not to commit to a time right now."

"That's fine, Mr Baines." She handed him a key attached to a disc showing the room number. "Room 23, up two flights of stairs then turn right, or the lift is just a little further down on the left. Do you need any help with your luggage?"

He reached down and picked up a small holdall in one hand and a laptop case in the other. "I'll be fine," he said, smiling. "If not, I'll make two journeys. Thank you, Emma. Catch you later."

He turned to climb the stairs and she felt the flutter and the flush return.

"I wish," she said, in a whisper, to herself.

*

"So, my question is, *if* Tom did go into The Minch somewhere between Ullapool and the Shiants, would you expect his body to turn up and, if so, where? Over to you, Mark." Tony shut down his laptop and leaned back in his chair. He'd been true to his promise and had shared *all* his thoughts with the Professor, without attributing any input to David Gerrard.

Mark had listened without interruption, edging further forward in his chair as the story unfolded. Now he got to his feet and stood looking out of the window across the harbour for a long time. He took a deep breath and exhaled loudly before sitting down again.

"Well, that confirms without any doubt that this and the other meeting *are* connected. Because that's exactly what my other two visitors wanted to know."

"Who did you say they were?"

"I didn't, and neither did they. You'd expect anybody – whoever they were and whoever they worked for – to make some sort of introduction. 'I'm Mr X and this is Mr Y.' But these men said nothing other than asked the questions. I asked them who I was talking to and they said I didn't need to know. They each showed me a sort of badge without any name on, just the name of an organisation. A branch of the Secret Service, they said, or Security Service or whatever, and they offered to show me a website – something-dot-gov – which would have provided a contact number which I could call and they would get me through the menus to someone who would confirm the legitimacy of their enquiries. All very exciting."

"Did you make the call?"

"No, I didn't. I asked why all the cloak and dagger stuff and they told me about their interest in Mr Brown. It all made sense and nothing they asked for was in any way suspicious."

"So, what did they want?"

"They said they needed confirmation of Tom Brown's death so *they* could close the case. The police had officially closed it, but they weren't the police. They said Mr Brown – given his role in government and, before that, as part of Special Forces – had vital classified information which, in the wrong hands, could present a threat to national security. It was imperative that they confirmed his death so they could be sure he had not, well... *defected*, I suppose you'd call it."

Tony could not stop himself laughing. "Tom, defected? That's nonsense."

"To be fair, that's what they said – that they didn't believe it. But this was a man who was not in a good state of mind – these are their words – who might feel he had been rejected by the country he had served so well and let down by the system of law and justice he had energetically supported. It was their job to confirm what everyone seemed to believe, that Mr Brown had drowned in The Minch, by recovering his body if at all possible."

"Can you remember what the organisation was they said they were part of? The dot-gov?"

"I don't, I'm afraid. It looked official, and there was nothing I told them that they couldn't have got from this." Mark picked up an A4-size booklet from the table in front of them and handed it to Tony, who read aloud the words on the blue front cover.

"Admiralty Tidal Stream Atlas NP 218, North Coast of Ireland and West Coast of Scotland." He looked up at Mark. "Not very exciting for two Special Branch officers to travel so far to see. Were you able to help them?"

"I'm not really sure. I was able to explain the charts in the booklet to them and make them aware of other factors and – as such – the limitations for their purpose. I'll take you through them if you wish."

"Yes, please."

Mark got to his feet and went over to sit at the PC. He pressed a button on the wall behind it and a white screen rolled down from the ceiling in front of the bookshelves on the opposite wall. A switch next to the button activated a ceiling-mounted projector. Mark smiled, clearly pleased with himself.

He booted up the computer, Tony noticing his screensaver was the same scene as the view from the window, and waited for the icons to appear round the perimeter of the image. He clicked on one, opening a file and projecting two maps, side by side in portrait format, onto the white screen. The maps included a large number of arrows of varying size and thickness around the sea areas, along with four-digit figures against some of the arrows.

"This is what you'll see if you open the tidal atlas at the second double page." Tony turned to the page then looked back at the screen. "The arrows show the strength and direction of tidal streams – the blacker and larger the arrow, the stronger the stream – and the numbers are the average neap and spring tide rates in tenths of a knot. So, this..." a red dot of light from Mark's laser pointer appeared next to the number *19,28* on the left-hand chart "... indicates a mean neap rate of 1.9 knots and a spring rate of 2.8. The comma in the middle is approximately the spot where the observations were made. With me so far?" Tony nodded. "It's the *right-hand* map we're interested in," Mark went on, "showing the Outer Hebrides, Skye and Wester Ross on the mainland. The Shiants are there, right in the middle." The red dot reappeared on the squiggle which was the small island group.

He moved the dot to a box at the top right corner of the screen which contained the data:

<table><tr><td>6</td><td>BEFORE
HIGH WATER
DOVER</td></tr></table>

"This refers to *when* these tidal streams occur. The atlas contains thirteen pairs of charts showing the status at hourly intervals from six hours before – which is this one – to six hours after high water at Dover. All tidal atlases use Dover as a reference point." Mark smiled. "I hope you're taking notes, Tony. There'll be a written test afterwards and this will count towards your degree in oceanography."

Tony laughed and tapped his forehead. "All saved in here."

"Okay. Let's move on. Get ready for a thirteen-hour, white-water experience." He clicked to the next pair of maps. "Remember it's just the right-hand one we're interested in. This is *five* hours before high water Dover. You can see the strength and rate of the tide increasing, still flowing north from the Shiants through

The Minch to the North Atlantic. Similarly, for four hours..." he moved through the maps "... and for three and two, although you can see the strength of the tide is weakening. When we get to *one* hour before high water Dover, the tide is flowing north *and* south from the area of the Shiants, as if the island group is the hub of a wheel and the tidal streams are the spokes. And at the *same time* as high water Dover – zero difference – the tide has turned and is flowing south through The Little Minch." He flicked on through the charts. "And you can see it's moving in the same direction for another four hours before it turns north again to complete the cycle. Any questions?"

Tony was silent for several moments, absorbing the information.

"And this is the same every day? Never varies?" he asked.

"Well, high water at Dover changes by one hour every day against the clock, but *relative* to Dover, yes, same every day."

"You said something about other factors; limitations."

"In some areas when the tidal streams are very strong you can get eddies and overfalls and even standing waves. It's not always possible to include them on the charts if these factors are unstable, or sometimes we just don't have enough information. They don't detract from the validity of the charts, but they could affect the direction of something washed along by the tide."

"What about wind speed? That must have an impact, especially with the gales they have out there."

"It would on a boat or anything floating on top of the water. But a body hardly breaks the surface so the wind wouldn't have anything to push against. It would just follow the tidal stream."

Tony paused again to gather his thoughts before continuing.

"So, these factors – eddies and such – would they apply in the case of somebody falling into The Minch?"

"Unlikely, and certainly not on the day in question."

"The day in question?" Tony interrupted.

"Yes, I can't remember which day exactly, but I can check my notes if you like and..."

"No, that's not my point," Tony said. "Are you saying they gave you a specific date to check?"

"That's right, and a time as well. It's nearly six months ago, so I can't remember the details, but they gave me a date and time – and a grid reference – and asked me to use them to explain a scenario. So, it was like, 'let's say, for example – date, time, grid reference – now take us through what this would mean'."

Tony got to his feet and walked over to the window, just as the Professor had done earlier, to draw in a long breath and exhale loudly. He turned back to Mark.

"Did you make notes of the meeting? It would be interesting to get those parameters."

"No problem. In fact, I typed them up and filed them; old habits. I can find them and put them on the screen, if you like." He turned to the PC again, then stopped. "Actually, if it's just the numbers you need, I think they're on a Post-it in the tidal stream atlas. Let me see."

He took the atlas from Tony and turned to the inside of the back cover.

"How did we ever exist without Post-its?" They looked together at the two hand-written rows of digits:

3/11, 04.00
N 57.50, W 06.25

"So that's four in the morning on the third of November," Tony said, "and where exactly?"

They both stepped back to look at the map on the wall above the PC. The red dot traced the grid lines from the top and then the side of the map, alighting on the intersection.

"The Shiants," said Tony. "And the exact spot where the boat was found."

"That's right," Mark said, "so let me take you through that same scenario. "But this time, I'm going to give you 'NP 218 – The Movie'."

*

The man took a sip of his beer as he waited for his call to be answered. He was seated at a table in front of the hotel, separated from the harbour wall by the width of the narrow road which ran around the bay. The sky was cloudless, the water as flat as a mirror and the sun bright enough to make him turn away from it despite the expensive Ray-Bans he was wearing.

He heard the phone being picked up, but no-one spoke.

"Hello, darling," he said. "Lucky me, getting through to you in the middle of what I'm sure is a really busy day. Just letting you know I've arrived safely. I know how you worry about me when you send me to these dangerous places."

There was a pause before the person spoke. "Have you anything interesting to tell me?"

"Well, I miss you terribly. I'm counting the minutes until I see you again. The hotel room is really nice but would be infinitely better if you were sharing it with me. How am I doing?"

"Please don't waste my time, Walcott."

"I do love it when you're really forceful like that. Our guy is here; he checked in around noon according to the hotel register. Don't know where he is right now; he's not in his room or the bar, so probably out for a walk somewhere. I'll catch him as he comes back."

"When's his meeting with the Professor?"

"Tomorrow morning. I'll fix everything tonight."

"How will you do that, just out of interest?"

"Trade secret. I might decide to fix you one day – wouldn't do for you to know what to expect."

"Just let me know when it's done."

"I'll phone you around midnight, okay?"

"*Not* okay. I'll be in bed by then."

"Perfect, we can talk dirty and…"

He heard the click as Grace replaced the receiver.

*

After the Professor had finished, Tony continued to stare at the map for a long time. Mark broke the silence.

"I suppose if you're going to choose a starting point just for the purpose of illustration, the location of the abandoned boat is as good a place as any?"

Tony snapped out of his trance. "I guess you're right, but what fascinates me is the *timing* they chose for the illustration." He turned to look at the paused image on the projection screen.

"Can we go through this again, Mark? Just humour me for the time being."

Mark smiled and nodded. "I've got the rest of the day. Off you go and take this..." he handed Tony the laser pointer "... it will tell me whether you've been listening."

On the screen was an image of the right-hand page only this time, with the box at the top right showing:

2	**AFTER** HIGH WATER DOVER

"This is the tidal stream two hours after high water at Dover. And on the date specified – third of November – high water at Dover was two o'clock in the morning. So..." he moved the pointer down to the map "... this is how it looked in The Minch at 4.00 a.m. – which was the time they specified. Right?"

"Right. I'll start the movie."

He clicked on the small arrow at the bottom of the screen.

Where the Shiants showed on the screen there was a red dot, part of the image this time. As the data in the box changed, the dot expanded, southwards, spreading into a narrow fan shape which passed through The Minch before widening to extend further south and east towards Skye and the mainland. The solid pink area created on the map was not uniform in colour, with some of the sections darker than others. Tony talked through the sequence.

"The tide is flowing down through The Little Minch. At a point opposite Benbecula it fans out, half flowing south then west into the Atlantic and the other half swinging east under Skye to the mainland."

He looked at Mark, who nodded again with a smile. "The terminology needs a bit of work, but yes, that's right again."

"The darker pink areas represent a higher probability of where something would be carried by the movement of the water. So, that would suggest Waternish or Duirinish on Skye, or it might even reach the mainland and come aground on Knoydart or Morar."

Tony shook his head as the moving sequence ended.

CAUTION:- Due to the very strong rates of tidal streams in some of the areas covered by this Atlas, many eddies and overfalls may occur. Where possible some indication of these has been included. In many areas there is either insufficient information or the eddies are unstable.

2 AFTER HIGH WATER DOVER

6h 15m before HW ULLAPOOL

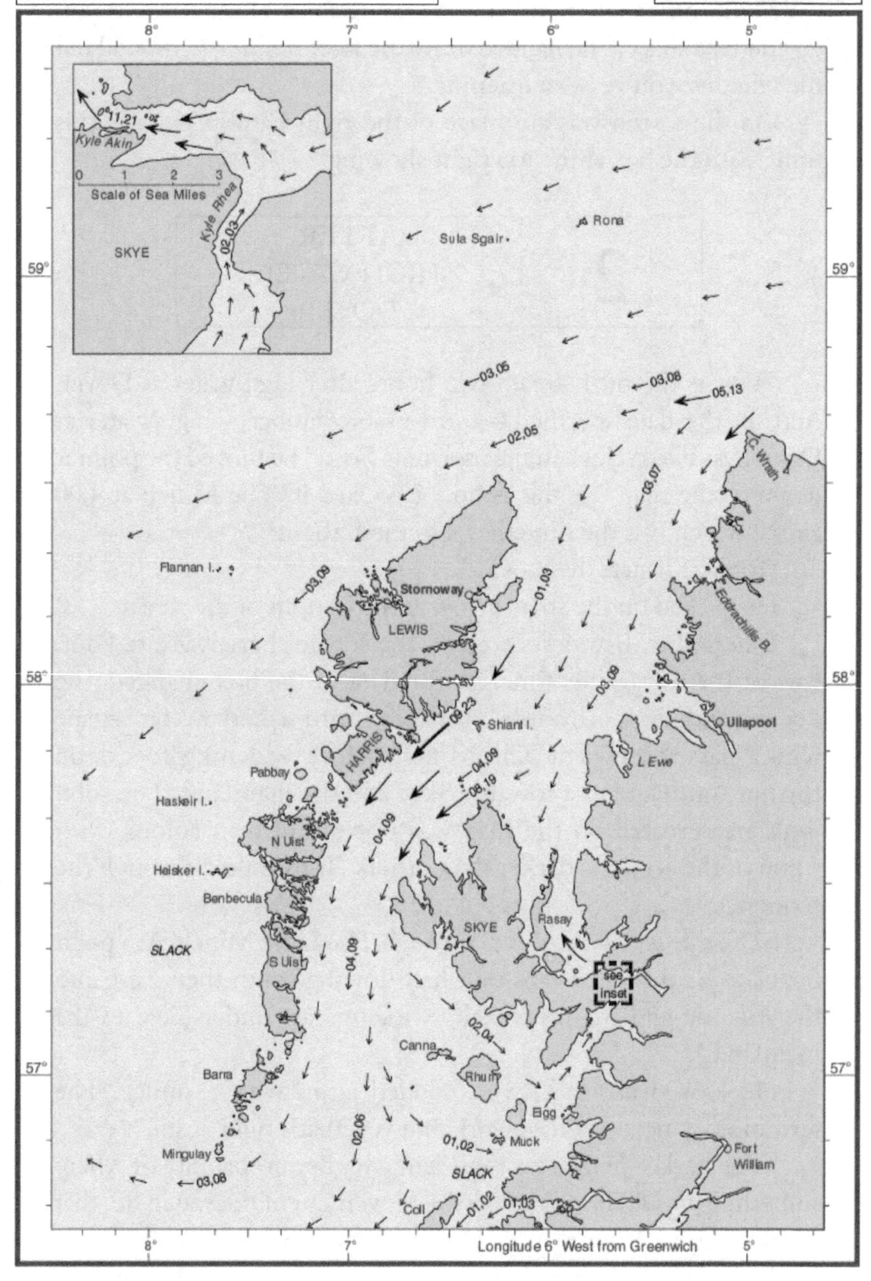

"That's a hell of a big area," he said. "But if that *was* the location and time and date that a body entered the water you would *expect* it to be washed up in one of those places. Right?"

"Expect is probably the wrong word. It's impossible to be sure of anything when predicting the effect of tidal streams, but assuming the flow was sufficiently strong to take it far enough south before the stream turned back to north – four or so hours later – it should be held in this area of sea until it turned up somewhere along there."

"How soon?" Tony asked.

"That's not possible to predict. If it became trapped within the tidal system, it could be any time from two or three days up to several months. Eventually, though, it would be more than likely to show up."

"So, if I understood you correctly, this would be the *optimum* status of the tidal streams for a body to enter the water and for it to turn up later?" Tony smiled. "I think you're right about terminology. I don't think I put that very well."

"Perhaps not, but you've got the idea. At any other time within the cycle, there would be little or no chance of *predicting* where a body might turn up. That's not to say it wouldn't turn up, but it would be hard to know where to start looking."

Tony paused again before speaking, his brow furrowed in thought.

"So, either these guys chose *at random* the one point in time when a body entering The Minch would have a decent chance of being found – a thirteen-to-one shot – or they know something we don't."

"That's right." After a few more moments of silence, the Professor spoke again, this time with a twinkle in his eye. "There's one other possibility."

"Which is?"

"Storm Kelpies."

"Storm…?"

"Kelpies. The Blue Men of The Minch got him."

*

Tony declined the offer of a lift from Mark and walked the couple of kilometres from the Marine Centre to the hotel. He exchanged a friendly smile with the man seated at the table near the entrance, who raised his near-empty glass and drained the last of his beer, letting out a satisfied "Aaaah" before placing it back on the table.

"What a fabulous place," the man said. "You're looking at a lapsed atheist. There must be a God for somewhere like this to exist."

Tony laughed. "Yes, it's a bit special. You staying here?"

The man got to his feet and reached out his hand. "Josh Baines, and, yes, I'm here for a few days. Doing a bit of birdwatching. This is the best time for it. Come here at this time every year."

"Tony Dobson. I'm here just for tonight. Wish I was staying for longer. And that looks like an excellent idea." He nodded towards the man's glass. "Ready for another?"

"Won't say no, but let me get them while you check in."

"I checked in earlier, actually, but thanks, I'll have what you're having. I'll drop this off in my room…" he held up his laptop case "… and see you in a couple of minutes."

"Okay."

When Tony returned, two pints of I.P.A. were resting seductively on the table gathering condensation and Josh was frowning at his mobile phone. He lifted one of the glasses as Tony sat down.

"Cheers, or *slainte*, I believe is the word up here."

Tony laughed. "In which case, *slainte*."

"What network are you on, Tony?" Josh was peering down at his phone again.

"EE. Why?"

"I'm on Orange and not getting a signal at the moment. I'm expecting a text from work that's quite urgent. Are you getting a signal?"

"Got four bars here."

"Right. Look…"

Tony handed Josh his phone. "Be my guest."

Josh took the phone and got to his feet. "Thanks. If you don't mind…" he nodded towards the hotel entrance "… I'll take it in there. Okay?"

"No problem."

Josh returned within a few minutes and handed Tony his phone.

"Sod's law," he said. "Just about to make the call and the text came through."

"Everything okay?"

"All sorted. Emergency over, or, should I say, *non*-emergency over. And they tell me in there that now's a good time to dine. Got a party of eight coming in about twenty minutes. Best get our order in before then, if you're ready to eat."

"I'm more than ready, I'm starving."

"Okay, let's go."

*

The sun had dropped low towards the horizon but seemed reluctant to disappear completely. Well after 11.00 p.m. it was still illuminating the harbour and reflecting off the white walls of the hotel.

"The main problem with this place," Josh said, "is knowing when it's time to leave the bar. Down in London, you get a hint with the fall of darkness, but here…"

"Well, I'm getting the message from inside. Really shattered, I'm afraid and got an early start in the morning."

"One more?" Josh lifted his empty beer glass. "My turn, I think."

"Go on, then. My arm has been effectively twisted. What about a dram of Shetland Reel?"

"Good idea. Always glad to sample local produce and help the island economy."

Josh disappeared inside and Tony felt his eyelids getting heavy. The sound of his companion's phone buzzing on the tabletop sprung him from his trance. Tony picked it up and glanced at the illuminated screen. But it wasn't the words of the message that took him by surprise.

*

"I thought I said *not* to call me at this time."

"You said not at midnight. It's only ten minutes to."

"So, tell me, quickly."

"Right. Good news and not-so-good news. The device is in place, but his meeting with the Prof has already taken place. It was brought forward to this afternoon – by the Professor, I understand – so we've no way of knowing exactly what they talked about. Unless Dobson types it up and files it, that is, which I guess he's more than likely to do. But you can get the guys to start monitoring right away. So, what next? Do you want the full works on Cottrell?"

"Not yet. We've got her phone calls and texts covered. Let's wait to see if she gets more involved."

"Great, so now can we get down to talking dirty?"

The tell-tale click gave him the answer.

CHAPTER SEVEN

Monday, 19 June

William Parks leaned forward, his elbows resting on the large mahogany desk and his fingers interlocked. He nodded his head slowly as he spoke, as if to force home the message he was delivering to the woman who sat across from him, and whose pale-yellow summer dress and golden-blonde hair lit up the wood-panelled office like a high-wattage light bulb.

"I really don't think this is a good idea, Mrs Tomlinson-Brown. I was unhappy with the arrangement in the first place, as you know, but… what?" Mags's wide smile and twinkling eyes brought his chastisement to an abrupt halt. His stern expression morphed into a puzzled frown. "I don't see what's so funny."

Mags laughed. "You know, I always hated the name Margaret and as soon as I was able to wilfully voice my opinion… I guess I'd be about three years old…"

"*That* I can believe."

"Thank you, kind sir. Anyway, I insisted on being called Maggie. My parents went along with this – probably to avoid the embarrassment of public tantrums – and the only time Mum ever called me Margaret from then on was when she was really mad with me and then I knew I was in big trouble. And you do the same, Will – or should I say, Mr Parks? – I'm always Maggie until I do something wrong and then I'm Mrs Tomlinson-Brown."

"Which happens very infrequently."

"Absolutely, which is why I know you're cross with me now."

"Not cross, frustrated, maybe, and certainly concerned. When someone is confirmed as… missing… presumed…"

"Dead – it's alright to say it, Will."

"It's the bank's policy – *every* bank's policy – to immediately cancel all cards held by that person. In fact, it's not so much a matter of *policy*, it's just common sense. That's why I was unhappy when you insisted on *not* cancelling Tom's Visa Debit card, even when it hadn't been used for over three months. By that time, it was clear that it wouldn't be used again."

"And yet the card *has* been used."

"I mean used *legitimately*."

"I can't get my head round how this could happen. Tom always carried that card with him in his wallet, and he would certainly have had his wallet with him when he disappeared. It wasn't with his bag on the boat and he hadn't left it behind at the apartment. He never went anywhere without it; he even took it with him when he went out running. And how does anyone get the PIN?"

"I can't answer those questions, Maggie, which is why I believe we must tell the police."

"But this can't be the first time it's happened to one of your customers, Will, so you must have some theory or opinion."

"Well, yes, in general terms. People can be mugged for their card and forced to disclose the PIN. Usually that means a quick one-off transaction at an ATM before the victim has time to report it. Some people – believe it or not – keep a list of PINs *with* the cards, then have their wallets or purses stolen with everything the thief needs right there. The most common cases are family members stealing from each other – kids from parents, spouse from spouse – and they'd often know the PIN because they'd used the card before. So, yes, I've got some theories, but none that come anywhere near to explaining this."

Mags sighed and shook her head. "You said you had a picture of the person who used the card?"

"Yes, if you're sure you want to see it."

"Well, I came a long way for this meeting so I guess I should tick all the boxes while I'm here."

"Okay. This was at our branch in Tottenham Court Road. The camera's behind the screen so we got a front view of the culprit." He took an A4 sheet of paper from a desk drawer and placed it in front of him. "Well, I say a front view, but you can't actually see his face at all. The bottom half is covered with a scarf and his hood is pulled down to hide the rest."

He turned the paper round and pushed it across the desk to Mags. It showed the head and shoulders of the person using the ATM. The width and squareness of the shoulders suggested a man, but, as Will had said, the features were completely obscured by the scarf and the hood. The picture was obviously a still from a CCTV recording and was grainy and indistinct. Mags screwed up her eyes and peered more closely. She gave a little gasp.

"What?" Will said. "Have you seen something?"

Mags recovered, blinking her eyes a couple of times. "No, it just suddenly hit me that this person could be somehow linked to Tom's… death. I'm okay now."

"Yes, I can understand it must feel strange." He hesitated for a moment. "So, what about informing the police, Maggie? The only reason I don't just go ahead and do it is because you're a long-term customer, and friend, I'd like to think."

Mags smiled at him again.

"So, as a friend, then, rather than my bank manager, can you give me time to think about it?"

"I don't really understand the downside of telling…"

"Just a few days? Please."

Will leaned back in his chair and sighed. "I'll do whatever you want, Maggie. You can take as long as you like. There is no legal requirement for me to take any action, I'm just telling you what I think is best."

"Thank you, Will." She got to her feet. "And now I really must go."

He walked her to the door, where they shook hands. Mags stepped forward and gave him a brief hug and a peck on the cheek.

"Thanks for calling me Maggie again."

"You're very welcome. Bye for now."

"Bye, Will."

She walked across the main floor of the bank, though the revolving doors and down the three steps to the pavement of the bustling street. She drew in a deep breath and leaned for a few moments against the railings in front of the building as she tried to come to terms with what she had seen in the picture.

CHAPTER EIGHT

Tuesday, 20 June

Tony looked from David to George, his eyebrows raised with the unspoken question. They were back in the snug again at the Dog and Duck. Both men nodded, their faces masks of confusion, as they all took their seats at the table.

"Becca sends her apologies. Called out on a photo shoot at short notice. She'll be disappointed because I know she was looking forward to seeing you again."

"Well, give her our regards when you see her," George said. "So how was the trip to the far north?"

"No luck with the Professor, I'm afraid. His name's Mark Fellows. Really nice guy, seventy-one years old, looks about forty-five. Very knowledgeable, as you'd expect for a department head at the uni, and a big noise with the British Oceanography something-or-other. Gave me a lot of information about tides and currents and probabilities, but nothing of any use, except he thought the Blue Men of The Minch must have got him."

"The blue…?" George said.

"Anyway," Tony went on, "I've come to a decision. I've done a lot of soul-searching over the past few days since getting back from Shetland and I keep thinking of the effect it's going to have on Maggie and Katey if I start dragging it up and force them to go through it again. They've lost half their family, and they'll still be grieving. It's only, what, just over seven months since Tom went missing and exactly a year since Jack died. They're strong people and they'll be determined to put it behind them and move on as best they can, and I don't want to get in the way of them doing that. I know for certain it's not what Tom would want."

"So, what next?" George asked.

"I'm going to drop it. I might let the police have the photographs and they can decide what, if anything, they want to do with them. But you're right, David, it's easy to fake a photo these days and as for the other stuff, well, I reckon your first scenario covered all that satisfactorily." He smiled. "Just put it down to natural journalistic enthusiasm for a possible big story. But, as I said, having balanced the small chance of a major scoop against what it might do to the remaining half of Tom's family, frankly, it's a no-brainer."

George and David exchanged glances. They all sat in silence for a few moments before Tony signalled with a "come on" motion of his hands for one of them to speak. It was David who broke the silence.

"Well, all I can say is I'm glad you've come to that conclusion, Tony. I think it's for the best and it's what I was going to suggest tonight. I don't know about journalistic enthusiasm, though, because *I* got a bit carried away with what you had. Probably more like nostalgia in my case. But given who we're talking about, I can't believe the police left *anything* to chance in tying up the loose ends."

"I'm sure you're right. What about you, George? What do you think?"

"I think we know that Tom is dead. The most anyone could achieve is finding out where and how, and that's not going to bring him back. So, yes, I'm with you two."

"Agreed, then," Tony said. "So, unless there's any other business, I declare the meeting closed and my apologies for dragging you out to the pub for no reason."

They laughed. "We don't take much dragging, do we, David? And we certainly don't need a reason. So, what now? Tell you what, it's a lovely evening, let's have a stroll around the village. Lots of points of interest – a village shop-cum-post office, village hall, church… help me out here, David."

"Fields, trees, livestock…"

"Amazing," said Tony. "Who would have thought it? Then back here for my round. What do you think?"

"Sounds like we have a plan."

"Let's go, then. I'll just put my jacket in the car…"

*

David removed the envelope from the back pocket of his jeans and unfolded the hand-written letter. They were seated around the low table in the living room of George's 200-year-old cottage. The room was small and cosy with an old-fashioned cast-iron range in the open fireplace and floor-to-ceiling shelves full of books in the alcoves at either side. On the mantlepiece, Tony noticed a picture of George and his late wife, Irene, laughing into the camera. He wondered if that was the last photograph of them together before her violent death outside the same pub where the three of them had just been drinking. The only other furniture in the room was the compact three-piece cottage suite positioned around the low table and currently occupied by the three men. George and Tony had each opted for a chair whilst David just about fitted onto the sofa. Their host was pouring coffee from a cafetiere.

"So, let's see how we did against our instructions." David read from the letter.

> Dear George
>
> Now we've set a date for our next meeting I'm going to surprise you with a request which will require you and David to do a bit of acting – it might even set you both off on a new career! The reason for our meeting, as you know, is to follow up my visit to the NAFC Centre in Shetland, and that's how it's got to seem. I'll explain everything when we leave the pub afterwards, but what I'd like you to do is this –
>
> 1. When I arrive at the pub, act naturally and one of you ask me how I got on with the prof.
> 2. I'll tell you I got nothing at all and that I'm going to drop the whole thing about Tom's disappearance.
> 3. You can act surprised, but I'd like both of you to agree that it's a good idea and you're glad I've come to that conclusion as well.

4. Then could one of you suggest we go for a walk around the village – to show me the sights or something. If it's raining, perhaps invite me round to yours or David's.

Why am I asking you to do this? I'll explain everything on the night but, briefly, I believe my phone is bugged. And if it is, then it's quite possible that someone could also be accessing my emails. Hence – this old-fashioned letter! I don't know David's address, but will you please share this with him before next Tuesday.

Thanks, George.

Tony

David looked up. "So, how did we do?"

"Perfect," Tony said. "And now – that explanation I promised you both." He took his mug of coffee from George. "First, thanks for going along with the little charade; I hope I can convince you it was necessary. Let me start by saying I have no intention of dropping this thing about Tom, and I'm sure I can keep Maggie and Katey out of it. That was just for the sake of whoever was listening, but I'm sure you've worked that out anyway."

He paused to sip his coffee. "As far as my visit to Shetland is concerned, I got a lot more from it than I expected. The Prof took me through the tidal flows and such which would affect a body floating in The Minch. That was interesting in itself, but what was more interesting was the fact that mine was the *second* enquiry he'd received about that..."

"Just before we go any further," David interrupted, "how come you can tell us all this here and now, but not before in the Dog? You're not suggesting the pub is bugged as well, are you? Because I'd be thinking along the lines of paranoia if you did."

Tony laughed. "Okay, I'm coming to that, David, and I will explain it, but let me take you through the story chronologically."

"It's what writers call 'narrative tension', David," George said. "Keeps the reader turning the pages to find out what's going on."

David shrugged. "Okay, so please *do* go on."

"Well, two guys turned up unannounced at Mark's – the

Professor's – house between Christmas and New Year, asking the same question – what would happen to a body, etc.? They didn't give their names but showed Mark badges linking them to a branch of the Secret Service or something. Definitely not the police, they said. They were trying to get closure on Tom's disappearance by turning up his body, so there'd be no worries about where he was and what he could be doing with all the highly classified information he had at his disposal."

"You mean they actually believed he might have defected?" George sounded incredulous.

"Mark said they *didn't* believe that but it was still important for them to make sure. Now here's the thing – they gave Mark a specific date, a precise time and exact co-ordinates for when and where a body might enter the waters of The Minch. They said it was for the purpose of Mark describing a scenario. That makes sense, if it was just to make it easier for them to follow what he was telling them. *But* the time they specified was the only hour in a thirteen-hour cycle when there was a good chance of predicting where a body would wash up. It's still a big area, but somewhere definite to look for it. Any other time, there'd be no way of knowing. With me so far?"

George and David exchanged glances. "Just about," David said. "You're thinking it's unlikely to be a coincidence, right? The time they gave, I mean."

"I'm not sure, to be honest. It *could* be a coincidence. And by the way, the co-ordinates they gave were exactly where Tom's boat was found on the Shiants, which, as the Prof pointed out, is as good as any place for the purpose of a what-if scenario."

David held up his hand for Tony to pause. "So, we have two guys turning up out of the blue and saying, 'where are we likely to find a body if it entered the water at this spot at such-and-such a time on such-and-such a day?' And it just so happens the Prof *can* tell them – approximately – because that's the one time in a thirteen-hour cycle on that day when it's possible to know. Is that what you're saying?"

"Well, not know for certain, but have a decent idea of where. And not necessarily right away, because it could be held within that area of sea for up to several months before it showed. But I can't come up with anything that would explain it other than it *is* a coincidence. Unless they got something from, say, a satellite at the time which showed them more than the public got to hear about."

They both looked at David. "No comment right now," he said, "but can we move on to diffuse this narrative tension that George seems to have identified. You know, get to the bit where we find out why we can talk now and not before in the pub?"

"Well, after I left the Prof, I went back to the hotel and met this guy who was sitting outside having a beer. First impression, I thought he was there for a photo shoot. He looked like a male model, straight off the front cover of a fashion mag. Wouldn't surprise me if his jeans, polo, trainers and shades had cost him upwards of a grand. Anyway, we got talking, had a couple of beers and ate together in the hotel. Said he was there for the birdwatching; went that time every year because it was the best time. That surprised me, because when I mentioned to the Prof I was thinking of doing a bit of birdwatching, he said it *wasn't* the best time of year – can't remember exactly why – between seasons or something. I didn't think much about it at the time – no reason to believe the prof knew more about it than this guy did. But then something happened.

"While we were sitting outside before dinner, he kept checking his phone, then he asked me what network I was on. I told him EE and he asked if I'd got a signal. I had four bars. He said he was with Orange and couldn't get anything. He was waiting for a text to come through and seemed very worried that he couldn't receive it. I can't remember whether he asked or I offered to lend him my phone, but he took it and went into the hotel to make a call in private. He was back in about five minutes; said he didn't need to use my phone because the text came through just as he got inside. I asked him if everything was okay and he said it was.

"We sat outside again after dinner – it was really warm and stays light until very late; doesn't gets properly dark, in fact. He popped back inside – to the loo or to get another round, can't remember exactly – and left his phone on the table. While he was gone, it buzzed with a text coming through. I picked up the phone, just instinctively, I suppose. The message was displayed on the screen. I didn't read it, but, guess what, I saw that he was on EE as well. I put the phone back on the table, exactly where it had been before, and when he came back, I said something like, 'I think you've just had a text.' He snatched up the phone, said, 'thanks', and put it straight into his pocket without checking."

"A different phone?" David suggested. "Could he have gone to his room sometime during the evening and changed phones? Perhaps a work phone and a personal one, on different networks."

"That did cross my mind, but I checked with reception as I left the following day and they said it wasn't possible to get a signal on Orange up there. In which case, the earlier text couldn't have come through on that network. I checked if he had, in fact, used my phone but, sure enough, there were no outgoing calls or texts at that time. So, the question is, why take my phone at all if he wasn't going to use it?"

"I assume that question is rhetorical, and you are about to answer it."

Tony smiled. "Absolutely. And remember, David, when it comes to conspiracy-theorising, your former colleague is probably way behind the average journalist. We don't just consider conspiracy theories as possibilities; we go out actively looking for them in life's every corner and hiding place. It's what sells papers and makes people watch documentaries. Something happening that shouldn't be; someone doing something they shouldn't. So, I checked my phone. Removed the back – which isn't all that easy with the new models – and found this..."

Tony reached into the back pocket of his jeans and took out a folded photograph, which he flattened out on the table then passed to David. George leaned across so they could both see it. It showed what was obviously a phone battery – in situ – but with a circular disc in the centre about the diameter of a pound coin.

"I guess you know what that is?" Tony said.

"I assume that question is directed at David," George said, "because I haven't a clue."

"Yes, I do," David said, "but I'm not sure *you* should know. These are illegal outside the police and secret services."

"Illegal but not unobtainable," Tony said. "And I'm sure the police are fully aware that, within press and media circles, they are used fairly extensively. But not by me," he added.

"So, this is a bugging device which enables people to listen in to other people's phone conversations?" George said.

"That's a picture of the one in my phone. It's a standard battery modified with a circular indent to enable the transmitter to be inserted without changing the battery dimensions. And this one does more than just eavesdrop on calls. You can listen to any conversations that take place within a range of around five metres of the phone."

"That's right," David said. "The more advanced models also allow you to disable the phone if you want to prevent calls and you can pinpoint the phone's location to within a five-metre radius without triangulation. And Tony's right, they are used extensively by the media for the purpose of getting to the truth and often – you could argue – the outcome justifies the means. But they're still illegal and even the police have to get approval to use them. Which, I'm pleased to say, since the introduction of the NJR is just a rubber stamp job. So, tell me, Tony, have you ever used one of these? And I'm not about to make a citizen's arrest or anything."

"I can honestly say I haven't, but I may have used information from sources who have used one to get it. If the info is what you're looking for and verifiable as true, you tend not to ask too many questions about where it came from. Best sometimes *not* to know, in fact. But it's such an obvious surveillance tool. I mean, these days nobody ventures more than a few feet away from their phone. I guess the majority of people are like me and even use it as an alarm clock at night. So, the device is with them *all* the time."

George took the photo from David and studied it closely.

"So where is your phone right now?" he said.

"In my jacket in the car. That's a fairly legitimate reason for being separated from it and why we can talk about it here and now. But the big questions are – why me and who's listening? Because I have to believe this has something to do with my looking into Tom's disappearance. Don't you think, David?"

"I suppose that would depend on what else you're into at the moment. You might have a few dodgy things in the pipeline. But it certainly looks that way, given somebody knew you were heading up to Shetland and, I assume, *why* you were going. But how could they know that if they only bugged the phone when you got there?"

"Well I made first contact with the Prof by phone but after that everything was done via email. So that could be how they knew I was going up there – and when – by hacking into my PC. But they must have had a reason to do that and, as far as I'm aware, we three and Becca are the only ones who know about what we found, other than the Professor, and he only knew a couple of hours before my phone was bugged. Unless you guys have mentioned it to anybody."

David raised his hand, a little sheepishly. "Guilty, m'lud. I spoke to Jo Cottrell – well, emailed her first, *then* spoke to her – just to sound her out about helping to set up a meeting for you with Harry Waters. She's still thinking about it, but I can guarantee she won't have mentioned it to anyone else. I specifically asked her not to."

They all sat in silence for a while, thinking through the implications of what David had said, before Tony spoke.

"Did your colleague know I was going to Shetland?"

"No, definitely not. How could she? Even we didn't know until you phoned George from the airport just as you were setting off."

Tony frowned. "Then the only way anyone would know about the trip if the phone *wasn't* bugged beforehand would be through my PC. I booked the flight and the hotel online as well."

"So, you were already being monitored before you went to Shetland. Is it possible you were under surveillance for something else? And the borrowing of the phone was just a coincidence, suspicious enough for you to check the phone, but perhaps the bug was already in place."

George got to his feet. "I need help with this," he said. "More coffee?"

As they sipped their fresh coffee, David was turning over in his mind the events of the previous year when Tom Brown emerged as a suspect in a spate of executions in Guildford, Cobham and Dorking. He recalled how Jo had refused to even consider his involvement as a possibility, just as she had never wavered in her belief that Tom's son, Jack, was innocent of Class A drug dealing. This had set her against the establishment, put her at odds with her colleagues and superiors. He also remembered the two occasions when Jo had been close to death, both accepted as accidental near-misses at the time.

First, an explosion in an apartment block would certainly have claimed her life had she not been delayed in traffic and arrived late to attend a meeting there. And, a week later, on the steps of Guildford Magistrates' Court where Mickey Kadawe had been gunned down by two shots to the chest as he entered the building, Jo had been saved from a third bullet by Tom himself reacting quickly and pulling her to the ground out of the line of fire.

At the time only David, it seemed, had linked the two events and expressed concern to Jo over her safety. Jo's reaction had been to dismiss it as his attempt at upstaging her in the conspiracy-theory stakes. A lack of any subsequent action seemed to bear this out, although there appeared to be some doubt, even in Jo's mind, as to who had initiated her transfer back to Leicester. Had it been her new superior officer in Leicester, eager for her to return and complete her interrupted assignment, or John Mackay, her own boss in Guildford, keen to get her out of harm's way?

Now his doubts returned. Had Jo's insistence at challenging the establishment and her reluctance to accept the jury's guilty verdict in Jack's case made her a target in some sinister plot? Surely not. But what if it had, and still did? What if someone was keen to know if she still harboured an ambition to set the record straight? That might mean she was under surveillance herself, and that his call to her or his email – or both – could have been picked up. He wasn't about to share these thoughts with his companions, but, of the five people who knew about Tony's investigation before he went to Shetland, Jo being the inadvertent source of the information seemed the most likely explanation.

"Listen, David." Tony interrupted his thoughts. "I don't want to point any fingers but I guess there must be things your ex-colleague is unable to share with you in her current job, in spite of how close you are as friends. Right?"

"I guess so, but…"

"So, is it possible that she may be officially involved in an ongoing investigation into Tom's disappearance? Perhaps a covert one. In which case, knowing I was going to dig into it, she could get the aforementioned rubber-stamped approval to bug my phone and computer, just on the off chance that I might get something they missed. That would fit with your suggestion that the device could have been in place before I went and the episode with this guy on the island was just a coincidence which led me to find it. Although, having said that, I can't imagine how and when it *could* have been done other than on the island."

David shook his head. "I don't believe Jo would be involved without telling me, *but…*" he held up his hand to stop Tony interrupting "… it's a possibility. Also, I'm not a believer in coincidence, and the mix-up with the networks in Shetland makes me think the deed was done at that time, whether or not it was at Jo's instigation."

"But *why*?"

"There can be only two reasons as I see it. Someone – or some organisation – wants to make sure you don't find out too much, or, as you suggested, thinks you might be able to help them solve the mystery of Tom's disappearance. Either way, it seems there are others who either know or believe there's something not quite right about Mr Brown's demise."

They each looked from one to the other in silence for a few moments.

"Just out of interest," George said, "how would this guy know what type of phone Tony had so he could have the right battery to insert?"

"That's a good question, George," David said. "It would be easy for the police or secret services to check that through the phone companies, but difficult for a private person or surveillance company, without raising a lot of questions. Which points towards an official job. What do you plan to do about the phone, Tony?"

"That's a question I was going to ask you. I could just transfer everything I needed from it to a new phone and throw it away, although I guess they'd find it almost straight away. I could change the battery…"

David shook his head. "If you do anything different with the phone right now it's a dead give-away that you know you're being monitored. Not knowing who these people are, we don't know how dangerous it would be for you if they found out. Now you know about the bug I think you should just manage the surveillance. You can tell them what you want them to hear, which is more of what you told us in the pub. Let them know that you've genuinely given up the chase, either by omission or by saying so whenever the opportunity arises. I would suggest, by simply not mentioning it again. And if it *is* Tom's disappearance they're concerned about, and not something else you're working on, then they'll stop listening. The only problem is you won't know *when* they've stopped listening."

They sat in silence for a while before David spoke again.

"Here's an idea. You need to keep your phone for the time being, as we said, but arrange to get it stolen or lost in, say, a couple of weeks' time. If you've mentioned nothing about this – by phone or email – during that time, chances are they won't go to the trouble of bugging a new phone. Make sure you get an upgraded model as a replacement, preferably with a new number, so even if you get the old one back, you can legitimately transfer all your documents over and keep the new one. Obviously, you'll download all the files, anyway, before it goes missing."

"Chances are I will get the old one back and fairly quickly," Tony said, "because, as I said, they'll know exactly where it is. I might not have time to set up a new one."

"Good point," David said. "It would be better to lose it, irretrievably. What about over the side of your boat? You could drop it and have it slide off the deck. Have Rebecca shout a warning for the benefit of anyone listening in. Even if they can salvage it, they're not going to return it, are they? That would take a lot of explaining."

"Sounds like a plan," Tony said. "I'll do that."

"One other thing," David said. "In the pub you mentioned you might let the police have the photos, which they will have heard, of course. It might look suspicious now if you *don't* do that, and Harry Waters would be the obvious person to send them to. But let me meet with him first with some hard copies. I got on well with Harry, so I think he'll agree to see me. Then I can prepare him for receiving them from you, presumably as an email attachment. It might prevent him from reacting in the wrong way." David shrugged. "Having said that, don't ask me what the *right* way is. So, what do you think, Tony? I'm not trying to take over or anything."

"No, that sounds good. I'm really grateful for your helping me out. What about DI Cottrell? Will she be in the loop at all?"

"I'm going to try to keep her out of it for now, especially as she seems to be the source of our leak."

They were silent again for a few moments.

"Shall I get some more coffee?" said George, smiling. "That being, it seems, my only material contribution to the proceedings."

⋆

Back in the car park of the Dog and Duck, Tony removed his jacket from the boot of the car and took his phone out of the pocket.

"*There* you are," he said in a loud whisper. He checked the missed calls – two from Becca, as planned. He smiled to himself as he touched the screen.

"Hi, Becca, I…"

"Where have you been? I've been calling you all evening."

"You've called me *twice*, in fact, and I'm sorry. I went for a walk with David and George then back to George's for a coffee. Left my phone with my jacket in the car. Thought I'd lost the bloody thing, nearly had a heart attack. Where are you?"

"Grosvenor Gardens. Where else? I know when I'm onto a good thing."

Tony laughed. "I guess I'm going to be the best part of an hour, but I'll get there as soon as possible."

"Okay, I'll keep everything warm for you."

He laughed again. "'Hot' would be even better."

"I'll do my best. What did David and George say?"

"They were genuinely relieved. They'd both come to the same conclusion and I think they were wondering how they were going to let me down gently."

"And you're sure?"

"Absolutely, Becks. Weight off my mind."

"Good. See you later."

CHAPTER NINE

Wednesday, 21 June

David drummed his fingers on the arm of the easy chair as he waited for his call to be picked up. The answering voice, as always, surprised him with its gentle softness as he imagined the mighty frame from which it came.

"DS Carter speaking."

"Hi, Seb. It's David Gerrard here. Are you with Jo by any chance?"

"Oh, hi, sir. I'm not, I'm afraid. I'm at a crime scene right now. Can I get her to call you when I see her?"

"Actually, it's you I want to speak to, Seb, and specifically when Jo's not there. And, by the way, it's David not 'sir'. I don't have a rank at all now. You're obviously too busy at the moment but..."

"No, it's okay, sir – David – we're just wrapping it up, so I'm okay to talk. Is something wrong?"

"I'm not sure. Nothing to be worried about I don't think but I don't want to say too much right now. Look, have you got a payphone in the village?"

"There's one at the pub – the Queen Anne."

"Any chance you could get Jo to phone me from there as soon as possible, preferably later today? You might want to be on the call as well. Don't worry, nobody's in danger or anything..."

"But you think someone may be listening to her calls."

"It's a possibility. Okay?"

"Okay. We'll speak to you from there later, after, say, eight o'clock."

"Perfect. Oh, and it's just possible if someone *is* listening, it might be more than just the calls. It might be any conversation within a few metres of the phone. So, take care how you let her know and make sure she leaves the phone behind when you go to the pub. Okay?"

"Okay."

"Speak later."

David ended the call and smiled to himself, imagining Seb going over in his mind all the intimate moments he and Jo had shared which just might have been enjoyed by a third party or parties.

He checked his watch – just after two o'clock.

Change of plan.

*

David glanced at the clock on the opposite wall; 7.55 p.m. The last time he'd been waiting in a similar establishment for this particular lady, she'd been late, and extremely wary of him. On that occasion it hadn't been his *unexpected* appearance that had surprised her; it was his *physical* one. He smiled to himself as he recalled his disguise – shaven head, earrings and tattoos – his street-fighter image for the job of tracking down Lawrence Harvey "Laser" Newhouse. Jo had seen David seated in the corner of the room in the Thonburi Thai restaurant in Guildford and looked quickly away, having failed to recognise him. She had climbed onto a bar stool with her back to him and he could sense her shaking inside as he approached her.

"You're late," he'd growled, and Jo had spun round on the stool, almost falling off it.

"Oh, my God!" she'd shouted, drawing anxious stares from every customer, before her alarm was swamped by laughter. Even so, the memory was tinged with sadness.

Laser had been the first of eight victims of a serial killer targeting seemingly harmless drug users. Sadness *and* guilt, in fact, because David had never been able to shake the feeling that his finding Laser – and extracting information from him about a wider network of dealers and suppliers – had been a factor in his death.

From his seat at a table in the main bar in the Queen Anne he watched two shapes appear behind the frosted-glass panel of the entrance door. It was pushed open and Detective Inspector Joannita Cottrell entered first, immediately followed by Detective Sergeant Sebastian Carter, who ducked his head instinctively to avoid colliding with the top of the door frame.

Jo was three-quarters Caribbean – her own description of her ancestry – five-feet five inches tall, with a trim figure, pretty face and shoulder-length auburn-tipped curls. Seb was a fraction short of David's height with a muscular, athletic frame. Six years younger than Jo, he had a fresh faced, schoolboy look about him. Both were wearing faded blue jeans and tee shirts. They walked across to the bar and Jo raised herself up on to a stool. David checked his watch; 8.07. He left his seat and walked over to them.

"You're late." The same growl.

Jo spun round. "Oh, my God! What are you doing here?"

"Well, as Spike Milligan famously said, 'everybody's got to be somewhere'. And, to be honest, I figured if I was ever going to meet this big guy here, I was going to have to take the initiative."

He reached out his hand to Seb, who took it. David noted the firm but gentle grip without any hint of trying to impress. He liked that.

"Great to meet you at last, sir..."

"David."

"David, sorry."

"No apology necessary. When my knighthood comes through, I'll be insisting on 'sir' again."

Jo had got down from the stool to embrace him. Being a little over a foot shorter than David meant her face was pressed against his chest. David bent to kiss her on the cheek. He took a small step back, lifting his right hand to his ear to make the thumb-and-little-finger sign for a phone. He pointed at Jo's bag with his other hand, raising his eyebrows.

"In the car," Jo said. "But why did you decide to come? Though, we're delighted that you did, of course."

"Of course," David said. "Mainly, I guess, because I figured there was too much to talk about for a phone call. Certainly, if you two had to stand in a public place for a long time. And I was right, I think. The payphone isn't exactly located in the interest of privacy, is it? I saw it on the wall in the corridor just outside the gents."

"Well, as I said, we're delighted you did," Jo said. "Partly, at least, because we weren't sure if we'd be able to work the payphone. It's been years since I used one and Seb's too young to even remember them."

Seb smiled. "Jo never misses an opportunity to remind me that she's older and wiser than me. I mean, it's only a ten-year difference." He winked at David.

"I *beg* your pardon." Jo nudged him in the ribs. "Anyway, are we going to talk or eat first? You must be hungry, David, driving all that way."

"It's not much more than a couple of hours and I had a snack on the way. But yes, I'm ready to eat if you both are."

"And you'll stay over with us?" Seb asked. "We have a spare bedroom."

"Which you'll just about fit into," Jo added.

"That's very kind but I need to get back tonight. Got an important meeting in Guildford tomorrow morning. I'll tell you about that later."

"Some other time, then," Jo said. "So, let's eat."

"I have a table waiting," David said, with a sweep of his arm.

A young man wearing a black polo shirt with the words "Queen Anne" in white on the breast pocket followed them to the table David had vacated and handed them each a menu as they sat down.

"Hi, Toby," Jo said. "Everything on tonight?"

"Yes, Jo, plus the specials on the board."

"Great. Just give us five minutes." The young man nodded and walked away.

"Jo's told me all about your achievements with Saracens," Seb said. "You made it to England Saxons as well, I believe?"

"Briefly, yes. Just enough games to get me on to England's radar and then I started falling apart – hips, knees, pretty much everything that moved. Saracens kept me on the coaching staff for a year or so after I stopped playing but it wasn't for me. You play yourself, Jo tells me, and same position as me."

"That's right, flanker. I was odds-on to play basketball up to my mid-teens. Over six feet before I was fourteen and thin as a beanpole. But I always wanted to play rugby, so I started working out and bulking up. Got as far as a trial for Leicester but missed out."

"You still play, though?" David asked.

"Yes, for Leicester Lions in the National League Two, a long way from the Premiership, I'm afraid. And for the police."

"I played for the police – bloody hated it. The only opportunity within the law for assaulting a police officer. And boy, don't they all take that opportunity."

The two men became aware of Jo jerking her head back and forth between them, with greatly exaggerated movement, as if she were watching a rally at Wimbledon. They both smiled broadly, pretending to ignore her.

"I was good at rounders until I left primary school, if anyone's interested," she said. "Then malnutrition took its toll, pretty much like it's doing right now, come to think of it."

They placed their orders – David, to Jo's amusement, gravitating to his standard haddock, chips and mushy peas – and ate in silence after Toby returned with their huge portions on large oval dishes. Afterwards, they leaned back from their empty plates and ordered another round of drinks as they were cleared away.

"Right, I'm ready to listen." Jo looked at David.

"No pudding?"

"I'm applying the twenty-minute rule. Don't order a dessert until you've given your stomach twenty minutes to decide if it's full. It takes that long for the brain to…"

"Yes, I've heard it many times," David said, "and always from the same source."

"So, shoot. Who do you think is listening to me, and why?"

⋆

When David had finished telling the story, he and Seb looked expectantly at Jo awaiting a reaction, which was not forthcoming. As she stared wide-eyed into space, Seb stepped in to fill the silence.

"Who suggested Dobson should go to Shetland?"

"He decided that himself later, after our first meeting in the Dog, and after I'd spoken to Jo. He thought it might be worth checking what would happen to a body if it went into the water close to where the boat was discovered and found this professor at the University of Highlands and Islands who would be able to help him. Turned out the Prof was based at the uni's Marine Research facility in Shetland."

"Right, so having listened in to your call to Jo or picked up your email..."

"Or both."

"Or both, they decided to put a tag on Dobson. They hacked his PC and found out about his trip to Shetland – when he was going, who he was seeing and where he was staying – all even before you knew about it."

"That's right," David said. "He was already on his way when he phoned George to tell him." They looked at Jo again, who shrugged her shoulders.

"If that's correct, then it's likely I've been monitored all the time I've been up here – and probably before. I don't know whether to feel frightened or angry. I mean, why would somebody do this and, more to the point, who *is* this 'somebody'?"

"Well, I'm not sure about the who, but I think the why is obvious."

"Do tell," Jo said.

"It must be because of you stirring things up about the verdict on Jack and Jason. They'll be keeping tabs on you to make sure you're not hiring handsome, retired detectives to keep digging, like you did before."

"But that was ages ago – last year. I admit, I still feel something wasn't right about the whole case, but I've put that behind me and even told Maggie 'case closed'. I only thought of it again recently when you got in touch."

"I know, but they don't know that and..."

"They? Now we're back to 'who' again. If – and it seems likely – my calls, at least, are being monitored, who's listening to them?"

"Well, perhaps the same people responsible for two attempts on your life."

"*What*?" Seb shot forward on his chair and grabbed Jo's hand. "What attempts on your life?"

"Oh, thanks, David," Jo said. "He's not going to let me out of the house now." She turned to Seb. "It's David's theory, his *opinion*. It's not what actually happened. I sometimes think he should be taking the creative writing course at Cullen College rather than the local government one."

"Okay," David said. "Let's get a *second* opinion. You decide, Seb. The first time was in Dorking, when..."

"Must we do this, David?" Jo pleaded.

David shrugged. "Not if Seb doesn't want to hear."

"Go on, David. The first time...?"

"Jo and her colleague turn up fifteen minutes late for a meeting with some guys under witness protection in Dorking, and as they arrive, the building where the meeting is to take place is destroyed by an explosion. If they'd arrived on time, they would have both been inside and – well – deceased, like the guys they were due to meet. I guess you knew this already, anyway, Seb."

"Yes, I did know, but I wasn't aware that it was Jo they were targeting as well."

Jo gave a loud, exasperated sigh. "That's got to be a coincidence, David. Only a handful of people knew Tina and I were going to Dorking for that meeting..."

"A similar-sized handful to the one who knew you'd be on the steps at Guildford?"

"That would be the second time?" Seb cut in.

"One week later, on the steps of Guildford Magistrates' Court, Mickey Kadawe was gunned down by a sniper – two shots to the chest, five centimetres apart. Pretty good shooting, wouldn't you say? What was not revealed to the public was that a third shot was fired, but this one hit the top step just below Kadawe's feet, and would have taken out a certain DI Cottrell had Tom Brown not reacted so quickly and dropped her out of the line of fire."

"There's absolutely nothing to indicate that the third bullet was intended for me, so..."

"It's the two incidents together, Jo. Just like we said about Tony's photos and the discovery of the boat. It would be relatively easy to dismiss either one, but together..." He spread his arms to seal the argument.

"You didn't tell me about the third bullet." Seb held on more tightly to Jo's hand.

"Because I don't believe..."

"Well I'm with David on this."

"Of course, you are, my darling." Jo smiled and leaned into him. "You're my champion, here to protect me. But that was nearly a year ago. Nothing's happened since then. If someone was trying to silence me, they wouldn't just give up because they failed with the first couple of attempts, now, *would* they?"

Seb was not ready to be appeased. "But think back to when you moved up here," he said. "John Mackay told you that Dotcom had requested that you be reassigned to your previous position here. But Dotcom told *me* that it was Mackay who suggested you came back."

"But does it matter?" Jo said.

"Not to me," Seb replied. "I'm just delighted that it happened, of course, but that might have been part of a plan. Your boss moves you away so you can't continue interfering, but arranges to bug your phone just as a precaution."

Jo looked from one to the other, eyes wide and incredulous. "You're not suggesting that it was Johnny Mac who was trying to do me in?"

"Of course not," David said, "but he might have suspected somebody was out to silence you. Seb could well be right. He moved you out of harm's way."

Jo sighed in conceding the point. "Okay, let's just say you're right, where do we go from here?"

David leaned forward. "I've thought of that. You need to take yourself out of the loop, Jo. It's important you don't get involved. They – whoever – will have heard you say you're still interested and mention the possibility of John Mackay meeting Tony. I think you need to do two things. One, don't mention this again to anybody, *except* – and this is number two – when I phone you to tell you Tony's dropping the case, do what he did, sound relieved and say something like 'I don't want to get involved again, either'. Say that life's too good at the moment…" he nodded towards Seb and smiled "… which I think is true, isn't it? But mention you think it's a good idea to let the police have the pictures; say they should go to Harry Waters but that you don't want to see them."

"But we don't know what Harry will do with them."

"I spoke to Harry today. I've arranged to see him tomorrow – that's my important meeting in Guildford. It will be off the record, before Tony sends him the photos. I'll have hard copies with me, so he'll know what to expect, and I'll take him through what's happened. But after that, you're right, we don't know what he'll do with them. Looking back, it would have been better if Tony hadn't said in the pub that he would hand them over to the police. But having said it, I think he has to do it." He looked from one to the other. "Are you both okay with that?"

"I guess so," Jo said. Seb nodded.

"Good, I'll phone you early tomorrow morning before I set off for Guildford. And, as soon as possible – stating the bleeding obvious – you should check that you haven't got the same bug in your phone as in Tony's. I think it's more likely that it's just your calls they're picking up, but worth checking."

They all sat with their own silent thoughts for a while before David spoke again.

"There's one other scenario, which I… sort of… hesitate to mention in case it signals the end of a beautiful friendship." He shrugged and spread his hands. "If you'd like to hear it."

Jo and Seb looked at each other and then at David.

"We'll take the risk," Jo said.

"One of Tony's theories is that you, Jo, might be officially involved in an investigation into Tom Brown's disappearance, and after I'd told you of Tony's discoveries, *you* authorised the hacking of his PC and bugging of his phone."

Jo's eyes opened wide again, this time in disbelief and indignation.

"I can't believe you just said that. As if I'd not tell you when we spoke on the phone. When have I ever *not* shared…?"

"Hold on, how could I possibly know when you've *not* shared something with me?" David interrupted. "Tony's point was, as a serving police officer, you must be party to information that you are not able to share with a civilian friend – me, in this case – or even other colleagues. And I accept that."

"Well, I think Mr Dobson is out of line suggesting that, but I can forgive him in his ignorance. On the other hand, *you*, David…"

"Hold on, Jo," Seb put in. "David's right, if you were on Tom's case and sworn to secrecy. I mean, it's only tonight that I've learned about David's phoning you about his meeting with Tony, because you respected him asking you not to share it with anyone. I understand that. So, it's a perfectly fair question."

"Gang up on me, why don't you?" Jo said. She looked at David. "Tell me, *is* it a question? *Are* you asking me if I'm actively and officially looking for Tom Brown? And if it is, what do *you* think the answer is?"

"I guess it would have to be no. Which is what I believed, anyway. I was just…"

"Right. Subject closed and the twenty minutes is up. You two can now talk about rugby again while I get the dessert menu."

She got to her feet, noisily pushing back her chair, and strode off to the bar. David and Seb looked at each other and rolled their eyes in shared relief and amusement.

⋆

David smiled to himself as the digital clock on the dashboard clicked over to four zeros. They had seamlessly navigated the awkward exchange with Jo, she had returned from the bar with the menu and more drinks, with her usual smile and demeanour and, true to her parting comment, the subject was closed.

In his ten years or so working with her, he couldn't recall a single occasion when a difference of opinion had escalated into an argument between them. He had always felt – and enjoyed the feeling – that, in spite of her blossoming career and growing reputation and independence, he had a duty of care for her welfare, and he had come to realise that his affection had been more than just platonic, or even paternal. So, he had been surprised tonight at how readily he had accepted Seb as the new major influence and protector in Jo's life. David's willingness to relinquish his role was testament to the young man himself and his obvious love for his former charge. And it wasn't just a doting infatuation but a mature embracing of his responsibility for her well-being, to the extent that he had supported David in pressing Jo to accept the vulnerability of her situation and even on his question about her possible involvement in investigating Tom Brown's disappearance.

It was, after all, a question that needed asking, but it wasn't until he was leaving the M25 for the short final leg of the journey to Meadow Village that it occurred to him that Jo had not answered it.

CHAPTER TEN

Thursday, 22 June

David looked at the faded frontage of the Westmore Guest House and then again at his iPhone with the address Harry Waters had sent him by text. Yes, this was the place. The two-storey white-rendered building was of an indeterminate age and lacking in any positive architectural features. The blandness of its exterior was accentuated by the chipped masonry and flaking paint of its windows, of which there were six at the front of the building on the first floor and two each side of the entrance at ground level. He walked up the three crumbling steps to the front door, which opened onto a dimly lit entrance hall about four metres square.

Opposite the door a thin woman in her early sixties was leaning with one elbow on a high, curved reception desk while turning the pages of a magazine with her other hand. Behind her on the wall was a line of twenty or so numbered hooks, mostly empty except for a few which held large metal keys. The woman didn't look up until he was standing immediately in front of her. Her eyes opened wide in surprise at his imposing presence and she took half a step backwards.

"I've a meeting with Mr Harry Waters. Am I in the right place?"

"That depends."

David sighed. "On what?"

"On who you are."

"David Gerrard. Will that do?"

She picked up a crumpled piece of paper from the desk and screwed up her eyes to read from it. "Is that double r?" she said.

"How many David Gerrards are you expecting?"

"It's my job to..."

"Yes, it's double r. Okay?"

"Okay. But you're definitely *not* what I was expecting. Room 17, first floor, stairs through there, no lift." She went back to her magazine.

David climbed the steep wooden staircase to a dark corridor with a worn carpet which was so threadbare it was impossible to discern the pattern on it. The only light was that from outside, forcing itself through dirty windows in the emergency exits at either end of the passageway. There were five numbered doors off in each direction and a sign on the wall pointed him to the right for "Rooms 15 to 19". The whole place smelt of a stomach-turning cocktail of damp walls, fried food and disinfectant. David knocked on the door of Room 17, hardly believing that Detective Inspector Harry Waters could possibly be on the other side of it.

He heard the sound of a chair scraping on the floor and light footsteps. A key turned and the door was pulled open. Harry Waters had changed his image since the first, and only, time David had met him. The thinning hair was disguised by a short, clippered style which was approximately the same length as his carefully sculptured stubble. Gone was the everyday grey suit to be replaced by chinos and a linen jacket worn over an open-necked shirt.

"David, good to see you. Welcome to our little hideaway."

They shook hands and David stepped into the room. In the centre was a small rectangular dining table with two chairs at one long side and another on the opposite side facing them. The only other piece of furniture was a sideboard on which was a double hotplate holding two Pyrex pots of coffee next to a tray containing three mugs, a sugar bowl and milk jug. The other item of interest in the room was a young woman in blue jeans and a white polo shirt, who got to her feet as he entered. A brown leather jacket hung on the back of her chair. She was the same height as Harry, with a slim figure, light-brown hair pulled back in a ponytail, and a round, friendly face.

"This is DC Natalie Crusoe," Harry said. "Nat, DCI Gerrard..."

"Retired," David said. "Good to meet you, DC Crusoe."

"You, too, sir, and it's Nat."

"And I'm David."

"Coffee?" Harry asked, walking over to the sideboard.

"Yes, please, black, no sugar." David looked around the room. "I'm struggling a bit wondering what to say about this place."

Harry laughed, placing a mug in front of David. "Claridge's was fully booked and, anyway, their coffee's rubbish. This is where we meet people who have something to tell us but who have a phobia about police stations. A place to unload – between fixes, usually – and get things off their chest without feeling any pressure."

"Makes sense," David said. "Which category do I fall into, phobias or fixes?"

"Well, that's what we're here to find out. I know you asked for this to be off the record – and it will be – but I asked Nat along because…"

"Fully understand," David interrupted, lifting his hands. "I expected it because I would have done the same. And three minds are better than two."

"Good. So, I assume you have taken up the Cottrell crusade to clear the Tomlinson-Brown family name and get Jason released. How's Jo doing, by the way?"

"Really well. She seems very settled in the job and in her personal life. She knows I'm meeting with you, by the way. Sends her best wishes."

"That's great to hear. We still miss her, don't we, Nat? Even though she did have a tendency to ask awkward questions at the wrong time. Looking back, though, I guess they all needed asking."

"Well, I can assure you this is not from Jo; it's from another source, and it's not the son but the father this time. It came about by accident. Tony Dobson, the journalist, and his girlfriend were on holiday last month sailing round Scotland and…" David reached into the inside pocket of his jacket and pulled out a number of folded sheets of paper "… took this photograph while they were in Ullapool." He unfolded the sheets and passed the top one across the table. "Well, more accurately, his girlfriend took the picture *of* Tony down by the shore."

Harry and Natalie studied the picture, then looked up at David.

"He then compared it with this picture of Tom Brown…" David showed them the second sheet "… which you'll probably recognise. It was taken last October and appeared in the press and on the news last November. Quite a coincidence, don't you think?"

He passed them a third sheet, a copy of the two side-by-side images.

Natalie screwed up her face in a frown. "And you say one was taken last month – May – and the other last October?"

"That's right."

"But that's not possible. They're exactly the same. They can't have been taken half a year apart."

"Well spotted, detective. That was a good ten seconds quicker than it took me to see it. And that was Dobson's point. Obviously, he can vouch for his own photo, so the October one is a fake. Questions are – one, where did it come from and, two, for what purpose? And I can answer the first one." He showed them the photo of Tom leaning on a car. "It was copied from this picture of him taken after a bender in Guildford earlier in the year."

Harry picked up the fake photograph and shook his head.

"I do remember this appearing at a time when we were still looking for Tom Brown," he said. "But there was other clear evidence he had travelled to Ullapool. I'm talking about his car and the stolen boat."

"Which brings me to Exhibit B." David passed them another sheet showing a picture of the boat with the remains of the crime-scene tape around it. "I guess you will have seen this for real. Dobson and his girlfriend spoke to a fisherman who works with boats in this area who thinks it highly unlikely anyone could have made it to the Shiants in this boat, especially at that time of year."

"That's one person's opinion, of course."

"Of course, but probably a valid one."

"No doubt, but just an opinion all the same." Harry continued to study the photos in silence.

"Just because the photo is a fake doesn't mean he wasn't up there," Natalie said. "There's the car as well, and the boat must have got to the island somehow, *with* Tom Brown's holdall in it."

"But anyone could have driven the car up there, and the boat could have been taken over in a larger craft and the holdall placed in it afterwards, although…" David held up his hands again to ward off their protests "… I'm not suggesting that *did* happen, just that it could have."

Harry and Natalie were silent again for a while.

"What do you – or Dobson – expect us to do with this?" Harry asked.

"Well before we get to that question, let me tell you the rest of the story." He pushed across the last sheet showing Tony's phone with the listening device in place. "I guess you guys know what this is, right?"

*

Harry rose from his chair when David had finished talking and walked over to the sideboard, picking up one of the coffee pots and topping up the three mugs. He sighed.

"So, Dobson will be forwarding these pictures to me by email saying I might be interested in them, but he isn't pursuing it himself?"

"That's right."

"And he's saying that with the belief that the message will be picked up by person or persons unknown."

"Yes."

"And that they will believe him?"

David shrugged. "That's the plan. Why?"

"Well, this guy, among other things, is a driven investigative journalist. Whatever he says to me in his email, whoever picks it up is going to assume – correctly – that he'll be pursuing this to the bitter end. Don't you think?"

"That would depend on how convincing he is with his reasons, but if he keeps his phone with him at all times and doesn't discuss it with anybody going forward – or text or email anyone about it – then I think he'll be able to persuade them that he means it. I take your point though, Harry. The email alone won't convince them."

"Okay, and how *is* he going to pursue it? Is he expecting us to take it on?"

"I've not asked him that. I know he uses a number of press offices around the capital. I'm sure he can do a lot on any number of borrowed PCs. He'll know for sure what he can and can't do now he's aware of the extent of the surveillance."

"Well, I can't commit any resources to this. The bugging of Dobson's phone is interesting – and Jo's, if that is the case – but I'm not sure it means anything in relation to Brown's disappearance."

David shrugged and look at Natalie.

"I guess it must mean that *somebody* is still interested in Tom Brown's disappearance," she said.

"I agree. I think that's pretty obvious," David said. "*Somebody*, but…"

"Hold on, I'm not so sure," Harry said, returning the coffee pot to its hotplate. "It could be linked to something else Dobson's working on. He hasn't risen to fame over the last few years reporting bicycle thefts and unfair parking fines. He's been into some big exposés and corruption issues involving very high-profile, influential people. He must have some powerful enemies out there. People who would have the means to do this without the need to fill in any forms. That's as likely – *more* likely – to be a reason than his stumbling on to a few scraps of information which don't add up to anything at all."

"I asked him that – about other stuff he was doing – and he said there was nothing like that. That's not to say he couldn't be getting too close to something without realising it, I guess. But it's the timing, Harry. He shares this with me and George, I share it with Jo, and suddenly someone's following him to Shetland to fix his phone."

"Yes, but…" Harry's voice tailed off and he stared into space.

"You okay, Harry?"

Harry blinked out of his trance. "Yes, fine. It was what you said about timing." He turned to his colleague. "Do you remember when we were up in Ullapool with Bonnie Prince Charlie…?"

"*Who*?" David interrupted.

"DI Charlie Stuart, Highland Police. I raised a question around the timing of Brown leaving London. Something to do with his car. Can you remember what it was, Nat?"

Natalie wrinkled her brow in concentration. "I think we initially assumed he'd headed up to Scotland to escape arrest. He was last at his apartment on the Sunday – not *seen* there, but he definitely made a call from there to John Mackay on that afternoon. His wife went to the apartment next day – Monday – and he'd already left, along with his car, overnight bag, whatever. You found the gun in the apartment two days later on Wednesday…"

"Actually, Jo found the gun and called me. That was in the afternoon."

"Right, and we put out an appeal for information about Tom and his car lunchtime Thursday. The car was reported in Ullapool within an hour or so after the appeal."

"But the person who reported it said it had been there for a couple of days, didn't they?" Harry said.

"That's right, in fact, Charlie said a lot of people came forward with that same information, not just the one."

"Sorry," David said. "The point being what, exactly?"

"Tom couldn't have known we were looking for him until Thursday afternoon, soonest," Natalie said. "And by that time, he'd already been up there for two days. So, the reason he ran away wasn't to avoid arrest."

David frowned. "You say *Tom* had been up there for a couple of days. Don't you mean his *car* had been there? I assume DI Stuart asked the people who came forward whether they had seen the driver?"

"Yes, he did, but most had only seen the car parked, empty, at the quayside," Natalie said, "and of the few who saw it arrive, none could give a description of the driver."

"So, when did this discrepancy with the timing arise?" David asked. "And what did you do?"

"It was shortly after we'd got up to Ullapool – the following Monday, I think it was," Harry said, looking at Natalie, who nodded. "What did we do? Well, we checked CCTV, ANPR and speed cameras on the routes from London to Ullapool. Captured enough images to confirm that it *was* the Tuesday when the car was taken up there. But it didn't register on camera at any of the motorway stops so he must have come off the main routes to refuel, and he would have had to refuel at least twice even if he started with a full tank. Not sure *why* he would do that because it's hard staying under the radar when you're zooming around in a silver racing car."

"Unless it wasn't Tom in the car, but the person driving it wanted you to assume it was."

"Well, we *did* assume exactly that. At the time we were just trying to establish *when* it was driven up there." Harry shrugged and spread his hands. "And to be honest, David, there's still nothing to suggest it was anyone else driving it. Although Charlie's lot checked out all the local hotels, B&Bs, camping grounds – *and* the ferries – and there was no trace of Brown at all. We also checked out a place on… where was it, Nat?"

"Knoydart peninsular. Margaret Tomlinson-Brown's godfather owns a house on there. They stayed there earlier in the year."

"That's right. We thought he might have just decided to get away from it all and it was just a coincidence that his disappearance was so close to when our call went out."

"And?"

"Whether it was a coincidence or not I can't say, but he wasn't on Knoydart. And then, a week or so later, the boat with his stuff in it was found on the island in The Minch and that sort of upstaged everything. The case suddenly turned into the search for a body."

"What about satellites, did they check if anything was picked up in The Minch?"

"There was a couple of weeks between his car arriving in Ullapool and the boat being found. They did check satellite images for that period, but nothing turned up. The weather was pretty good for the time of year, but it was still mostly overcast – or dark, of course. Brown would know enough about surveillance to choose the right time for the trip."

They sat in silence for a long time, Harry with the same vacant expression as before, deep in thought, staring at the wall behind David. Eventually, he turned to Natalie again.

"Mackay phoned while we were up there, didn't he, Nat? About Brown trying to stop the transfer vessel."

"Yes, it was a few weeks before he went missing, the day Mickey Kadawe was shot, in fact. Tom left the scene while he was waiting to be questioned about his possible involvement in the killing. We didn't find out where he'd gone until sometime afterwards through his wife telling John Mackay. It was also the day the final group of exiles was being taken to Alpha and, apparently, he'd hired a private jet and attempted to stop the vessel."

"Why the hell would he want to do that, and *how*?" David asked.

"He believed Jason Midanda – his daughter's boyfriend – was on board," said Harry. "And with the new evidence against Kadawe, he had asked Mackay to take him off passage. At that stage, Midanda was supposed to be at an intermediate destination awaiting shipment at some future date, but there was no record of him ever having reached that destination after leaving Guildford. Brown put two and two together. Whether he was right or not, we've no way of knowing."

"But how could he have hoped to stop it in a private-hire jet? I assume they're not fitted with air-to-surface missiles."

"Apparently, he'd tried to contact the vessel – and Lochshore – but there was a radio blackout or something," Natalie answered. "So he was going to try to parachute onto the ship and… well, I'm not sure what he thought he could do."

David was wide-eyed with incredulity. "I'm not really built for parachuting," he said, "so I'm no expert, but I'd guess that jumping out of a jet onto a ship out in the Atlantic is something to be avoided. I'm amazed he could get a pilot to agree to help him."

"Well, the pilot wasn't aware of what he had in mind," Natalie said. "From what Mrs Tomlinson-Brown told John Mackay, he saved Tom's life by stopping him trying. They were then escorted away from the vessel by a couple of fighters who had threatened to shoot them down."

"Bloody hell. How did I miss that on the news?"

"You didn't," Harry said. "The Home Secretary put a block on it. The police were planning to make a statement, but Hewlett stepped in. From what I understood from Mackay, she felt there was nothing to gain by tarnishing Brown's reputation further. I think he and Hewlett had been close friends in government, so it never came out. We knew nothing about it until Johnny Mac contacted us in Ullapool."

"So why *did* he tell you this while you were up there with DI Stuart? What did he expect you to do?"

Harry and Natalie looked at each other and laughed.

"I seem to remember asking Charlie exactly the same question after we finished the call," Harry said. "I guess the possibility of him trying to storm Alpha to save Jason wasn't any less likely than him parachuting onto a ship to do it. Anyway, Charlie got the area around Alpha checked out and there were just a couple of boats taking water samples or something… Nat? Do you remember?"

"British Oceanographic Society testing water quality around the platform and the St Kilda island group. Checking for any adverse impact of the platform, I'm guessing. Tell you what, though, sir, do you remember they reported that a woman on one of the boats had done a striptease or a pole dance or something. Charlie suggested we bring her in for questioning."

"And I suggested for an encore. I do remember that. Strange behaviour, to say the least, for a scientific expedition."

"But a classic diversionary tactic for something else," David said.

"What do you mean?"

"I went on a course once about hostage rescue tactics and one of the handouts was a book – a manual, in fact – by some American guy, I think. Anyway, he was a leading light on hostage rescue and VIP protection and such. Really interesting, and after the course I read it cover to cover. In the section about rescues from ships there was an author's note saying something about girls in skimpy bikinis on a boat nearby being used to distract the hostage-takers while swimmers or divers attacked from the opposite side."

Natalie smiled. "Forgive me for asking, David, but is that the only thing you remember from the course?"

David laughed. "No, that wasn't part of the course itself, it's what I read afterwards. And it would *never* work with me, Nat, because I'm always too focussed on the job in hand."

Natalie laughed. "I believe you."

"That sounds feasible for a ship, David," Harry said, "but there's no way on to the platform, as I understand it, except via the elevator for disembarking prisoners. And that can only be used from the transfer vessel. There's a helipad for access to services on the satellite platform, but neither of those would allow anyone to gain access to the main platform – and certainly not without being seen. Then, once on, there's no way off, anyway – other than another chopper ride. And there are cameras all the way round the structure pointing seaward. It would take more than a stripper to distract *them*."

"Just someone deciding to give the lads a bit of a treat, then, you think, sir? It wouldn't harm, though, would it, to check if the boats *were* part of a survey? What do you think?"

"I think it would be a waste of time," Harry said. "I admit there are one or two questions around the timing of Brown's disappearance, but I can't see the survey boats could be anything to do with it. We appreciate you coming, David, to give us advance warning of Dobson's email, and we will give it some thought, but I don't think we've enough to take it further. And, look, to be honest, I don't know where any of this is leading us. There's a weight of evidence pointing in one direction and a few scraps pointing the other way, but to what? Are you suggesting that Brown might still be alive? Or that he's dead, but by someone else's hand? I'm not sure that I see..."

"*I'm* not suggesting anything, Harry. Just being... not much more than a postman, I guess. I'm certainly not proposing that he's either alive or somebody killed him. But you know as well as anyone that when you put enough scraps together, they make something that's difficult to ignore."

Harry smiled. "You know what, it could have been Jo saying that. I know now where she gets her words from." He gave a loud sigh and leaned back in his chair. "And that takes me back to around a year ago, when Jo *was* saying all those things. When the evidence against Jack and Jason Midanda was so great and Jo built her own personal case for the defence around the look on Jack's face when she confronted him with the drugs they found in his room. No way, she said, could he possibly have been guilty reacting as he did. And, as I remember telling you, we all desperately wanted her to be right, but we had done such a great job building the case against them..." He spread his hands and shrugged. "Then, when it was too late, the other stuff started to come out, thanks in no small part to you, David, who sort of set the ball rolling. And though I wouldn't go so far as to say it keeps me awake at night, it's something I think about a lot."

"I guess the great irony," Natalie said, "was the impact of Tom Brown's NJR. That required us to work to tighter timescales and perhaps we took certain things more at face value than we would have prior to the new regime."

"Who knows, but if so, that certainly wasn't your fault," David said. "I think you did a great job. But talking about irony, one of my cases that I still think about from time to time goes back twenty years. The guy I helped put away – my first time as an SIO – definitely *was* guilty, of some of the most brutal murders in my experience. But as we built the case against him, it occurred to us that every one of his victims was a villain who we were glad to see the back of. The guy went down for twenty years for doing our job for us."

Harry and Natalie laughed. "And yet you never learned, did you, David?" Harry said. "You did the same with John Deverall, when he was about to clean up the East End. But thank you for your generous appraisal of our performance on the Jack and Jason case. Even so, that was then, and this is now. I really think that Dobson's surveillance will turn out to be about something he's already working on rather than anything to do with Brown's disappearance, and if that is the case, I wouldn't be surprised if it turns out Jo's phone isn't bugged at all. But, as promised, we will think about it, and thank you again for meeting with us."

David spread his hands and sighed. "Okay." He got to his feet and smiled across at Natalie, who stood to take his handshake. "Tell you what, though, Nat, you've got me intrigued about this pole-dancing scientist. I know of someone high up in the British Oceanographic Society. Tony Dobson's Professor Mark Fellows, based at the university on Shetland. You should give him a call. He'll be able to tell you whether that survey was legit or not. And if it was, he might even have the dancer's phone number. You may yet get your encore, Harry."

CHAPTER ELEVEN

Saturday, 24 June

The office of the Ministerial Director of Justice, on the eighth floor of Seacole Building in Marsham Street, SW1, was large and rectangular, with two floor-to-ceiling windows overlooking St John's Gardens. Grace Goody was seated in an antique tilt-and-swivel behind a large mahogany desk, facing a half-circle of four leather-upholstered wing chairs in front of it. In the other half of the room, three two-seater, brown-fabric sofas were arranged around a low glass-topped square table in front of a black marble fireplace. The white-painted walls displayed a number of gilt-framed portraits of various parliamentary dignitaries from the distant past, all of whom were unknown to Grace and most of her visitors.

Jamie Walcott had been staring out of the window closest to the desk for nearly two minutes without speaking. It was a welcome change, Grace thought, from the usual stream of innuendo which seemed to fill their conversations, but, even so, the silence was beginning to grate on her nerves. She coughed, loudly, and he turned towards her.

"Didn't it occur to you that this might be more than a coincidence?"

"Of course, it occurred to me that it *might*..." she began.

"So why wait so long to mention it?"

Grace bristled, getting quickly to her feet. "Why so long? It was only two days ago. And let me remind you that *I* decide who gets to know what – and *when* – around here," she added, thinking immediately how pathetic and frustrating it was that she always felt the need to say something of that nature at every meeting she had with this man.

"Okay, let me put it this way. What was the basis of your decision to wait *two* days before sharing this information, when it seems fucking obvious to me that both surveillances have been compromised?"

"Now look, Walcott…"

"For God's sake, Grace, does our every meeting have to be a vehicle for you telling me who's the boss? We're on the same fucking side, aren't we?"

Grace sighed and sat down again.

"So, tell me why it is *fucking obvious* that something's wrong rather than they've simply decided, independently, they don't want to pursue it."

Jamie left the window and took one of the chairs across the desk from her. He nodded at the small black box on the desk.

"May I?"

Grace turned the recording machine round and pushed it over to him. He pressed the rewind button and watched the digital display changing before hitting pause.

"Right, this is from their phone call two days ago." He pressed play.

David's voice…

Hi, there, and how's my favourite…?

Then Jo…

Oh, David. I'm so *sorry. I was supposed to get back to you on this thing with Dobson, wasn't I? What with all…*

Hold on, that's not why I'm phoning. Well, it is, but not to chase you up. I met with Tony a few nights ago and he's dropped the whole thing. Says he doesn't want to cause mother and daughter any more grief by dragging it up again, just when they're trying to move on. So, I'm just letting you know.

Oh, that's great news, David.

You think so? I wasn't sure what your reaction would be, but that one wasn't on my list.

Well, to be honest, the real *reason I hadn't called you back is because I'm not sure I want to go there either. In fact, I'm sure I* don't *want to go there. Life's good for me here, David, and Tony's right, Maggie is getting her life together again and there's no way we can bring Tom back, so… You're not disappointed in me, are you?*

Of course not. I happen to think you're right to leave it alone. I just didn't expect you to feel the same. And I'm glad life's good for you, Jo. He's a great guy.

Three seconds of silence.

And how could you possibly know that?

Two seconds.

Because I believe everything you tell me, DI Cottrell…

Jamie pressed pause again, frowning at the recorder then at Grace.

"Did you hear that?"

"I heard what you just heard. Why?"

"Listen again." He took it back fifteen seconds.

… just didn't expect you to feel the same. And I'm glad life's good for you, Jo. He's a great guy.

Three seconds.

And how could you possibly know that?

He stopped it again. "That."

"I still don't know…"

"These two are like an old music-hall double act. Their conversations are like…" He clicked his fingers rapidly several times. "No pauses, it's as if they rehearse or something. But just there, a three-second pause. Cottrell didn't know how to respond, what to say. As if he'd confused her somehow, then…" He backed it up a few seconds and restarted the recording.

…for you, Jo. He's a great guy.

Three seconds.

And how could you possibly know that?

Two seconds.

Because I believe everything you tell me, DI Cottrell…

He stopped it again.

"Another pause. Like *Gerrard* wasn't sure this time."

"Okay, but let's assume they *don't* rehearse…"

"Listen to the first call again."

Jamie wound back the recording, this time to the beginning of Jo and David's previous conversation. He moved it forward, stopping and starting until he reached the place he wanted. He pressed play again.

David's voice…

… Anyway, to more important things – how's the incredibly lucky Mr Carter?

Seb's fine, thank you, and still looking forward to meeting you. I really can't believe I've failed to get my two favourite men together for so long. Perhaps I'm not sure I can deal with all that masculinity in one place at the same time.

Jamie stopped the tape.

"Now do you get it?"

Grace nodded. "Gerrard hadn't met lover-boy before the first call, but 'glad life's good for you, he's a great guy' suggests he'd met him before the second call."

"Right. I think he made a mistake and Cottrell picked up on it, but only after a few seconds. And when she let Gerrard know about the mistake – 'how could you know that?' – it took him a couple of seconds to realise and respond. I reckon they met up between the two calls and they *did* rehearse the second call. But Gerrard screwed up by mentioning the boyfriend."

Grace frowned and drummed on the desk with her fingers. "O-kay…" She drew out the word as she thought through the implications. "Which, if that's true, would suggest someone knew, or suspected, Cottrell's calls were being monitored. But how does that lead you to conclude that *both* surveillances – Cottrell *and* Dobson – have been blown?"

"Too much of a coincidence. Two people who passionately state an interest in following up a couple of discrepancies relating to Brown's death suddenly decide, within a few days, that they can't be bothered. And, if we're right, Cottrell changed her mind – or *said* she'd changed her mind – after a clandestine meeting with Gerrard."

"How the hell would she know she's being monitored?"

"No idea."

"And, I ask again, why do you think Dobson knows he's under surveillance? We've listened to every word he's said since you fitted his phone. He's never once mentioned the photo, the boat, Tom Brown, anything, except to tell Gerrard and Holland that he'd given up the chase, so why would he lie to them? Why would he say he's giving up if he's not when he set up the initial meeting specifically to ask for their help?"

"Well, obviously, if he knew or suspected he was being monitored, he'd say that to get whoever was listening off his trail. And perhaps, like Cottrell, he met with them separately to tell them the true story."

"Or he was telling the truth and he *is* off the case and Cottrell is going it alone. Dobson's initial interest might just have fanned the flames for her."

Jamie got up from his chair and walked back over to the window, as if he might find the answer outside. "I don't buy it," he said. "Journalists don't just park a potentially sensational headline for sentimental reasons. This stuff about the wife and daughter, he could still go after his story without involving them. It's a wonder he didn't go straight to press rather than to Gerrard."

"But presumably Gerrard *believes* he's given it up. Dobson hasn't told him otherwise, and don't forget we're tracking him and he's been nowhere near Meadow Village since that second meeting. So, Gerrard must have passed on to Cottrell what he thought was the truth."

Jamie stared in silence out of the window before walking back to the desk and sitting down again.

"Has there been any time when Dobson's been without his phone? Could he have had a secret meeting with Gerrard, like Cottrell did?"

"I'm sure he hasn't, or someone would have flagged it." She turned to her PC and clicked the mouse to bring the screen alive. She moved it round so they could both see the rows and columns of words and figures on an Excel spreadsheet. "These are the times and duration of the recordings." She pointed to the column headings. "Date, time, nature of contact – that is, whether it was face-to-face, call made or call received – duration, other party or parties, and call reference, which links to the actual recording."

Jamie pointed to a cell highlighted in yellow. "Why is that blank and highlighted?"

Grace frowned in thought for a few moments.

"Ah, that shows a time when he *was* away from his phone, but there was nothing suspicious. He just left it behind by accident."

"How do you know he was away from the phone?"

"Well, there was virtually no sound from it except for a couple of incoming calls from his girlfriend which weren't picked up. But we know mainly from what we heard just before and just after that period of time."

"Which was?"

"Just before, Dobson saying he was leaving his jacket in the car, then afterwards phoning his girlfriend back to say…"

Grace stopped speaking and opened her eyes wide. She turned to Jamie. "And guess why he left his jacket in the car."

"Go on."

"To take a walk round Meadow Village with Gerrard and Holland, *just after* he had told them he was dropping the case."

"Leaving him…" Jamie checked the "duration" figure in the column next to the highlighted cell "… just under two hours to talk to them without anybody listening."

They were both silent with their thoughts for some time.

"So," Grace said, "I guess that does suggest he knows he's under surveillance."

"It most certainly does."

Grace smiled. "Then there's the other piece of circumstantial evidence we have."

"Which is?"

"Dobson and his girlfriend always seem to have sex in the shower, where they can legitimately leave the phone in another room and have any sounds of ecstasy drowned out – literally, you might say."

Jamie shook his head. "I just knew we couldn't get through a full meeting without you talking dirty."

Grace laughed.

"So, what else is Dobson up to at the moment, other than shagging in the shower?" Jamie asked. "What *have* we managed to hear?"

"Not a lot other than what you'd expect a busy and popular journalist to be doing: interviews, meetings, casual conversation, lots of paper-rustling and key-tapping. Works freelance, as you know, but has an office at the premises of the *London Evening Standard* in W8. Certainly not heard anything of interest to us and he's not been anywhere we'd not expect him to go given the stuff he's working on. He's heading up to the north coast of Scotland next week with the girlfriend – leaving here Thursday, I think – to retrieve his boat."

"So, let's hope for high seas and stormy weather – and a freak yachting accident." He paused. "And at that second meeting in the pub, what do you think he meant by the blue men? He said the Professor thought they might have got Brown."

"No idea. A reference to the police, perhaps, although it doesn't make any sense."

They both became silent again for a while, before Grace spoke.

"Okay, we have Dobson and Cottrell, let's assume both still interested but each with their hands tied. So, what do they do? How do they connect? How do they *both* go forward with this? No prizes for spotting the common denominator."

"David Gerrard. He's the one we have to deal with."

*

Jamie Walcott pushed his chair away from the desk and leaned back, stretching his legs and arms and yawning long and wide. He checked his watch. It was just after 3.00 p.m. and he had spent the last two hours and two minutes working at his PC. That was about how long it took him to run sixteen miles – which he did twice a week – and after which he felt a lot less tired than he did now. But the time spent had been necessary and ultimately productive. Trawling through the records of a thirty-five-year career in a little over two hours was pretty good going, he thought, especially when you find what you're looking for.

Still in a sitting position, he used his heels to manoeuvre the chair on its castors across to a small fridge under the sloping window. He took a bottle of water from the fridge then stood up and stared out across the green expanse of Kennington Park to the Oval cricket ground beyond. The attic of his three-storey Georgian terraced had been converted, at no personal expense, into a high-tech office which also served as a store for Jamie's impressive arsenal of guns and ammunition. These were stowed around the edges of the room where the roof met the floor, behind low, upright wooden panels secured in place by tiny locks like Phillips screw-heads, giving the appearance of permanence and inaccessibility. Except, he knew, to expert eyes which would not be deceived by something so simple. But he also knew that no-one with such eyes was likely to be aware of his existence, let alone where he lived and the tools he used in his employment.

He went back to the desk, pushing the chair and carrying the bottle of water. He sat down at the PC again and reached across to switch on the printer just as his phone sounded. He recognised the number.

"Well, hi. So soon after the last time. Does this mean we're friends?"

"No, but, as you said, we *are* on the same side."

"So, to what do I owe…?"

"I was thinking after you left this morning about these secret meetings. Around three weeks ago, when he first met with Gerrard and Holland, Dobson said something about possibly meeting with Harry Waters. Since then he's managed to drag himself away as far as Shetland, and Guildford is right on his doorstep, so it might be worth checking whether he did get together with Waters. It would have been before he went to Shetland, otherwise we'd have picked it up on surveillance. It should be on the station Corporate Time schedule, unless Waters has got sucked into the shadowy world of clandestine liaisons as well. Can you check that?"

"I certainly can, and if you wait, I might be able to answer that right away."

He clicked the speaker button on the iPhone and turned to the PC. His hands flowed over the keyboard past menus and passwords for less than a minute before he was speaking again.

"I'm in their CT now, hold on." Ten seconds later, "No, I've gone all the way back to the date of that first meeting with Gerrard, and Waters doesn't appear to have met with him."

"Oh, well, it was just a thought and…"

"*However*, it *is* showing that Waters and a DC Natalie Crusoe had a meeting at 10.30 a.m. on the twenty-second of June, just two days ago, with an un-named person. That's well after we fixed Dobson's phone, though. The venue is down as 'WGH'. No idea what that means, but should be easy to check, if you think it's relevant."

"Only in that the place might have been chosen because one or more of the parties thought it was better not to meet at Guildford New Station. So, yes, check out the venue. Oh, and just one other thing. When you said, 'deal with Gerrard', I hope you have something a little more subtle in mind than when you usually use that expression. I mean…"

"You mean, you wouldn't want to hear that something, let's say, *terminal* had happened to him?"

"Yes, that's exactly what I mean."

"If that's how you feel, then, of course, I'll do all I can to ensure his ongoing safety, but I can't be held responsible for anyone *else* taking action against him. He must have a lot of pretty nasty enemies out there. It's what you get after a successful career putting bad people away, don't you think?"

There was a long silence before Grace replied.

"Well, thank you for that reassurance, Jamie, I'll sleep much better now."

"Hey, you called me Jamie. That *must* mean we're friends."

The call ended. He smiled to himself.

*

It had taken him only a few minutes to establish what "WGH" referred to, and then less than an hour to drive the twenty-five miles along the A3 from Kennington to Guildford. He parked in front of Westmore Guest House a few minutes before five o'clock. The thin woman behind the reception desk gave him the sort of smile that suggested it was an expression she used very sparingly. Jamie waved an ID badge in a battered leather wallet at her, returning it quickly to the inside pocket of his jacket.

"Good afternoon. Detective Inspector Whitelock, Guildford CID. I wonder if you can help me. We're trying to locate someone who attended a meeting here on Thursday with two of my colleagues, DI Waters and DC Crusoe. We just want to check that the person who attended the meeting was indeed the one we were expecting. He's missed a couple of appointments since then and we think he may be in trouble. His name is Tony Dobson."

The woman frowned at him. "I'm not meant to give that sort of information out. This is supposed to be a secure venue for meetings."

"I should hope it is, too," Jamie said. "You could call DI Waters to check it's okay, if you wish. Not sure he'll be too pleased because he's away for the weekend, which is why I'm here. But I can try to get him on the phone, and you can have a word…"

"Thursday, you said?"

"Yes, at 10.30. Were you here on that day?"

"I was. I'm doing Wednesday to Sunday this week."

Jamie smiled his best smile. "So, I'm in luck." He reached into the same pocket and took out a photograph which he placed on the desk in front of her. "This is Mr Dobson. Do you recognise him?"

She shook her head. "He looks a bit familiar, but not because he's been here. Is he famous or something?"

"Not yet, but he might be soon for all the wrong reasons if we can't find him. Can you check the diary or whatever for that day?"

She took out a small stack of A4 sheets from under the desk and flicked back to the one for Thursday.

"Oh, I remember this man alright – the one who came to the meeting," she said, peering at the sheet. "Definitely not the one you're looking for."

"He might have used a different name."

"It's nothing to do with the name. This bloke wasn't anything like the one in the photo. He was much older, and bloody *huge*. Scared me to death when I looked up and saw him just a couple of feet away."

"Really? And what was the gentleman's name?"

"Well, I'm not sure I should…" Jamie gave her his smile again. "Gerrard. David Gerrard."

"Thank you." He turned to go.

"With a double r," she called after him.

CHAPTER TWELVE

Sunday, 25 June

The two men stood in silence on the cliffs above the shore. One was tall, with a dark complexion and handsome features; the other short and stocky with blond hair and eyelashes. They watched as the fishing boat glided through the still waters of the Storvika fjord towards the small jetty below them. The slowness of its approach reflected the nature of its cargo: far more precious than its usual haul of fish. It pulled alongside the jetty where two men in a flatbed truck waited to receive the delivery. A number of wooden crates were handed across from the boat and placed with care onto the dense bed of straw which filled the back of the truck. The men pressed more straw in between the crates and covered the whole with a tarpaulin which they secured tightly in place.

The boat pulled away and the men with the truck climbed into the cab and waited. Two minutes later, the driver's iPhone trilled with an incoming call.

"In position. Ready to leave."

The truck moved off the jetty and turned right onto the road which would take them south to where their load would be stored for the next few days. In front, their escort, a Land Rover Defender long-wheel-base pickup, moved ahead of them. In the back, under the canvas cover, one of the four men seated on the bench seats, each with an automatic weapon, gave the driver a thumbs-up sign.

The two men who had been watching from the cliff picked their way down the rocky path to where their own transport awaited them. Neither had spoken throughout the operation, but when they had settled into the front seats of the jeep, the smaller man turned to his companion.

"So, just one week to go. It's been a real pleasure working with you." He gave a little shrug. "And I'm still not sure how I'm supposed to address you."

"Well, as we've finished our business together – for which I am sincerely grateful – you will not need to address me at all from now on, so it doesn't matter, does it?" He paused, then turned to the other man and smiled. "However, if the occasion does arise, 'Abu' is fine."

CHAPTER THIRTEEN

Wednesday, 28 June

The man seated at the bar of the Remington Arms public house in Clapham was relaxed and quietly sipping his beer, savouring every drop and seemingly at one with the world. Even so, his large bulk and battered features were an intimidating presence on a quiet lunchtime when most of the other customers were smartly dressed business people on their midday break. His face sported a number of deep scars, the stubble around it uneven and clearly there through lack of grooming rather than as a fashion accessory. His eyes were dark and brooding in a shaven head which had the appearance of being attached directly onto his shoulders without recourse to a neck. The black Iron Maiden tee shirt strained to contain bulging biceps and pecs, but a circle of flab pushed its way into view below it over the belt of his faded blue jeans.

Danny Weaver had felt their eyes on him as he entered, sensed the hush of interrupted conversations as they watched him pull himself up on to the bar stool. He was used to this reaction; it always happened when he entered a pub for the first time – and usually every time after that, in fact. He knew it couldn't be because they recognised him, unless they put up posters these days, announcing the latest releases. *Coming out on the first of May, "Weaver the Cleaver", in public houses near you. Certificate* X. No, it was just because he didn't belong anywhere – not yet – and everyone could tell.

Since "Her Majesty's pleasure" had ended and he had stepped out again into a world which was vastly different from the one he'd left, he had made it his quest to visit every pub in Clapham and

Southwark, his previous stomping grounds, in the hope of finding some of his old cronies and picking up some sort of meaningful life again. The problem was, of course, it had been his definition of "meaningful" that had got his life taken from him in first place. At fifty-eight years old, another twenty-year stretch would significantly reduce his enjoyment of the time he had left. Anyway, in the two months since his release, he was well down the list of pubs but without sight of anyone he knew. Not surprising, of course – twenty years was a long time to be out of circulation, and the lucky ones move on and away.

He held up the empty glass and the barman raised his eyebrows with the unspoken question.

"Same again, please," Danny said. "Good pint, that."

The barman topped up his glass and Danny raised it as if for a toast.

"Here's to Timothy Taylor, God bless him and long may he brew."

The barman laughed, picked up the three pound-coins from the bar and walked off to serve another customer. Danny surveyed the reflection of the room in the mirror behind the bar. No-one was watching him now, but he had been observing – through the mirror – two men seated at the table closest to him. They reminded him of two of the characters from his favourite movie, *Goodfellas*. The Ray Liotta lookalike was a dead ringer, same classic good looks, perfect build, ice-blue eyes. His companion was a little too tall and too athletic for Joe Pesci, but he had a similar swarthy complexion and displayed the same simmering menace. The scar above the right eyebrow was a little out of context, but the effect of the two men together was close enough.

He wondered to himself how many times he had seen that movie. Twenty years inside, once a month – say, about 250 times. And it came out when? Around 1990, he seemed to remember, ten years before his social life had changed so dramatically. How many times as well, then, during those years?

Thinking, as he was, about the movie and his extended incarceration, it was a shock to hear one of the Goodfellas mention the name of the man who had put him there. In fact, at first, he thought he must have misheard him or simply brought the man to mind subconsciously. As if for reassurance, Joe Pesci mentioned his name again.

"… Right out of the blue, large as fucking life, smiling at me over the top of his pint as if we're best mates. Fucking bastard."

"Keep your voice down," his companion set the example with his quiet admonishment, but not so quiet that Danny couldn't pick up more of their conversation. "We can deal with him if he gets too close. He's been out of the picture now for a couple of years, anyway."

"Still has his contacts though, doesn't he? Guys that would do stuff for him if he asked them."

"*If* he asked them. What he *doesn't* have now, though, is a bunch of buddies surrounding him twenty-four-seven watching his back. He's out on his own, no protection."

"And if we have to 'deal with him', as you put it, who's going to do that? Not me."

"Well I wasn't suggesting unarmed combat. And there are guys around who will do stuff for *us* – *if* we ask them. Look…" he glanced over his shoulder at Danny "… let's talk about this some other time, somewhere a bit more private. Another pint?"

Danny swung round on the stool and dropped to the floor, towering over their table before Ray Liotta could get to his feet.

"Let me get these," Danny said. He looked from one to the other. If most people in the room did find him intimidating, it took only a couple of seconds for him to realise that these two were different. They displayed not a trace of anxiety or even interest. It was satisfying for him in a way that the link to the movie was complete. They were perfectly cast.

"Now why would you want to do that?" Joe Pesci said.

Danny smiled. "Just being friendly. And anyway, I think we might have a mutual friend."

"I doubt that."

"Acquaintance, then. Someone, it seems, we feel the same about. And you just might have stumbled onto someone who could do the *stuff* for you that you just mentioned."

CHAPTER FOURTEEN

Saturday, 1 July

At 8.30 a.m., Tony and Rebecca reeled out of the Ferry Inn into a gale, blowing straight off the Pentland Firth, turning mid-summer in Caithness, temporarily, into something more like mid-winter in Greenland. They were both already feeling much the worse for having spent two hours in the downstairs bar of their hotel in Scrabster the previous evening, followed by the same amount of time again in the Upper Deck restaurant before getting to bed well after midnight. Their pride in keeping pace with the intake of the local drinkers and diners, which seemed so important last night, now felt idiotic in retrospect.

They struggled along the concrete jetty, past the line of boats towards their own bouncing and swaying craft, which they'd had the foresight to prepare for departure before last night's festivities and had positioned in readiness close to the harbour entrance. The thirteen-metre Bavaria Cruiser 41, with its sleek lines and luxurious cabin features, was Tony and Rebecca's pride and joy, but right now the thought of boarding her represented a challenge in itself, without the prospect of having to take her out to sea.

The alcohol-induced grogginess, which had destabilised their first few steps, was now replaced by the physical challenge of staying upright and on-course in the high wind. They threw their rucksacks and holdalls onto the deck and followed them with a precarious step-cum-leap from the iron ladder on the harbour wall across the watery gap, which seemed to change every second from a couple of centimetres to half a metre. They each dropped flat onto the narrow deck area between the cabin and the rail, turning onto their backs and giggling like children.

After a few minutes, Tony sat up and made his way to the bow, holding on to the rail to steady himself. He looked towards the harbour entrance and across to Dunnet Head, the eastern promontory of Thurso Bay and the most northerly point of the Scottish mainland. Beyond the bay, the Firth awaited them, with its reputation – on a bad day – for emptying the stomachs of the most hardened seafarers in the world. Tony was only too aware that he and Rebecca were not included among their number.

"I'm not sure about this," he said.

Rebecca sat up and followed his gaze to the churning, white-crested waters.

"Why, what's wrong? Just a bit bouncy, that's all. We'll be hugging the coast, won't we? And anyway, it'll make for a great piece of film."

"Yes, I'm aware of the need to complete your video for Channel Four, but I'd like to think I'll be around afterwards to see it. Whether we hug the coast or not, it's still the Pentland Firth out there. Do you know that seven currents…?"

"Come together in the middle from different directions creating a corkscrew effect and making it one of the most hazardous… et cetera, et cetera, et cetera. Yes, you have apprised me of that geophysical phenomenon on more than one occasion, I believe."

Tony smiled. "Tell you what, though. This weather's a pretty good cure for a hangover, don't you think? Or at least it takes your mind off it. Let's give it an hour or so. The forecast said it would get calmer later this morning."

"Aye, aye, cap'n. I'll get me below and make a brew."

*

"No way we can make sail in this."

Tony's statement of the blinding obvious did little to convince Rebecca of her captain's command of the situation and his qualifications as custodian of their immediate safety.

Once they had left the relative shelter of the harbour, even now whilst they were still in the bay, her initial bravado had been replaced by a state of high anxiety, if not actual fear. She was half-sitting, half-lying on the deck in the bow with her legs stretched out and spread in front of her and her arms locked around the rail in a crucifix position. Tony was a good sailor – she kept telling herself – but everyone had their limits, and this was definitely out of his comfort zone.

"Let's see what it's like when we get round Dunnet," he said, "and we'll turn back if it's too much. Okay?"

Rebecca decided to say nothing, being uncertain what would come out of her mouth if she opened it to reply. She nodded vigorously.

"Right." Tony managed a weak smile, presumably of reassurance and encouragement. Rebecca felt neither reassured nor encouraged. She closed her eyes, knowing that would make it worse but desperate to try anything, then opened them again quickly as the bile rose in her throat.

Tony was steering almost directly away from the Head using the powerful 40hp Volvo engine to compensate for the force of wind and tide driving them towards it. Rebecca, facing the stern, had an excellent view of the towering cliffs as the gap between them and the boat narrowed.

As it turned out, they made it round into the open water of the Firth with plenty of clearance to spare and, almost miraculously, the sea flattened to a gentle swell and the boat steadied itself. The wind, still strong but moderating, was now behind them and Rebecca loosened her grip on the rail and grinned at Tony.

"There you are, told you it would be okay."

Tony smiled back. "It helps when you've got a master mariner handling the boat, of course. Right, let's have a photo of me looking totally in command to put on Facebook and Twitter tonight."

"Okay. Pass me my rucksack."

"Take it with my phone, it'll be easier to share later."

"As you wish, but I don't want my name on the credits. I have a standard to maintain, you know."

"Understood."

He took his phone from the pocket of his jeans and held it up for her to see, miming, "Ready?"

She gave him the thumbs-up sign with both hands and nodded.

★

Jamie Walcott pressed the green phone symbol on the steering wheel of his BMW to take the call on his hands-free.

"Yup."

"Walcott…"

"Miss Goody, what a nice surprise. I was just thinking about you. Shouldn't really when I'm driving – I mean, one gear-stick is enough to…"

"I want you to listen to this. If you're in traffic, you might have to call back when it's more quiet because the recording isn't too clear. It's on a boat at sea. I'll play it, stop me if you can't make it out."

"Okay."

Even against the background of waves and wind, Tony's voice was clear enough.

… let's have a photo of me looking totally in command to put on Facebook and Twitter tonight.

Okay. Pass me my rucksack.

Take it with my phone, it'll be easier to share later.

As you wish, but I don't want my name on the credits. I have a standard to maintain, you know.

Understood.

After a few seconds' pause, Tony again.

Here, ready?

No, don't throw it, you know I can't catch.

Okay, I'll slide it across.

No, wait!

The scraping sound of the phone sliding across the deck, then voices further away.

I said, NO!

Grab it, Becca. Quick. Oh, SHIT!

What followed sounded like an untuned radio, loud crackling and rushing sounds, the source of which was obvious to both listeners. Grace stopped the recording.

"Shit, indeed," Jamie said, "Where and when did that happen?"

"Around eleven this morning. Just after setting off from Scrabster to sail round the coast to Inverness. It seems you got the freak yachting accident you were hoping for."

"What I had in mind was something a bit more fatal. So, what do we think? *Was* it an accident, or was it staged?"

"It's ten days since Dobson told Gerrard he was quitting his interest in Tom Brown and since then he's said nothing, written nothing, texted nothing about it. It could be that leaving his phone in the car immediately after that same conversation might have been a genuine oversight after all and nothing to do with creating an opportunity to talk without us hearing."

"Sorry, but..."

"I know you don't believe that, but I'm just saying it's possible. One thing for sure, we won't find out from this incident on his boat. We need to get together as soon as possible and decide where we go from here. Within the next few days perhaps."

"What about the next few *hours*, Grace? If he does believe he's being leaned on and decides to pursue this through the press, the worst-case scenario for you and me doesn't bear thinking about."

"Okay, tomorrow then. And what about Gerrard – if they start putting their heads together again?"

"I have a feeling the Gerrard problem might very shortly disappear." There was no response. After five seconds or so, Jamie spoke again. "Grace, are you still there?"

"Speak tomorrow."

*

The discussion in the main bar of the Dog and Duck in Meadow Village had increased in both volume and animation as voices became more lubricated and opinions more polarised and entrenched. The news from Glomfjord in Norway had sparked a debate on human rights and the whole moral issue of abandoning young males in the confused, testosterone-fuelled, identity-seeking period of their lives.

Earlier in the evening, just about everybody in the pub had crammed into the rear bar to watch the news item on the huge TV screen. There had been audible gasps and a lot of headshaking in disbelief at the magnitude of the logistical challenge they were witnessing. Even the person doing the voice-over commentary seemed astonished at what she was seeing.

"Earlier today, just north of the Arctic Circle at Glomfjord on Norway's west coast, preparations were being made to move the former Saint Olaf production platform. This huge assembly will shortly begin its two-thousand-kilometre voyage from Glomfjord to the structure known as Hotel St Kilda in the Atlantic close to the island group, where it will become the second annexe of the off-shore establishment for the detention of life exiles. It will be called Platform Beta."

A drone-cam showed the structure from a fly-past high above, before swinging down and round to capture the awesome dimensions of the platform against a backdrop of the towering heights to the south of the fjord. The voice-over continued.

"This second platform, though slightly smaller than Alpha, is the same semi-submersible design and the second largest of its type in the world. It will provide accommodation for six hundred more exiles. The operation deck has been cleared of equipment and once the former rig is attached to the satellite platform of the existing structure, work will begin air-lifting the housing units in modular form to build the eight-storey accommodation blocks which will surround and secure the recreation deck."

A CGI sequence was showing how giant helicopters would lower the building blocks into position like huge Lego pieces. The screen image changed again to actual pictures of the platform in its present position, before morphing back to CGI in order to follow the reporter's commentary.

"But before all that happens, they have to transport the platform over two thousand kilometres of sea. Towing it all the way would take up to eighteen days even using the most powerful ocean-going tugs available. So, Beta, like Alpha, will be taken on the deck of the *Mastodon*, the largest heavy-lift ship in the world, which will reduce the journey time to between seventy-five and eighty-five hours, depending on weather and sea conditions. At present, the *Mastodon* is awaiting its load ten kilometres offshore in the Norwegian Sea.

"Within the next hour, the platform will be towed out of the fjord. To stabilise it for this short journey to the awaiting transport vessel, the semi-submersible structure will be ballasted down to a draught of around eight metres. The *Mastodon* itself will be ballasted deeper still – to around eighteen metres, at which point only the forward bridge and aft towers will remain above water – to allow the platform to be towed into position above the ship. Once that has been achieved, the *Mastodon* will be de-ballasted to raise it up and lift the platform clear of the water before setting off, at around 6.00 a.m. British Summer Time, tomorrow, Sunday, the second of July, on its journey to become part of the extended Hotel St Kilda.

"We will, of course, keep you up to date with the progress of Beta and bring full coverage of its arrival."

The CGIs had taken the watching group through the full jaw-dropping sequence and remained the subject of conversation as people returned to their previous places in the two bars and restaurant.

The argument in the main bar had begun at a table in one of the bay windows, where eight people were occupying their usual Saturday evening seats, and had spread round the room. The exchanges progressed good-naturedly, with George Holland – one of the group of eight – *gently* targeted as the guilty party. It had been George's lecture tour and, later, his bestselling book, *The Meek's Inheritance*, that had helped focus national support for Tom Brown's NJR – the New Justice Regime – one feature of which was the establishment of the offshore prison. The *gentleness* came from the knowledge of all present that writing the book had been part of George's way of dealing with the tragic death of his wife, Irene, a victim of the type of violence the NJR was introduced to address.

"Well, I think the whole thing should be settled sensibly," George said. "I propose an arm-wrestling contest to decide who's right, and I nominate my good friend here as our champion." He placed his hand on the shoulder of the huge man sitting to his right as the room filled with jeers, boos and laughter. David Gerrard got to his feet and raised his arms for silence.

"I accept the nomination," he said, "but only if it's best out of three."

More laughter. Someone shouted across to the landlord. "It'll have to be you that takes him on, Jed, or it'll be no contest."

"It can't be me," Jed called back. "I'm on George's side,"

"Thank God for that," David said. "I was about to withdraw my services." He sat down again, and his smiling companion, seated next to him on the bench seat, slipped her arm through his and nestled a little closer.

"My hero," she said. David beamed back at her.

Marie Lockwood was petite, pretty and fifty-four years old; her hair was naturally curly and slightly greying amidst the light brown. The skinny jeans and close-fitting top showed off to good effect a slim but full figure which someone half her age would have been more than happy with.

The conversations became localised again and the noise level had already fallen when the stranger entered, bringing a further hush to the room. He walked over to the bar and surveyed the selection of beers and lagers on draught.

"Pint of San Miguel, please."

He turned and leaned with his back against the bar as he surveyed the room. Several people who had been watching him looked hurriedly away; others – braver or just more curious – were encouraged to do so when his eyes met theirs. David, whose seat was facing the bar, continued to watch him, struggling to retrieve some recognition from a distant memory. Eventually, the newcomer's searching gaze alighted and locked on his face, reflecting for a few moments David's own expression. His mouth widened into a smile which didn't reach his eyes.

"Three pound twenty, mate." He turned back to face Jed and took a wallet from the back pocket of his jeans, pulling out a five-pound note and handing it over.

"Not seen you around here before," Jed said.

The man turned away from Jed to answer, his voice loud enough to reach all parts of the room. "No, I've been away for a while. A very long while, in fact, thanks to one of your customers."

He was staring at David now. He picked up his drink and his change from the bar and walked over to the group of eight, all of whom had now turned and pushed their chairs away from the table. David got to his feet, his right hand resting gently on Marie's shoulder.

"Danny Weaver," he said. "Long time, no see."

"You're right. Twenty fucking years *is* a long time." He reached forward and slammed his drink down onto the table.

"Are you hoping to join us, or is that for me?" David said.

"Don't get fucking smart with…"

"Yes, certainly a long enough time to come to terms with the error of your ways, I would have thought. What's the point in your coming here? You miss it that much, being inside?"

Jed had moved quickly from the bar and was standing close up behind Danny.

"Right, mate," he said. "You're out of here, *now*."

"And I thought this would be a good place to have a nice quiet drink."

"It is, but only for nice quiet people."

"I'm not sure that's true. From what I read a couple of years or so ago, it's like Dodge City here. Gunfights in the street, women and children shot dead. Real friendly-like…"

George jumped to his feet. "You watch your mouth. It was my wife who was killed out there. I won't listen to you making jokes…"

His voice tailed off. David watched Danny's scowling face give way to a genuine softening of his eyes.

"I'm…" he said. "I'm truly sorry, friend, I didn't mean…" And then he was quickly back in character. "Not planning to stay, anyway – tonight – but I'll leave when I'm ready."

"Wrong," Jed said. "You're leaving now."

"I've not finished my drink, and I've never left a pint yet."

"So, this will be a first, then. I feel sort of proud that it's going to happen in my pub."

"It'll take more than a fucking jumped-up…"

Jed's arms went around Danny's chest, his right hand grabbing his left wrist, locking them in place just as he seemed set to move. Danny flung his head back, but Jed had moved his to one side in anticipation. He spun Danny towards the door.

Marie grabbed David's hand with both of hers as he set off round the table.

"No, David!" He pulled away from her.

He was alongside the two struggling men in a couple of strides, towering over both of them. He forced Danny's head down hard with his left hand and wrapped his right arm around his neck in a headlock. He tightened his grip and set off for the door, with Jed's arms still holding firm and helping to propel him forward. Someone opened one of the double doors, another stepping across to pull back the other. They struggled through into the car park outside, shoving Danny hard as they released him. He shot forward, just managing to keep his balance before turning to face them, eyes blazing and rubbing his throat.

"That was a big fucking mistake. This isn't the end of this. You forget who you're dealing with…!"

"Danny, *Danny*, *DANNY*. For Christ's sake, *calm down*. You'll give yourself a fucking heart attack." David's booming voice shut out everything else. Danny seemed to be shocked into silence.

"Okay, Jed, thanks for that. You can leave us now."

"*What?* I'm not sure that's a good idea,"

"It's alright, Jed. Really." David's voice was quiet and calm. "Danny and I need to talk." The anger in Danny's eyes had receded a little although his stare was just as intense. Jed backed away to the open doors where George and Marie stood watching them.

"David, come back in… *please*."

"Just two minutes, love. Promise."

David heard hurrying footsteps behind him, and Marie was suddenly by his side wrapping her arms around his waist. He half-turned and pulled her to him,

"Nice lady," Danny said. "Just right for me, I reckon, if something was to happen to you."

"What the hell is all this about, Danny? Who's the big loser tonight, do you think?"

"Time will tell, I reckon."

"How *much* time? Look, you're about my age, aren't you – mid, late fifties, right? You've got twenty-five, maybe thirty years left. You've already wasted twenty. You're an intelligent guy, you *know* there was nothing personal in what happened between us. You broke the law, fully aware of the consequences if you were caught and found guilty. Me, I was just doing a job. Don't make it personal now, Danny. There's no future in it for you going down that route, just a repeat of the past."

Danny said nothing, the silence between them lasting for a long time. Finally, he turned and walked away towards his car. David called after him as he opened the driver's door.

"Just ask yourself this question. Am I going to look forward… or am I going to look back?"

Danny started the car and eased it out of the parking space, stopping alongside David and Marie. He wound down the window.

"It's not over yet between me and you, Gerrard, but tell the little guy I really am sorry about his wife. I didn't mean to upset him."

*

As he walked home, alone, David considered the last few hours with mixed feelings – good news and bad news. Danny Weaver's appearance had certainly spoiled what had been, until then, a very enjoyable evening. Everyone had made an attempt afterwards to get the conversation and atmosphere back on track and, he supposed, it hadn't been a complete disaster, but the tension was never far away and surfaced every time the doors opened to admit a new customer.

That was the bad news.

The good news came with the appraisal of his feelings for Marie. Their blossoming affection was something they had taken for granted, right from their first meeting six months ago at the local education authority's Christmas dinner dance. They had never openly discussed their relationship or examined their feelings for each other; they had just got on with feeling happy together, with no demands on either side for statements of love or permanence. Their intimacy had been natural and satisfying rather than passionate, and, given their difference in size, a source of curiosity among their friends, leading to some gentle teasing.

But that had changed tonight – for him, at least.

It was the look of stark panic on Marie's face when she saw him – through her eyes, anyway – heading into danger. How she'd followed him into the car park to face that danger at his side. The way she had pressed herself against him on the bench seat when they went back inside and for the rest of the evening, as if she would never let him go. The tears in her anxious eyes when he waved to her as she was driven away, home, in the taxi, after pleading to stay with him when he explained that he wanted her safe whilst there was a chance that Danny was still in the village. And the realisation that all this evidence of her feelings for him was a simple reflection of the depth of his affection for her.

He had always been cynical about the L-word. How could four letters strung together in a particular sequence be symbolic of such a giant leap forward in a relationship? But right now, that didn't matter. He would tell her he loved her the next time they met. He smiled to himself, looking forward to it and relishing the thought.

The final couple of hundred metres past the last house in the village up to the entrance to Neville Farm Fold often seemed dark and sinister, with a short stretch of the lane squeezed between high hedges on each side. Tonight, the full moon threw down its light from a clear sky and David picked out its reflection on a metallic object just off the lane in the gateway to a field. David slowed, treading more softly and moving closer to the hedge on the same side. A few more careful steps and he made out the bumper of a car. He crept forward and was within a few metres of the vehicle when a figure walked out from behind it and stood facing him in the middle of the road.

"Mr Gerrard. I did say it wasn't over between us, didn't I? That was an excellent speech you made back there, and a really good question. 'Are you going to look forward or are you going to look back?' Well, I'm here to give you the answer. But before I do, let me remind you what I said to you twenty years ago. I never killed anybody who didn't deserve to be dead."

CHAPTER FIFTEEN

Monday, 3 July

Harry Waters picked up his iPhone from the desk in his office at Guildford New Station, his eyes widening in surprise when he saw the caller's name.

"Charlie! What a nice surprise. How are you?"

"Hi, Harry. I'm very well, thanks, and you?"

"Also well. We were talking about you with someone only a few days ago. This person couldn't believe that DC Crusoe and I had met Bonnie Prince Charlie. A couple of things had turned up around Tom Brown's disappearance and..."

"Well, whatever they are, I bet I can top them."

"Okay, then, you go first."

"Right, are you ready? What about Tom Brown's body, can you beat that?"

Harry took a couple of seconds to process the information. "Really? When and where?"

"Just this morning, about four hours ago around ten o'clock. And where? Near Elgol in southern Skye, close to the site of – you're not going to believe this, Harry – Bonnie Prince Charlie's cave. The last place they hid him after he'd escaped from Culloden, before they rowed him back to the mainland. No charge for the history lesson. A group of walkers getting an early start from Elgol spotted it through the bins and called it in right away. Amazing that they saw it, actually, in amongst some rocks a good way past the cave."

"And we're sure it's him?"

"The CSIU guys are still with him. The body's not identifiable as you'd expect, but the bits of clothing that are still on it seem consistent with what you believed he must have been wearing. And they've retrieved a wallet from a money belt, which has credit cards, driving licence and such, all his. So, I guess we're as sure as we can be at this stage."

"And where are you now, Charlie?"

"I'm at the scene; chopper over straight away from Inverness. Signal's not so clever here so I might get cut off any time, but as it was your case now we have a provisional ID, I thought you'd want to know a.s.a.p. and possibly see the body for yourself. If it is him, he's been in the water for… what… eight months? So, a day or two more won't make any difference. We can secure it against the tide."

Harry was silent for a while before answering. "I wish you hadn't suggested that, Charlie, because now you have, I feel I ought to. Can't imagine they'll pay for a private jet with a well-stocked drinks cabinet. So, what's the best way to get to – where did you say? Elgin?"

Charlie laughed. "Elgol. Elgin's much easier to get to but it's a hundred miles or so from Elgol. If you fly to Inverness, I'll meet you there and we'll fly back here together."

"By chopper?"

"By chopper, but I'll make sure I've a half-bottle of The Macallan with me to dull the senses."

"Okay, but better make it a full seventy-mil. I'll be with DC Crusoe again. I'll let you have our flight details as soon as. First, though, I'd better get it up through the ranks at my end. I guess you'll do the same there. They're going to want to work together on how and when to release this to the press. It's going to be the main story everywhere."

"Okay, Harry, see you soon."

"Yes, see you, and thanks for thinking about me, Charlie. I can't wait to climb aboard one of those bloody death-traps."

He ended the call then pressed the first digit on his speed-dial list.

"Hi, Abby, can I speak to the Super, please? Very urgent."

"She's on her way back from a meeting at the town hall. Should be here any minute. I'll let you know when she arrives."

"Thanks, Abby. Right away, please, so I can see her before she starts anything else."

"Okay, sir, will do."

Harry walked over to the door and into the Major Incident Team room. Natalie was at her desk.

"Nat, got a minute. I've a surprise for you."

*

"So, who knows about this so far?" Natalie had sat in silence as Harry gave her the news and his plans for their trip to Elgol.

"Well, down here, just you and me right now. Abby's going to let me know when the Super gets in and then it's over to her, and they'll need to liaise with Charlie's lot to get this out. I imagine the PM will want to make some sort of statement. Before that, of course, we'll have to let his wife know. Bit of a coincidence, don't you think? All that stuff David brought us, casting doubt on what happened to Brown, and a few days later, this."

"I thought you didn't believe in coincidence."

"I don't, but at times like this, it would make life a lot simpler if I did."

A figure appeared behind the frosted glass of his office door.

"Come in," Harry called.

The door opened and his boss stepped into the room. Detective Superintendent Lynsey Hargreaves was of Indian ancestry, taller than both her colleagues, with a strong athletic build, and was in full uniform, which included a close-fitting knee-length skirt instead of her usual trousers. Her dark hair was pulled into a neat bun on top of her head, adding to her already impressive height. Harry and Natalie both got to their feet. "Please, don't get up. You wanted to speak to me, Harry?"

"Yes, ma'am. I was going to come to your office, but thanks for…"

"Well, I'm passing, aren't I? So, fire away." She took the vacant chair next to Natalie's.

"I've just taken a call from DI Stuart of the Highland and Island police. He's the one who found Tom Brown's car for us last year. It seems he's now found the driver. A body was discovered washed up on the Isle of Skye this morning, which seems to be that of Tom Brown. Body's in a bit of a state, as you'd expect, but they've recovered stuff from a money belt that seems to confirm ID. I'm arranging to go up to the scene with DC Crusoe. We will, of course, need to speak to Mrs Tomlinson-Brown as soon as possible because the body was found by some walkers who will, I have no doubt, be desperate to share the excitement with others, although I guess they won't know who it is yet."

Lynsey was wide-eyed with surprise. "Wow, that's how long since Brown went missing? Six months?"

"Exactly eight – end of October last year."

"I assumed we'd gone beyond the time when we'd expect him to show up."

"If a body gets caught in that particular area of sea, it can wash around for a long time but, eventually, it's likely to show up." Both women were staring at him. "Apparently," he added.

"How do you happen to know that?" Lynsey asked.

"Well..." Harry looked across at Natalie.

"DI Stuart told us when we were up there in October," she said. "When we were trying to work out what could have happened to him."

Lynsey was still looking at Harry. "I see. Well, I'd better alert the powers that be. Who would be the best person to tell his wife, do you think? I guess it's you or me, Harry, unless it would be better from someone else."

"What about DI Cottrell?" Harry said. "I think they became quite close during the course of last year. I don't know whether they're still in touch."

"Or perhaps Mr Mackay, ma'am?" Natalie suggested. "I know he's not part of this anymore, but he's a very close friend of the family. He might prefer to be the one to break the news."

"Fine with me. You okay with that, Harry?"

"Yes, I think that would be a good idea – to ask him, I mean."

"Okay, I'll give him a call." Lynsey got up to leave.

"We could do that, ma'am, if you like," Natalie said, also getting to her feet. "I mean, you'll have enough calls to make."

Lynsey looked from one to the other and shrugged. "Okay. Let me know what you two decide between you." She left the room.

Harry waited a short while then opened the door a crack to check she had gone.

"You were very forceful there, detective, taking charge of the conversation like that. Something I missed?"

"Well, firstly, you only knew about the body being trapped in that area of sea from what David told us in an *off-the-record* meeting."

"Yes, I realised that a bit late."

"*And*, in the highly unlikely event of you being wrong and everybody else being right about Jo's calls being monitored, whoever is listening would find out about the body before they were supposed to if we contacted her. So probably best to keep her out of it altogether."

Harry was silent for a few seconds, then smiled and shook his head.

"Thank you, DS Crusoe. And in recognition of your excellent intervention, I've decided not to give you a written warning for sarcasm. Now let me make this call to Johnny Mac while you organise our flight to Inverness. Get as big a plane as you can, will you?"

*

"How many people are in the loop up to now?"

Jackie Hewlett, the Home Secretary, was sitting with her PA, Jenny Brittani, on the terrace of the Palace of Westminster. The senior minister was an attractive woman with a trim figure and was, as always, immaculately and fashionably dressed, today in a dark suit with a short straight skirt and double-breasted jacket. Jenny, a small, twenty-something Somali, with large appealing eyes and dark-brown hair in loose curls, had just delivered the news about the body during the afternoon recess of the Commons sitting.

"You, me, DI Waters – he took the call from Skye – one of his DCs, his immediate superior and Chief Constable Mills, who passed the message through for you. And the Highland police, of course, but I understand they are holding back on any communication until you can get together with them on this."

"Has Mrs Tomlinson-Brown been informed?"

"Not yet, but Chief Superintendent – I mean, *ex*-Chief Superintendent – John Mackay has agreed to do that. Oh, yes, he's the other person who knows. Maggie's living away from London at present and he needed to get a contact number for her through her business office. He's going to let me know when he's given her the news."

Jackie noted the little catch in Jenny's voice and turned to see the tears welling in her eyes. "Why, Jenny…"

"I suppose it really *is* him, isn't it? I mean, what with the things they found in the money belt. Only, until they actually *found* his… body… I was still hoping… you know?"

Jackie sighed, also feeling the loss of a close friend all over again. She put her arm around Jenny and leaned into her. "I think we have to assume it's Tom and try to see this as some sort of closure."

"I guess so." Jenny swallowed hard as the trill of her iPhone stopped the tears escaping. "This is Mr Mackay," she said, checking the screen. "Do you want to take it?"

Jackie nodded and took the phone, getting up from the table as she answered the call.

"Hello, John, this is Jackie Hewlett. I'm with Jenny on the terrace at Westminster. Just hold on one minute, please, while we find a bit of privacy inside, then I'll put you on speaker."

They walked off the terrace and into the quiet of the library.

"Okay, John. We're both listening."

John Mackay's voice seemed to fill the room. "Hi, to you both. I'm not sure if this is a sad day or some sort of watershed."

"We've just been wrestling with the same thoughts, John. I suppose it's not a shock, exactly, but it now means we've lost him for sure. Not just *presumed* dead anymore. Have you spoken to Maggie?"

"Yes, about twenty minutes ago."

"And?"

"Well, to be honest, the delay in phoning you has been due to me trying to get my head round her reaction. I expected tears or a strained silence or some sort of out-pouring of pain and grief, but she took it very calmly. Within a couple of minutes, she was asking how I was enjoying retirement, if I was keeping well. She even joked about me getting my weight down, which I'd always said was my number one priority when I got out from behind my desk. So… I'm not sure what to make of it."

Jackie looked at Jenny and frowned before replying. "Perhaps she's in denial still, or, more likely, she'd come to terms with this a long time ago and this confirms what she'd already accepted. Still a strange reaction, though."

"Perhaps I'll call her back in a couple of days, check how she is then."

"Good idea. Where is she, by the way? Jenny said she's living away from London."

"She didn't say where. Said they were just taking time away together. 'They' being mother and daughter, I assume."

"They probably want as few people to know where they are as possible. Maggie's always been a magnet for the press and the paparazzi even before all this, so I don't blame her. Let me know how she is when you've spoken to her again, then I'll get in touch with her. You can get me easiest through Jenny on this number."

"Okay, will do. When will this go out? It's not something you'll want leaking."

Jackie checked her watch. "Four-thirty now. I'll need to speak to the PM as soon as possible, so earliest six o'clock news but more realistically ten o'clock. In fact, we'll definitely go for ten o'clock. It's not something that we need to rush through, so we'll take our time to get it right. And we'll give a press statement just before the news bulletins go out on air."

"Sounds good – well, you know what I mean. Great to talk to you both, shame about the subject."

"Bye, John."

Jackie got to her feet and handed the phone to Jenny.

"Must get back and get this moving. I think the PM first then…" she screwed her face up in a grimace "… probably Wonder Woman next. Well, I suppose they did work together for a long time. Tell you what, I'll see you later in my office. We'll have a brew and a chat, and perhaps something a little stronger to drink to a lost friend."

She gave a brief smile then walked away before stopping and turning back to Jenny.

"That's assuming it *is* him, of course," she said.

*

Marie Lockwood leaned forward on the sofa and picked up the remote from the coffee table, turning up the volume on the television as the ten o'clock news began, before leaning back again.

"The main news story tonight: police are investigating the discovery of the body of a man near Elgol, on the Isle of Skye. They were alerted to the find at around ten o'clock this morning by a party of hillwalkers following a coastal route near the Cuillin range of mountains. It is believed the person was a victim of drowning and that he had been in the water for several weeks if not months.

"Although the police say they are still in the process of identifying the body, initial signs point to its being that of Mr Tom Brown, former Home Secretary, who went missing at the end of October last year. Mr Brown's car was found abandoned in Ullapool around that time, and shortly afterwards a holdall containing items of his clothing and other personal effects was discovered in a rowing-boat which had been grounded on the Shiants, a small group of islands in The Minch, between Skye and Harris.

"At the time, the police were looking to interview Mr Brown in connection with a number of fatal shootings in Cobham and Guildford, and an explosion in Dorking, which killed three people. The police pronounced Mr Brown 'missing presumed dead' at the end of December last year and the case was closed when they said they were not looking for anyone else in connection with the murders.

"We're going over now to our Highlands and Islands reporter, Annie McKinnon, in Elgol. Annie, tell us how the discovery was made earlier today."

The screen showed a young woman with wind-swept hair speaking into a handheld microphone against a backdrop of the Cuillin beyond a stretch of water.

"Well, Sophie, at around 8.30 this morning a group of six walkers set out from here to visit Bonnie Prince Charlie's cave a kilometre or so away on the southern tip of the Straithard peninsula. This is a popular walkers' target, although getting into the cave itself involves quite a difficult scramble and just two of the party undertook the climb down. On the way, one of them noticed something near the waterline on a small headland just beyond the cave. He checked it through his binoculars, then handed them to his companion and they came to the conclusion that it was a body, and most probably a human body. They were unable to get a signal on any network in the area, so it was not until they got back to Elgol that they were able to report their find."

"So could the body have been there for some time, Annie?"

"The police can't tell us that and will probably never know. What they do say is that it is amazing it was spotted at all. Very few of the people who do this walk actually climb down to the cave, and there is only one point on the descent where the site of the find is visible. I spoke earlier to one of the two men after he had given his statement to the police."

The head and shoulders of a man in his early sixties appeared on screen, tanned and bearded, and wearing a Tilly hat, checked shirt and khaki gilet. A caption at the bottom of the screen identified him as Mr Stuart Bowker.

"Mr Bowker, you were one of the two walkers who climbed down to the cave. Tell us what happened."

"Well, we never got as far as the cave because it was on the way down when Jack – Jack Arnold – saw the body. He pointed it out to me, and I couldn't see it right away. It was hardly visible at all. Almost the same colour as the rocks themselves."

"But you finally made it out."

"Yes. He passed me his bins and... well, it was certainly something odd. I wasn't sure what it was at first, but Jack was convinced it was a body, and the more I looked at it... And he was right, of course."

"So, what did you do then?"

"We climbed back up and told the others, then we abandoned the walk. Well, I suppose we'd completed the walk, anyway, except for me and Jack going into the cave and, to be honest, we just didn't feel like it anymore. It was pretty upsetting. Even Jack was all for getting back although it had been him who suggested the walk in the first place. Said the cave was somewhere he'd always wanted to visit."

Annie McKinnon was back on screen.

"How long, then, Annie, before the police confirm – or otherwise – the identity of the body? I understand Mr Brown's family have already been advised of the discovery."

"The police haven't said, Sophie, but everything seems to be pointing towards who they already believe it is. One small mystery, though. Mr Arnold was a stranger to the group until yesterday when he joined them where they were spending the evening in a restaurant in Broadford, not far from here. It was he who suggested they all do this walk, but, immediately after they got back to Elgol following the discovery, he disappeared before the police from Inverness had arrived and had chance to take his full statement.

"The police are not suggesting there is anything untoward about this, because he had told the group he would have to leave immediately after they completed the walk. But one of the walkers told me she'd been surprised because, had they not seen the body, the two men were expecting to spend at least thirty to forty minutes exploring in and around the cave until the incoming tide would have forced them to climb back. So, they would have finished the walk much later, anyway. No doubt we'll find out more soon."

"Many thanks, Annie." The news reader turned back to camera. "And it goes without saying that we'll keep you up to date with any developments with that story.

"And now, the rest of the news."

Marie muted the sound and leaned forward to replace the remote on the coffee table.

"Well, I guess that draws a line under that," she said.

"I guess so."

*

George Holland switched off the television and sank back into the armchair, struggling to come to terms with the discovery of his friend's body after all this time. It made him realise that he had never accepted that Tom was dead, not until now. After all, he had told himself, this was a man who had cheated death many times in the Royal Marines and Special Forces. He supposed he had been waiting for this moment before he would believe it – but hoping it would never come.

He got to his feet and went into the kitchen, taking a bottle of Famous Grouse and a glass from one of the cabinets. He smiled to himself, remembering how Tom used to scold him for never having a decent single malt in the house. It hadn't prevented Tom taking copious amounts of the blend, however, on his numerous visits to his home. He looked with sadness at the bottle of Laphroig, sitting on the same shelf of the cabinet, which he'd bought shortly after his friend's last appearance in order to surprise him on his next visit.

He eased himself back into the wing chair as his iPhone sounded. It was a number he didn't recognise.

"George Holland speaking."

"Hi, George. Tony Dobson here. Just phoning to let you know that I'm free. *Freeee!*"

"Hi, Tony. I'm very pleased to hear it, although I haven't a clue what you're talking about."

"We've ditched the phone, like David suggested. *Accidentally* washed overboard as Becca and I were sailing round Dunnet Head, the Scottish equivalent of Cape Horn. Anyone listening would have heard the final few moments before it died, me sliding the phone across the deck to Becca and our shouts of dismay as it went into the sea. So, as I said, we're free. *Freeee!*"

"So where are you now?"

"Still on the boat, in Inverness. Just this minute arrived and tied up. This is Becca's phone and the first time we've had a signal."

"Well the timing of your freedom couldn't be better." George looked across at the wall clock. "Have you seen or heard the news at ten o'clock?"

"No, why. What's happened?"

"They've found Tom's body, or what they think is Tom's body. On Skye, earlier today."

There was a long silence before Tony spoke again.

"*Shit*. Not a surprise, but you hope for things, don't you? Even when everything tells you there's no point. I just thought he might have survived somehow, what with the thing with the boat and the photo."

"I don't think they pointed towards him being alive, though, Tony. More to do with the circumstances of his death. But I'm pretty sure David is still looking into it. It doesn't change anything, does it?"

"I guess not, but there doesn't seem much point anymore."

"Hey, Tony, you're an investigative journalist or had you forgotten? You're *freeee* to follow that story now with no-one listening in. Well not on your phone anyway. In fact, Inverness, did you say? That's where the Highland and Island police are based and they're the ones on point for this. Don't know where the main police station is, but it can't be far from where you are right now."

*

They sat in silence for a long time, snuggled together, before Marie suddenly pulled away and turned to face him, remembering what they had been arguing about before the news item.

"Look, *are* you going to tell me what happened after I left on Saturday?"

He smiled and pulled her to him, wrapping her in his arms and kissing her long and gently. Eventually they drew apart, Marie's eyes wide and shining.

"I *will* tell you, very soon," David said, "But in the meantime, I've got something much more important to say to you."

CHAPTER SIXTEEN

Tuesday, 4 July

The pilot of the police helicopter did Harry no favours by flying them to Elgol low along the jagged ridge of the Cuillin and over Loch Coruisk "to enjoy one of the finest parts of the whole of Scotland". "Enjoy" was not the word that Harry would have used. Natalie's reaction could not have been more opposed.

"Right, that settles it. Next holiday, I'm coming here."

"Skye is like Scotland in miniature," DI Stuart said. "It's got everything the mainland has and you can see it all in a couple of weeks. Scotland itself, a couple of years at least, and I'm talking the full hundred-plus weeks, not just two lots of annual holidays."

"What do you think, sir?" Natalie turned to her boss.

"I'll let you know when I see it from ground level. Nothing looks good to me from up here. I hope you've not forgotten the malt, Charlie."

Charlie laughed and patted his pocket. "As if," he said.

The chopper landed on the grassy top of Suidhe Biorach, which Charlie informed them was Gaelic for "pointed seat". Harry suggested somewhere flat would have been preferable. As the rotors slowed to a stop, they donned the walking boots that had been provided for their short trek to the location of the cave, then dropped onto the soft ground below the aircraft.

Since the discovery of the body, temporary ropes had been installed to facilitate the rock scramble down to the cave entrance. A local police officer met them and guided them along the rough, steep path, with another bringing up the rear of the small party. Halfway down, the leading officer handed Harry some binoculars and pointed to something secured by nets to the rocks at sea level.

"There he is," he said. "Amazing how anyone would see him while they were climbing down here. I mean, you'd be watching where you put your feet and hands all the time. And bear in mind, the nets holding him in place make it much easier to spot, and it's still hardly visible."

In fact, it took Harry nearly a minute to pick it out among the rocks and seaweed swaying back and forth on the tide.

"And the man who spotted it?" Harry said.

"Disappeared straight afterwards," the officer said. He looked across at Charlie. "Unless he's surfaced again, sir?"

"Not yet, Callum. We're still looking." He turned to Harry. "I don't think it's necessary to go all the way down, unless you want to see my cave, of course." Harry and Natalie smiled and shook their heads. "Okay, Callum. Let's get him out of the water. He'll catch his death."

*

Back at Inverness Airport, as they waited for their flight to be called, Harry pulled out a folder from his shoulder bag.

"Take a look at these, Charlie." He placed two sheets of paper on the low table in front of them. "These were brought to our attention recently by a retired DCI." He pointed to each picture in turn. "This was taken in Ullapool last month, and this is one of Tom Brown in exactly the same place last October. What do you think?"

Charlie pointed straight away to the picture of Tom. "I know Ullapool really well and it doesn't look like that in October. It's a fake. Where did he get these?"

"The one of Brown appeared in the press down south last November, and the recent one, of a journalist called Tony Dobson, was taken by his girlfriend while they were on holiday. And this is how the fake came about." He placed a third picture next to the others showing Tom Brown leaning against the car. "Brown's image superimposed on the same scene."

"And this was brought to your attention, you say, by a *retired* DCI?" Charlie asked.

"That's right. A friend of Tony Dobson's is a neighbour of ex-DCI David Gerrard, so he arranged for them to meet so he could get his reaction."

"And Mr Gerrard obviously thought there was enough intrigue in it to make it official by bringing it to you."

"Well, *semi*-official, I suppose. He didn't seem to have much of an opinion either way, but felt that we should see the pictures, right, Nat?"

"Yes, Dobson was a close friend of Tom Brown's and I imagine that's what fired his interest as much as the possibility of a story."

"Well, I guess yesterday's event puts paid to any doubt about Mr Brown's demise," Charlie said, "if not the circumstances thereof. Remember when we were in Ullapool after the car had been found, wondering where he might have gone from there? My sergeant, Izzy Macken, mentioned that a boat had disappeared just north of the town but there would be no way – she said – that anyone would put out into The Minch in it at that time of year. Not with the wind, the waves and the blue men working together to take it down. Well, that *was* the boat that we found on the Shiants with Tom Brown's stuff in it."

"The blue men?" Natalie said.

Charlie smiled. "Fallen angels, also known as storm kelpies. Mythical creatures, who live in that stretch of water between mainland Scotland and the Outer Hebrides and who prey on sailors and stricken boats."

Harry and Natalie looked at each other, then back at Charlie.

"But am I right in assuming that we are not actively looking for one of these creatures in connection with Mr Brown's death?"

Charlie shrugged. "No point, Harry, they're impossible to catch, even for the elite Highland and Island police. But *something* caused him to end up in The Minch, and eventually on the shore near Elgol."

They were silent for a while, with Harry deep in thought.

"There's something not right here, Charlie," he said. "A guy – a stranger – attaches himself to a group of walkers and suggests they pay a visit to your cave the next day. We have to assume he was pretty persuasive for them all to agree to go along. On the walk, as they climb down to the cave, he spots the body. God knows how. The guy who was climbing down with him couldn't see it at first even when it was pointed out to him, and, even *then*, he wasn't certain it was a body. The local police say it was amazing that anyone would see it from there and it took me what, a minute, to see it today knowing exactly what I was looking for and where to look.

"*Then*, when they all get back to Elgol and after this mysterious person has informed the local police, giving them the precise co-ordinates of the find, he disappears with some story about having to get away quickly, when they weren't supposed to have got back to the start of their walk yet, anyway. I mean... what do you think?"

"My thoughts to the letter, Harry. I believe this guy knew exactly where the body was and took the party along with him so they could *all* find it – as if by accident."

★

Six hundred kilometres due north of Inverness, the man sitting with his back to the low metal rail pulled the woollen blanket more tightly around him and hunched his shoulders against the cold. Mid-summer meant little in terms of temperature at 9.00 p.m. British Summer Time at the edge of the Norwegian Sea. Three days ago, at the start of the adventure, the sheer enormity of the drama unfolding around him seemed to numb all the physical senses, but that had only lasted until they were underway.

It had begun with loud, metallic sounds, echoing around them in the dark space of their confinement, signalling that their mission was underway, and there was no turning back. Then, after the long, exhausting climb, the brightness of the daylight and the coldness of the air had hit them like a blunt instrument as they emerged onto the steel-mesh floor which hung below the main platform deck. They had crawled on their stomachs to the edge of the floor and taken in the heart-stopping scene with involuntary cries of amazement.

Far below and ahead of them, the four powerful ocean-going tugs looked like a child's model boats on a vast pond. The reinforced steel towing cables – fifteen centimetres thick – appeared no more substantial than domestic washing lines to the far-distant eyes. The towering southern side of the Glomfjorden glided past them as the huge structure was eased towards the open sea to prepare for the 2,000-kilometre journey to its final destination.

Beyond the battery of tugs, ten kilometres offshore, their main transport vessel awaited them. The 250-metre-long *Mastodon*, with a beam width of seventy metres, was the largest heavy-lift ship in the world by some margin. Right now, it rode like a colossus on top of the sea, but shortly its vast deck would sink below the waves as it positioned itself to receive its cargo.

On clearing the fjord, they watched as the two rear tugs turned away from the platform – to the north and south – then doubled back to act as a brake for the forward movement. Once stationary, they could feel the platform ballasting down to a level where the cables attached to the vertical columns were just above the surface. Once the structure had stabilised, the four tugs moved back to their original positions and headed for the ship.

It had taken the best part of two hours to reach the vessel, during which time the deck of the *Mastodon* had disappeared completely, leaving the forward superstructure and the two stern towers still visible, looking like three detached and completely separate objects. The feeling of vulnerability at this stage, looking down from a height of around one hundred metres, had made the man feel decidedly queasy. It was as if he was on a giant building being shaken by an earthquake or landslide.

As they approached the submerged vessel, the tugs carried out the same braking manoeuvre to position it over the deck. The *Mastodon* began to rise out of the sea, like a modern manifestation of the Kraken, the legendary sea monster from Norse folklore. The platform had jolted and swayed as it was lifted from the water and was hurriedly secured by a network of wires and chains to hold it in place.

The vessel, with its massive load, had finally got underway a few minutes after 6.00 a.m. BST – 7.00 a.m. local time – the following day, Sunday. That was just over sixty-three hours ago, and since then the sameness of the surroundings and the lack of activity had allowed cold, hunger and anxious anticipation to dismiss that initial feeling of awe. And they were still twenty hours away from their journey's end.

The man leaned forward and looked down through the mesh floor to the deck below. He knew the exact distance he would need to travel in order to reach it; 121 metres, just under 400 feet and many times further than he had ever descended on a loose rope before. He was getting too old for this sort of thing, he told himself, looking round at the other twelve members of his group. At closer to fifty than forty, he was older than any two of their ages added together. He had started out on this life before any of them had been born and had held his current position of power for most of their lifetimes. And though normally be would not be actively involved in a mission like this, he knew that this was how he would maintain the respect of, and authority over, his charges, by demonstrating he was prepared to do anything he asked of them.

Even so, it was getting harder.

He looked again at the task in hand. An abseil would have been preferable but was not an option. The vertical surfaces of the columns, which would have made it a straightforward descent in other conditions, were moving too much to make it possible to maintain contact for more than moments at a time, with the attendant risk of someone being dashed against them. No, it would have to be the loose rope with a descender, and in darkness, which was in short supply in these latitudes at this time of year.

He checked his watch; it was showing 21.23, confirming that it had made the automatic adjustment when they had moved out of the mainland time-zone. It would be nearly two hours before the light faded enough for them to go, which would leave around eighteen hours for them to manage the situation before they were in position to achieve their objective. That was a long time to be living on a knife edge.

He took some assurance looking again at his team. They were the best; hand-picked by him to tackle what was a little outside the scope of their training. What they were about to do – if they were successful – would mean they would not be entering the life beyond, not yet.

He was still a believer himself, although his motivation had shifted from purely religious to more material drivers over two decades. He knew inside that the glorious afterlife was there waiting for him and he looked forward to that as much as ever. But there seemed no reason why it shouldn't go on waiting a little longer while things were going so well for him as a mortal entity. Just like the work he had done during his service to the cause, the really important things shouldn't be rushed.

The Shadow got to his feet and clapped his hands, just loud enough to attract the attention of his companions. He gestured for them to come to him and the twelve men obeyed quickly, sitting cross-legged in front of him in a tight semicircle, heads upturned to hear the latest words of wisdom and encouragement from their leader. He turned and addressed two young men seated to his left.

"Khaled and Mahmoud, talk us through once more the location of the communications room and Bay 24."

⋆

By 11.00 p.m., the light had faded and some welcome cloud had billowed up along the western horizon blocking the rays of the setting sun. The huge area of the deck was in near darkness. The thirteen men leaned over the rail of the mesh floor and watched the three 150-metre ropes snake downwards. Immediately below them, close to the forward superstructure, was one side of the platform's hull pontoon, stretching across the deck and overhanging it by twenty metres on both port and starboard sides.

The pontoon, in the shape of a square doughnut, was that part of the platform which gave it its semi-submersible design, and would allow it to be ballasted down and stabilised by a network of chains and wires attached to the seabed. The four sides of the giant tubular square had a cross section of twelve metres, which was the height above the deck where the ends of the rope landed. The first three terrorists clipped their descenders to their belts before attaching them to the ropes. They swung over the rail and dropped swiftly and silently through space, landing on top of the pontoon, then abseiled the last few metres down the side closest to the superstructure.

They fastened the ends of the ropes to the heavy rings set in the deck, which held the cables securing the pontoon itself. Pulling them as taut as possible, they signalled for the next three to follow, the rope now angled so they avoided the pontoon and alighted directly on to the deck. The three duly arrived, each with a chest-pack and back-pack, while the first three watched carefully to deal with anyone arriving unexpectedly on deck.

Fifteen minutes after the ropes had been lowered, all thirteen men were on deck along with the same number of automatic weapons and handguns, and twelve packs of equipment.

CHAPTER SEVENTEEN

Wednesday, 5 July

12.03 a.m. BST (01.03 a.m. local time, Norway)

The Norwegian city of Stavanger, close to the southernmost tip of the country on its west coast, dates back to Viking times and grew and flourished during the age of sail. With the twentieth century oil adventure came a period of investment which saw the influx of foreign companies as well as the growth of Norway's own oil industry. The modern port now accommodates a cosmopolitan population in excess of 100,000.

The headquarters of Scandoil Search & Production ASA in the commercial sector was a huge single room, eighty metres square and eight metres high, which topped a five-level car park, three levels of which were underground. Around three sides of the room the walls were completely of glass, frosted up to a height of one-and-a-half metres and plain above. The fourth wall was solid and featured a number of large screens displaying the latest information on a variety of factors including weather conditions, stock market data, productivity, gross and operating profit, and commodity prices, plus a map of the Norwegian Sea and North Atlantic showing the sites of production platforms and supply routes. The high ceiling was partly to balance the extensive floor area but also to allow the dissipation of the heat generated by 180 desktop computers, one for each of the workstations which were clustered around the room in groups of four and five, and all but a few of which were currently unoccupied.

In one corner of the room in a large, frosted-glass cubicle, a group of three men and four women were gathered round a fourth man seated in front of a bank of ten monitor screens on a semi-circular workstation. He was speaking anxiously into a microphone on a stand on the worktop.

"Control to *Mastodon*, will you respond, please? What is your position?"

The speaker in front of them crackled into life.

"Control, this is *Mastodon*. I'm hearing you. Can you hear me?"

The group exhaled a collective sigh of relief and looked around at each other, smiling. A couple of them tapped the seated man on the shoulder as if to congratulate him.

"Hello, *Mastodon*. Kurt Olafsen here. Yes, we can hear you now, but we lost you for twenty-four minutes. What happened?"

There was a pause.

"Problem with comms."

"Understood, but what type of problem?"

An even longer pause. The group looked round at each other again, this time with questioning frowns and shrugs.

"We think interference from static on the rig. Or conflicting frequencies or something. Seems to be okay now." The voice was monotone and mechanical.

They were all silent for a while before one of the group leaned forward and picked up the mike. She was tall, with blonde hair pulled back in a tight bun behind her head, and, unlike her companions, was dressed formally. She wore a dark-blue, business trouser suit and high heels.

"*Mastodon*, this is Director Alicia Stenson. Who am I speaking to?"

"Comms Officer Ove Fossen, ma'am."

"Is Chief Engineer Johansen available, Ove?"

There was a shuffling of feet and murmuring among the group. She turned and held up her hand for silence.

"Well actually, the Chief…" Ove hesitated again, for barely a second, "… is up on deck, ma'am. Still trying to find the cause of the problem, I assume."

"Okay," said the woman. "Well, whatever it was it seems to be okay now. I'll hand you back to Kurt to confirm your position. Safe journey."

Alicia replaced the microphone in its stand in front of Kurt and stepped back a few metres, turning to one of the women and speaking in almost a whisper.

"Get Josef here right away, Lisa."

The others looked at her, eyes wide and anxious.

"Well, Chief Engineer Johansen," she said, addressing one of her colleagues, "would you mind telling us how you happen to be in two places at once?"

★

The Norwegian Coast Guard vessel *Sonja* had changed course within a minute of receiving the message from its Sortland Naval Base headquarters at 12.22 a.m. BST. Unlike its sister organisation in the UK, the Norwegian coast guard is a maritime military force which is part of the Royal Norwegian Navy. Its main task is to assert and uphold Norwegian sovereignty over its inland and territorial waters, and Norway's 2.4 million square-kilometre exclusive economic zone. The organisation's structure is centred around a peacetime role, but the country's Coast Guard Act also grants it law enforcement jurisdiction in certain circumstances.

The NoCGV *Sonja* was one of the coast guard's three *Nordkapp*-Class vessels, a class of ship designed with a secondary role as wartime naval escorts, and used predominantly to patrol the Barents Sea. It was equipped with one Bofors cannon, six machine guns, torpedoes and depth charges, and carried an NH90 military helicopter. Its current assignment was to shadow the *Mastodon* on a parallel course, maintaining a distance of ten kilometres.

By now, at 3.40 a.m., first light, following the intelligence from HQ, it had closed to within four kilometres and was ready to investigate.

★

Abu el Taqha – a.k.a. The Shadow – stood at the very centre of the *Mastodon*'s huge deck, his feet planted wide apart to compensate for the swaying motion as they headed due south, cutting through the strong eastward rush of the Atlantic. Around him, resting on the deck and overhanging the sides of the ship, was the massive pontoon which formed the stabilising base of the platform's structure, whilst, above, the 120-metre-square canopy of the former production deck created the impression of his being inside a huge, airy building.

He was encouraged by how the mission had progressed so far. The initial seizing of the communications room had gone exactly to plan. Cutting contact with the ship's land-base had been an essential first step before taking full control of the vessel. The inside knowledge provided by two of his team, employees of Scandoil, had been critical to achieving their goal.

He checked his watch; 3.48 a.m. Still thirteen hours to go if they kept to schedule, but radio contact had been re-established to the apparent satisfaction of the company's HQ, a situation which was unlikely to change. If the pistol currently held close to Communications Officer Fossen's head was not sufficient incentive for him to play along, the knowledge that a vehicle containing two members of Islamic State was parked outside his family's house in Egersund should be more than enough.

The fact that there had been no casualties was a bonus. Also, Ove Fossen aside, who was isolated from the rest of the crew, anyway, his team had gone to great lengths not to intimidate and threaten their captives. They were well trained and practised in the handling of hostages, knowing how important it was to establish rapport – and empathy – as soon and as much as possible in such circumstances. Controlling a relaxed bunch of prisoners was many times easier than with an agitated group gripped by a collective feeling of nothing to lose.

As he rehearsed again in his mind the first contact with their targeted representatives of the enemies of Islam, his attention was caught by a large seabird, drifting across the deck, its wings barely moving in relation to its body as it appeared to utilise the wind and thermals with exquisite skill. He was drawn to it as much by the noise of the other birds, who seemed to perceive it as a threat, diving and pecking at the larger bird as it continued, totally indifferent to their attentions, on its elegant way. It circled the deck several times, before gliding almost to deck level and heading directly towards him, then soaring over his head, continuing up and around one of the stern towers before turning with the same easy motion to head westward, out over the open sea.

*

In the observation cabin of the NoCGV *Sonja*, Captain Haugen and two of his senior officers watched on the monitor screen the images transmitted to them from the drone. A voice from Sortland Coast Guard HQ filled the room.

"You say he's been the only one to come up on deck? So, we've no idea how many there are on board?"

"I'm afraid not," the captain said. "We'll keep swinging Gully round, but I guess they'll be fully occupied below decks. It's a massive area to control. And no contact, yet, you say? So, we don't know what they want – or even whether it's us or the Brits they're after."

A different voice cut in.

"Captain, this is Agent Elsa Tongan of the Police Security Service. I'm with the team at Scandoil in Stavanger. We're getting your pictures through here now, and I can confirm that you were correct, the man on deck is Abu el Taqha, that's one hundred percent. We need to make sure we don't give him cause to think he's got a problem. The comms guy on the *Mastodon* did a great job letting us know they'd been taken. I only hope he's not been found out yet, and we have to assume that he *hasn't* and the hijackers don't suspect we know anything. So, don't send your bird out again yet. Keep a visual from the ship, and if it looks like there's more movement on deck, then use your discretion based on what I've just said. If he's not planning to do anything until he reaches St Kilda, that gives us over twelve hours to get things in place to deal with this. We don't want to precipitate any action before we're ready. Okay, Captain?"

"Okay, Agent Tongan. In fact, I'll check with you first before we send her out again."

"Thank you, that's great. And excellent work, tell your birdman."

"I will, ma'am."

Above them, the great black-backed gull was landing gently – and vertically – onto the deck. One of the crew stepped forward and threw a switch under its belly, after which the gentle whirring of its concealed propellers slowed gradually into silence.

CHAPTER EIGHTEEN

6.40 a.m. BST (8.40 a.m. local time, Cyprus)
The five men in black running shorts and white tee shirts crashed through the coarse grass and ferns of the woodland floor, parrying low branches as they went. The two men in front, racing stride for stride, were similar in size and build and both in their mid-forties. Two metres behind, keeping the same pace and distance, a tall black man, supremely athletic and totally relaxed in his running style, had been talking in his beautiful French accent and without a trace of breathlessness throughout the whole of the ten-kilometre run.

Several metres back from him, and dropping further behind, two huge men – each approaching two metres in height – were engaged in a good-natured battle of words which was becoming more difficult to sustain with each challenging stride and gasping intake of breath. The younger of the two, slightly ahead of his running companion, called over his shoulder in a strong Glaswegian twang.

"Come on, Seggy. Remember, there're only four camels and there are five of us. You dinna want to miss out! It's that fucking beard that slows you down."

The three men ahead of him laughed at the Russian obscenity that exploded from the trailing man's lips. Gradually, they climbed out of the wood up to the rough track that ran parallel to the road, increasing their pace as the running became easier. The black man slipped past his two companions to take the leading position. As they lengthened their stride, a military jeep pulled up alongside, keeping pace with their running. A young soldier in the driver's seat called across to them.

"Mr Kade, you're needed urgently at the base. I'm to take you there right away."

The man running in second place checked the stopwatch on his wrist and spoke with an American accent.

"Tell them I'll be there in nine minutes forty seconds; make that… thirty-five… thirty. You get the idea."

"Yes, sir, but I need to take you *now*. Otherwise, by the time you get back, I will have lost my position and will be packing to return home. Can you live with that… sir?"

The American laughed. "You got real style when it comes to getting your own way, soldier."

The jeep pulled ahead, stopping after fifty metres or so, and Kade slowed to a halt beside it and climbed into the front passenger seat. He shouted across to the leading runner as they pulled away. "Don't win by too much, Jules. You know what Brig's like when things don't go his way."

The man laughed and waved as the jeep accelerated away in a cloud of dust and fumes.

*

Ex-US Colonel Marty Kade and the other seven members of his team were pressed back into their seats as the Cessna Citation X+ jet climbed steeply and fast above the military base at Akrotiri in Cyprus and wheeled away over the brilliant blue of the eastern Mediterranean before turning half-circle onto its course for Stornoway. The military version of the world's fastest executive jet would take just over three hours, flying at a fraction under Mach One, to reach its destination 3,000 kilometres away at around 11.30 a.m. BST. From there, a Eurocopter X3 awaited them for the onward journey to St Kilda, unless something happened in the meantime to change their plans.

With an in-flight briefing scheduled for two and a half hours' time, to ensure it reflected the most up-to-date circumstances, all eight members – six men and two women – settled into the lush seats for as long a sleep as possible, knowing it could be their last for some time.

*

Two Sikorsky S92 UK coast guard helicopters touched down on Benbecula in the Outer Hebrides to join the pair of Agusta Westland AW189s based there. Within an hour of their landing, all four aircraft lifted off for the twenty-minute flight to the helicopter standing area on Hirta, the main island of the St Kilda archipelago. They were in the vanguard of a small fleet of vessels assembling in readiness for the *Mastodon* reaching its destination in an estimated nine hours' time.

Three seventy-five-metre Boskalis ocean-going tugs out of Stornoway and one from Oban were on course for the island group at their top speed of thirty kilometres per hour.

HMS *Jura* had left its temporary mooring off Uig, Isle of Skye, and was heading across The Little Minch towards the Sound of Harris and, once through there, on into the Atlantic to meet up with the tugs. The *Jura* was a River-class patrol boat, eighty metres long with a displacement of 2,000 tonnes, converted into a hospital ship, specifically for covert operations.

A second Norwegian Coast Guard vessel – NoCGV *Ursula* – had set off out of Bergen shortly after midnight with an estimated journey time of around thirty-six hours to link up with her sister ship.

Ahead of all of them, two naval offshore patrol vessels – OPVs *Spey* and *Kintyre* – had already set out from Tobermory on their five-hour journey to St Kilda with an ETA of around noon. Each carried a full complement of thirty-four crew members, a 30mm cannon, machine guns and a Merlin MK3 Commando helicopter. This was the new hi-tech crafts' first mission, the nature of which was still unknown to all on board.

CHAPTER NINETEEN

2.05 p.m. BST (3.05 p.m. local time, Norway)

The frosted cube enclosing the bank of monitor screens in the corner of Scandoil's open-plan office was crowded with people, all following what uninformed ears would assume was a routine communications link to a vessel out in the Atlantic. Those present, however, were very *well* informed, and were waiting anxiously for the scenario to change to reflect the impending crisis.

Present, from Scandoil, were Alicia Stenson, along with Head of Security Josef Solheim, Chief Engineer Mikel Johansen and Communications Supervisor Inga Larsson, who had taken over from Kurt Olafsen at the end of his shift. Inga had been in contact with Ove Fossen on the *Mastodon*, as normal, for the scheduled half-hourly updates on weather and sea conditions, and any changes to their estimated time of arrival. These regular checks were also being routed through to the central unit of the PST, the Norwegian Police Security Service, in Oslo and to Thames House in Millbank, London, the home of MI5.

Attention in Stavanger was focussed on a large monitor screen displaying a map of the area and showing the *Mastodon*'s current position on a projected line representing the route to its destination. At the edge of the screen, a table of figures showed its actual and scheduled journey times and ETAs.

"They're behind by a couple of hours," Alicia said, "and all that slippage has been in the last fourteen hours since the comms blackout when, we assume, the hijack happened, So, they must have slowed deliberately to give us more time. New ETA seven o'clock. That additional two hours will be hardly noticeable in a journey of over eighty, but it makes a hell of a difference to those preparing to receive them."

In the room with the Scandoil group were agents Elsa Tongan and Erik Sundstrom of the PST, along with Agent Silas Horne of the CIA. In between Inga's contacts with the *Mastodon*, during which the need for absolute silence had been diligently observed, the conversations had been animated and heated at times.

"Let's make sure we're both on the same page, Silas," Elsa said, addressing her CIA counterpart. The diminutive Norwegian was in her early thirties, with short-cropped blonde hair above a round, attractive face. Her dark, piercing eyes hinted at an underlying toughness. She wore dark chinos and a denim jacket.

"You are here because we felt it was a matter of courtesy to inform you of el Taqha's presence following his alleged involvement with the Willis bombing. That's the *only* reason you're here and..."

"We've been through this, Elsa," Silas jumped in. "And remember, *we* tracked him here to your country. Your guy wouldn't have ID'd him from the drone if we hadn't put his mugshot out there for people to see. So, I'm not sure I agree that this is a *big favour* you're doing us. The US has a policy, as you know, Intelligence Community Directive 191 – a legal *duty* to share information with our allies. I just thought – official policy or not – it should work both ways."

"It *is* working both ways. We do *not* have an ICD 191 equivalent, which is why this is a *courtesy*, but it does the same. It keeps you informed and..."

"Our concern," Elsa's colleague, Erik Sundstrom, put in, "is that, at this stage, until we hear anything from the hijackers, it remains within our control. There are Norwegian and Dutch nationals on that ship. Our only objective at this moment is their safe return. You're perfectly entitled to remind us that it was your agency that tracked The Shadow to Norway, *after* he had successfully staged the attack in Chicago. But this has nothing to do with the Willis bombing, so..."

"Oh, you don't think so? Silas Horne interrupted. "You don't think we have the right to get involved in bringing to justice someone who has delivered death and misery around the world, including playing a big part in 9/11? And this emphasis on *after* they bombed Willis. Is that a subtle way of saying we screwed up? Well, it's not so fucking subtle, Erik."

"You can have him as soon as you like, after we deal with this," Elsa said, her voice rising. "They are less than five hours from St Kilda. We don't want anything getting out yet about him being on board before they talk to us. My guess is, when they make contact, they will not reveal that he's there. *We* know he is, so it doesn't matter what they say, but we don't want him to know that we know."

"Why the hell not?"

"Because it just changes the dynamic," Erik said. "Raises the stakes. If it gets out, we'll have the whole of the US of fucking A baying for his blood with total disregard for anyone else's situation. Because nobody over there will give a shit what happens to the guys on the ship. They're not Americans so they don't matter."

"Hey, come on, Erik," Silas said. "That's not fair…"

"Not *fair*, maybe, but *fact* all the same. And you know it, Silas. If you leave this room and pass this information back to Langley, it will be on CNN before the *Mastodon* reaches St Kilda…"

"Now that's not…"

"… *because* everyone in the US wants revenge for 9/11 – and now the Willis – and someone will decide they'll look really good if they get to break the news. Big hero. Not exactly in the same league as 'we got him' but 'we know where he is' will do for now."

Silas gave a thin smile. "You're such a fucking cynic, Erik. You'd do well in the CIA."

The comment diffused the tension a little.

"Thanks, Silas, I'll give the offer some thought."

"Look," Elsa said, "can we agree that until we hear from the hijackers, and understand what their demands are – that's if they have any – until then *no-one* says anything to anyone about who's on the ship?" She looked around the room at all present. "Once we know, we take it from there, working *together.*"

"Okay," Silas said, "If that's…"

"Which *might* mean," Elsa continued, "you guys taking a back seat in the short term. Okay?"

Silas shrugged. "Still okay. Look, I need a caffeine shot." He turned to leave the room. "Should I hand over my cell or do you trust me not to phone Fox News?"

Elsa smiled. "That won't be necessary, because I need a coffee as well, so I'll come with you."

Silas laughed, opened the door and waved Elsa through ahead of him with a low bow.

The refreshment area was a screened-off central square containing fifteen rectangular tables with a seating capacity for exactly one-third of the employees occupying the floor, enforcing a voluntary, self-regulated system of staggered breaks. In the centre of the square, the circular kitchen area, surrounded by a continuous stainless-steel counter, served hot and cold light meals, tea, coffee and chilled drinks. They found an empty table in a quiet part of the area.

"When are you guys going to join the real world and get burgers on the menu?" Silas asked, with a smile, cradling his coffee cup in both hands. The CIA agent was around forty years old, shortish and stockily built, with craggy features and thinning hair cropped very short. He wore a dark suit and black tie.

"Probably as soon as you stop asking," Elsa said.

Silas shook his head. "You all don't have a particularly high opinion of us, do you?"

"Who's 'us'? If you mean you, personally, then you couldn't be more wrong. If you mean the mighty CIA, then sometimes we have issues. But, honestly, Silas, it's nothing personal – Erik and I agree – we couldn't wish for an easier guy to work with."

"Well, I'm flattered, Elsa – truly. So, what then? I'm part of 'the mighty CIA' as you put it. Why am I different?"

"It comes down to individuals, doesn't it? In any organisation there are good and bad and all points in between. My grandfather fought in World War Two. Norway declared itself neutral and the Germans stomped all over us anyway. But Grandpa told me there were some really good guys among them who just didn't want any part of it, and after the war he used to meet up with a few every springtime for a holiday right up to his death two years ago. So good guys in a bad organisation."

"Christ, Els, we've had our critics in the past, but no-one's ever compared us to the Third Reich before – well, not that I'm aware of."

Elsa laughed. "What I mean is, we can be frustrated with the CIA as an entity and like the guys we work with who are part of it."

"So, why do we frustrate you – or why does the *entity* frustrate you?"

"Rushing too quickly to conclusions, because you're always so desperate to *reach* a conclusion, and the one that you *want* to reach. Which is why untruths lead to the wrong actions. Look at Colin Powell with his famous PowerPoint presentation, stolen from a post-grad thesis, which was supposed to prove conclusively that Saddam had WMDs stashed somewhere. If someone had taken longer to investigate, instead of charging in because that was exactly what they *wanted* to believe, then a few more of your young men would still be alive, along with some French, and Canadians and Brits and Australians."

"I see, so it wasn't just us, then? And I seem to recall the general feeling was that Saddam got what he deserved. Right end, wrong reason, isn't that okay? Or am I mistaken?"

"He probably did, but at least with him around there was some structure to people's lives; far from ideal, I admit. But there was no planning at all for what would happen when the conflict was over. For the ordinary Iraqi, things were a lot worse."

"I'm missing a link, here."

"I guess we just get tired of feeling that the US is all that matters so it can do what it likes. Let's tell the world what we've done, what we've found out, how well we've handled it. How fucking great we are."

Silas snorted a laugh. "Tell you something, Els, I don't actually disagree with you. We're exactly as you describe us and when I listen to myself – and other guys – here and in places where there are calm, unexcitable, dignified people like you…" he held up his hand as Elsa leaned forward to interrupt "… no, I mean it. I can understand why we get under your skin. We're brash, arrogant, cocky, but one hundred and ten percent on your side. Try not to forget the last bit and cut us a bit of slack. It's how we were brought up. Society is to blame, as they say."

Elsa laughed. "I'll definitely remember that next time."

"Thank you, because you've got to accept, I cannot sit on this information and not tell anybody, even for a few hours. I have a boss who will crucify me if I don't let him know. And I've got mouths to feed back home."

"I thought we just agreed, if I understand what 'still okay' means. So why…?"

"I guess I just wanted to get through that little fallout in there, bearing in mind we had an audience. Couldn't stand the thought of the Brits listening in, chuckling away over there and choking on their tea and scones. I wanted to tell you one-to-one, but…"

Elsa leaned back on her chair and sighed. "Oh, shit, Silas, this is exactly…"

"*But*," Silas interrupted, "if you'll let me finish, Agent Tongan, I'll make it clear to him that it must go no further. Okay?"

"Still *not* okay, Agent Horne. Because *he'll* have a boss who must be told and this is exactly what we've just been talking about. It will quickly get up the chain of command to someone who is *so* big and *so* important that he or she doesn't have to worry about what we want – and when I say 'we' I'm including you, by the way. Before you know, the President will be addressing the nation and the press will be all over it."

"Interesting that you should mention President Weston and the press, because when he visited Oslo on his European tour just prior to the Willis bombing, he was swamped with questions about his alleged relationship with a very senior civil servant in the UK judiciary. And when he failed to confirm it – pretty much denied it, in fact – your press guys went ahead and printed the rumour: front page, top story. So, just think before you vilify the US media. 'Let he who is without sin…' or 'she' in this case."

"Come on, Silas. You've been here long enough to know that the people of Norway have a great liking for President Weston, and the story was born out of a genuine desire for him to find love again. It was an affectionate bit of… well, mischief, I suppose, but totally harmless."

"*Harmless*, you say, and I guess you're right. But it could have caused all sorts of shit to fly in the UK if they'd picked up on it and looked at a possible conflict of interest."

"But they didn't, Silas. So why are you making this comparison with what will be one of the biggest global stories of the day? Nine-eleven was two decades ago. Can't this information wait for a few more hours?"

Silas shook his head. "Sorry, Elsa, but you'll have to trust me, and my boss. You also have a rather flattering view of how quickly information gets around over there. My guess is we'll be through this crisis before the general public find out it involved The Shadow at all."

Elsa sighed.

"And, for the record," Silas continued, "the ICD 191 works both ways, at least the *principle* of the directive does. As soon as we knew for certain el Taqha was somewhere in your country, we were in touch with you and Delta *within minutes*."

"At which time," Elsa said, getting to her feet, "unless my memory fails me, we were *not* in the middle of a delicate, life-threatening emergency."

As she turned away, Alicia Stenson opened the door of the corner office and beckoned for them to go back. They hurried over to find Inga still at the table, but now joined by Erik Sundstrom, who was typing messages for her to read on a laptop immediately in front of her. She was speaking slowly and clearly in English to someone who *wasn't* Ove Fossen.

*

DC Natalie Crusoe checked the name on the display of her iPhone before answering. It was a name that had been on her list of contacts for only a couple of hours.

"Professor Fellows. That was quick. Thank you for phoning back."

"Please call me Mark, and it's no problem. I really don't mind helping the police with their enquiries, as long as it doesn't mean what it usually means."

"Which is?"

"That I'm suspected of something."

Natalie laughed. "Well, I'm very grateful and, I promise you, you're not."

"Good. Well, as I said when you phoned this morning, the survey didn't ring any bells but it's not like they consult me before they undertake these adventures – more often the exact opposite – don't bother to tell me about them at all. But I thought I'd be aware of the one you described because the subsequent analysis of the samples would most likely be carried out here. It's the sort of work we've done around the production platforms in the North Sea, and as far as I was aware we hadn't undertaken that sort of project in relation to your offshore prison. Sorry, I'm rambling."

"Not at all."

"Anyway, I was right. There hasn't been any such sampling or testing done in the area of St Kilda or the platform on any date, including the second of November last year. I hope that helps."

"Thank you, Professor, err... Mark. It sort of completes a picture for us."

"You didn't explain why you were interested in that date. Can you tell me? My guess would be it's something else to do with the disappearance of Tom Brown. And now his body has been found..."

"Well, you'd be right about that, Mark, and I understand you've had a couple of enquiries about where his body was likely to turn up. This survey thing, as I say, now completes the picture, but it's not linked to your two visitations."

Mark chuckled. "Thanks for telling me nothing, Natalie, but I do understand. I will say this, though, if a body went into the sea close to St Kilda or the prison, its chances of turning up at Elgol would be exactly zero."

CHAPTER TWENTY

2.45 p.m. BST (3.45 p.m. local time, Norway)

"You still haven't told us who you are. We do not know who we are talking to, so please identify yourself." Inga Larsson continued to speak into the radio telephone in front of her, reading from the screen and clearly articulating each word. Everyone in the room was staring silently at the table-mounted speaker, as if an image was about to emerge from it to go with the new voice from the *Mastodon*.

"We are Brothers of Islam. We are here to show that the presence of Allah is total and knows no limits, and very soon you will witness his power as well as his presence."

"I see. Can I assume that you are the spokesman for the group?" Inga was still reading from the screen. "And if so, and as we may be talking for some time, please tell me your name so I can address you personally."

The man laughed loudly and harshly. "Do you think I don't know your pathetic tricks. To try to make friends and gently appeal to my – how do you say – better side. But, if we are playing these psychological games, then you tell me who you are."

"My name is Inga."

"Ah, *Inga*?" he said, as if he had suddenly recognised an old friend. "So, tell us what you do, *Inga*."

"I am a communications supervisor here at the company's headquarters. So now it's your turn, who are you?"

The harsh laugh again. "Tell me, *Inga*, who is telling you what to say?"

"No-one. Why do you say that?"

"Because you hesitate each time after I have spoken, like you just did then."

"It's because this is all new for me and a little frightening. I'm wondering what I *should* say. There are some other people here now. Would you like to speak with someone else?"

"Tell me who is there."

Inga looked around the room. Alicia pointed to herself, then to Josef. Inga relayed the names. "Production Director Alicia Stenson and Head of Security Josef Solheim." She looked at Mikel Johansen, raising her eyebrows. The Chief Engineer shook his head.

"So, your Head of Security is still there. Not for long, I think."

The laugh again, a little forced this time. Alicia leaned forward, speaking over Inga's shoulder.

"This is Alicia Stenson. Would you please give us your name – or *a* name – so we may properly address you?"

Inga made way for her to sit at the table next to Erik Sundstrom.

"With respect, Director Stenson, I need to speak to someone with the authority to meet our demands. And that is not you or any of your Scandoil colleagues. Nor is it your police, politicians or military. We need to discuss our objective with the British authorities, so you can relax. We want nothing from you except to set up the appropriate channels of communication. Then we will leave you alone."

"I'm afraid it is not as straightforward as that." Alicia was reading from Erik's script. "You have thirty-six Norwegian nationals on board along with seventeen Dutch nationals who are our contracted employees. Until we have proof that they are unharmed, we cannot proceed further with any requests."

The man laughed again. "You are not in a very strong position to be making the rules, Alicia. I *can* assure you, in fact, that no-one has been injured. But I would say that, wouldn't I, if that is a condition before we negotiate? So, tell me, how can I convince you I'm telling the truth?"

Alicia glanced at a screen to her right, displaying an Excel spreadsheet with columns of data. "I have a list of names here of all fifty-three crew members who are on board. I will need to speak to each of them personally. They can identify themselves by answering two security questions. It will take less than a minute each, so if you can organise that quickly, an hour at the most."

"But that is impossible, you must realise that." The brash confidence in his voice had evaporated.

"And we will start with Mr Fossen. Please let him speak to me."

"Certainly, Director Stenson." A different voice, deeper and more confident. "Ove, speak to your colleague."

"I'm here, ma'am."

"Are you okay? Have they...?"

"*Two* questions you said. You've already used up one."

Alicia sighed. "Date of birth, Ove?"

"December twelve, eighty-four."

"Mother's maiden..."

"That's all," the new voice interrupted. "Date of birth was your *second* question. Now we will leave you and consider your request, but I suggest, in anticipation of our likely response, you should think of another way we can move forward."

The connection was cut and no-one spoke for a long time, each absorbing the situation and contemplating the next steps. It was Inga who broke the silence.

"I'm sure I know that first voice, and that laugh. I've heard them before, more than once."

"An employee?" Josef said. "That would make sense of how they managed to occupy the platform."

"How's that?" Silas asked.

"We checked the whole structure just an hour or so before the start of the loadout operation – top to bottom, inside out. Found what we expected, nothing and no-one. I've been thinking up to now this must have been some sort of mutiny, or they've parachuted in during the hours of darkness. Both highly unlikely."

"As unlikely as the hijacking of a ship carrying a redundant production platform," Silas put in.

"Agreed, but there's another possibility. Two of the four columns – adjacent, not opposite – are double-skinned. A column within a column, in effect, for added strength. These are at the side of the platform which housed the loading facility when it was operational, so the double skin is for protection in the event of the service vessel colliding with the structure during a loading operation. Which leaves a top-to-bottom cavity between the skins, serviced by a ladder, accessed from the steel-mesh floor below the main deck, and containing a number of floors running round between the outer and inner columns to bind them together. That cavity, when you add up the total area of all the floors, could easily accommodate a group of up to, say, twenty people in each column. That is the only place they could have hidden themselves on the platform."

"Could they have hidden on the ship itself?" Alicia asked.

"No chance of that," Josef said. "There would have to be a good number of them to take over and control a ship that size, and there's nowhere to conceal more than one or two people away from the vessel's surveillance systems, and not even as few as that for nearly three days."

There was a collective shuffling as the group looked around at each other with a few murmured comments.

"I have to say," Alicia said, "I knew nothing about this cavity."

There was a general shaking of heads.

"No reason why you – or anyone – should, Ali," Mikel Johansen said. "It's not part of the living quarters or the storage capacity of the platform. It has no operational function; it's an engineering modification to address a specific risk."

"And that's my point," Erik said. "Other than the South Koreans who built it, only an offshore production or maintenance worker employed by this company would be familiar enough with the platform to be aware of that feature. The cavity doesn't serve any operational purpose, but it *is* on a scheduled, in-situ inspection roster."

"What about one of the contract employees from the Netherlands?" Alicia asked.

"Unlikely, because they are only there to drive the ship. No reason for any of them to know that level of detail about the structure of their cargo."

"No prizes for guessing who the second guy is," Elsa said.

Another voice. "Millbank here, MI5 Agent Joe Kilby speaking. Seems it's our problem so we'll pick it up at our end a.s.a.p. I'm going to raise it through to ministerial level right away. I heard what you said about the hostages, Ms Stenson. If it looks like it's going to be a long job, we'll try to negotiate an exchange with our own people, so we can release your fifty-three. Although we will need to retain a minimum crew level to operate the ship."

"Is that likely to happen," Alicia asked, "their agreeing to an exchange? Doesn't it weaken their position?"

"It depends who we offer up and whether they think the replacements give them at least as much leverage as the original hostages. We've been successful doing that in the past, in somewhat different circumstances, I must admit."

"Hi, Joe, it's Elsa here."

"Hi, Elsa."

"Will it be Millbank conducting the exchanges, so we know where to set up the channel, and do you want to be part of the dialogue when they come back on here?"

"Yes, to the first question – ongoing, anyway. But I think, Ms Stenson, when they come back you should continue to insist on the individual one-to-one IDs. It sounded like they might not agree, but I think you should push for it as hard and long as it's safe to. It's a great stalling tactic. If we can get that extra hour without any further developments, that will be invaluable. We've already got a lot of stuff mobilised, but time could be the defining factor. And anything you can tease out of them at this stage about what they want would be useful, but my guess is we'll only find that out when they're talking directly to us. All okay with that?"

Elsa looked round the room at the nodding heads before replying.

"Yes, all okay."

"Great. One more thing: latest ETA?"

"Alicia again. You know it's been revised from the original estimate?"

"Yes, I heard. Your guys slowing the ship – good job."

"Well, no change since the last estimate. Still 7.10 p.m. your time."

"And we're at... what... 2.53 p.m. BST. So, four and a quarter hours. A lot can happen."

"Amen to that," Silas said. He turned and left the room.

Elsa watched him go.

*

The phone rang on Jackie Hewlett's desk in her office in Marsham Street. She pressed the speaker button to take the call.

"They're on the line, Home Secretary. Shall I put them through?"

"Yes, please, Jenny."

The two people seated opposite her across the desk leaned forward in anticipation. Ruby Weller was in her early fifties, shorter than medium height and sturdily-built. Her hair was in a bob-cut style and she wore her trademark navy trouser suit over a white blouse. The other person present, Sir Roger Ashpole, ex-army and special forces, was in his sixties, tall and slim with a full head of grey hair, neatly groomed, He wore a dark-grey suit, cream shirt and blue-and-yellow striped tie.

"You're through now, sir." A brief silence was followed by a deep male voice speaking perfect English with only the slightest hint of an accent.

"Jackie, Klaus Lundquist here. Are you well?" The speaker was the Norwegian Minister of Justice and Public Security.

"Hello, Klaus. Very well, thank you. And you?"

"Also, well. I have with me Milena Bakke, Director of PST, our Security Service."

"Hello, Milena. I think you both know Ruby Weller, our Minister for Security and Counter Terrorism. And, Milena, I know you have previously worked with Sir Roger Ashpole, Head of MI5."

There were greetings on both sides before Klaus spoke again.

"I think we are all on the same page, but the purpose of this call is to be sure. The main contact so far has been through Scandoil, only because that was the established channel of communication with the *Mastodon*. The dialogue with the hijackers has been by Erik Sundstrom, prompting the Scandoil people who are in contact with them. Erik is one of Milena's agents and an experienced hostage negotiator. So, Scandoil voices, Erik's words. It was important, of course, that the hijackers were not aware we were in a position at this stage to respond to their actions. Also in attendance in Stavanger was a member of the CIA, although he will not be involved in any part of the process. That, I understand, has been made clear to him by Elsa Tongan, another PST agent."

"That's good," Jackie said. "If el Taqha hasn't identified himself yet, it's best we don't make him aware we know he's there. And the last thing we need at this stage is the US whooping and cheering because they've found the guy who bombed the Willis."

"That's the point that Elsa made to him," Milena said. "The CIA have taken a pounding from the press for letting the Willis happen and they'll be desperate to grab any chance to show the world – or the US, at least – how good they are."

"And we have no idea yet what they want," Ruby Weller said, "except whatever it is, it seems we – the UK – are the ones who have it. Nor do we know what they have on board with them, whether it's just a hostage deal or a bomb or what."

"That's right," Milena said. "It's around fifty minutes since they broke off communications with Scandoil HQ. They've tried to contact the *Mastodon* but there is no response. We're still awaiting a reply to Alicia Stenson's request for individual confirmation of the crew's well-being. Your agent Kilby has been in touch with us throughout. When they do come back, Sundstrom will talk directly to them. There will have been enough time for him to have been 'coptered in from Oslo, so they'll expect a new voice. In fact, it could be what they're waiting for."

"And I think I'm right, Milena," Klaus said, "that Millbank can take over direct contact whenever they're ready."

"That's right. Kilby can activate a direct link to the *Mastodon*. But I suggest we try for that extra time with Stenson's ID suggestion."

"Agreed," Jackie said. "Roger and Milena can move it forward together for now, I think." She looked at Ruby, who nodded. "We have hostage rescue personnel already in place on St Kilda, which will likely become the command centre, assuming they stay in the area around Alpha."

"It will be necessary, though," Sir Roger put in, "to have somebody in place at the command centre who knows the *Mastodon* inside out. Could you arrange that, please, Milena?"

"That's a good point," Jackie said. "We'll need to know every inch of the ship. So, perhaps Johansen, or someone from the Netherlands with experience of the *Mastodon*."

"Leave that with us," Klaus said, "we'll make sure you get the right person." He gave a little chuckle. "I must say, Jackie, I'm impressed that your troops are in place already. We only heard an hour ago that it's you Brits that they're after."

Jackie laughed. "Yes, it makes me look good, doesn't it, but I could have looked just as bad? They left Cyprus around 8.30 this morning – our time – and would have been on Hirta well before first contact. But if they'd then said that Norway was their objective, the PM would be jumping all over me for wasting the Service's budget. Speaking of the PM, I believe he may take this to COBRA, depending on the nature of their demands and particularly because there are non-UK nationals involved. We're all standing by here in case that happens.

"And, by the way, the PM has confirmed that we'll offer an exchange of hostages in an attempt to release your people and the Dutch contractors, but, as Kilby said, I think, we will need a skeleton crew to manage the ship." There were a few moments of silence. "Does anyone have any theories at this point as to how this is going to develop?"

Sir Roger answered. "If this whole thing is to get some deal or concessions from the UK, then MI5 believe it is certain to involve Alpha. Right now, there are only non-Brits at risk, which doesn't give them the best leverage to negotiate with us."

"I agree," Milena said. "But if that's correct, the only way they can use your exiles as hostages is from the outside. And the only way to put them at risk as part of a bargaining tool is to have a bomb on board the *Mastodon* or some other means of capsizing Platform Alpha."

"Not a very comfortable thought," Klaus said. "Okay, so we are now at 3.35 your time and we sit and wait for… one moment."

They could hear another person entering the room to join Klaus and Milena, then an excited exchange of anxious voices. They heard Klaus say "thank you". He spoke into the phone line. There was a frantic edge to his voice.

"That was one of Milena's colleagues. The hijackers have been back in touch with Scandoil and what they said will change *everything*."

*

David took the call on his way home to Meadow Village after dropping off Marie at Shenfield railway station on her way for a shopping expedition with friends in the West End.

"Hi, David? This is Harry."

"Hi, Harry."

"What's that noise? Are you in the car?"

"Yes, on my way home."

"Well, I hope you're on the hands-free or I'll have to ask you to pull over."

David laughed. "What can I do you for?"

"It's just an update on the Tom Brown thing. Natalie phoned our friend in the North – the Prof – as you suggested, and he says there was definitely *not* a survey taking place around the platform on that date, or any other date, in fact. So, it just gets more confusing. It makes you wonder whether he really did try to get on to Alpha, but what the hell could he possibly have hoped to achieve? And how did he persuade whoever was with him to give it a go? Still makes no sense."

"But if he *did*, perhaps things went badly wrong and he got swept away."

"A reasonable suggestion except the Prof said if anyone went into the sea close to Alpha, there would be no chance at all they'd be washed up at Elgol. Apparently, there's this thing called the Outer Hebrides in the way."

"And then there's the mystery of the empty boat in The Minch. With hindsight, it's surprising DI Stuart didn't check the survey out at the time."

"He did, but not with the Oceanographic Society. They contacted the service centre on St Kilda who said the society had been in touch with them in advance and given them full details. And everything that happened on the day checked out. The boats arrived at the island group at the scheduled time, did a full circuit taking water samples – they watched them do that from the observation tower – and then they left for Alpha. Lochshore confirmed they had been informed as well, so they were also expecting the boats, if not the floor show. So, they figured there was no point in taking it further."

"Fair enough, I guess. Any news yet from the post-mortem?"

"There wasn't a lot to post-mort, but no signs of broken bones or head trauma, so unlikely a violent death. Drowning seems the most probable, the doc said, but not enough left to make a definitive assessment."

"Well, at least we know where he is now, which is more than we can say for your pole-dancing scientist, Harry. That avenue of discovery having been closed, a nationwide APB might be your only way forward."

"Either that or I could forget about her altogether and get a restful night's sleep for a change."

David laughed. "So, do we have as a possible scenario? Any idea how a clandestine water survey links to a drowned ex-Home Secretary? This is where we need our mutual friend and colleague, Ms Joannita Cottrell. She'd be sure to come up with a theory."

Harry gave a little laugh. "That's for certain."

"Anyway, thanks for the heads-up, Harry. See you soon, no doubt."

"No doubt. Any contact yet?"

"Not yet. You'll be the first to know."

CHAPTER TWENTY-ONE

4.00 p.m. BST

The Cabinet Offices in Whitehall, at the rear of 10 Downing Street, are the normal location for meetings of the UK's emergency response committee, which convenes when a major crisis hits the UK or involves British nationals abroad. These are popularly referred to as COBRA meetings – being the acronym for Cabinet Office Briefing Room A – because they are usually held in Conference Room A at the main building at 70 Whitehall. And, whereas there is no basis to the story that it was originally referred to simply as Briefing Room A and the words Cabinet Office were added to give the acronym a more adventurous character, that doesn't mean that the regular – and occasional – attendees are not in favour of the two extra letters, and for that very reason.

Conference Room A can seat up to thirty people – at a squeeze – and is only ever used for COBRA meetings. Like all the Cabinet Office rooms, it is fitted with video and audio links to provide all relevant information for the situation being addressed. On this occasion, only eight people would occupy the room and there were no data links in use, except for a telephone connection to MI5 at Thames House.

Prime Minister Andrew Donald entered the room at exactly 4.00 p.m. and took his place at one end of the large table which almost filled the room, leaving just enough space around it for attendees to take their seats. He nodded to the committee members, who were already present and had got to their feet on his arrival.

"Please, be seated."

He was flanked by his two senior Cabinet ministers; Jackie Hewlett to his right and Jonathan Latiffe, the Justice Minister, to his left: a huge black South African, in his trademark grey-striped three-piece suit, the colour of which exactly matched his neat beard and close-cropped hair. Also present were Lawrence Harding, Permanent Undersecretary of State for Prisons, Ruby Weller, Sir Roger Ashpole, Major General Alan Cooper-Brand, Director of Special Forces, and Grace Goody.

"Good afternoon, ladies and gentlemen," Andrew said. "I believe we are all up to speed, so we will dispense with any preliminaries given the urgency of the issue we face. Roger, do we have any word yet regarding the demands of the hijackers?"

"Not yet, Prime Minister. Since the bombshell half an hour ago, all attempts to contact them have failed."

"Right. I assume the reference to 'bombshell' was an *unintended* pun."

Sir Roger coloured a little. "Yes, my apologies, Prime Minister, it *was* unintended."

"Can you recap, then, on all we know from the last – the *second* – call they made to Scandoil?"

"If the Prime Minister agrees, I have MI5 Agent Joe Kilby on the line from Thames House. Joe was party to the call from the hijackers."

"Then let's hear him."

"And he has a recording of their dialogue with Erik Sundstrom of the Norwegian Police Security Service.

"How long was the call?"

"Just under five minutes."

"Okay, play it back."

Sir Roger reached forward and depressed a button on the compact rectangular box in the centre of the table. "Joe, are you on the line?"

"Yes, sir." Joe Kilby's voice came out of four speakers angled down from the corners of the room.

"You already know who are present here, so could you play the recording?"

"Yes, sir. Good afternoon, Prime Minister, ladies and gentlemen. This call came through to the headquarters of Scandoil at 3.24 p.m. our time."

They heard a faint click then a voice speaking in clear English with just the trace of an accent.

This is the Mastodon. *Please acknowledge you are receiving me.*

This is Scandoil HQ, Erik Sundstrom speaking, and receiving you. Do you have an answer for Director Stenson regarding her request for confirmation of the safety of the crew members?

We have a statement, which I hope will convey, by implication, the answer to Alicia's question.

I must emphasise that we would need an assurance regarding their safety before we would be willing to discuss any requests which you may have.

Perhaps, Herr Sundstrom, you should listen to the statement first. Shall I go ahead or shall we end this conversation right now?

Very well, go ahead with your statement.

There was silence for a few seconds, then the same voice.

We, Brothers of Islam, children of Allah, will speak shortly to the authorities of the United Kingdom about what they must do to ensure a safe conclusion to this current situation. We assume, in fact, that by now, representatives of that country will be listening in to this conversation, and what I have to say will be of more interest to them than to you. We, contrary to popular belief, do not set out to destroy all infidels but we require a reciprocal tolerance on behalf of our comrades, some of whom are persecuted and incarcerated by servants of western evil. Shortly, we will tell you what our demands are, but we will share with you now information which will leave you in no doubt as to the seriousness of the situation and the lengths to which we are prepared to go to ensure justice for our brothers.

On board, we have a nuclear device which will shortly be prepared for activating, using what your military people would call an MRTD. You may be interested in the following facts:

The device is powerful enough to vaporise Hotel St Kilda many times over.

The prevailing westerly wind speed is currently ten miles per hour, only a gentle breeze for this part of the world.

Allowing for the natural lag of the wind-blown radioactive cloud, it will take approximately six hours to cover the forty miles to the Outer Hebrides.

The population of the Outer Hebrides – I am informed – is just over twenty-seven thousand people, plus an estimated two thousand tourists at this time of year.

To save you the calculation, the total number of hostages we will, in effect, hold in just over three hours' time, when we complete our journey, is about thirty thousand. That is how many lives are at stake, even before you add those on the inner islands and the mainland who would doubtless join their brothers and sisters as victims in the near future.

Be sure to understand that it is not our intention to die on this mission, nor do we wish anyone else to die. But you know for certain that my brothers and I do not fear death and would welcome it if it helps our cause, knowing as we do of the life that awaits us beyond. So, be sure we will *explode this device if you do not meet our demands.*

That is the end of the statement and I hope, Herr Sundstrom, that you can read into that our response to Alicia's request. However, I can confirm that none of the fifty-three Norwegian and Dutch nationals on board have been harmed. That will have to suffice by way of assurance. I have just been told, a few moments ago, that the nuclear device has now been armed, so any attack on this vessel, or attempt to retake control of it, will result in the immediate detonation of the bomb.

I do not wish you to respond. I will make contact again at midnight when I expect to be speaking to a senior minister of the United Kingdom.

Goodbye.

There was a slight click on the line as the recording was stopped, then Joe Kilby's voice.

"Sundstrom tried to speak to the man before he went off the call, but he had already disconnected."

The silence lasted almost half a minute as the seven other people waited for the Prime Minister to speak.

"Mr Kilby," he said. "How many people were on that call, other than Sundstrom?"

"They'd set up the link to the *Mastodon* away from the main comms centre at Stavanger because that is used for all offshore communications, so they received the call in the office of Josef Solheim, Scandoil's Head of Security. Also present with Sundstrom and Solheim were Alicia Stenson, Scandoil's Production Director and PST agent Elsa Tongan. And, of course, me over here."

"No CIA?"

"No, sir, and we agreed to keep the information about the nuke with only the people on the call until we had time to consider it here, except, of course, to alert immediate superiors. I assume, Prime Minister, you will be making a press statement soon about what the terrorists are telling us, including that they have a bomb on board, which is what everyone will assume anyway, but the nuke dimension would cause such a panic…"

"Thank you for the advice, Mr Kilby, which is *good* advice, by the way, but how long do you think the Norwegians will keep that sort of information to themselves? I mean, it is *their* people who are at risk, just as much as ours, if not in the same numbers."

"I don't think for very long, Prime Minister. But I *am* sure Elsa Tongan will make certain the CIA don't get to hear while things are still in the balance. She's told Horne that he's out of the loop for now, because he's made it very clear that any info they get has to go straight back to the US."

"Horne?"

"The CIA agent working with the PST. To be fair to him, the CIA were responsible for tracking el Taqha to Norway in the first place, but they seem to believe that gives them the right to take over the situation, And with the sort of bloodlust prevailing in the US right now that would probably involve sending in their own nuke on the end of a rocket. So, Horne's been side-lined and not a threat to disclosure at the moment."

"That's good. It buys us some time before we have to go public. Thank you."

He paused again to collect his thoughts.

"So," he said, "we have a weapon of mass destruction on a ship heading for an offshore establishment which is the home of nearly eight hundred British citizens, none of whom will know a thing about it, of course, if the bomb is detonated near them. Plus, a further twenty-nine thousand who may die afterwards, and more agonisingly. Plus… however many others. He didn't mention the few hundred of your people, Lawrence, on St Kilda itself." He turned to Sir Roger. "And *what* is an MRTD?"

"A manually-restrained trigger device, sir. It normally involves two terminals, which activate the trigger, held together by a spring mechanism. The trigger is deactivated by manually holding them apart. The trigger man reactivates the trigger simply by releasing his grip. In the case of a nuclear bomb, it could be someone holding back a sub-critical mass of uranium, to prevent it coming together with another sub-critical mass to create a divergent chain reaction."

"You mean like the famous laboratory incident. The lecturer

holding apart two hemispheres of nuclear fuel and accidentally letting them come together. Killed himself and his whole class, didn't he?"

Sir Roger nodded. "That's right."

"So, the rationale for this type of trigger is what?"

"From the hijackers' point of view, you mean? Well, if we gain access to where the detonator is, we can't take out the trigger man because that will cause him to release his grip and allow the explosion to take place."

"So, what *can* be done?" Andrew asked.

"We can sever the link between the trigger and the fuel, or somehow get a non-conductive material between the electrodes or a neutron-absorbing medium between the sub-critical components. There are ways, in theory, but we'd need to know how the bomb is constructed to do that. This would be unprecedented. No terrorist group has ever used a nuclear device before. It's the worst-case scenario from a rescuer's point of view." Sir Roger spoke into the rectangular box. "Joe, are you still there?"

"Yes, sir."

"Can you tell us the situation re the IAEA?"

"The what?" Andrew said.

"Sorry, Prime Minister," Sir Roger said, "the International Atomic Energy Agency."

Andrew sighed and nodded. "Yes, go on, Mr Kilby."

"Well, Prime Minister, the IAEA is responsible for ensuring the distribution and usage of nuclear material complies with the non-proliferation treaty and the safety standards laid down for all member states."

"Yes, I know this."

"So, the Agency knows exactly how much uranium is in circulation and where it comes from, where it went for processing and where it is put to use. This means, then, that if terrorists got hold of a nuke and set it off, there'd be slightly different radioactive traces depending on who made it, because there are different ways to make weapons-grade uranium. So, you can trace the bomb back to its source."

"That's very interesting, Mr Kilby, but I think we'd rather the bomb didn't go off in the first place."

"Yes, Prime Minister, and also, of course, if you've got a supply of uranium nobody knows about, then you're screwed, anyway. So, the IAEA have introduced a new arm to their operation, more *pro*-active. They have a registered inventory of all nuclear materials and can track their movement through their NMTS. Which means that..."

Andrew banged the table with both palms. "*NMTS?*"

Sir Roger answered. "Nuclear materials tracking system. Sorry, Prime Minister."

"Look," Andrew said. "Can we just stick to English instead of wading through the alphabet? Get to the point, please, Mr Kilby."

"Yes, sir. They should be able to tell us whether any nuclear material is missing from any source. The only country with nuclear capability that is not a member state of the Agency is North Korea and the likelihood of it being the source is virtually nil."

"So, this means what, Agent Kilby? Have I missed something, or have you still not made your point yet?"

"The IAEA should be able to tell us if any weapons-grade material is missing. Not with *absolute* certainty but as a percentage risk factor."

"Thank you. We seem to have got there at last." Andrew turned to the Special Forces Director. "Does that make sense, Alan?"

"Yes, Prime Minister. I don't doubt they have a bomb on board – it's the only way they can threaten the exiles on Alpha – but acquiring nuclear fuel, then making and transporting an a-bomb would be almost impossible."

"*Almost.*" Andrew said. "Not sure how *possible* it is to hijack the world's largest heavy-lift vessel carrying the second biggest production platform on the planet, but they just did it. Roger, have we been in touch with the IAEA yet?"

"Not yet. It only takes a phone call."

"Then why not?"

"Because we haven't released anything about the hijack yet and as soon as we go outside our inner circle, we lose control of communications. I am assuming, Prime Minister, that there will shortly be some sort of statement to the media, and I also assume, like Agent Kilby, you will not be telling people there is a nuclear bomb floating in UK waters. But if we ask the Agency to check this out for us, it will be a significant task for them, and we will have to tell them why we are making the request."

Andrew looked down at the table in front of him and was silent for a long time. The others in the room shuffled in their seats. When he looked up, he spoke with calm assurance.

"Roger, get Mr Kilby to speak to the agency right away. Tell them on no account should this go any further than those checking the data. It's a risk, as you say, but if there are steps we could take before the public gets to hear about this, they'll want an assurance that we have already taken them. We can manage the fallout later." He paused. "That was another unintentional pun, by the way. Ruby, Roger, I'd like you to oversee the hostage rescue teams on St Kilda. Communication, co-ordination, not hands-on, of course. They'll know what they need to do, just be there to help with any decisions outside the scope of the actual mission. Alan, I'm not cutting you out of this, but I want a small team on it. We don't want more chiefs than Indians, if that isn't too politically incorrect these days."

Alan smiled and nodded.

"And, as we are *not* able to move thirty thousand people in just a few hours, then Roger and Mr Kilby are right, there's no benefit in creating panic and a public demand to evacuate the area by announcing the nuke right now. We wait until we know the extent of the problem. A question to you, Mr Kilby, as the fountain of knowledge for all things nuclear. I'm aware that very few countries possess nuclear capability when it comes to weapons, but I seem to have the number seventeen in my mind as the total using nuclear fuel for peaceful purposes; and of the seventeen, I do know that Finland generates around a third of its electricity this way. Is it possible that Norway's close neighbour could be a source? It would be relatively easy for such a determined group to sneak it over the border in the north."

"That's why I specified 'weapons-grade', Prime Minister. Because the domestic use of nuclear energy in all seventeen countries is so well-regulated and regimented that removing even a small amount would be virtually impossible. It's in the secretive world of weaponry where inventory and location need monitoring."

"Okay, understood. Let's make that call right away."

"Speak later, Joe," Sir Roger said, as he reached across and switched off the connection. "There's one more piece of circumstantial evidence which might give us some food for thought, Prime Minister," he continued. "Abu el Taqha has been around for more than two decades, which means, of course, he doesn't do suicide missions."

"And…?"

"My point is, *if* we assume el Taqha wants to carry on living and has no intention of blowing himself up, we just need to keep him on the ship. Resist any approach by air or sea transport, even if he threatens to detonate if we intercept. Something to think about, that's all."

"Okay," Andrew said. "Let's think about it, then, but we must move on now. I need to brief Defence. Jackie and Ruby, you come with me. Roger, I want you to take the next call from *Mastodon*, which, from what they said last time will be at midnight. They've asked for a senior minister, but I want to leave that as a possible bargaining concession in any negotiation. I understand you'll have Lydia van Roden from Kade's team in attendance and acting as adviser throughout, which means, ideally, we'll need you with her on Hirta before then.

"Jonno, Lawrence – not much you can do right now, except let's make sure we know exactly how many of our people are on Hirta and who they are – Lawrence, you do that. Grace, could you draft something for the media and get it in front of me within the next half hour, and I want you to co-ordinate all internal communications within this group. Anyone has any new information, let Grace know and she will get it to all of us. Let's keep the nuclear dimension within this group as much as we can. If we have to include subordinates – which I accept we may – let's make it as few as possible and make it clear to them it must go no further.

"This goes against every instinct. Something like this, you feel we should be throwing military personnel at it – troops on to St Kilda, navy swarming all over the area in a show of strength. But if they have got a nuke, why would you put them all at risk when there's nothing practical they can achieve anyway?"

He sighed and got to his feet.

"Thank you."

They all stood as he walked from the room, Jackie and Ruby following him out.

*

"The time is 6.30 p.m. and we return to our main story tonight: British and Norwegian naval and coast guard vessels are responding to an incident in the Atlantic involving the hijacking of the heavy-lift vessel, *Mastodon*, en route to the offshore exile establishment known as Hotel St Kilda, where it is due to deliver the second platform, designated Beta. It is thought the hijacking took place around midnight during a communications blackout. The hijackers, believed to be an Arab-based group, identifying themselves as 'Brothers of Islam', initially contacted the headquarters of Scandoil Search and Production in Stavanger, Norway, just before 2.30 p.m. British Summer Time today, and again at around 3.30 p.m. The group gave no indication as to what their plans were for the ship and its load, nor did they make any demands, except that they wish to negotiate with British authorities and have requested that a senior minister is involved in the dialogue. And, whereas we understand that further dialogue is either scheduled or already ongoing, we have no information at this time as to who such a senior person or persons would be, if indeed the Home Office accedes to this request. What we do know is that the Prime Minister held a COBRA meeting this afternoon at 4.00 p.m. to discuss the emergency.

"The *Mastodon* was scheduled to reach its destination within the next hour, at which time it was due to re-float the new platform, allowing tugs to guide it and hold it in place whilst it is secured to the existing structure, In the meantime, the *Mastodon*'s progress is being monitored by the Norwegian Coast Guard vessel *Sonja*. Two British naval offshore patrol boats, HMS *Spey* and HMS *Kintyre* are also heading out to the island group of St Kilda to intercept it."

David had been glued to his computer screen in his small study/ bedroom for the last half hour, watching and listening to news of the events unfolding in the North Atlantic. His mind was so focussed on the drama that it took him a few seconds to realise that the sound interrupting his thoughts was that of his phone signalling an incoming call. He muted his PC.

"Hello, this is Gerrard,"

"Ah, Detective Chief Inspector Gerrard, this is…" It was a young-sounding male voice.

"*Ex*-Detective Chief Inspector Gerrard."

"Yes, sir, as you say. This is DC Jay Lauder from Guildford New Station. I'm phoning on behalf of DI Waters. He'd like to meet with you at the guest house where you met before. As soon as possible, he said. Would you be free…"

"Hold on a second… By the way, what does the 'J' stand for?"

"Nothing, sir."

"Nothing?"

"That's my name, sir. Jay. J-a-y."

"Okay, Jay, why isn't DI Waters phoning me himself to set up this meeting. I know he's a busy man but it's not like him to delegate a phone call, or is it? I'm sure you know him better than I do."

"It's a bit delicate, sir." Jay's voice descended, rather pointlessly, to a whisper. "He believes his phone has been bugged. I understand that's the reason he wants to see you 'off-line' as it were. He said you'd probably guess what it's about – what you discussed there last time. Oh, and he asked me to say not to call him until after you've met, for obvious reasons."

"Okay, Jay, when does he want to meet?"

"He'd prefer early tomorrow, if possible. He said to apologise for the short notice, but suggested 9.30, if you can make it for then from Meadow Village. That would give him time for the early briefing and then he and Nat – DC Crusoe – could meet you right after that."

David was silent for a while, thinking of all the times he had accused his former sergeant of inventing conspiracies.

"Are you still there, sir?"

"Yes, still here. That will be fine. Same room as before? Room 15?"

"Room 17, sir. That was the room last time."

"Of course."

"So that's a wrap, is it, sir? And DI Waters said if they're delayed, please wait for them in the room. Okay?"

"Yes, Jay, that's a… *wrap*. Bye."

"Bye, sir."

David placed his phone on the table in front of him and sat, deep in thought for a long time. He checked the time – 6.40 p.m. He picked up the phone again, went to his recent call listing and touched the last number. He was answered immediately by a familiar voice.

"New Station CID, DC Lauder speaking."

"Hi, Jay. It's David Gerrard again. Sorry to bother you but is DC Crusoe there?"

"No, it's just me, sir, holding the fort, so to speak. Everyone's out on this missing mum and toddler case. You've probably seen it on the news, mum picked up her youngest daughter from nursery in Shalford at midday and no-one's seen her since. Should have picked up her other daughter from school at three but didn't show. Husband's just been stopped boarding a plane at Heathrow. So, the whole team's out looking and talking to friends and neighbours, and I can't see them coming back here tonight, to be honest. I'll be away myself soon."

"Okay, Jay, no problem. I'll see her tomorrow morning anyway, won't I? Hope you find the mum and toddler. What happened to the other daughter, by the way?"

"Staying with grandparents. Used to spending a lot of time with them, apparently, so hopefully she should be okay for now."

"That's good. Fingers crossed, eh? Bye."

"Bye, sir."

David put the phone down again, turning back to his PC and accessing Local News for Shalford. The first item headline read:

Woman and child missing, husband arrested at Heathrow

He logged off and checked the time again, deciding to wait an hour before making the next call. Then he went through to the living room and switched on the TV, selecting the BBC news channel.

CHAPTER TWENTY-TWO

7.10 p.m. BST

By the time the *Mastodon* was close to its destination, just over two hours behind its original ETA of 5.00 p.m. BST, the air around it was host to a small flock of aircraft. Military jets – Typhoons from the RAF Quick Reaction Alert station in Lossiemouth – conducted regular fly-bys, screaming past close to the ship at a few metres above the waves. The Eurocopter X3 – Kade and his team's transport from Stornoway – was being used to observe their progress, sending a continuous stream of images back to St Kilda, from where they were being transmitted to the PST's HQ in Nydalen, Oslo, and Thames House in London. Light aircraft, including helicopters, chartered by the press and all the main television channels, circled at a discreet distance to capture their customers' share of the excitement.

For the past two hours, the vessel had been reducing speed, finally slowing to a halt one kilometre from the platform, just outside the ring of fifty-five massive wind turbines that formed a circle round it, spaced around the circumference at ninety-metre intervals – with a single 180-metre gap to allow access for additional platforms. Each turbine reached 110 metres into the air to the top of its tower and over 150 metres to the tip of a vertical blade.

During that time, the pictures relayed to the watchers had shown a flurry of activity on the deck, as people loosened the heavy chains and removed the dense matrix of steel cables which secured the platform in place. The *Mastodon* and Hotel St Kilda were now close enough for the captured images to show both in the same frame. As the excitement in households across the UK mounted with the unfolding drama on their TV screens, none of those circling close to the action to bring the scene into the millions of living rooms had any idea that they were just possibly rubbing shoulders with oblivion.

⋆

In one of those living rooms in one of those households, David Gerrard leaned in closer to the TV. It occurred to him that he was watching the same few square kilometres of the Atlantic Ocean that he and Harry had been discussing just a few hours ago. That incident – the strange case of the pole-dancing marine scientist – had been fascinating enough, but, right now, something extraordinary was happening. And for the second time in the space of an hour, the sound of his phone took several moments to penetrate his concentration.

⋆

In the observation tower on Hirta, Kade raised his binoculars and inhaled loudly.

"Here we go. At least they were good enough to wait for you, Sir Roger."

The man at his side had landed only a few minutes ago after his two-hour flight in the V22 Osprey from the heliport in Battersea. He had barely recovered his breath after a sprint up the tower's spiral staircase.

Like the big man in the armchair 1,000 kilometres away, Kade had also been thinking back to that same day, eight months ago, when he and his team, in their two Archer patrol boats with the initials of the British Oceanographic Society displayed on their hulls, had been under observation from this very tower. He tried to conjure up a picture in his mind of how those two small boats would look against the floating monster close to the horizon, a monster which was now visibly sinking into the sea, as if its massive load was forcing it under.

In the middle distance, halfway between the island group and the *Mastodon*, the four tugs which had been patrolling back and forth for the last hour or so, turned simultaneously in a show of synchronised unity as their orders came through, and headed south-west towards the sinking ship. Just ahead of him, from the standing area to his right, Kade heard a mechanical roar as the engines of the four coast guard helicopters started up and the main rotors and tail props wound up to their lift-off velocity. Two minutes later he watched them rise in unison from The Cambir, a grassy promontory which reached out diagonally from Hirta's north-western extremity towards the island of Soay. The four machines set off in nose-to-tail formation in the direction of the tugs.

"Colonel, we need to talk." Sir Roger placed a hand on Kade's shoulder. "Right now, in private."

⋆

"So, what have you been doing while I've been spreading my meagre income around the West End?" Marie asked, having taken David through her afternoon's shopping experience in close to real time as he drove her home from Shenfield station.

"Oh, just drumming my fingers and counting the minutes until your return," he said.

"Which is why it took you so long to answer my call, I suppose. Might be dangerous to *suddenly* stop drumming when you've been doing it for three hours."

"Very true. Did you get my text, by the way?"

Marie frowned. "No, I didn't." She took out her phone and switched it on.

"Well, there's no point in reading it now," David said. "It's too late."

"Why, what did it say?"

"It was just a list of things I'd like if you decided to get me a present while you were out. But it's okay… I suppose."

"Oh, *poor* David," Marie laughed. "What a shame. I'm *so* sorry."

"It doesn't matter." He reached across and took her hand. "I've got everything I'm ever going to need right here."

She placed her other hand on his and squeezed hard.

"Are you coming in for a bit?" Marie asked, as they pulled up in front of her house.

"A *bit*? Can you be more specific?"

"A *while*, I meant." They looked at each other with exaggerated frowns, then burst out laughing. "Come to think of it, I do have a present for you, but it's not something I bought today."

"And how do you know it's something I want without checking the list?"

"Because it's something you *always* want."

"Then I think I can guess what it is."

"Oh, that's right, spoil my surprise."

They laughed again, then leaned together and kissed for a long time.

"Well, are you, or aren't you?" Marie asked.

"I shouldn't really. I've got an early start tomorrow to get to a meeting in Guildford."

"A meeting? Guildford? Not with Danny Cleaver?"

"*Weaver*. No, with a police colleague. Well, a colleague of Jo's actually. Nothing remotely exciting. And I've also got a call to make which might take a while."

"Tell you what, make the call now from the car. I'll go in and make us some coffee, then you come in and unwrap your present."

"You know, I think that plan might just work."

"See you in a few minutes."

Marie got out of the car and went inside.

★

It was exactly 10.00 p.m. when David finally got home. He went straight through to the living room to catch up with the latest on the hijacking. The ten o'clock news was just beginning and the first item featured edited sequences from the BBC eye-in-the-sky helicopter, strung together in a summary report of the action from the moment when the *Mastodon* began ballasting down to release its load. The reporter in the aircraft captured the excitement with a commentary which was pitched at the same level as someone covering a horse race or a boxing match, his voice rising and falling, quickening and slowing to reflect the action.

"What we're seeing now is the deck of the vessel almost completely under water. The platform was itself ballasted, of course, down to a depth of eight metres, so it will stay on the deck until the ship drops below that level, but you can see it is already swaying slightly with the effect of the current. Soon, the forward superstructure and the two stern towers will be the only parts of the *Mastodon* visible above the surface.

"Look! Over to the right of your picture, the tugs are moving closer. We don't know at this point how they will secure the platform when it comes free of the ship and starts to drift due west with the Atlantic current towards Benbecula or South Uist, seventy kilometres away. Thankfully the wind is light, and we are told that, with luck, the platform should not capsize and will be moving quite slowly, but if it is not secured in time by the tugs it could do considerable environmental damage when it reaches land."

The report moved forward to the point at which the platform drifted clear of the submerged vessel. At which stage the commentary reached fever pitch.

"What is happening, as you can see, are the coast guard helicopters hovering above the tugs. We believe they will be taking on a towing cable from each tug and effectively lassoing… yes, we can make out the first chopper lowering a line with a hook down to the leading tug and now that is being repeated with all four tugs. We can see heavy steel cables being looped over the hooks and… now what?"

The report skipped some more minutes and focussed on one helicopter and tug working together to wrap the cable around one of the columns.

"Well, we're now witnessing first-hand how they plan to harness the platform. The helicopters each flying round one of the columns and returning the cable to the tug, lowering it back onto it where it will be secured with the other end. So simple and obvious, but we'll see if it works in the next few minutes. It appears the cables are lagged with something. We have on board with us Desmond Wakeham, a salvage expert and recovery consultant. Des, what is the lagging for, some kind of protection?"

"No, what you see is a series of inflatable sleeves along the length of each cable which will prevent it from sinking below the water. Remember, the columns don't stop at the surface but continue down for five or six metres before they connect to the base, the pontoon. Without the floatation aides the cables would each sink to that depth, so the tugs would be pulling at an angle. This way, the cables will be horizontal – as near as makes no difference – and, just as importantly, all four will have the same tension."

"Right, I see. And how, in your opinion, Des, is the operation going up to now?"

"It's just about perfect. The big test is when they rein it in, if it remains stable and upright, and that will depend on the skill of the crews. But from what we've seen so far, I'm confident they won't have a problem."

"Thanks, Des, and now comes the tensioning of the cables as the tugs get into formation."

The report moved on again to show the platform upright and stable, moving gracefully through calm waters with the tugs neatly in formation around it. Two of the coast guard helicopters had landed on the former production deck, their rotors slowly turning, and a number of figures could be seen checking the area.

"We understand that the plan is to tow the platform through the Sound of Harris between the islands of Harris and North Uist and anchor it temporarily in The Minch, close to the Shiant Islands...

"But, look at the *Mastodon.* While our attention has been focussed on the platform, this huge monster of a ship is now being de-ballasted to raise it to the surface again. And it's an awesome sight, isn't it? Although we've been watching the ship for some time now, to see its deck becoming visible under water and rising to the surface. We are astonished – all over again – at just how vast this heavy-lift ship is."

David watched with the same awe as the reporter at the sheer scale of the action on his screen. He also reflected on the irony of the situation, of the significant locations in the report. The area around Hotel St Kilda, where a mysterious survey – *non*-survey – took place on that day last November; the same day, quite possibly, when Tom Brown met his fate. And, the giant structure whose destiny Tom, more than any other single individual on Earth, was responsible for, was about to be taken to the probable site of Tom's demise. Not for the first time recently, he would like to have heard

Jo's take on the situation; how she would have woven the disparate factual threads into a meaningful tapestry. Meaningful to her, that is.

Perhaps what surprised him above all else, in spite of the remote feeling of dread the current situation in the Atlantic was giving him, was how totally contented he felt. His earlier present – and its unwrapping – had been, as Marie had said, *exactly* what he wanted. He went over the evening again in his mind and felt the slightest prick of tears as he smiled to himself.

This might just be the happiest he had ever been in his whole life.

CHAPTER TWENTY-THREE

Thursday, 6 July

12.07 a.m. BST
The call came through seven minutes later than promised, and was answered by Sir Roger Ashpole in what was now established as the incident command centre in the tower of the Alpha Administration Centre on Hirta. This new building, close to the village, was single storey except for the square tower, which reached one floor higher and had windows to all sides, providing a 360 degree, wrap-around view. Two further floors were below ground and comprised the staff's accommodation and working facilities: offices and meeting rooms. Scattered around the Centre were the crumbling remnants of the concrete and steel buildings from the mid-1950s, when a military base was established as a missile tracking station during the Cold War.

With Sir Roger were Kade and Lydia, and the call was also picked up at three other locations in two different countries.

In London, at Thames House, Jackie Hewlett, Ruby Weller, Lawrence Harding and Grace Goody sat with Joe Kilby in its central communications room, around a table covered with speakers, TV monitors, microphones and digital recorders.

In Stavanger, Alicia Stenson, Josef Solheim, Elsa Tongan and Erik Sundstrom still occupied the Security Director's office at the company's monitoring centre, their role having been reduced to listeners, but with the Scandoil contingent, in particular, still focussed on the safety of their employees and contract workers.

In Oslo, Milena Bakke, Head of PST, and her two most senior direct reports sat in comfortable wing chairs at a low coffee table, listening to the latest exchange with the terrorists through a speaker in front of them; passive observers for the moment.

"Who am I speaking to?"

"My name is Roger Ashpole, and I have been assigned..."

"Roger Ashpole? I am not familiar with the name. I can only assume you have been promoted to your senior ministerial position very recently. Of which ministry are you a part?"

"I have been assigned to speak with you by the Prime Minister himself as someone who can help progress any..."

"You have not answered my question. Of which department of the British government are you a senior minister? Defence? Home Office? Foreign Affairs? Am I getting close? And if you are none of these, what is your position?"

"I am Head of MI5, and the Prime Minister believes..."

"It was nearly nine hours ago that I indicated that I wished to speak to a senior minister of your government. *Nine hours*. It seems that you are not taking this very seriously, so the time for action has arrived rather sooner than I expected. *However*, I will extend this deadline in the interest of preserving life. We will call again at 5.00 a.m. and hope that progress has been made on your side. In the meantime, we will take our next step in convincing you of our intent."

The connection was cut, and, in all locations, people sighed and leaned back in their seats.

⋆

The two Sikorskys hovered fifty metres above the Atlantic between Platform Alpha and the *Mastodon* as the gap between the two giant structures narrowed. The night sky was moonless and, a few minutes after 2.00 a.m., still dark as the searchlight beams from the helicopters illuminated the upper foredeck with a piercing intensity. They picked out figures on the deck, impossibly small in comparison to the immense size of their host. A few aimed their weapons, threatening, it seemed, to shoot out the lights. The choppers edged closer, as if daring them to do so. Some of the figures waved and, through binoculars, the co-pilots could make out smiles and laughter on the faces of the hijackers.

Two kilometres astern of the ship, at an altitude of 600 metres, the huge glider, with its black underbelly, drifted past, disgorging from the sliding door on the right-hand side of the aircraft five figures dressed head to toe in midnight-blue assault gear. They free-fell towards the dark waters for ten seconds before the chutes opened and they adjusted their descent to land, as lightly and silently as butterflies, on the starboard tower at the stern of the ship.

A few minutes later, the helicopters rose and turned back towards St Kilda as the *Mastodon*'s bow edged under Platform Alpha.

★

Jackie Hewlett was awoken from a deep sleep by the sound of her phone and took a few moments to identify her surroundings. She had stayed over in Marsham Street in the small apartment which formed part of her suite of rooms within the Home Office building. Perhaps apartment was too grand a description for an ensuite bedroom off a small dining kitchen/sitting room, but it more than sufficed in both comfort and convenience for the few nights each year when work demanded a sleepover.

The wake-up call to her iPhone, a few inches from her head on the bedside table, was from Ruby Weller.

"Hi, Ruby, what...?"

"Sorry to disturb you, Jackie, but our worst fears about our US brothers-in-arms have been realised. CNN just reported el Taqha being on the *Mastodon*. Not just a possibility, but a cast-iron ID. Our man in Washington has just sent through a recording of the news item. You might want to get over here and check it out, like, right now, because we all know what's going to hit the fan within minutes."

"Oh, *shit*."

"Yes, exactly."

"Why the fuck do they have to do this? When Elsa asked *specifically* that they don't release the information. We shouldn't even *need* to ask them; you'd think they would work it out for themselves. They're like a small child with a secret. When was this, Ruby?"

"News item was about twenty minutes ago, 2.50 a.m. our time – 9.50 p.m. yesterday in New York, which I guess means it might take a few hours to get to full hysteria. They interrupted a programme to share it, and presented it as though they're demanding some sort of action. You'll know what I mean when you see it."

"Please God, no mention of the nuclear device?"

"No, nothing, so let's hope that knowledge is still under control. But you know what CNN are like. They might be holding that back for a later report. Makes them look good, like they're finding stuff out for themselves."

"Well, let's hope they simply don't know about it. According to Elsa, the CIA were out of the loop before that information came through to us. Where are you now?"

"We're in the same room as before."

"We?"

"Grace is here, Lawrence as well, and people are arriving as the news gets about. We'll start the recording again when you get here. We're tuned in live on another monitor to see what else comes out of CNN. And we've got another on Fox. Nothing from them yet."

"And Ashpole? Has anybody…?"

"I contacted him before I phoned you, Home Secretary, I hope you don't mind."

"Of course not. Right thing to do. Important he knows before they send the fucking B-2s over."

Ruby chuckled. "That's your second 'fuck' in the last five sentences. Must be serious, And Sir Roger already knew. They'd picked it up live at the time of the broadcast."

"Okay. On my way. Is there any coffee there?"

"Gallons of it. Ready and waiting."

*

Silas Horne rolled over and squinted at the clock display on the bedside table. It told him it was 04.35.

"Jeez. What the hell?"

He groped under the pillow for the vibrating iPhone, which disconnected before he could answer. He placed it next to the clock as he reached for his glasses. He put them on and picked up the phone to check the number, almost dropping it as it started vibrating again. The caller's name was known to him, which meant the call was unexpected.

"Elsa, what's going…?"

"We need to talk, right now. Won't wait."

"Okay. Just hold on while I go to the bathroom and…"

"I'll see you in the lobby in five minutes."

"You're *here*, in the *hotel*? Can't we talk over the phone?"

"No. Five minutes. I'll get coffee."

When he arrived in the lobby in a hurriedly assembled outfit of baggy jeans, Chicago Cubs sweatshirt and sandals, Elsa had her back to him, looking out of the picture window across the hotel gardens to the sea, shimmering in the soft, early-morning light. He coughed quietly, so as not to startle her as he approached, but she did not turn to face him until he spoke.

"Morning, Elsa." He tried to make his voice light and friendly. "If you've come to say sorry and that I'm back on the case, then it *could* have waited until…"

She turned towards him, her face like stone and her expression as far from apologetic as was possible.

"Let's sit," she said, the words just escaping through her clenched teeth. She waved to the low table in front of the window, on which there were two polystyrene cups of coffee and an open laptop. She took one of the armchairs next to it.

"Am I to understand, then, that this is *not* an attempt on your part to re-establish ourselves as good buddies?"

Elsa did not speak but tapped a few keys on the laptop before turning it so Silas could see the screen.

"Enjoy," she said, and tapped another key with a dramatic flourish.

The sleepy expression fell away from Silas's eyes as they widened to take in the text sliding across the bottom of the screen… *Abu el Taqha, terrorist leader… responsible for 9/11 and Willis bombing… found on Dutch heavy-lift vessel…* below the words in large letters – *CNN – SPECIAL REPORT!* The presenter began speaking.

"We have received information from a government source relating to the hijacking of a heavy-lift vessel from Holland, currently en route to the British offshore prison in the Atlantic known as Hotel St Kilda, to deliver a decommissioned oil production platform to add to the facility. Pictures taken from a Norwegian Coast Guard vessel confirm conclusively that one of the hijackers, presumed to be the leader, is Abu el Taqha, the mastermind behind the recent bombing of the Willis Tower in Chicago."

Silas raised his hands in a gesture of surrender. Elsa reached forward to pause the playback.

"Listen, Elsa, I laid it on real hard about..."

"You should listen to it all, Silas, at your leisure. It's got a lot of detail, including some that even *I* wasn't aware of and I was right there in the fucking room. But this is the bit you'll really enjoy."

She dragged her finger across the screen to advance the report.

"... failure of the security services to prevent the attack. So, with the strong feeling that exists of being let down by the very people who are supposed to be protecting us, it will be interesting to see how the US responds to this information. Will they exercise a watching brief while our allies across the Atlantic are allowed to address their own priorities? Or, is this the time for real action, a time for us to take the initiative and administer our own terms of justice for the acts of barbarism that this man has perpetrated on American soil? The country tonight and in the days to come will be watching carefully to see just how imperative the safety of our people is to those in power, and how seriously they view the importance of national security.

"Stay with us on this channel and we will bring you all developments as they happen – out there in the Atlantic and here, in the corridors of power. This is Margo Stanton on CNN."

Elsa had got to her feet and was standing again at the window, her back to Silas. He walked across to stand beside her.

"What can I say, Elsa? Except you were right. Someone decided they'd look good breaking the news the whole country was waiting to hear. I'm not making excuses, but you can't know what the intensity of feeling is like over there. The outrage, the accusations, the... vitriol."

"A few hours, Silas, a couple of days absolute max, that's all I asked. To wait before you passed it on." She turned to face him. "How come I knew what was going to happen and you're claiming you didn't? You knew *exactly* how it would go. I might as well have let you phone Fox News like you said at the time. I didn't want any fucking coffee, anyway."

"Hey, Elsa. It's five in the morning. Not the most positive time of day. We don't know how this is going to pan out yet. It might not make any difference. It might even scare the bastard."

"Oh, I'm sure it's going to scare the bastard. It's just what a *scared* mass-murdering bastard is likely to do compared to a relaxed one that bothers me. So, the decision that this is all off-limits now for you is more important. We can't risk any more sensitive information…"

"Hey, Elsa, you don't understand…"

"I do, Silas. I *really* do. I understand *and* I sympathise, believe it or not. You've got a job to do. The next thing you know, they'll be *ordering* you to take over here, with that weight of public expectation pushing you on. Well, we'll deal with that scenario if and when it happens. But right now, in the absence of any directives from your chain of command, you're still off the case. In fact, you're *further* off the case, if that's possible. I don't expect you to be happy about it, but are you clear?"

"Come on, Elsa." Silas was getting angry now. "You can't do this."

"Oh, yes I can. And you could do yourself a favour and accept it from me, so someone higher up in the Service doesn't have to get involved. Then it might just remain a *minor* international incident."

She walked back to the table, closed and picked up her laptop, then left the lobby. Silas remained at the window, looking at the same view, without actually seeing it.

★

The same clusters of people in the same rooms in the same countries leaned forward in their seats again in anticipation of the 5.00 a.m. call. Ruby Weller, in Thames House, waited to receive the call as the designated contact with the hijackers. She adjusted the earpiece in her left ear as the voice of Doctor Lydia van Roden asked for confirmation that the connection was good. Lydia waited in readiness as the prompt for Ruby's anticipated dialogue. Her voice came through the earpiece.

"Keep watching the screen, Ruby. It will be easier than listening and speaking simultaneously. And please, use your own words; these will just be bullet-point prompts and only when I feel they may assist you. I'll only use the voice connection if necessary."

Ruby checked the monitor in front of her and the same words, from Lydia, appeared on the screen.

"Okay, Lydia. Thanks." In the corner of the screen the four digits showed 04.59.

The hour past, the quarter hour, then the half hour. Ruby said she knew now how Scrooge must have felt waiting for the appearance of the first of the Christmas spirits, prompting a trickle of nervous laughter in several locations.

There was nothing; not a sound from the *Mastodon*.

As the time approached 6.00 a.m., Sir Roger's voice came over, angry and clipped. "No surprise! Thanks to our so-called *friends* in the CIA, this is a game-changer. They will have picked up the news item on the *Mastodon* and know now that the US will be involved. We should seriously consider taking legal action against Horne, and demand an apology from the CIA. Some chance."

"I think we need to try and understand his position, though, before we get on his back," Elsa said. "Agents are required to provide information to Langley as part of their ongoing responsibilities. It's up to their superiors to handle that sensitively. Remember 'don't shoot the messenger'. That's what Silas is, just doing a messenger's job."

"Come on, Elsa, you were the one who banished him from these link-ups because you couldn't trust him to play ball. Have you changed your mind all of a sudden?"

"Certainly not, Sir Roger, and if you'd been in the Amundsen Hotel lobby at five o'clock this morning, you'd have witnessed me giving Agent Horne a hard time. But the banishment is for his own good as much as ours. What he *doesn't* know, he can't feed back; what he *does* know, he has to. This way we can still be friends."

"Friends!" Sir Roger sounded incredulous. "You have a strange idea of what…"

"This isn't helping." Jackie Hewlett's voice was loud and carried authority. "There *will be* an inquest afterwards, because this leak of information *is* a screw-up, but right now the situation for fifty-three crew members on the *Mastodon* and nearly eight hundred exiles on Alpha is exactly the same. Nothing has changed for them. They are all sitting on a nuclear bomb, a bomb which will detonate if the wrong person sneezes. We must work with that assumption until we know differently. Which means…"

The fifteen people spread thinly around north-west Europe all started at the sound of the now-familiar voice.

"Good morning. Please tell me who I will be speaking to."

"This is Ruby Weller. I am a senior minister in the Home Office. I will be your designated contact going forward. How can I help you?"

"Thank you, may I call you Ruby?"

"You may. What is your name?"

There was the sound of a deep chuckle. "I think you know my name, Ruby. I think the whole world does by now. Which is unfortunate, for everybody."

Lydia prompted. Ruby said, "So how do I address you?"

"For simplicity and expedience – 'Abu' will be fine."

"So, Abu, how can we move forward to resolve this?"

"Well the rules have changed, Ruby, as you may have expected. I have to assume now that everything I say – indeed, everything that *you* say, as well – will be broadcast by CNN shortly afterwards. And whereas I accept that, when I am speaking with you now, other people are listening to our conversation, I did hope that those observers would be a small, discreet number, who would understand the delicacy of the situation. Not the whole of the lying western media, manipulating and twisting words to further their own self-justification."

"All CNN have done is report you being aboard the *Mastodon*," she said, paraphrasing Lydia's words on her screen. "Your face is well known, and I'm sure you would have expected that when images we received confirmed it was you. There has been no twisting of words – in fact, none of the exchanges with you has been reported at all. So, I'm not sure how this changes things."

"I think you do, Ruby. The demand for information by the American media will be too great for their agencies to resist. I'm sure you realise that, and I'm also sure it will be causing some friction between you and your US counterparts. So, here is how the rules have changed. You and I will not be negotiating over what is now effectively an open line to the world. We shall be negotiating face to face on board the *Mastodon*. And this time I will be even more specific as to who I intend to talk with. I will give you a name, and you can rest easy, Ruby, that it will not be yours. I will speak to you again at 9.00 a.m. In the meantime, you must find a way for me to get this name to you without the rest of the world hearing who it is. This person's identity must remain a secret until we have a negotiating party in place on this vessel. Do you understand, Ruby?"

"I understand what you are *saying* but, of course, I cannot guarantee we will comply without knowing more of the conditions attached to that arrangement." Lydia's words were arriving fast in front of her. "One condition we wish *you* to consider during the next two hours. *If* we were to land a negotiating party on the *Mastodon*, we would insist on the release of hostages in exchange. That is for you to agree when we next speak. Do *you* understand, Abu?"

"I do, but, like you, I can guarantee nothing."

The connection was broken.

The spontaneous chorus of voices across the locations was interrupted by Jackie. "Thank you, everyone. We are going off-line here now. We have much to consider and discuss. I suggest we all connect again in one hour's time, well ahead of the call. Unless someone has anything to add right now. Oslo?"

"No, Home Secretary. That suits us."

"Stavanger?"

"Okay here."

"Good. Thank you all, again. St Kilda, we'll get right back to you in a few minutes."

*

Jackie had ensured that, when Abu el Taqha next made contact, it would be with a much-diminished audience. Ahead of the next scheduled call, through Elsa Tongan, she had cleared the way for a direct link from *Mastodon* to Thames House rather than a relayed connection from Stavanger. Milena Bakke in Oslo accepted the need for secrecy at this stage, having been assured of frequent and regular timed updates. The only remaining link-up, then, was with the official mission command centre on St Kilda.

Elsa had also provided the vehicle for the terrorists to communicate the name of their preferred contact for negotiation. A coded message was sent from Stavanger to the *Mastodon* with an iPhone number and a request to text the name to Jackie. At 6.45 a.m., as she waited in a side office off the main communication room in Thames House, the text came through. She gasped, her eyes wide with surprise and shock; she opened the office door and called across to the one whose name was displayed on her iPhone's screen. The person walked across into the office and sat down at Jackie's request.

The Home Secretary gave a loud sigh. "You and I need to speak to Andrew as soon as possible."

CHAPTER TWENTY-FOUR

David Gerrard had set his alarm for six o'clock, well ahead of the time he would have to leave for his meeting in Guildford. He was eager to get the latest on the drama unfolding around Hotel St Kilda. The news of Abu el Taqha's presence on the heavy-lift vessel, picked up from CNN and delivered as the opening item from that network, did not carry the same air of revelation as it had in the US. The American news reporter's excitement reflected a far greater significance in a country where the terrorist leader's deadly influence had been only recently evident in the Willis bombing.

What had seemed more unsettling was the second report, shown just before he set off for Guildford, also picked up from the same US network but this time presented as a UK bulletin.

"We are just receiving reports that the American aircraft carrier, USS *Ronald Reagan*, is on its way from its current station off Iceland on course for St Kilda. The vessel is a nuclear-powered Nimitz-class supercarrier with ninety fixed-wing aircraft and helicopters on board. At its cruising speed of around thirty knots, it will cover the seven hundred or so kilometres in just under fourteen hours if, indeed, the island group is its destination. At this time, we have no information regarding the nature of its mission, but it seems certain it is linked to the hijacking of the *Mastodon*.

"Neither do we have news of any further progress with the hijackers. There have been no demands at this stage from the terrorist group and we understand discussions so far have centred around who the hijackers wish to negotiate with, and how and where."

David checked the time: 7.28 a.m. He turned off the television, set the house alarm and got into his car. He switched on the engine, then turned it off. He went back into the house, picked up one last item of clothing, reset the alarm and got back in the car. After turning on the radio and pressing the key to switch from Classic FM to BBC 5 Live, he took a deep breath and pulled out of the double gates of Neville Farm Fold en route to do battle with the M25.

★

David reached his destination with time to spare, affording him the opportunity to park up and listen to the exact same item of news about the carrier for – he estimated – the sixth time before vacating the car. At just after nine o'clock, he renewed his acquaintance with the receptionist at Westmore Guest House.

"Remember me? I'm the Gerrard with two r's, here to see DI Waters. I'm a bit early, but..."

"Oh, good morning, Mr Gerrard. Nice to see you again."

David's eyebrows shot up in surprise, He was tempted to look behind him in case one of those other Mr Gerrards had followed him in.

"And good morning to you."

"They said to wait in the room – Room 17 – if you don't mind. First floor, stairs through there, no lift, I'm afraid."

"Still no lift?" He gave a little laugh. "Oh, well..." He set off for the stairs. The woman called after him.

"Oh, by the way, Mr Gerrard, did they ever find that young man they were looking for? They thought it was you, but I said it couldn't have been. This one was younger."

"Er, I'm not aware of... Who did they think was me? And who's 'they'?"

"A detective. Came here saying they needed to find the man who met DI Waters here on the twenty-second of June. That was you, of course, but when he showed me this photo, it was of someone else, a much younger man. So, I told him he was mistaken."

"Did he say why the police were looking for me?"

"Like I said, it *wasn't* you. It was someone else."

David walked back to the reception desk.

"Okay, but did he say why they were looking for the man in the photo?"

"He said he'd gone missing and they were worried something had happened to him."

"And what did he look like, the one asking the questions?"

"Real handsome he was, actually, but a bit smarmy. Said he was a colleague of DI Waters."

"Name?"

"He did say his name – and showed me a badge thing – but I can't remember. He was only here a few minutes, then shot off again."

David nodded then turned away again.

"Right, thank you. I'll wait upstairs."

*

Andrew had been pacing non-stop around his private inner office at Number 10 ever since his two visitors had stepped through the door.

"And you're confident that Weller will be able to delay this with no consequences?"

"I'm confident Doctor van Roden will be able to if necessary, *through* Ruby." Jackie checked her watch. "Ten past nine. If the call came through on time at nine o'clock and she *hadn't* managed it, we'd have heard by now. We are just saying we need a bit of time to consider their request. They're not going to abandon all the planning they must have put into this for a couple of hours."

"Okay. So, just to recap, who else has seen the name?"

"At this end," Jackie said, "only we three and Ruby. No-one at Scandoil, although that's where the direct link to the *Mastodon* was set up."

"And so, indirectly, where the name came from."

"No, that's not the case; they passed on my iPhone number to el Taqha so he could send it to me, *by-passing* Scandoil."

"Depends how you define 'indirectly'. Having got the number, they could have intercepted the text."

"They could, but I don't think so. Firstly, I don't know what they would gain by knowing who the terrorists want to talk to and, more to the point, I trust Elsa Tongan. She was keen to make up for the leak to CNN, given that it came from over there, though it wasn't in any way her fault. In fact, I understand she did everything she could to block the CIA agent reporting the sighting to his superiors."

Andrew sighed. "Let's hope you're right." He finally sat down at his desk. "Anyway, it isn't going to happen, so how…?"

"Don't I have a say in this?"

Andrew and Jackie turned to the third person in the room, who had just spoken for the first time since the meeting started.

"Well, no, you do *not* have a say, in fact. It is not your decision, so…"

"Prime Minister," Jackie said, "under the circumstances, I think the owner of the name is at least entitled to express an opinion."

Andrew glared at Jackie for a long time, then leaned back in his chair and sighed.

"So be it." He smiled thinly. "Go ahead, Ms Goody, regale us with your opinion."

*

The door to Room 17 was unlocked. David went in, leaving it half-open and taking the seat that Harry had occupied at their last meeting so he could see anyone approaching from the stairs. He checked the time – still eight minutes to go. He felt hot and sticky in the still, stale air of the room, and, he realised, anxious.

He heard footsteps in the corridor outside. He expected to see the person before they reached the room, but when he appeared suddenly in the doorway, it was from the other direction.

It was not the person David was expecting, and he wondered why the man was wearing soft-leather gloves on such a hot morning.

*

Harry checked his watch as he and Natalie emerged from the front of the main building of Guildford New Station and raced across the courtyard to their unmarked car.

"Shit, we need to get a move on. We should have left about ten minutes ago."

"We'll be okay," Natalie said, settling into the driver's seat and starting the engine. They were moving almost before her DI had closed the passenger door. She clipped on her seatbelt as they turned out through the main gates.

"Let's make it quick, Nat, we need to be close enough to be the first response."

"Understood, sir." Natalie sounded a little hurt. "Perhaps you should have had DC Grantham drive you."

Harry glanced across at her and snorted a laugh. "I think Alice shaves about twenty minutes off my life expectancy for every minute I spend in the car with her. You'll do fine. Is the doc up to speed?"

"Yes, sir. She'll try to keep herself free."

"She's got to do more than try, for God's sake."

"I'm sure she'll be ready, sir."

*

It was the first time Jamie Walcott had encountered David Gerrard in the flesh. He had seen photographs of him, of course – mainly head and shoulders – in his file, and he was aware of his imposing size. Even so, the huge stature of the man took him by surprise. As well as his towering height, his upper body was notably bulky, like that of a lapsed bodybuilder. There was nothing slow about his movements, however, and he was quickly on his feet, eyes challenging. Jamie pushed the door closed, backing up to it and feeling behind him to turn the key.

"Whoever you are, locking yourself in here with me might not be the smartest thing you've ever done," David said.

Jamie smiled and reached inside his jacket, taking out the handgun, A Glock 17 with silencer already in place.

"I'm not here to sumo-wrestle you, Mr Gerrard. I'm definitely too smart for that."

David grabbed the edges of the small table, lifting it high in front of his face and tilting it so the legs were aimed away from him. Whether he was just protecting himself or planning to use it as a weapon, Jamie didn't wait to find out. He fired six times into his upper body. David shot backwards, dropping the table and crashing over his chair. He lay twisted on the floor, his head pressed hard against the angle of the floor and the skirting board.

Jamie turned, unlocked the door and left the way he had arrived, walking quickly away from the direction of the stairs, but only for a few metres. Turning the knob on the door of Room 19, he slipped inside.

CHAPTER TWENTY-FIVE

9.25 a.m. BST

Andrew was pacing again.

"At least we agree on one thing," he said. "The reason he wants to negotiate with you *on the ship* is because of your affair with Romeo Weston."

Grace struggled to stay calm. "I repeat, it is *not* an affair, it is a relationship which began during my assignment in the US last year. I have hardly seen him during the period since then, but we have kept regularly in touch, mainly by phone, and we have found our friendship mutually satisfying. So, I wish you wouldn't keep…"

"Look, does it matter? Jackie interrupted. "Grace's relationship with President Weston is her own business. For what it's worth, I think he is the most charming of men and I'm happy for Grace – and him, for that matter."

Grace's eyebrows shot up in surprise. "Thank you, Jackie. I really didn't expect…"

"But are we sure that's the reason el Taqha wants Grace there?" Jackie went on. "As a hostage, I mean." She turned to Grace. "Is it generally known that you and the President are… close friends?"

"Yes, we're sure that's the reason alright," Andrew said, before Grace could reply. "They were big news in Norway when Weston was over there. She flew out to meet him for dinner…"

"Along with half a dozen other people," Grace put in.

"And that's all the press wanted to talk to him about."

"I know that, but he denied it at the time, didn't he?" Jackie said.

"With a big cheesy smile on his face and a twinkle in his eye, and probably a twitch in his boxers as well."

Grace smiled at the Home Secretary, ignoring the Prime Minister. "The fact is, Jackie, I'm not having an affair with John Weston – *yet* – but it may be heading that way and I hope it is. Although it won't be an *affair*, as such, it will be open and transparent. And Andrew is right – assuming el Taqha has been in Norway recently, he is certain to have seen the speculation, *and* the conclusions drawn from the rumours, all over the Norwegian media. It's flattering, really, because they love John over there, and they seem to think this… liaison… is good for him."

Jackie smiled. "Well, I hope it works out, Grace, I really do."

"And that's why Taqha has chosen her as chief hostage," Andrew said, "because it safeguards him against any direct action by the US."

"That's what el Taqha might *think*, but…"

"Oh, come on, Grace. Weston's not going to send a flight of Raptors to blow up his chance of happiness. It's as clear as anything and…"

There was a faint tap on the door.

"Come," Andrew said.

The door opened a few inches, just enough for one eye and a nose to come into view.

"Yes, Marcus?"

"I'm sorry to disturb you, Prime Minister, but I have Sir Guy Cartwright on the red line. I think you should hear what he has to say."

"Very well, put him through." He sat down again. "I wonder what the Head of MI6 has to offer to further complicate things?"

The desk phone rang and he pressed the speaker button.

"Prime Minister, I'm sorry for…"

"It's alright, Guy, but can you be brief, please? I have Jackie Hewlett and Grace Goody with me and you are on the speaker. Please go ahead."

"Okay, good morning to you all. Ten minutes ago, I had a call from Annie Lyndon, CIA Director. She has made it clear that under no circumstances must we allow Abu el Taqha to leave the *Mastodon* alive unless it is to hand him over to the US. That's close to verbatim. The call lasted about three minutes."

Andrew was back on his feet, leaning over the desk and shouting into the phone.

"*Made it clear! Under no circumstances!* Who the fucking hell does she think she is? She's a front-office bimbo who looks good on TV and whose main job seems to be passing on messages."

"Then perhaps that's what she's doing, Prime Minister – passing on a message. Presumably from the President,"

"Not the President's style," Andrew said. "Weston would speak to me direct, not delegate to some mouthpiece. She's just jumping on the populist bandwagon."

"Even so, we have to assume it's official, don't you think?"

"Not necessarily. Anything else?"

"That's all. I told her I'd pass the message on to you."

"Well, you have. Thanks, Guy." He pressed the same button to end the call before sitting down again, slumped forward, his arms flat on the desktop. "Jesus, with friends like that..."

"Who needs enemies?" Jackie completed the cliché. "I think we can assume that was the CIA's response to CNN's call for action. Now they'll be able to say, 'Rest assured, we have el Taqha exactly where we want him and we've made sure he won't escape justice this time...', etc., etc."

Jackie's iPhone pinged with an incoming message.

"It's Ruby. Next scheduled call at midday." She looked up. "Look, I need to get back to Thames House as soon as possible. So, *whatever* Grace's relationship is with the President, *whatever* the reason el Taqha wants her on board, we need to decide within the next half hour or so, who, if anybody, is going up there and onto the *Mastodon*. It might be that the only way forward is to comply with their request for on-site negotiations, *and* it would be a major diplomatic coup for you, Andrew, if, as a result, they release those hostages."

Andrew smiled. "Playing to my vanity again, Jackie?"

"I wouldn't say 'again'. I can't remember another time."

"Let Grace and I talk about this further and you get back to the nerve centre. We'll both join you over there within the half hour. Are you okay with that?"

"Fine." Jackie got to her feet. "I will say one thing, though, Prime Minister. I suggest you *listen* to Grace for a change instead of just *telling* her things."

She turned and left the room.

★

Danny Weaver checked his watch: 9.42. He'd seen David Gerrard enter through the front door nearly an hour ago from where he was parked on Washbrook Road, since which time he had been waiting for an ancient road-sweeping vehicle to finish crawling along Westmore Street, the narrow, tree-lined thoroughfare at the side of the guest house. Now it had gone, and it was time to make his move.

He got out of his car and walked down Westmore, then turned up the alley which ran behind the building. Entering the rear yard through the creaking door in the high wooden perimeter fence, he ascended the rusted, metal fire escape to his left which gave access to the upper floor. The emergency exit door opened easily with no alarm. The corridor was empty and quiet, as he had expected, and he walked softly forward to Room 17. He knocked gently on the door and waited, slipping the Smith and Wesson pistol from the inside pocket of his jacket. There was no sound. He tried again, a little more loudly. Still nothing. He opened the door and stepped inside.

★

"I know you think I'm a total bastard, Grace, and I guess you've got plenty of evidence to support that conclusion, but I am not prepared to land one of my closest associates on top of a nuclear bomb. And certainly not a woman."

Grace gave him a twisted smile. "I wondered when you'd get around to that. So, you'd land a man on the *Mastodon* but not a woman. In the context of equal opportunities and the twenty-first century, would you mind explaining your thinking behind that?"

"For God's sake, let's not descend into bickering over lost values…"

"*Lost* values. I'm talking about *new* values. Christ, they've taken long enough to get here."

"Do you want to die, Grace? Is that it – just to show that you, as a woman, have got the same right to be blown to bits as a man? *I* don't want you to die, and it's got nothing to do with which sex you are – as I'm sure you know. It's because I'd never get anyone else to do the job as well as you do."

"You just said 'and certainly not a woman'... and you're saying that's got nothing to do with which sex I am? Look, Andrew, I was *trained* for a role like this. A long time ago, I know, and circumstances sent me on a different path, but this sort of assignment was what was intended for me at the time, before you produced your little incentive for me to join you on the campaign trail. So, why...?"

"Well you're right about one thing: it *was* a long time ago. What, twelve, fifteen years? Things have changed since then."

"*I* haven't changed. I work with the same group every week. Have the same personal trainer, lift the same weights and shoot just as straight. You don't seriously believe I could have done the things I've done for you in the past year or so if I *had* changed." Her voice failed a little as she spoke, then recovered quickly. "God knows, I might as well have been pulling the triggers myself for all the difference it makes. That's the sort of thing I was recruited for. Just because I wear high heels and a business suit doesn't make me fundamentally different."

Andrew sighed.

"The woman thing, Grace. You know their culture, how they treat women. As machines for breeding terrorists. Can't you see how vulnerable...?"

"Christ, Andrew, they've *asked* for me in person, to negotiate with, not to ravish." She hesitated. "Having said that, I'm not suggesting I go there alone. I'd expect a fully armed team of bodyguards. Please tell me that was in your mind as well."

"What's in my mind is that you don't go at all. Look, here's what we do." He leaned forward in his chair, elbows on the desktop. "We will agree to his demand for you to meet him on board, accompanied by your minders as a non-negotiable condition. Except it won't be you, personally, but someone who looks like you. One of the Brigadier's doppelgangers, if necessary. It won't make any difference to what is said, she'd be wired to the van Roden woman, who'll be with Weller and Ashpole. They'll be pulling the strings whether it's you or someone else. Can we agree on this, as a compromise?"

"Compromise? I thought what we – you, me and Jackie – agreed, was that they probably want me on there to discourage an attack by the US military. So how is putting someone else on there in my place going to achieve that?"

"Come on, Grace. *Obviously*, we will tell everyone, when the time comes, that *you* are the one they asked for and we have agreed to that demand. *You* are in place, on the *Mastodon*, to negotiate with the terrorists."

"When the time comes?"

"Yes, once you – I mean, your double – is on the ship. I understand one of el Taqha's conditions was that the name mustn't be disclosed until then. At the moment, as far as I am aware, only we two, plus Hewlett and Weller, know the name, other than Taqha and his buddies."

"So, your proposed substitution of Miss Doppelganger for me is intended to fool *everybody*, not just the terrorists, and including the President of the United States?"

"*Especially* him, because, ultimately, he'll be the one calling the shots. Another unintended pun," he added. "You just said yourself, it doesn't work unless he believes you are on board. Obviously, some of our guys on the mission will need to know – Ashpole, and the guys in the bodyguard, for instance. You'll have to go up there, of course, to Hirta, so we can show you leaving here and so you're not visible anywhere else."

Grace was silent for a while before speaking again, slowly, as if choosing her words carefully.

"It's almost touching, Andrew, that you are prepared to lie to the President in order to protect me from harm, even though, as you say, it's purely for professional, not personal, reasons. Especially as you are correct in believing that I think you're a total bastard. In fact, given the number of times I've heard you say 'we put them on Alpha to die' I'm surprised you don't view this whole thing as an opportunity to hasten the process."

"It's funny you should say that..."

"But it wouldn't look good in the opinion polls, would it? I quite understand. Going back to my substitution, let's just consider one possible outcome. She – would it be a 'she', by the way, or a 'he' made up to look like a 'she'?"

"It would be a woman."

"I suppose it would have to be, just in case they do intend to ravish me. They'd fairly quickly spot the difference. So, this possible outcome… if something goes badly wrong and the woman is a casualty, a fatality, let's say. Would I then have to be eliminated to complete the charade? Otherwise, how do you explain to the President that I'm still around? He'll know he's been conned. It wouldn't do a lot for the so-called 'special relationship', would it?"

Andrew was on his feet again, looking angry. "Special relationship! Like when we ask them not to reveal that el Taqha is on board the *Mastodon*, so they put it out on the biggest global news channel in existence. You mean *that* sort of special relationship? It's only come to this because they couldn't keep their fucking mouths shut."

Grace looked down at her hands, resting on her lap.

"Okay. But where does that put me? And this *is* personal and not professional. The President will know that I was party to the deception, that I used his… feelings for me to trick him. What do you think that will do to *our* – mine and John's – 'special relationship'?"

Andrew sat down. It was his turn to remain silent for a few moments. When he spoke, his voice was soft, almost gentle. "So, what are you suggesting, Grace?"

"We do it as requested, *without* the substitution. I have to go onto the *Mastodon*."

*

When the call reporting the shooting came into the main switch at 9.48 a.m., Harry and Natalie were just a few minutes away and first on the scene, closely followed by two marked police cars each with two uniformed officers. The receptionist was sitting wide-eyed and ashen faced behind her desk when the two detectives hurried in through the front door. A youngish man stood behind her, a comforting hand on her shoulder. She raised a shaking arm, pointing to her left, but with her eyes still staring ahead.

"Room 17, first floor, stairs… no lift."

They stopped briefly to address the man.

"Mr Kemp?" Harry asked.

"That's right, I'm the one who…"

"Yes, thank you. Please wait here with Evelyn for a moment. We'll be with you very soon."

They went through the reception area. At the foot of the stairs Harry stopped. "Nat, stay here and sort out the uniforms, get the place sealed off. Keep everyone down here for now, including the SOCOs, and get somebody to make Evelyn a cup of tea or something. She must think we're all mad. Then wait for the doc and bring her up. Just the two of you at first. Paramedics?"

"Specials, sir. Already briefed."

"Good. As of right now, we go as planned, depending on…" Harry frowned and shook his head. "Christ knows what we'll find up there. Surely to God, Weaver hasn't… I can't believe… please don't say we've lost David."

"Best go and find out, sir."

Harry turned and raced up the stairs.

CHAPTER TWENTY-SIX

10.05 a.m. BST

The people in the main communications room at Thames House sprang to their feet as Andrew entered with Grace at a little after 10.00 a.m. In the room were Jackie and Ruby, Lawrence Harding, Joe Kilby and Jonathan Latiffe. They had been joined by the Defence Secretary, Bernard Wilson, who was in an adjoining office making a phone call which he ended on Andrew's arrival in order to join the group.

"Could someone get me a coffee?" Andrew said, prompting a minor stampede for the cafetière on one of the cabinets at the side of the room. Ruby moved to one side to allow him to take the middle seat at a long side of the conference table as the coffee cup, with saucer, was placed in front of him. He turned to Jackie as they all took their seats around him.

"Home Secretary, is anyone here other than you and Ruby aware of the name on the communique from the *Mastodon*?"

"No, Prime Minister. We thought you should be the one to share the identity of the person."

Andrew nodded. "Quite, thank you. The person requested by the terrorists is the Ministerial Director of Justice, Grace Goody, and, after a discussion with the aforementioned nominee, it has been decided that Grace *will* be fronting the negotiations."

Grace looked across at Jackie, who frowned the unspoken question. Grace gave a little smile and nodded.

"Along with whom, Prime Minister?" Lawrence Harding asked the question, leaning forward intensely. He was tall and distinguished-looking, with a mane of steel grey hair.

"She will have a concealed radio link to the control centre on Hirta where Doctor Lydia van Roden…"

"No, I mean, who will be with Grace on the *Mastodon*?"

"A group of armed special forces personnel will accompany her on board as her personal bodyguard. That condition is non-negotiable, she will not be embarking without full and visible protection. Only the *number* of operatives is up for discussion. We'll propose eight, but concede to, say five or six if it looks like a deal-breaker. The person who will be leading the group will advise on the minimum number. And, of course, we'll have other forces on board in addition to the negotiating party. I believe some are in place already. Mr Kilby?"

"I'm not familiar with the operational details, Prime Minister, but, yes, I believe Blue-One is in place."

"Blue-One? Don't tell me we've moved from letters of the alphabet to colours of the rainbow."

"No, sir. I expect Ms Goody's group will be given the designation Red-One; the two covert teams are Blue-One and Blue-Two. It's standard coding for this type of op." He smiled. "Not my fault this time, Prime Minister,"

As he spoke, he touched his right trouser pocket in response to a faint buzzing sound.

"Thank you, Mr Kilby. What is it?" he nodded to the iPhone as Joe took it out and checked the screen.

"May I take this, Prime Minister? It will be very relevant to the meeting."

"Then I think you can guess my answer." Andrew smiled. "Please do."

Joe went onto the office recently vacated by the Defence Secretary to take the call.

"I think we should link with Hirta before we continue this meeting," Andrew said. "It will save duplication of communication with its attendant danger of misunderstandings. Can someone get them back on the speaker while we eagerly await Mr Kilby's revelation?"

Joe's re-emergence and the establishing of the connection happened at the same moment three minutes later.

"Could you identify who is present, please?" Andrew spoke into the metal hemisphere in the centre of the table which was the conference phone.

"Roger Ashpole speaking, Prime Minister. I have with me Colonel Kade and Dr Lydia van Roden of IHRS..."

"International Hostage Rescue Services." Ruby put in quickly as Andrew's jaw muscles clenched. He nodded a thank you before running through those present around the table.

"I wanted you in on this meeting, Sir Roger, to confirm the name of the chief negotiator as requested by el Taqha. It will be Grace Goody, who has agreed to take on that role, with a bodyguard in attendance on the *Mastodon*. Grace has requested that you, Mr Kade, will lead that group. I don't propose that we discuss the details or logistics of the mission now, that is for the participants to agree later. Grace will be travelling with Ruby Weller to join you after this meeting. But before we proceed, MI5 agent Kilby has just received some news which I believe he is anxious to share." He looked across at Joe and raised his eyebrows in an invitation to speak.

"Yes, Prime Minister. That was the monitoring arm of the Atomic Energy Agency in Vienna. They can confirm with ninety-five percent certainty, that no nuclear material is missing from their global inventory. They have looked specifically at Iran, for obvious reasons – bearing in mind the personnel who are claiming they have the device – and Finland, given the country's proximity to Norway, but are confident that stocks of materials are all present and in their assigned storage locations."

"That's ninety-five percent confident?" Andrew said.

"The five percent represents the level of risk, a one-in-twenty chance that regulations have been deliberately by-passed, but undetected."

Andrew was silent for a long time, long enough for Sir Roger to ask if the connection was still in place. When he spoke, it was with a shaking of the head.

"Just indulge us for a few minutes, St Kilda. How many people in this room buy lottery tickets? Raise your hand." All raised a hand. "Bernard, tell us why you buy lottery tickets." He smiled. "It's not a trick question, I promise you."

The Defence Secretary screwed up his face in thought before replying. "I guess it's a form of escapism. The lure of the big prize. The only chance readily available to make an instantaneous quantum leap into life-long financial security and luxury for yourself and your family."

"That's a good answer, from which I assume that you're not in it for the three-numbers, thirty-pound prize. Am I right?"

"Yes, Prime Minister, although it's always welcome if it happens."

There was a ripple of laughter, joined by Andrew.

"It seems," he said, looking round, "that all can identify with that. You may or may not know that the odds of getting three numbers on the lottery are around a hundred to one – ninety-seven to one, to be exact. That's on any one line. So, if your card has, say, five lines on it, you've got a twenty to one chance of getting three numbers. And I'd guess, if you do buy five lines every week – or twice a week, or whatever – you wouldn't necessarily be surprised if you had three numbers come up. My point being a one-in-twenty chance does not represent particularly long odds, especially when the prize is instant death."

No-one spoke, all eyes on Andrew waiting to see where his argument was going. After a half-minute's silence, Joe Kilby raised his hand.

"If I may, Prime Minister?"

"Go on."

"The ninety-five percent relates to the certainty that no nuclear materials have been unlawfully acquired. The other – and possibly *main* – factor which must be considered, although it may not be quantifiable, is the likelihood of stolen material being made into a bomb capable of being manually handled across borders and onto the vessel. Gut feel, the odds for that stage on its own, even assuming the material is available, must be longer than the ones for the actual acquisition. In terms of your lottery analogy, Prime Minister, it must stretch easily to four numbers."

"The odds for which are over two thousand to one, in case anyone is interested."

"Just out of curiosity, Prime Minister," Jackie asked, "how come you are familiar with this stuff?"

"A fascination for statistics, Jackie, and personal investment." He turned to Joe. "A fair point, Mr Kilby. Anything else?"

"There was one other piece of news from the Agency, and it touches on a question you raised yesterday." He consulted a hand-written note. "They uncovered this when they checked the Finnish nuclear stocks. A few months ago, a discrepancy arose between the recorded and counted stock of nuclear fuel rods at the Loviisa power station. Some fuel rods appeared to be missing. It turned out to be an administrative error due to a duplication of a batch in the stock records. The error was rectified by deleting the duplicated record. But it coincided with a breach of security twenty-four hours earlier, when a section of the station's steel-mesh perimeter fence had been holed. It was initially assumed this had been done to allow entry for intruders. However, nothing was captured on CCTV within the perimeter, and there was no physical evidence of anyone either."

"So, what are they thinking? A coincidence? And more to the point, what are *we* thinking now? Should we be reviewing those odds in the light of this? I'm surprised you added this almost as an afterthought, Mr Kilby. It seems pretty relevant to me."

"If I can share what I believe, Prime Minister? Because…"

Grace leaned forward in her seat, as Joe began to reply.

"Just hold on," Andrew said, holding up his hand to stop him. "Grace, have you got something to say?"

"I don't think the admin error and the hole in the fence coming together is a coincidence, but I don't believe it points to anything other than a sort of tactical red herring. They – el Taqha and co – must know we will be sceptical about their having a nuclear device on board, and that on balance we'll believe they don't. We won't know for certain, of course, until this thing plays out, but anything they can do in the meantime to test that belief will give them more leverage. My feeling is they sent someone to just cut the fence and disappear, and immediately afterwards, they hacked into the logistics software at Loviisa and made a change to the inventory. Not easy, but not that difficult for someone at the top end of the hacking community pyramid. I know I've got at least one guy working for me who could do it. Remember, these systems are designed to stop nuclear material going missing, not to prevent admin errors."

"Okay. But it's interesting if they did have the same idea as I did yesterday. I'm not sure how worried I should be that my thinking seems to be aligned with the world's number one terrorist."

"It could prove very useful over the next couple of days, Prime Minister," Jonathan said.

Gentle laughter rippled around the table and over the speaker from St Kilda, coming as a welcome relief. Grace turned to Joe.

"Agent Kilby, you were going to say something."

"You just said it for me, ma'am, word for word."

"Excellent," Andrew said. "So, does anyone else have an opinion on the Finland thing? Roger?"

"It makes sense," Roger replied, "We're all nodding heads here."

"Right. We'll keep the odds as they are for now then, and you ladies had better get ready for your journey north." He nodded to Ruby and Grace. "Let's take five minutes."

*

By 10.35 a.m., everything was in place. The whole of Washbrook Road was sealed off with solid barriers, as were the other three streets around the block which contained the guest house. A police vehicle with its blue lights flashing was stationed at each corner. Police crime-tape sealed both ends of the alley which gave access to the rear of the building, the route used by Danny Weaver just over an hour ago. Three more police cars and two ambulances were parked along the road in front of the guest house.

Harry and Natalie were seated side by side on the bed in Room 19. The young man who had called the emergency services earlier was sitting opposite them on the threadbare wingchair which, apart from a small bedside table, was the only other piece of furniture in the room. The man, who introduced himself as Nathan Kemp, was of average height, smartly dressed in dark-blue trousers and a button-through, short-sleeved white shirt, which was close-fitting enough to show a slim but muscular upper body. His hair was dark, as was his stylishly trimmed beard. He had a horizontal scar over his right eye which showed up white against his tanned skin. The man looked more agitated than distressed by the events of the morning, and it became clear why.

"So, you claim you arrived here with… A N Other, we'll call her for now… at around eight-thirty," Harry said. "You had planned to use the room until midday for, let's say, recreational purposes, right?"

"Look, I don't need these little barbed comments, thank you. Whatever you think about the moral issue here…"

"We're not thinking about anything of the sort, Mr Kemp," Natalie said. "But so far you've refused to give us the name of the person you were with. She has disappeared, apparently, that's if she was ever here at all. The receptionist has been here since eight o'clock and claims she did not see either of you arrive. There is no record of this room being booked and we've got two bodies just along the corridor which we haven't even got around to talking about yet. So, please, let's get this thing moving."

"Look, you should be thanking me. I caught the fucking murderer for you."

"And we appreciate that, Mr Kemp. You were very brave; it took a lot of guts to do what you did."

"Let's just go through this again from the beginning," Harry said, "and see if we can tease out a bit more information. Let's start with the arrangement you made to meet your friend here today."

"Okay, from the beginning, *again*. I don't know if you're aware of it – although I guess you are – but this place is bookable by the hour, the day, overnight… for, as you call it, *recreational purposes*. The lady I was with is married, she works nights at a supermarket, stock-taking and stacking shelves. Sometimes she works an extra half-shift until twelve o'clock. And sometimes she tells her husband she's working the extra hours when she's not. That gives us the opportunity to meet without anybody wondering where she is."

"Nice and neat," Harry said.

"Yes, well… but today was different. This week she's been covering eight to twelve for someone who was absent. She was expecting to do that for the remainder of the week but today the person returned to work. So, she contacted me at eight o'clock and we arranged to meet here. Because of the short notice, I didn't bother to book the room because I knew it was easy to get in from the fire escape and the rooms are always unlocked." He gave a little laugh. "Except when people are in them, of course. Then they're always locked, but on the inside. Anyway, that's why the receptionist didn't see us today."

"And what about other days? She tells us she doesn't recognise you at all."

"When I had this place recommended to me, I was assured she was very discreet, so it doesn't surprise me she tries to protect the customers by saying she hasn't seen them here before."

"Okay, so where is your friend now?"

"Well, when all this happened, I told her to go straight away. I don't want her identified. We're having an affair – yes – but she has two children that she loves, and has no intention of leaving her husband and splitting up the family. This is just a bit of an adventure for her – for both of us, in fact – and you can think what you like, but *I* don't believe she deserves to be compromised because I was… 'brave', I think you said… when I could have just left with her."

"Mmm…" Harry said. "You say you're married as well, Mr Kemp. Where does your wife think you are right now?"

The man sighed. "I've already told you that."

"Yes, I know, but we're going over it again, aren't we?"

"I'm a merchandiser for a food company."

"Which is…" Harry checked his notes "… Peregrine Pickles and Sauces?"

"That's right."

"And just remind me what a merchandiser does."

Mr Kemp sighed again. "I visit outlets – distributors and retailers – taking orders and dealing with any issues around timing, shortages, quality, etc. Right now, my wife believes I'm on my way to visit a customer in Wolverhampton, for a meeting at two o'clock. And, hopefully, I'll still make it. Look, I can't see how my job description has any bearing on this case."

"It doesn't, Mr Kemp," Natalie said. "But we have to establish why you just happened to be in the right place at the right time with the right weapon to bring what would seem to be a rapid conclusion to this case. The Crown Prosecutor will be keen to ensure there's no chance that a clever defence counsel could bring something new to the court at a critical time. You do understand, don't you?"

"Prosecutor? Court? What do you mean?"

"Well, we'll have to arrest and charge you. You attacked a man from behind with a heavy weapon without knowing why he was there. He could have been an innocent person in the wrong place at the wrong time."

"Or a member of the police," Harry put in.

"Oh, come on!"

"We'll just finish going through this," Natalie said, "and if what you said before is true, I can't see there being any conviction. So, I ask again. You do understand, don't you?"

"I suppose."

"Good," Harry said. "So, you were in Room 19 with Mrs…?"

"With my friend, when I heard a crash from just along the corridor. Just before that there was a sort of fast drumming, like *dum-dum-dum-dum*, but quite muted. I looked out towards the stairs and noticed Room 17 door was open. I took the lamp from the bedside table – it's got a really heavy base – wrapped its cord round my hand and snuck along to see what the noise was. *Shit*, it scared me half to death. There was this guy lying against the wall, and just inside the door, this other guy with his back to me holding a gun. He must have heard me or sensed I was there, because he started to turn around, so… so…"

"Go on, Mr Kemp." Natalie leaned forward.

"I swung the lamp and hit him as hard as I could. He just went down without making a sound. I thought I'd killed him. I'm not sure about being brave; it was more to do with self-defence."

"Then what did you do?" Harry asked.

"I went back to our room, told her what had happened, and to get out fast. She left by the fire escape, the same way we got in. Then I phoned you – the police."

"So, if no-one saw her come or go, why did you tell us about her at all if it's so important to keep her out of it?"

The man smiled. "I was thinking about that while I was waiting for you to arrive. Then I thought, what are they going to believe? Why else would I be hanging round in a shithole like this? As I said, I assumed the police knew about the place, anyway." He snorted a laugh. "We didn't even get started. No fuck-*ing*, just a fuck-*up*." He looked up at Natalie. "Sorry."

"I've heard worse, Mr Kemp."

*

The group settled back into their seats with replenished cups of coffee.

"Are you guys still there?" Andrew spoke into the phone.

"Still here… and re-caffeinated," Sir Roger said.

"Okay, to summarise. Grace and Ruby will be arriving at Stornoway, I'd guess, in around three hours or so. They've already left to get their stuff together for the trip and they will be contactable to go over any details at all times during their flight. Grace will want to speak to you, Mr Kade, about the bodyguard. As I said, she has asked specifically for you to lead the team, but she is also planning to have with her an associate who she'd like to be part of that group. I'm not sure how that fits with your plans and I'm certainly not going to insist from here. You and Grace need to talk. Okay?"

"Understood, sir." The clipped American accent was in sharp contrast to the dulcet Etonian timbre of Sir Roger Ashpole.

"Ruby will attend essentially as an observer, but has the authority to decide on any concessions and conditions when negotiations get under way. Should there be a need to refer up to the Home Secretary or me. Ruby will know when.

"I cannot emphasise enough the need for secrecy. Only the people in this room, you three on Hirta, and Ruby and Grace know the identity of our chief negotiator. It must stay that way. It irks me on the one hand to think we have readily acceded to el Taqha's request for Grace, but I see nothing to gain by creating a stand-off before we even start. And part of that request was to release her identity *only* when the group was in place.

"Finally – for now – we will be demanding that all hostages be released in what will effectively be an exchange for the negotiating party – Grace and her bodyguard. To affect that we need transport. I doubt they will agree to a fleet of helicopters or a ferrying operation with one making multiple trips, so I'm looking to you, Roger, or Mr Kade, to arrange for a Chinook or similar to take them all at once. When I say all, I mean all but a skeleton crew to operate the ship. We are liaising with Scandoil to establish how many and who. And just to confirm, an engineer from Boskalis, the Dutch company who operate the *Mastodon*, is already on his way to Stornoway and will transfer to Hirta with Grace and Ruby. He is due to arrive when, Jackie?"

"He will get to Stornoway around 3.30. I assume he will be given only limited information about the mission, but I understand his input on the layout of the ship will be crucial to our success. I'm guessing the three of them will be on Hirta by, say, four-fifteen."

"Are we all okay so far?" Andrew asked.

There were nods around the table and verbal agreement through the speaker.

"Good." He checked his watch. "We are thirty-seven minutes from our next scheduled call with el Taqha at high noon. Jonathan will take the call here at Thames House this time, as Ruby will be in transit. Dr van Roden, you will be on the call as before, and, I say again, many thanks for your input so far. If any new information comes to light any time and from any source, then contact agent Joe Kilby here at Thames House. He will be co-ordinating all communications from all sources going forward. Thank you, ladies and gentlemen."

Andrew got to his feet to the sound of chairs scraping on the wooden floor as the rest of the room's occupants did the same. He turned to leave the room, nodding to Jackie to follow him.

CHAPTER TWENTY-SEVEN

11.45 a.m. BST

Abu el Taqha leaned back against the short length of rail, which extended five metres or so along the starboard edge of the deck from the forward superstructure. That, and a similar section on the port side, were the only lengths of rail on the whole of the main deck, to allow its standard cargo of giant semi-submersible platforms to rest securely on, and overhang, the wide, flat surface.

He craned his neck to survey again the monstrous structure above him. Even partly submerged with the stabilising pontoon well below the hull of the *Mastodon*, he could still appreciate the greater size of Alpha when compared with the platform they had recently cast adrift. It was hard to imagine that nearly 800 people, who were the key to his success, were just beyond the metal-latticed floor he could see a hundred metres above his head. There was no visible or audible evidence that they existed at all, just the certain knowledge that they did; confined and vulnerable.

His attention was drawn to the sound of screeching seabirds, the same scenario that had played out yesterday at first light. A huge gull with black wings, slowly circling around the fore and aft superstructures before gliding down over the deck, all the time mobbed by twenty or so other birds, some much smaller, but others of a similar size and colouring. Not an inter-species dispute, then, he thought, so why the animosity towards this one bird? It dropped down to within a half-metre of the deck itself, and began to glide back and forth across its the full width, working its way forward towards him from the stern. The other birds were almost frantic now as the chaotic scene moved closer.

He checked his watch: 11.52. Time to prepare for the midday call. He opened the door leading to the comms room, with a last backward glance at the furore which had by now travelled the full length of the deck and was just a couple of metres away from him. The birds had forced their quarry onto the deck and were pecking furiously at it, attacking each other as they jostled for position.

He stopped and stared. The large bird was making no attempt to defend itself. Nor was it moving its wings at all. At first, he thought it was badly injured and had succumbed to its attackers. He took the Browning Hi-power pistol from inside his coat and fired two shots into the air. The mass of birds scattered in all directions. For a few seconds, the one on the deck remained perfectly still. He stepped towards it, leaning over to check for signs of injury. He could hear a low-pitched buzzing sound and stepped back as the bird rose from the deck. It soared vertically past him and he could see beneath its wings the three rotors and swivelling camera, plus a flat square plate with a pattern of circular indents, everything in miniature.

He raised the Browning, getting off seven shots, all missing, as the drone wheeled away to the west. Footsteps sounded on the stairs inside and four of his men burst through the door on to the deck, guns out and ready, to see what was wrong. Abu el Taqha ignored the salvo of gabbled questions and stared out to sea at the diminishing dot heading towards the gently flapping Norwegian flag.

*

Alerted by the gunshots, the five men eased up the flap of their improvised shelter on the top of *Mastodon*'s starboard tower at the stern of the vessel. They looked down on the deck nearly fifty metres below. Blue-One had been concealed beneath a canopy, no more than a metre high constructed from their five parachutes, for the past ten hours, out of sight of media cameras in the circling aircraft. The familiar sound of a discharging weapon was a welcome relief to a group not disposed to long periods of inactivity.

The Major, leader of the group, was a man in his mid-forties, tall, slim and with broad soldiers. In place of his beanie, he now wore his hallmark black baseball cap pulled low over his forehead. He eased his rifle forward and shouldered it into position resting on the bottom bar of the low rail which ran round the edge of the tower. He lined up his weapon with el Taqha's head in the centre of the reticle. He recalled in painful detail the only previous occasion he'd had the same man in the sights of the same rifle.

"This takes me right back." He spoke to the group in general who waited for him to continue, but the story stayed inside his mind, active but silent…

He was with the SBS, eighteen years ago – was it *really* that long? – on a ridge in Afghanistan, as part of Operation Ptarmigan trying to flush out the Taliban. They had been out on patrol with some Navy SEALs under the overall command of a US major – one Marty Kade. The Taliban were spread very thinly in that area, in small cells which were difficult to track. The patrol had decided to split up into two groups – SBS and SEALs – to cover more ground more quickly, but not expecting to find anything.

It was about thirty minutes after they had separated that both groups received intelligence that Abu el Taqha was close by, about a kilometre from the SBS patrol's current position, but more than twice that distance away from the SEALs. The Brits got there well ahead of Kade's group, finding el Taqha down in a dry basin with around fifty Taliban. The patrol took up a position on a ridge above them less than 500 metres away. El Taqha was standing on the back seat of a jeep, the others in a semicircle in front of him. He had a clear shot; he couldn't miss.

It was at that point their patrol leader contacted Kade to tell him of their status. Kade had said to wait until they – the SEALs – arrived, they were *only* twenty minutes away. The SBS guy asked "Why?" Answer – "VTI." "What the fuck is VTI?" "Verification of target identity." The patrol leader had emptied his vocabulary of expletives into the field radio and turned, crimson-faced with rage to tell the Major – then a sergeant – to lower his weapon. He had held The Shadow in his sights – exactly where he was right now – for a full minute before finally complying with the order. By the time the SEALs arrived, el Taqha was invisible inside a distant cloud of dust kicked up by his departing vehicle.

It was not Kade's fault. The Major knew it then and never doubted it since. The American was every bit as angry as himself at what transpired, something that contributed to his leaving the military at the earliest opportunity to take over IHRS. Someone behind a desk in Washington, desperate for the Americans to get el Taqha for his role in 9/11, rather than anyone else get the credit, had taken the decision. It remained the Major's enduring regret that he had not disobeyed that order and taken him out.

"Major, you still with us?"

He came out of his trance at the sound of Sergeant Sam Hudson's voice. His four companions were staring at him,

"Sure. As I said, this takes me right back."

He lowered the rifle.

*

In her office at the PST central unit in Nydalen, Oslo, Milena Bakke studied the data scrolling across the monitor on the desk in front of her. Twelve hundred kilometres away, Captain Jonas Haugen – the source of that data – was watching the same image on his own screen in the observation cabin of the NoCGV *Sonja*, now steady at a distance of two kilometres from the *Mastodon*.

"So, what are we looking at, Captain?"

"Well, very little, in fact, which is good news, of course. The small bubbles of activity at the bottom of the chart are just normal noise – a limitation of the measuring device, if you like. Not significant. We'd be seeing sharper peaks, and much bigger, if it was finding anything."

"But wouldn't you expect the material to be fully contained anyway? I mean, it would have to be for them to handle it. And if it's in one of the cabins it will be surrounded by substantial walls and ceilings. Am I right? Or am I asking the wrong person? No offence, Captain, but I guess you don't have a lot of experience trying to find WMDs."

Jonas gave a little laugh. "You are right about bombs, ma'am, but we do have experience monitoring vessels for radioactivity. We have intercepted traffic in the Barents Sea many times when we have suspected them of transporting nuclear waste, for example. And we have been right on most of those occasions. But to your point, yes, the material will be fully contained for safety purposes, but with enough uranium on board for an explosion on the scale they're threatening, we would expect to be picking up traces. And the thickness of the walls and deck are no barrier to escaping neutrons. I'm not saying there is nothing on board, just that we didn't find anything. But I assume you will be getting one or more of your experts to analyse the data. Please don't act on my opinion alone."

"We will do that right away. Many thanks, Captain, for this. And I'm pleased your great black-back escaped unhurt. He's certainly taken on celebrity status over the last couple of days. Please pass on our sincere thanks to him."

"I'll do that," Jonas laughed. "I'm sure he'll be glad to see the Geiger-counter go and to get back to just taking pictures. Although I guess he's off duty for now. We can't send him out again."

"A well-deserved rest, I think."

Milena ended the call and pressed the speaker button on the red phone on her desk. It was answered immediately.

"Thames House. Agent Joe Kilby speaking."

*

Doctor Amy White signalled for the body to be removed from the scene at just after midday. With no lift in the building, it was a major logistical challenge to ease the body bag containing the 112 kilogram bulk of David Gerrard, strapped to a stretcher, down the steep, narrow staircase to the ground floor where a scissor-jack trolley awaited it, to the immense relief of the four paramedics and two scene-of-crime officers who had managed to get it that far.

Outside, a small crowd had gathered at the barriers on the corner of Washbrook and Westmore, swelled, Harry had no doubt, through social media, and including local press and a TV crew. Cameras and iPhones clicked and people shouted questions without any expectation of getting answers at this stage. The trolley was manoeuvred through the front door, down the three steps and across to one of the ambulances.

Natalie and Amy climbed into the back with it and a paramedic closed the rear doors. Harry, standing in the guest house doorway, watched it drive away. He looked across at the second ambulance, where paramedics were still working on Danny Weaver, before turning back inside.

Evelyn, the receptionist, was being comforted in the small residents' lounge by a female uniformed officer while they waited for a car to take her home.

"How are you feeling, Evelyn?" Harry asked.

"Not so good. Just want to get away."

"Well I believe you've given a full statement to DC Crusoe, so, as soon as the car arrives, PC Marriott here will make sure you get home as soon as possible. I'm so sorry about this. Will you be okay on your own? Penny can stay with you for a while if you wish."

"It's okay. I'm sure I'll be fine."

"That's good. For the time being, please don't tell *anyone* about what's happened. One of the team will want to go through it with you again later, just in case you remember something else. We could do that at home or we could send a car to bring you in to the station, whichever you like."

"Oh, you can send a car. That would be fine. Just give me half an hour or so notice and I'll be ready."

"Okay, Evelyn. You're almost one of the team yourself now, aren't you?" He smiled and Evelyn attempted a smile back. He nodded to the uniformed officer. "Thanks, Penny."

Harry's iPhone signalled an incoming call.

"Hi, Alice. What news?"

"Well, sir, Peregrine Pickles and Sauces certainly exists," DC Alice Grantham answered, "but they have no-one called Nathan Kemp working for them. Nor do they have any customers in Wolverhampton."

"Thanks, Alice. Look, Nat has gone with the ambulance; can you or one of the guys get over here right away. I think we need to make it clear to the man with no name that we don't like people lying to us, whether he's a hero or not."

He ended the call and went upstairs again, passing Room 17, where the SOCOs were still working, although their terms of reference had now changed significantly. He left them to it and went to Room 19.

It was empty.

"Where's Mr Kemp?" Harry addressed the young uniformed officer standing in front of the emergency doors at the end of the corridor.

"Just stepped outside, sir, onto the fire escape for a smoke."

Harry rushed forward, almost elbowing the policeman out of the way, and crashed through the doors.

"Sir? Something wrong?" The young man looked nervous and followed Harry out. Mr Kemp was nowhere to be seen.

"How long ago?" Harry snapped.

"I didn't realise..."

"*How long?*"

"Five minutes, perhaps a bit longer. I didn't know he wasn't allowed out. I mean, he was the one who called it in, the one who..."

"You're right, son," Harry sighed. "You did nothing wrong, but I think our hero is having second thoughts about the wisdom of being so public spirited when he doesn't want his wife to find out he was here. And it seems that Kemp is not his real name."

"Oh, right. I see..."

"Well, he must be around here somewhere; we've got the perimeter sealed off. But where he definitely *isn't* is where I told him to wait for me. I'll check around. Let me know if he wanders back in."

"Yes, sir. Sorry, sir. It just seemed obvious that as he was the one who is helping us, it was okay to..."

"As I said, you did nothing wrong, and you're not the only one who's confused by what's happened. Since I saw some bloody photographs recently, it feels like *nothing* is what it seems."

CHAPTER TWENTY-EIGHT

12.40 p.m. BST

Jonathan was checking his watch for about the twentieth time when the call finally came through.

"And who has been selected to speak with me this time?" The voice was clipped and angry compared to his previous cool, relaxed manner.

"This is Jonathan Latiffe. Could you explain, please, why...?"

"Ah, the Minister of Justice. How very appropriate. I seem to be going up in the world."

"Could you explain why you have kept us waiting for forty minutes? If we are to trust each other discussing what I anticipate will be some very delicate issues, it is not a good start when you cannot respect a simple arrangement like the timing of a phone call. We are disappointed, especially as we have been working hard in considering your requests in order to meet the midday deadline, which *you* stipulated, so we could provide you with an answer."

"You talk about trust, Minister. The reason for the delay is because *we* have been working hard considering any repercussions of the incident which took place just as I was about to contact you. The Norwegian vessel which has been following us since we set out from Glomfjord seems to be spying on us. I now understand how I was identified – by a drone with a camera. I can accept that at that early stage, but I thought we'd moved on from there and had established, shall I say, a state of equilibrium in readiness for our discussions. And yet this thing is still flying round taking pictures. I don't know whether it was checking for blood on the deck or what, but if we see it again, it will be shot to pieces, that is a promise."

Jonathan was silent for a moment before replying.

"I can only assume our friends at Scandoil are still concerned about their colleagues. You have denied them the opportunity to confirm that they are safe and it is not unreasonable that they should see your refusal to mean that they are *not*, in spite of your personal assurance. Given that you have hijacked a ship, imprisoned its crew and are threatening the lives of – in your own estimate – thirty thousand innocent people with a nuclear bomb, sending a harmless drone to check for signs of life is about the least response you could expect. I find it amazing that you believe righteous indignation and a sense of betrayal are appropriate reactions."

There was a long silence before Abu spoke again. "A very well-argued point, Minister. Can we now proceed?"

"Yes, if you are ready to enlighten us to your requests."

"We are, Minister, although we see them more as demands than requests. Firstly, can you confirm that the named person will be the one leading the negotiations here on the *Mastodon*?"

"I can confirm that. The person is en route to St Kilda, accompanied by Ruby Weller, who you spoke to on the last call, which is why I am speaking with you now. However, we have three non-negotiable conditions attached to that. They will not be detrimental to your position and we fully expect you to agree to them."

"Go ahead, Minister, although I am a little surprised at the phrase 'non-negotiable' so early in the proceedings."

"Firstly, the person will be accompanied by eight armed personnel. I assume you would expect this, but I think it is important we fully understand each other and avoid any surprises. Secondly, the meeting will take place on the deck of the ship, not in one of the cabins below. We expect you to make appropriate arrangements for the comfort of the party as much as you can in the circumstances. This is so all parties involved are at all times visible for verification that there is no foul play."

"On either side, you mean?"

"And thirdly, we expect you to release all the hostages except a small number who will remain to carry out essential duties on board relating to the operation of the ship."

There was a further period of silence, even longer than before. Jonathan heard Lydia's voice through his earpiece. "Wait, Jonathan.

Do not be tempted to fill the silence. Leave the onus on him to respond."

It was well over a minute before Abu spoke again.

"We will need to consider the final condition."

"Non-negotiable," Jonathan read from his screen. "It will be forty-six people released and you get nine in return. That's a net reduction of thirty-seven from *your* total of thirty thousand *and* that will leave you a smaller group to manage in situ. Your main hostages, I assume, are the people on Alpha, otherwise there would have been no point at all in this whole adventure. If the fifty-three people on board were all that were important to you, you didn't even have to leave the fjord."

"Your numbers are correct, Minister, but you miss the main point of what you call our 'adventure', which is a demonstration of what we are capable of. To acquire a nuclear bomb is unique in the history of this sort of conflict. To hijack a high-profile vessel of this size is almost unprecedented, as well. But to put the two together is nothing short of miraculous. So do not demean the importance of the on-board hostages, Minister. They are part of this great show, which we felt deserved a better stage then a quiet inlet in the Arctic Circle."

Jonathan checked his screen before responding.

"If putting on a show is what this is all about – and I am not in any way trivialising your achievement, Abu – then is it now over? Do your demands, which we have no hint of yet, relate to your being granted a safe passage out of there. And if that is so, why do we need the further drama of an on-board negotiation?"

"Wishful thinking, Minister. Our demands are very specific and set out to redress injustices against our brothers by western tyrannies in multiple Islamic communities. I'm sure in your position you will be sympathetic to the righting of wrongs. In a few minutes I will give you a list of the victims of these crimes against Islam, men and boys wrongly imprisoned, who must be released to save the people on this ship, this platform and, most probably, the islands of St Kilda and beyond. We are providing you with the list now so that your negotiating team can be briefed in advance, and business can start promptly on their arrival. The list of personnel is, to use your own term, non-negotiable. What *is* negotiable – and what will constitute the agenda for the meeting here on the

Mastodon – are the timescales and logistics for their release, and a way of demonstrating that they are free, and out of danger. We are not stipulating deadlines at this stage because only you – I mean, your side – are in a position to know the processes and complexities involved. But once we are made aware of those details, and have agreed the timescale, we will hold you to it against the threat we have already communicated. Are you clear on that, Minister?"

"At this point…"

"As a demonstration of good faith and co-operation by us, we will agree *in principle* to your three conditions, but please be aware that once we have made the exchange – the hostages for the negotiating party – no-one will leave this ship unless our demands are met. If they are *not* met, they will die along with the rest, including me. You are quite right, I *did* expect that your chief negotiator would be accompanied, but I will only accept on board an escort of half your number – the negotiator and four others. And you can take comfort in the fact that you are putting less people at immediate risk. I ask again, Minister, are you clear on this?"

"Yes, I am clear on what you are *saying*, but I have two questions."

"Go ahead."

"Firstly, what of timing? We can have our negotiators ready to meet you tomorrow morning, though we are not in a position to give a precise time right now. Also, until we get the list of detainees, we will not be able to identify how long it will take to access and relocate them. We need to schedule a further call to finalise everything."

"Shall we say eight hours' time at nine o'clock. In the meantime, we will send the list as an attachment using the same contact number as before. And your second question."

"The device which you claim you have…"

"Claim? You don't believe…?"

"How can we be sure it is safe? You say it is currently on some sort of hair-trigger, that it is fully activated all the time and prevented from detonating by human restraint. Do you intend that the whole of the negotiations will take place under those circumstances? Because we feel such conditions are not conducive to productive dialogue. As one of my colleagues put it, 'if the wrong person sneezes'."

"All I will say, Minister, is that my mission has one objective – to secure the release of the people whose identities I am about to share with you. After achieving that, I intend to return to my family – I *do* have a family, you know – and arrangements are already in place to enable me to do that. Nowhere in that scenario is there room for me to turn myself into tiny organic fragments. So, as far as the safety of the device is concerned, let me worry about that."

★

Grace listened to the chirpy-sounding voice for the fifth time.

No-one here right now. Leave a message and you just might get lucky.

The person wasn't able to identify himself by name, she knew, because his identity depended on who was trying to contact him. She didn't leave a message. She was already annoyed at herself for leaving the second message, the second plea for him to get in touch. Because it *had* been a plea, in the sense that it must have sounded as if she was pleading with him. And being in control of her exchanges with Jamie Walcott was always important to her. Sounding that she desperately needed him had surrendered that high ground.

Even more frustrating was the unshakeable feeling that she really *did* need him; that there was no-one she would feel safer with, stepping down onto the deck of the *Mastodon*, than the brash, over-confident and spectacularly attractive man who was both the bane of her life and the focus of her fantasies. The last part at least until recently, when John Weston had taken over that role in her mind.

She checked the time on her phone: 1.55 p.m. There was still time. If he contacted her in the next few minutes – couple of hours, even – they would be able to get him to Hirta in time. Kade would not be pleased, either way, with or without Walcott. Their last parting had been acrimonious to say the least. It would be a difficult reunion, especially in a situation where there was more than enough tension and anxiety without the added dimension of personal vendettas.

Ruby suddenly dropped into the seat opposite her, interrupting her thoughts.

"Just had some news from Thames House. The Norwegians have run a scan over the *Mastodon* and have come up with no radioactivity."

Grace frowned. “Is that good? I mean, is it relevant? I’m not a nuclear physicist, but wouldn’t you only get that when a bomb went off, anyway?”

“That’s what I said, but apparently they would expect to pick up at least some low-level radiation if a nuclear device was present. ‘Not absolutely conclusive, but strongly indicative’, as the Head of PST put it to our Mr Kilby. So, we have three factors pointing towards there not being a nuclear device on board. The degree of difficulty, no record of any missing material and no evidence of radiation.”

“That’s great, I’ll just get blown up, but not atomised.”

Ruby shook her head. “You don’t have to do this, Grace. Jackie told me that Andrew had suggested they send a double. It’s probably not too late to change your mind. I can hardly believe that you *are* doing it.”

“Me, too, but it’s going to happen.”

Ruby sighed. “Okay, I’ll leave you in peace, unless you want to talk?”

“No, thanks, Ruby. I’m fine.”

Ruby returned to her seat and Grace looked out of the window of the Cessna Citation as they approached their destination on Lewis, the most northerly part of the string of islands which comprised the Outer Hebrides. The nine passenger seats in the private jet were arranged in two groups of four, two pairs facing each other across a table, plus a fold-down seat opposite the external door to the passenger compartment. As the only two passengers on this trip, Ruby and Grace each had a table to themselves. It had served both their preferences to use the time for inward reflection rather than conversation.

Below them the mighty structure of the new platform, Beta, anchored in the lee of the heights of Harris close to Tarbert, dominated the scene. Grace hardly gave it a glance. As they began to lose height over The Minch, her eyes were fixed on the group of three small islands known as the Shiants, where, eight months ago, an incident occurred that caused her life to take an irreversible step into darkness. The islands were the site of the worst thing she had ever done in a career during which she had done many bad things.

They descended further, now less than a hundred metres above the water, passing over Eilean Mhuire, the island to the east, where, just a short distance off its northern tip, Tom Brown had breathed his last. She had watched him die, not right there in The Minch, but on the screen in the monitoring suite on HMS *Jura*, as his vital indicators flatlined. Her doing; her accountability for the death of one of the best men she had ever known. A man who, without knowing it, had rescued her from a life of bitterness by unlocking feelings she had suppressed for half her existence.

★

DC Alice Grantham appeared in the doorway of Harry Waters's office. Harry was gazing, unfocussed towards the window, deep in thought. She gave a little cough bringing him out of his trance. Alice was in her early thirties, a tall, slim woman with a mass of brown curls framing an attractive ebony face.

"Are we ready?"

"Yes, sir. I've briefed Detective Sergeant Carter. He said to call at 2.15 and he'll be with her in a room away from the rest of the MIT. So that's…" she checked her watch "… six minutes from now."

Harry drew in a long breath. "Okay. This, I am definitely *not* looking forward to."

"I know, sir, but it has to be done."

Harry stared at the wall clock, not knowing whether he wanted it to race through the next few minutes or stop altogether.

"Where's Nat?" he asked.

"Still at the mortuary, then she's going straight round to Marie Lockwood's, David Gerrard's partner. She's expecting to meet you there later."

"And Mr Kemp. Any sign?"

"Afraid not. Last I heard the uniforms were checking the wheelie bins behind the guest house. I think they're in denial that he got past them."

"Well, make sure they keep on looking." He checked the time. "Three more minutes. I think I'll get myself a coffee."

"I'll do that, sir. You can work on your speech."

Alice returned two minutes later with a Styrofoam beaker and placed it on the desk in front of him.

"Don't worry, sir. Think how many times you've done this before."

"I'm not so much worried about the call as I am about the next time I meet her."

He picked up his phone and stared at it for a long time, gathering his thoughts before scrolling through his contacts. He glanced up at his colleague. "Okay, Alice, I'll see you later."

"Right, sir."

Alice left the room and Harry pressed the name on the screen. The call was answered straight away.

"Hey, Harry. This is a surprise."

"Hi, Jo. Is DS Carter with you?"

"Well… yes." A pause. "But he won't be jealous, so just go ahead and…"

"Jo, there isn't an easy way to say this. There's been an incident, earlier today, involving David. A shooting. I'm so sorry, but I'm afraid he's dead."

CHAPTER TWENTY-NINE

2.30 p.m. BST

The Prime Minister leaned back in his chair and spread his hands.

"So, that's the story so far, ladies and gentlemen. You now know as much as I do of what has gone before, and I repeat – the identity of our chief negotiator is not to be mentioned outside this room until such time as I say."

The mood in the Cabinet Room at 10 Downing Street was, understandably, tense. Since the meeting began, on the hour at 2.00 p.m., Andrew had been the only one in the room who had spoken as he brought the twenty-eight members of his inner circle up to date with developments. The two people missing from the meeting were Jonathan Latiffe, who was still at Thames House, in case of any unscheduled contact from the *Mastodon*, and Ruby Weller, currently in Stornoway, along with Grace Goody, awaiting the arrival of the Dutch engineer, before their onward journey to Hirta.

"So, what happens now?" Andrew continued. "Well, the plan, as it stands, is for Grace to arrive on the *Mastodon* tomorrow morning at a time yet to be established. Accompanying her will be an armed escort, which I understand will comprise five people – one man and one woman from Special Forces, along with three members of the International Hostage Rescue group, one of whom, an American, Colonel Kade, will be in overall charge.

"We had proposed a guard for Grace of eight people, el Taqha said four, and we've settled on five, but Kade is satisfied with that number. At this moment in time we are still trying to locate an individual who may join them, displacing one member of the Special Forces. That's a detail which, I am told, will not affect timing or operational plans. The terrorists have agreed to the three conditions Jonathan put to them, so we are, as the Americans say, good to go. However, since that was all agreed, we have received two more pieces of information.

"Firstly, and most significantly, the names of the people they want released, eighty-seven in total. And along with the names came the rather chilling statement that no-one will be allowed off the ship until we have released *all* of those on the list. If we fail to agree to their release, they will detonate the bomb, killing all on board the vessel, including the negotiating party. We have MI6 working with that list right now, but their recommendation is – as always – that we should not release any, let alone all, of the people named. No surprises, we have always said that we do not negotiate with terrorists. And let me assure you all, while I am Prime Minister, that will never change."

There was a turning of heads as people looked at each other and back to Andrew; a few half-murmured comments.

"So why are we sending Grace Goody to her death on the *Mastodon*, Prime Minister?" The murmurs were replaced by an expectant silence after Lawrence Harding asked the question. "I mean, with respect, that is more or less what you have just said, isn't it?"

Andrew smiled. "You seem to have a great regard for the welfare of Ms Goody, Lawrence." The silence gave way to knowing chuckles from one or two around the table. "Which is very commendable, by the way. But you must have been aware – all of you – even before we knew what their demands were, that we would never accede to them. This mission is *not* a negotiation; it is a rescue. And by asking to meet face to face on the *Mastodon*, el Taqha has played right into our hands. But before we go into that, let me share with you the second piece of information.

"Our MI5 colleagues at Thames House have received information from the Norwegian Police Security Service that – as far as it is possible to tell – there are no nuclear materials on board the *Mastodon*. The whole length of the ship was scanned at deck level for traces of radioactivity and they found nothing. But I repeat, that is *as far as it is possible to tell*."

A short period of reflective silence was ended by Reggie Greyburn, Chancellor of the Exchequer, seated on Andrew's immediate right.

"Does this mean we can effectively rule out the possibility of their having a nuclear device on board?"

"Even with the other evidence, or perhaps we should say informed speculation, I still don't believe it is safe to assume that, but the odds are decidedly against it. That doesn't mean they don't have a bomb on board, but if it is a conventional weapon, it reduces the potential number of hostages – according to their own estimates – from thirty thousand to around eight hundred. They still need saving. They are British citizens, and our responsibility."

The Defence Secretary raised a hand. "Excuse me, Prime Minister, but if we have no intention of releasing any of the eighty-seven people named by the terrorists, why are there key players in the military and secret service going through the list of names? Isn't that a waste of time?"

"Good question, Bernard," Andrew said, turning to the person on his immediate left. "Jackie, would you like to answer that, please?"

Jackie leaned forward in her seat as Andrew leaned back, so she could see everyone around the table.

"It's important, obviously, that we give the impression that we are genuinely considering the release of these people. It won't be easy to convince this man, unless we can get into some detailed discussion with him. He is not expecting it to be straightforward, because these individuals he has named are scattered around Europe in six or seven different locations. Some are not directly under our supervision at present and are being held, in effect, by proxy until we decide what action to take against them.

"Which means, even if we were prepared to release them, there are miles of red tape to unravel. Given that Grace's true role is decoy rather than negotiator, in that she is there to hold attention and buy time, this sort of complexity will stretch the proceedings and make that extra time available to the rescue teams, if necessary. So, we need detailed information on every one of the eighty-seven people on that list to be able to convince el Taqha that we are seriously addressing his demand."

"Does everybody understand that?" Andrew asked. He looked round the room to acknowledge the nodding heads, then turned back to the Home Secretary. "Jackie, could you briefly tell us –

without compromising anything – what happens next on the way to saving our lost souls."

"Well first, just to clarify what the Prime Minister meant about the terrorists playing into our hands. As I said, the so-called negotiating team will be, in effect, a decoy to focus the terrorists' attention. Without el Taqha's insistence to negotiate on board the *Mastodon*, this option would not have been available to us. As the main event progresses on deck, this will allow two covert assault teams – one of which is already in place – to do their work. I cannot tell you more because I am not aware of the details of the plan, nor do I wish to be. It will need to be fluid and adaptable, anyway, and we can take much comfort from the fact that the teams carrying it out are world-class, if not the very *best* in the world. I am, however, party to its objectives, which are threefold. To find and nullify the threat of the explosive device, to ensure the safety of Grace, her escort and the remainder of the Scandoil hostages and, once and for all time, to take the world's most dangerous terrorist out of circulation."

"Capture him, you mean, Home Secretary?" someone asked.

"Preferably."

"Or kill him," Andrew added.

*

"So, you didn't get to tell her any details?" Alice glanced across at her boss as she edged the unmarked police car through the heavy mid-afternoon traffic along Southway towards the Royal Surrey County Hospital on Egerton Road.

"No, a lot of shrieking and I could hear Seb talking to her, trying to calm her down. She'll be okay when he gets her away from there."

"And he's bringing her down here?"

"That's right. They're going to Marie Lockwood's. It's going to be quite a party."

They had been reduced to a crawl, but Harry had declined Alice's offer to use the blue light to hasten their journey. There's enough chaos, he said, without a hundred cars trying to create an extra lane out of nothing. And anyway, it gave him longer to think about their forthcoming interview with Mr Weaver.

They eventually parked in a place reserved for them close to the main entrance and were met by the doctor who had tended the injured man's wound when he arrived a few hours ago. He introduced himself as Dr Asif Khan.

"He took a hell of a hit," Dr Khan said. "But his skull must be exceptionally thick, and I don't see any sign of lasting damage. We'll need to keep him in a couple of days just to be safe. I haven't asked him anything about the incident, as you requested, but he does keep saying he can't remember what happened. This is quite common. The brain always takes time – a few hours sometimes – to transfer stuff from the short-term to the long-term memory. If that process is interrupted in circumstances like this, people often can't recall things right up to the point they lost consciousness. Over the period of a day or two, much – if not all – of that memory may return, but right now he might not be able to tell you what you want to know.

"I just mention this, so you don't think he's being evasive or unco-operative. He might be both of those things as well, of course, but, please, just bear in mind what I've told you and don't push him too hard if he gets confused. I'll pop my head in after about twenty minutes or so to check everything's okay. If you need me before then, I'll show you where I'll be. Okay?"

"Thank you, doctor. We'll be gentle with him."

Dr Khan smiled. "I'm sure you will. This way, please."

He led them up a flight of stairs to a private room, outside of which two uniformed police officers sat side by side on a couple of chairs, staring into their iPhone screens. Inside, Danny Weaver lay propped up on pillows against the angled bedhead watching *Antiques Road Trip* on the huge wall-mounted TV. His hospital robe covered his chest up to his throat, but his powerful tattooed arms were bare from his shoulders and crossed in front of him. Harry noted he automatically flexed his biceps as they entered as if instinctively sending out a message to his visitors. His head was heavily bandaged to just above his eyebrows and there was dark bruising around his eyes.

Harry introduced himself and Alice and looked across at the screen.

"Sorry, we're going to have to terminate your entertainment for now, Mr Weaver." He picked up the remote from the bedside table and turned off the set. "How's the head?"

"Aching, but the same shape as before, they tell me. No harm done, according to the medics."

"It was a hell of a thing he hit you with. I understand they'll be keeping an eye on you for a day or two."

"Fine by me. This is a lot better than my place. TV's three times as big for a start."

Harry pulled a couple of chairs across to the side of the bed and he and Alice sat down.

"We need to go through with you what happened today, as much as you can tell us. Do you feel up to having a chat right now?"

"Sure, but as I told the doc, I can't remember anything that happened after driving past the guest house on Washbrook Road and parking near the corner of Westmore Street. I remember seeing this road-sweeping thing working its way along Westmore towards Washbrook. I switched the engine off and decided to wait until it finished, and, after that… nothing."

"Okay, but can you remember what you were *intending* to do?"

"Well, yes, of course. I can remember the *plan*, because that came *before* all that."

"Right, well let's go through that, then."

CHAPTER THIRTY

At a few minutes after 4.00 p.m., the Sikorsky S92 UK coast guard helicopter began its decent down to the helipad close to the observation tower on the western slope of Mullach Mor, the highest point of Hirta, and of the whole St Kilda archipelago. Grace could see the cluster of people standing well back from the giant "H" on the flattened area. Most were looking up towards the aircraft but it was impossible to identify anyone from an angle which gave a view of just head and shoulders, the rest of their bodies tucked underneath.

Given the ordeal that was facing her over the next few days, it was surprising that the only thing causing her any anxiety at that moment was her first contact with Kade. She went over in her mind again their last parting, the details of which had come more into focus the closer she got to the time of their meeting. Was there anything in that final exchange which would serve as a suitable bridge to their renewing what until eight months ago had been a fruitful association based on mutual trust and respect? It was not her fault. His reaction to that last assignment had been unreasonable; he knew the rules; it was a job, just a job; that's what they were trained for and what they had to do.

The objective of the mission had been straightforward enough, albeit a significant challenge to carry out. Get Jason Midanda – a.k.a. Oliver Wangari – off Platform Alpha. He had proved himself a threat to the security of the platform. A hacking superstar, he had interfered with control systems and communicated – through a transmitter/receiver he had constructed himself – with a number of diverse organisations, many of them politically active. Quite possibly including – for all they knew at the time – Islamic State terrorist cells. Kade's team on that occasion had included Tom Brown, former Home Secretary, ex-special forces, but more importantly a close acquaintance of Midanda – a prospective father-in-law, in fact. That was before Jason had been convicted of dealing Class A drugs, an offence which, under the provisions of the NJR, carried a mandatory expulsion as a lifetime exile.

The first part of the mission's objective was successfully completed. Jason was removed and the transmitter he had constructed destroyed. Kade's failing had been with the second part of the plan, which was to leave Tom behind on the platform. Following his son's death, the Home Secretary had become a liability in his outspoken condemnation of his own New Justice Regime, and, as a result, a risk to the stability of the government, which had come to power primarily on the promise of its implementation. Tom's disappearance would have been irreversible and his life expectancy almost certainly very short. The exiles would soon realise that this newcomer was the very man who was responsible for putting them there. Kade, she had learned, had the chance to do it; he even went so far as to isolate Tom with the exiles before changing his mind and bringing him back with the rest of his team, plus Jason.

It was hardly surprising, she realised in retrospect, that Tom would make a favourable impression on Kade. After all, they were two of a kind, birds of a feather. But the American should have been professional enough to put any personal empathy aside and do his job. He *had* done it in the end – under protest – dropping the comatose Tom Brown into The Minch to end his days "through natural causes". A case of drowning, pure and simple, if the body was ever found. They would never be able to detect in his bloodstream the minute quantities of the drug which inhibited his regaining consciousness even as his lungs filled with water. Just to be sure, however, they had had their own forensic team standing by to carry out the post-mortem if required. It had been an unnecessary precaution. Tom had co-operated by taking eight months to make his reappearance; by which time there was hardly a trace of anything left, let alone any evidence of medical assistance.

So, everything had worked out: Tom out of the way and the threat to the smooth running of Alpha negated, but Kade's parting exchange with her still grated on her memory.

"Don't screw up this time, Kade," she had said, as he prepared to leave with Tom's unconscious body. She had held out her hand to him and he had looked at it in disgust for a long time before shaking his head.

"Sorry, ma'am, daren't risk it," he said. "Whatever it is you've got, it might be contagious."

She came out of her trance to see Ruby already standing at the door as the rotors slowed and began to dip. Next to her, the engineer from Boskalis, Jens Reinhardt, tall, blond and very Dutch in his good looks, waited to disembark. Jens smiled at Grace as she got to her feet and collected her shoulder bag and briefcase. He waved an arm in a flamboyant "after you" gesture as one of the cabin crew slid back the door and leaned out of the aircraft, anchoring against the fuselage the set of steps that was wheeled up to it.

Grace watched Sir Roger duck under the slow-spinning blades to welcome them. She looked past him at the twenty or so other people around the edge of the helipad, hoping to see Kade and get this confrontation out of the way. He was nowhere to be seen, but there was a face she did recognise although it now sported a neat goatee beard. Mike Needham was around average height and in his mid-sixties, and was the designer responsible for taking the largest oil producing platform in the world and converting it into the eight hundred self-contained apartments known as Hotel St Kilda.

Mike seemed not to notice her, however, and walked across to introduce himself to Jens. That was fine by her, because his presence did nothing to address her feelings of guilt and anxiety. The last time she had been in Mike's company was in the IT suite of HMS *Jura* where they had sat, together, just the two of them, and watched Tom Brown die on their monitor screen.

*

The two kilometres of bouncing and zig-zagging in the first of the three Army Range Rovers taking the arrivals and reception committee to their meeting place, was an unpleasant contrast to the smooth flight from Stornoway. By the time she and Ruby were approaching Village Bay in the west of the island, after only a few minutes in the vehicle, Grace was feeling quite travel-sick.

"Has anyone thought of building a proper road between the two sites?" Grace asked the driver.

"An accident of timing, ma'am, I'm afraid. The old military road is under repair right now, which is why we have to take the scenic route. It really needs a completely new link road building but that's not part of the MOD's agreement with the National Trust of Scotland. St Kilda is a dual World Heritage site, one of only twenty-four in the whole world, and we can only do so much development above ground. But it does have the longest street in the whole of the outer isles, which, as a special treat, I'm about to drive you through now."

The two women looked in fascination as they passed the row of thirty or so houses, all uninhabited and mostly just stone shells, but a few with thatched or corrugated-iron roofs.

"Hard to believe that these islands were self-sufficient for centuries up to less than a hundred years ago," Ruby said.

"And now we're back" Grace said, "and mainly underground this time."

"Another one of the rules, ma'am," the driver half-turned to speak. "And a hell of a lot warmer in winter down there. You spend a winter here and you realise just how amazing it was that people survived. Nothing could get on or off this island for seven, eight, sometimes nine months of the year. October through to May it was a no-go area because of weather."

"So how *did* people survive?" Ruby asked.

"Living on things they'd collected and saved during the summer – the *so-called* summer. Seabirds mainly, I believe, ones they'd caught and salted away underground and in cleits. Those are the little stone stores you can see behind the houses along the street."

Grace and Ruby's minds were transported to another simpler, if harder, world, before the Range Rover slowed to a halt in front of a low single-storey building. Its squareness and regularity were evidence of its being a new build, but it had been cladded with local stone in an attempt to blend it into the surrounding primitive architecture. It was certainly more aesthetically pleasing than the scattered ruins of the Cold War era.

Two people were already standing outside the front door of the building. The man and the woman approached the car as Grace and

Ruby half-stepped, half-slid out of the vehicle. Grace's first contact for eight months with ex-Navy SEAL Colonel Marty Kade proved to be an anti-climax. He extended his hand, first to Ruby, then to Grace. The American, in his mid-forties, was tall and slim with dark hair and the classic features associated with Hollywood movie stars in the 1950s and 60s. His eyes were ice-blue and intense.

"Welcome to the wild side of life, ladies," he said with a wide smile, showing perfect teeth. "This is Doctor van Roden, one of my team and…" he turned to Grace "… with no apology, Lydia will be putting words into your mouth, Ms Goody. But only to help and only when necessary, of course."

They both shook hands with Lydia. "You must be drained after your journey," she said. "Let's go inside and drink some very good coffee before we get started."

Kade opened the door to the building and waved the three women inside ahead of him. Lydia led the way through a pair of automatic sliding double doors to a landing with a central descending staircase and an escalator on each side: one up, one down.

"Shall we walk or ride?" Lydia smiled.

"Walk, I think," Ruby said. "Our lower limbs have hardly moved for hours."

"I need to make a call first, in private," Grace said. "Just a few minutes. Better now before we start."

"No problem. In here." Lydia opened the door to a small meeting room off the landing. "Ms Weller and Kade can go ahead; I'll wait out here."

Grace stepped through into the room and Lydia closed the door behind her. She pressed the last name on the list of recent calls.

No-one here right now. Leave a message and you just might get lucky.

"Fuck," she said, then turned to the door, wondering if the woman outside might have heard. Not that it mattered, she thought; given what she was about to put herself through, she was probably allowed a few expletives along the way. She checked her watch: 5.05 p.m. Still enough time to get him there, but running out.

She called again, this time leaving a message.

"I don't know what the fuck you're playing at, Walcott. It's five minutes past five in the afternoon. If you haven't phoned me back by seven o'clock – that's within two hours – don't count on *ever* being able to make another phone call in the future."

At least not pleading this time. She opened the door. Lydia was leaning against the rail at the top of the stairs. Grace stopped, feeling there was something disconcerting about this confident, statuesque woman. She walked across to join her.

Lydia smiled. "Any more news?"

"Yes, but about another matter. I'd just about forgotten I had a proper day job before this happened."

"Let's ride," Lydia said, stepping onto the escalator. She turned to Grace from the moving step below her as they set off on the long descent. Her smile had gone and her expression was hard and serious. "Kade tells me you had a different job altogether before the one you're doing now. Not a lot different to the one we do, in fact. It explains a lot. For example, how you could do what you did to someone you'd worked so closely with for so long. It makes a lot more sense now."

Grace glared straight back at Lydia. "Now is not the time for accusations and recriminations, doctor."

Lydia raised her hands in a placatory gesture. "Hey, no criticism intended, just a statement of fact. No-one in Kade's team is in a position to moralise about what you did. Your job, isn't that right? *We've* been paid for doing a lot worse, and just because I don't pull any triggers, we're all equally responsible. For what it's worth, Grace, we think it's an amazing thing you're going to do. I'm not sure I'd be willing to stand on that deck with Abu el Taqha a few metres away. You don't know what he might be wearing under his coat, for a start."

Grace gave a thin smile. "Not my idea of a good time, either, Lydia, but you'll be there in spirit, won't you? It will be your words coming out of my mouth, like Kade said."

"Your words, my suggestions. And, that's about as close as I want to get."

"Yes, well, there is a lot at stake for me, which I won't go into now."

"John Weston. Yes, I know. You must think a lot about him to take this sort of risk just so you don't have to deceive him."

Grace opened her eyes wide. "You're very well informed."

Lydia turned and they stepped off the escalator, moving aside and standing together.

"It's not difficult to work out, Grace. You're going on to the *Mastodon* to deter a US attack. Normally we'd send a double, but then what happens if the double gets killed? What's Mr Weston going to think when you call him to say you're okay?"

"I'm impressed, unless you've been talking with our Prime Minister."

"It's sort of my job, Grace. Trying to see into people's minds." She gave a little laugh. "I remember Tom saying..." Her voice trailed off leaving an uncomfortable silence.

"Saying what?" Grace spoke in hardly more than a whisper. "Something wrong?"

Lydia shook her head and sniffed a little laugh. "Nothing. It's just... well, I guess I liked working with him. He's funny, and kind... *was* funny and kind, I mean." She paused for a moment. "Just a job, right?"

"Right. So, what did he say?"

"Sorry?"

"You were going to tell me what Tom said about you seeing into people's minds."

"Oh, yes. He said something like, 'I'd better be careful what I'm thinking, then'. That's all."

"And what was he thinking?"

"No idea, but nothing about me, if that's what you're asking. Anyway, I promised you some coffee. We'd better go."

They set off along a short, wide corridor through another set of automatic doors into an expansive cafeteria. Around the walls were large glass panels with backlights to give the impression of daylight outside. There were about a hundred people in the room, filling most of the tables. Heads turned as the two women – one dark, one blonde, both beautiful – made their way to the far end, where Kade, Ruby and Sir Roger awaited them. Kade pulled out a chair for Grace, so she was sitting with her back to the room.

"Okay, Kade," Lydia said. "Do you want to show off your waitering skills, or shall I pour?"

"Let me." Kade filled two more beakers from the coffee pot on the table and placed them in front of the late arrivals. Grace swivelled in her seat and looked around the room. Most of the faces were turned towards them. Some nodded, some smiled, some did both. At the far end of the room, close to the door, one man sat alone. He did not acknowledge her with a smile or a nod, but she sensed an intensity in his look behind the dark-tinted lenses of his glasses. She turned back to the table and took a sip of her coffee.

She froze, putting the beaker down and turning back to the room. She looked across at the same table; it was now unoccupied. But she was sure there had been someone there less than half a minute before. Just the one person. She had not recognised him, as such, but there was something familiar… or had she imagined him, or at least the familiarity? She turned back to the confused looks on her companions' faces.

"Sorry," she said, smiling. "I don't suppose there's any chance this place is haunted?"

★

The traffic had got much worse by the time Harry and Alice set out on the drive to Marie Lockwood's home on the Cullen Field estate, in Marlburgh, East London. After suffering the white-water experience of joining the anti-clockwise M25 at a little after five o'clock, then having slowed to a crawl, Harry had given way to Alice's persistence and she lowered the window, placing the magnetic light on the roof. Responding to the blue flashes and the siren, the traffic ahead parted like the Red Sea and they had arrived at the estate before 6.00 p.m.

"Great driving, DC Grantham. Close to a world's best time, I shouldn't be surprised." He looked across at the door of Marie's small townhouse. "They must be here by now, I guess. It's what, a couple of hours from Leicester?"

"About that." She smiled at him. "Best get it over with."

He reached for the door handle as his phone bleeped to signal an incoming text. He checked the screen.

"It's Nat," he said, showing Alice the screen. "*Be there in 5 mins*". Do you think we should wait and all go in together?"

Alice gave a little laugh this time. "No, I don't, sir. We should go in now. You did what was necessary. Jo will know that."

He looked again at Marie's front door and noticed a curtain twitching in the window of the room next to it.

"Okay, let's go. They've seen us, anyway."

They got out of the car as the front door was opened by a woman they assumed was Marie. The muscles in her jaw and neck were taut and she looked stressed and anxious, but she stepped forward and extended her arm to greet each of them with a friendly handshake.

"DI Waters?"

"That's right, and DC Alice Grantham. And you must be Marie. We're very pleased to meet you."

Marie stepped back inside and waved them into a tiny hall, not much more than a metre square, with a door off to the right and one straight ahead. She edged round them to close the front door.

"You can imagine what it's been like getting David through here."

She gave a little laugh.

"I take it they've arrived?" Harry asked.

"Yes, they're in there," she said in a hushed voice, nodding to the door on the right. "Please, go through."

Harry took a deep breath and pushed open the door to enter a tastefully furnished through room. Immediately in front of them was the dining area with a table and four matching chairs. In the rear half of the room, on the left, a door led off to what Harry assumed was the kitchen, and an open-plan staircase climbed back towards the front of the house to the first floor. Three wing chairs formed a shallow semicircle at one side of a long, low table facing a large leather sofa which almost spanned the full width of the room and on which sat Jo Cottrell and a very large man who Harry knew must Seb Carter. They were sitting apart and the tension in the room was tangible. They both got quickly to their feet, Jo's arms stiff by her sides and hands clenched into tight fists. Her face was flushed and her eyes red-rimmed.

"Jo, I'm really..." Harry began. Alice stepped past him and walked over to Jo; they hugged each other in silence as Jo's eyes filled with tears. Seb stepped forward and held out his hand to Harry.

"Detective Sergeant Carter, sir. Very pleased to meet you."

Harry shook the enormous hand without taking his eyes off Jo. "And you too, Seb. Please call me Harry."

The doorbell rang and they all turned to look at Marie. She gasped and held her hands to her chest, then turned and hurried through to the hallway, closing the door behind her. They heard the front door pulled open, and Marie's quiet sobbing. Another woman's voice, and Natalie stepped into the room, closing the door again. She went over immediately to Jo, and repeated Alice's silent embrace.

They all turned as the door opened.

CHAPTER THIRTY-ONE

6.00 p.m. BST

Given the urgency of the situation, a coffee break of a little over an hour seemed to Grace a bit of a luxury, although they had used the opportunity to each express their private thoughts about the pending drama, and the shared concerns served as a form of therapy. So, when they eventually rose from the table to leave the cafeteria the mood was calm and relaxed. They exited through a side door to a large reception area with a suite of rooms leading off it through a pair of frosted-glass doors. Another short, wide corridor gave access to a large meeting room at the end and two smaller ones to either side.

Grace's phone trilled. She took it from her shoulder bag and checked the screen. It was from her surveillance team.

"Sorry, I need to take this… in private, I'm afraid."

"No problem," Lydia said. "In here." She opened the door to one of the smaller rooms on the left. "If you all go through to the main meeting room, I'll wait here and make sure Grace doesn't get lost."

Grace answered the call as she stepped through into the room, Lydia closing the door behind her.

"Connor?" she said. "This is not a good time. It needs to be very quick, whatever it is."

"Okay. We picked this up at 2.15 this afternoon. Harry Waters calling Jo Cottrell. I'll just play the first bit of the call. Okay?"

"Go ahead."

There was a click on her phone, followed by the recording.

Hey, Harry. This is a surprise.

Hi, Jo. Is DS Carter with you?

Well… yes. A pause. *But he won't be jealous, so just go ahead and…*

Jo, there is no easy way to say this. There's been an incident, earlier today, involving David. A shooting. I'm so sorry, but I'm afraid he's dead.

There was a brief silence followed by a scream of despair. The recording was paused.

"There's a lot more anguish and distress and shrieking," Connor said, "but that's the end of their conversation. It sounds like the phone was dropped. The boyfriend – Seb – must have picked it up because next you can hear him ask when and where. Waters says around 9.30 at a place in Guildford, and that the shooter was a guy named Danny Weaver, ex-con, someone who Gerrard put away for a long time. Tells Seb to look after Cottrell and to call him back if he wants to know any more details. Then the phone gets switched off. Do you want to hear the whole thing, ma'am?"

Grace didn't answer; she felt physically sick. She thought about the last conversation she had with Walcott. This had to be his doing – even if he didn't pull the trigger.

"Ma'am, are you still there? I said, do you want to listen to the whole recording?"

"No, not if that's all that was said. No call back since then?"

"No, ma'am. The phone hasn't been used again. If the boyfriend did phone for more details, he must have used his own phone, or a land line at the station."

Grace's mind was racing.

"Look, can you contact Jamie Walcott and…"

"Been trying, ma'am, for nearly four hours, since we heard the call. When we couldn't get him, we forwarded him a copy of the recording, asking him to confirm he'd received it. Not heard anything back yet. We're only calling you because we can't get hold of him, otherwise we wouldn't be bothering you, what with all that's happening. I guess you might be involved with the hijack in some way. Am I right?"

"Just a bit."

"In which case, I'm sorry if I've interrupted anything but I thought someone should know about Gerrard's death."

Grace was silent again for a while, her stomach recovering from the shock.

"No, you were right to tell me, Connor. Keep trying to get Walcott and when – *if* – you do, tell him he *must* call me right away. Okay? And keep listening for Cottrell's phone."

"Yes, ma'am, that's what we do *all* the time."

Grace ended the call without registering the hint of sarcasm in the caller's last remark. She waited for a couple of minutes before joining Lydia, turning things over in her mind. A coincidence? David Gerrard's death and – on the same day – the first time, for as far back as she could remember, she had been unable to contact Walcott. Sometimes she'd had to leave a message, but he invariably got back to her – within minutes, usually, and always in less than an hour. She checked her watch: 6.08 p.m. It was seven hours since she first phoned him.

Not a coincidence, then.

*

Marie entered the room, her arm trailing behind her as she held on tightly to the hand of David Gerrard. Jo flew across the room into his arms, then stepped back half a pace and pounded his chest with her fists.

"Don't you ever do that again, you big, stupid bastard."

David pulled her to him and swayed back and forth holding her close to his chest.

"Do what again? Die, do you mean? Well, perhaps just *once* more but not for a long time yet."

Jo broke away and turned to Harry. "And you're a bastard as well. How could you *do* that?"

"Didn't Seb explain?"

Jo pointed to Seb without looking at him. "And he's the biggest bastard of all."

Seb spread his arms wide and shrugged in a gesture of innocence.

"That's not true. David's at least an inch taller than me."

"Don't you make a joke of this, you… you…"

"Bastard?" Seb prompted.

"I've got an idea." They all turned to look at Marie. "Let's sit down, I'll make us some tea, and then we'll listen while someone explains what's going on. I'm sure there are enough seats for everyone if Jo and Seb can manage to sit a bit closer to each other this time. Okay?"

Everyone looked around sheepishly and gravitated to the chairs and sofa.

"I'll help," Alice said, and followed Marie out of the room.

They returned a few minutes later with a tray each, Alice's holding seven china mugs plus a plate containing a pile of chocolate digestives, Marie's with the largest teapot any of them had ever seen, a milk jug and a sugar bowl. They set them down on the coffee table, and, when the refreshments had been administered to all, Harry turned to David.

"I guess it's your story to tell, if you're up to it."

David rubbed his chest. "Still a little sore when I breathe, but I guess I need to kick it off at least. And it actually starts before any of us in this room got involved, with a certain Danny Weaver in a pub in Clapham."

He reached over and took Marie's hand.

"Last Saturday, Marie and I were in the Dog and Duck in Meadow Village with the usual Saturday night crowd, when Danny Weaver came in. Danny was a big noise among the criminal element in and around Clapham back in the nineties. Did a few favours for the police, in fact, by getting rid of some of the baddest villains around at the time: his competition, in effect. Anyway, I was working at the Met then and it was my first case as Senior Investigating Officer. Long story short, we put him down for twenty years and he got out just a couple of months ago. He was the one I told you about, Harry. Like Deverall…" he smiled across at Jo "… we put someone away who was doing our job for us."

He rubbed his chest and took a couple of deep breaths.

"You okay?" Marie said, squeezing his hand.

"Yes fine, thanks." He took a sip of his tea. "Anyway, he started making a nuisance of himself so Jed, the landlord, and I threw him out…"

"Oh, is Jed still there?" It was Jo who interrupted.

David smiled. "Yes, he's still there. You'd better watch her with this guy, Seb. He makes Jean-Claude van Damme look like Gollum out of *Lord of the Rings*."

They all laughed.

"Anyway, he made a few threats against me outside and as I was walking home later, he was waiting for me in the lane. He said to me, 'I never killed anybody who didn't deserve to be dead'. And, like I said, he's probably right. Then he said, 'and I've decided that you *don't* deserve to be dead, but I've just met a couple of guys who think different'."

He paused and took another deep breath.

"So, we went back to my place, had a couple of malts – bizarre really – and he told me about these two he'd met in the Remington Arms in Clapham He'd been having a quiet pint and overheard them talking about me. They were saying I was getting too close to something and that they might need to get someone to take me out."

Marie drew in her breath and shuddered, pushing herself closer up against David.

"Danny said he got curious and sort of introduced himself, not *as* himself, but as someone who might be interested in helping them. He said they tried to ignore him at first, but eventually they started taking him seriously and agreed to meet him again – at a place called Middleton Green. Do you know it?"

Harry turned to Natalie. "That's where George found Sammo's body in amongst the ducks, isn't it? And where Mrs – what was her name…?"

"Thornbury," Natalie said.

"Thornbury, that's right. Where Mrs Thornbury saw a guy *with* Sammo a few days earlier. She put a mugshot of him together with the e-fit guys. Said she thought he looked like a film star, didn't she?"

"That's right," Natalie said.

"A film star?" David frowned and reached for his phone. "Speaking of which." He switched it on and opened the photo file, scrolled through it, then enlarged an image with his finger and thumb. He held it up for them all to see then passed it to Harry. "Danny sent me some pictures this afternoon, ones he'd taken of the two men he met in the Remington Arms, He waited in his car after he left the pub and took them when they came out. This one is the guy who shot me. Danny reckons he looks like Ray Liotta, the main man in the *Goodfellas* movie."

The phone was being passed around the group and stopped with Natalie, who gave a little gasp.

"What, Nat?"

"I'm sure I know him, sir. Or someone very like him." She frowned in concentration, then looked up and passed the phone back to Harry. "Unless – because you just mentioned it – I'm thinking of Mrs T's e-fit picture. What do you think?"

"Couldn't say. I don't remember it that well."

Alice leaned across. "Could I see it again, please, sir?" Harry held the phone out for her to look. "I'd have to see the e-fit again, but it *could* be the man Mrs Thornbury described."

"One way to find out," Harry said. He checked his watch. "Six-forty." He took out his phone and scrolled through his contacts. "Let's see if George is still awake."

He made the call, which was answered straight away.

"DC Clancy speaking. Oh, hi, sir. What a nice surprise so *late* in the day."

"You'll thank me when you hear what I want, George. You know that really nice lady who helped you find Sammo and made you into a hero? Well, I'd like you to go and see her again. I'm going to text you a photograph of a man we're looking for. I'd like you to check if it's the same one she described for the e-fit boys."

"You mean *now*, sir? It's a bit late. She's got a little girl…"

"Who's about five or six, I seem to remember. You're not going to wake her up or anything. Where are you now?"

"At home, just about to start a seven-course meal, but I suppose it will keep. I'm only about fifteen minutes away. I guess I should phone first."

"We need her to ID him as soon as, George. So just go round, don't give her the chance to put you off. She won't even have to invite you in; she can tell you on the doorstep."

"Right, on my way. Send me the photo."

Harry ended the call and handed David's phone back to him. "Can you do that, please, David? Here's George's number." He held up his own phone so David could enter it before attaching the photograph and sending the text.

"Having done that," Harry said, "I'm not sure what it's going to tell us if it is the same guy. Can we see a picture of the other one, David?"

David changed the image and gave the phone to Harry, whose eyes opened wide. He passed it to Natalie.

"Mr Kemp. Our pickled merchandiser."

"This is the man we interviewed," Natalie explained. "The one who crocked Weaver. Which is a good link back to your story, David."

"Yes, please carry on," Harry said. "You'd got up to where you were getting pissed with a murderer."

Alice got to her feet and topped up their mugs from the bottomless teapot. David continued.

"A couple of days after the first meeting in the Remington – the day before he turned up at the Dog – Danny went to Middleton Green for the second meeting, but only Ray Liotta turned up this time. He gave Danny five grand in fifties with the promise of a further ten when he'd completed the job."

"Bet you didn't think you were worth fifteen grand, did you?" Harry said.

"Well, obviously I'm not, because it never happened, did it? He told Danny they'd set me up with a phoney meeting and let him know where I'd be and when. He'd just go along and dispatch me. So, there'd be nothing to link Danny with the hit because he'd have no part in setting it up. No way it could be traced back to him."

"Danny Weaver told you all this over a wee dram at your place?" Jo said.

"Well, not so 'wee'. I'd like to claim the credit for his crossing over from the dark side. Outside the pub, I gave him the benefit of my standard question to potential re-offenders. 'Are you going to look forward or back?' But he'd already chosen his way forward and saw this chance meeting with the two guys as an opportunity to prove that... he said."

"Well he didn't sound much like a reformed character when he confronted you in the pub," Marie said. "I thought he was going to start on you there and then."

David laughed, then grimaced and rubbed his chest again.

"Danny explained that. He said that was his insurance. After making a big scene like that, there was no way he'd be able to change his mind and take me out without everybody pointing the finger straight at him. So that scene on Saturday blew the Goodfellas' plans right out of the water."

"So up to then he was still thinking about it?" Jo asked. "He couldn't trust himself *not* to make the hit?"

"I can't say for certain, Jo, but, as I said, I *believe* he had made up his mind before he came to the village. I must have been pretty certain about him, because he stayed over at my place..."

"*What?*" Marie pulled away and turned to face him. "That was a ridiculous chance to take, an hour after he'd threatened you in the pub!"

David smiled and pulled her back against him. "I guess it must sound like it, but I really felt we'd moved on. And anyway, I wanted him around when I phoned Harry, which I did the next morning." David inhaled another painful breath and gently rubbed his chest again. "Good place for you to take over, Harry. Okay to give me a break?"

"Sure." Harry leaned forward. "Well, as David said, he phoned me, with Weaver, on Sunday morning and we hatched a plan. Quite simply, whatever these guys set up, David and Weaver would go along with it, except for the actual hit, of course. But so these guys would think Weaver had done the job, we initially planned to put out a statement that a killing had taken place, but that we were not able to name the victim until his family had been informed. These guys would know it was David from the time and place, and we'd be there to nick them when Danny turned up to collect the ten grand."

"It all sounds a bit too simple to me," Jo said.

"In hindsight, it probably does, and in reality it didn't work. But Weaver had given us a chance to get two villains off the street. We couldn't just ignore it, we had to try."

"I guess so. Sorry, Harry, go on."

"So, David got a call last night, allegedly from someone on our team, asking him to meet me and Nat at the guest house this morning. That was a big enough shock – how would whoever it was know that this was a secret police meeting place? And he also knew what we'd been talking about at the meeting, because he referred to the phone bugging. But we had no time to worry about that because we had only about twelve hours for us to plan the logistics and brief everyone who would be involved – police, paramedics, CSIs, Doc White and our little friend on reception.

"It turned out Evelyn had already received a call from, we assume, the same person who phoned David, claiming to be one of our team, booking Room 17 and asking that no other bookings be made for that day. Incidentally, only a few of the people we briefed knew *all* the details of what was planned, the others – and as few 'others' as possible – were told it was a training exercise, to test how quickly we could seal and service a crime scene. I even told them I'd deliberately chosen someone large for the victim, just so it would make the exercise more challenging."

"You must have been very persuasive to get them to believe all that," Jo said.

"It's because I've got such an honest face, Jo. Also, when you think about it, there would be no actual crime committed on the day, so technically it *was* a sort of training exercise. Anyway, David turned up at the meeting place – Westmore Guest House – as agreed, around nine o'clock and was told by Evelyn to wait in the room. As planned, Danny sneaked in the back way and went to Room 17. We know this because we found him there, although Danny himself can't remember anything that happened in the ten minutes or so leading up to then."

"And do you believe that?" Jo again.

"The doctor said it was very common in cases of concussion and…"

"I know that," Jo put in, "but the question is, do you believe it in *this* case?"

"Well, yes, because I can't think of a single reason why he would make it up. He was *expected* in the room, so he's not going to incriminate himself by telling us he went there. I'm pleased to see you've not lost your natural dislike of the blinding obvious, Jo. Why do *you* think he would claim he's lost his memory?"

"It's just that the whole thing seems a bit… unlikely. This multi-murderer suddenly turns good guy. But the outcome is still that David's almost killed. Anyway, sorry again, Harry. Please go on… Danny sneaked in and went to Room 17."

"But instead of David sitting there with a broad smile waiting to meet his new friend, he's lying absolutely still up against the wall.

Danny gets bashed from behind by Kemp and he – not Evelyn, as planned – calls in the hit. And that's when we realised it had all gone tits-up. The real shame is that we didn't have Danny's photos earlier in the day. If we had, then we'd have got one bad guy – Kemp – off the streets and we might be part way to finding his motive and perhaps even his accomplice. But as it was, this guy sounded very credible, didn't he, Nat?"

Natalie nodded.

"He took a hell of a risk, didn't he, this Kemp guy?" Seb said. "I mean he *had* to get away, didn't he? If he hadn't, it would have been so easy to blow his story right out of the water. I don't understand why they didn't just let Danny get on with it, unless they *suspected* he was going to double-cross them."

"Except this way," Natalie said, "they'd get the target *and* the killer at the same time. I think they probably intended to kill Danny as well. Case closed; nobody looks any further."

"Why did they need two to do it?" Alice asked. "One guy could have shot David and then crocked Weaver."

"Someone had to leave with Danny's gun," Harry said.

"Why was Danny carrying a gun, anyway?" Jo asked.

"In case anyone was listening close by to check it was going to plan – from outside at the back or even in the house itself – Danny was going to fire a few shots – blanks, of course."

"I think Seb might have something, you know," David said, "The photos of the guys are full-face, like they're looking towards the camera. Perhaps they saw Danny photographing them and suspected he might not go through with it. Or, even if he did, they'd know he could ID them in future."

"Either way," Harry went on, "Kemp downs Danny, takes his own gun from him and places the murder weapon – *attempted* murder weapon – in his hand, pressing his fingers and palm against it like they do in the movies. Well, I'm *assuming* that's what must have happened for Danny's prints to be on the gun, which, incidentally, they've already confirmed was the one that fired the shots."

"The guy who shot me was wearing gloves, by the way," David said. "Not sure I mentioned that. Probably Kemp was as well, leaving only Danny's prints on the gun."

"It's a bit Agatha Christie, isn't it?" Harry said. "I thought those stories were all a bit far-fetched until today. And talking about far-fetched, that's the exact expression our DC Crusoe used when we found the mess at the guest house. Right, Nat?"

"Yes, a couple of things occurred to me. One – what's the likelihood of it being a *chance* meeting in the Remington Arms? A bit of a coincidence, isn't it, that two people should be talking about David Gerrard in a public place, loud enough to be overheard by someone he'd put away for twenty years. And if it wasn't a coincidence, then these two must have tracked Weaver down with the premeditated intention of priming him to put David away.

"And two, why would anyone want an all-round nice guy like Mr Gerrard out of the way? These two pub-crawlers wouldn't tell Weaver that, apparently, said it wasn't something he needed to know. The only thing we could come up with was this stuff about Tom Brown. Two phones bugged – Jo's, possibly for a long time – and Tony Dobson's, since he'd come up with a couple of anomalies surrounding the circumstances of Mr Brown's disappearance. So, David being the third person involved in this latest development, they had to do something about him as well." She looked across at the puzzled expression on DC Grantham's face. "Apologies, Alice, but we've not had time to brief the whole team on that yet."

"That's okay, go on."

Harry was looking at Jo, who was sitting *very* close to DS Carter now.

"And this is where I come in," Jo said. "If you were right about these two being linked to Tom Brown, then they would likely be part of the surveillance set-up listening in to me and Dobson."

"Exactly, got it in…"

"And, as such, they would hear me receiving the news of David's demise."

"Yes, so…"

"It made sense to give me the official version *before* telling me it's not true so they'd get a genuine reaction and believe David really *was* dead. Then Tom Thumb here takes my phone off me…"

"Well, you dropped it, actually," Seb said.

"And whisks me out of the room to tell me the wonderful news that David's absolutely fine and I was just being used in a plan to catch a couple of baddies. That about right?"

There were a few moments of uneasy silence before Harry spoke.

"*Exactly* right, Jo, and pretty cruel when you put it like that, I guess. Phoning you wasn't part of the original plan. But if Nat was right about the link – and I believe she is – then we figured we could let them know of David's death much sooner through you, and possibly avoid making any public statement, which we would have to retract later."

"Yes, it was *fucking* cruel," Jo said. "I know I'm not frigging Helen Mirren, but I reckon I could have convincingly acted out being a bit upset."

"Point taken," David said, "and for what it's worth, Jo, I'm really touched by… well… you know."

"Don't get too mushy about it, David. That was *before* I knew that you were still alive."

Marie giggled, putting her hand over her mouth. "Sorry, Jo, it's not funny, but good for you. Tell 'em like it is. I'm on your side."

Jo smiled back and shrugged. "Okay, I've said my piece. So, where did it all go wrong?"

David was frowning and looking at his phone.

"David?"

"Just a thought when you mentioned Tony. When he was telling me and George Holland about meeting the person who he thinks bugged his phone, he said that when he first met him, he thought he might be up there for a photo shoot or something, because he was like a male model, right off the front of a fashion mag. Same description as your Mrs Thornbury, and how Evelyn described the man who came looking for me a few days ago. And it certainly fits the guy with the gun this morning. Might be worth sending Tony the picture and see if it is the same person."

"I thought Tony couldn't use his phone?" Jo asked the question.

"Apparently he lost it overboard last weekend whilst sailing with his girlfriend. Very careless. So, he's now contactable on a burner that he's planning to change every week. George will have his current number." He looked at Harry. "Worth a try?"

"Let's do it."

CHAPTER THIRTY-TWO

6.15 p.m. BST

When Grace and Lydia entered, the twelve people already present rose, as one, from their seats. The meeting room in the Central Conference Suite of the Hirta facility was even better equipped than the Cabinet Office Room where the COBRA meeting had taken place around twenty-six hours ago. It had the same facilities for displaying information but each place around the table had its own mini laptop, with flip-up screen, inserted into the tabletop in front of it. These were each linked wirelessly to the continuous screen which ran from one side of the entrance door in an unbroken line round the four walls to the other side of the door. Each laptop had a designated area on the wall-screening which allowed participants to project notes, images, charts and general information through their keyboards for the benefit of the full meeting.

Most of that would be superfluous to today's requirements, with Kade and Sir Roger leading the meeting. It was Kade who opened after Grace and Lydia had taken their reserved places at the table.

"First, let's all get to know who we're working with. To save time, I suggest I do the honours and as I introduce you, just raise your hand, and if you wish to say something, please do, just so long as it's not 'I've changed my mind'. Okay?" The laughter was genuine and welcome, but brief, as Kade pressed on. "I'll start with the one I know best." He raised his hand. "Ex-Colonel Marty Kade – just Kade will do – former US Navy SEAL, now operational director with International Hostage Rescue Services. On my right, Sir Roger Ashpole, Head of MI5, ex-Special Forces, who will be overseeing the mission, and on my left, clockwise round the table, my team.

"Lydia van Roden, doctor of psychology, the best-known – and *best* – hostage-situation negotiator in the world." Lydia rolled her eyes. Kade continued. "Sergei Rouschek, Russian, ex-FSB and Robbie Burns, ex-SBS. Combined height, about thirteen feet. These two little guys will be part of your escort, Grace, on the *Mastodon*. Shirley-Anne Donnelly – ex-US Navy SEAL, Jules Cartier – former GIGN, French counterterrorism, Enrico Santana – ex Peruvian commandos." Kade smiled. "Don't be fooled by the mild expression and rimless glasses; Rico's the meanest of us all. These three guys will be part of Blue-Two. I'll tell you what that means very soon.

"Centre-stage – appropriately, at the end opposite me – Grace Goody, our chief negotiator. Without making a meal of this, Ms Goody, I think we are all in awe of your courage in taking on this role, and it will be our privilege to ensure that we get you back safely."

Grace smiled through her surprise, feeling her heart lift. "Thank you, Kade. I'll *definitely* hold you to that promise," she said.

Kade moved on. "On Ms Goody's left, Ms Ruby Weller, Minister for Security and Counter Terrorism. Here to advise as necessary on any protocol we may risk over-riding in our excitement." Ruby returned his smile.

"The other two members of Ms Goody's escort – Holly and Daz – both current-serving SBS and members of the same action cell, having served together for a long time – including missions with us on several occasions. Daz is fluent in Arabic, so he's our translator for any covert messages passing between the bad guys.

"And finally – and crucial to our success – our engineers. Mike Needham, the man who designed Hotel St Kilda, and an honorary member of IHRS. Mike has worked with us many times. And, Jens Reinhardt." He nodded to the man on Mike's immediate left. "Could you help me out, please, and introduce yourself?"

The man next to Mike got to his feet.

"Good afternoon, everybody. Jens Reinhardt, Senior Engineer at Dockwise, which is now a subsidiary of Boskalis. We are the company who own, operate and maintain the heavy-lift ships, including the *Mastodon*, and I was personally involved in modifying the vessel three years ago so it could accommodate Platform Alpha.

Also, I have visited CSBC Corporation in Taiwan, who built the vessel, on an exchange assignment with one of their senior designers. So, I have observed the construction of the current ship they are building, which is to the same specification as the *Mastodon*."

"Thanks, Jens. No doubt you will be playing a big part in our preparations over the coming hours."

As he finished speaking, a buzzer sounded on the door behind him.

"Ah, sustenance," Sir Roger said, getting to his feet. "Jolly good."

He opened the door to reveal two stainless-steel catering trolleys full of food and drink, which he pulled into the room, one after the other. "This has to keep us going until we finish," he said. "It is now 18.40. God knows when we'll get our next proper meal, so we need to make this lot last. There's tea, coffee, still and sparkling water, sandwiches, pizza – nothing to get cold – or warm, for that matter. I'll leave the trolleys here, just grab what you want whenever. Might be an idea to get a drink now at least."

"You didn't mention Bourbon, Sir Roger. Was that just an oversight or a… what?"

"It's a 'what', I'm afraid, but I promise you can have as much as you want when you get back."

"Ah, well… Ten minutes, guys, then we circle the wagons again."

*

Sitting directly opposite Grace at the meeting table made it impossible for Kade not to look directly at her for a good part of the time. He had been unsure as to how they would work together after his parting shot, and his refusal to shake her hand at their last meeting. He was the one who was out of order, however unsavoury the task she had set him. His acceptance of the assignment should have been one hundred percent and any reservations needed to be voiced and resolved before he undertook it. A change of mind part-way through was unprofessional and, as such, unacceptable. Grace's request for him to lead her escort had come as both a surprise and a relief.

As Sir Roger stood to address the meeting, Kade caught her eye briefly and smiled, receiving a raising of the eyebrows in response. He decided that was okay.

"Right, everyone," Sir Roger said, bringing the group to order. "Time to get serious. Kade will now take you through his plans for tomorrow, but first, something for your benefit, Jens, as the newcomer to the mission. The terrorists are claiming that they have a nuclear device on board and are threatening to detonate it if we do not comply with their demands. Let me say right away, we will *not* be meeting those demands, *but* nor do we accept they have such a device, for three reasons. One, because of the degree of difficulty in constructing such a device, two, there is no record of any materials missing from anywhere that would be needed to make such a bomb, and three, a Norwegian Coast Guard vessel has scanned the ship for a radioactive source and found none.

"So, although we *believe* we are in no immediate danger of being vapourised, there is no absolute guarantee. We have made arrangements for you, Jens, to be flown out of here and back home once we have finalised the planning phase. We have not yet agreed a time when Red-One will land on the *Mastodon*, but it will be some time tomorrow morning or early afternoon. We will have you out of here well before then."

Jens raised a hand. "Excuse me, Sir Roger, you said 'red something'?"

"Sorry, I'm jumping ahead. Red-One is the designated call-sign for the negotiating party. Kade will explain that very soon. In fact, if there are no questions…?"

Ruby raised a hand.

"Just one, Roger. I know it's nearly two hours away, but we need to decide who will be on the nine o'clock call with el Taqha. You took the first, I took the second, Jonathan Latiffe the third. If it hasn't been decided yet, I think, it makes sense for me to take it here. That will assure el Taqha that we are moving closer – geographically, I mean – to meeting with him. And also, of course, Grace, Lydia and the full Red team are here."

"That makes sense. I'll clear that now with the Justice Minister and Home Secretary. They'll want to be linked in anyway, I'm sure."

Sir Roger left the room and Kade looked around at the expectant faces.

"Aside from Jens, the rest of you will be familiar with most or all of what I'm going to say, but this will put each of us on the same page before we get into the minutia. Let me begin by reassuring the people just joining this group that we are not starting now, at this moment, in planning the mission. The basic plan is already in place – this is essentially fine-tuning plus the opportunity for you – any of you, to ask questions or challenge. It's really important, if you are concerned about anything, to voice those doubts here and now.

"This mission is about rescue, *not* negotiation. Let's understand that right away. Our objectives are fourfold. To take as many hostages off the ship as we can at the outset, to deactivate whatever explosive device they have on board, to ensure the safety of Ms Goody, the rest of the escort and the remaining hostages, and to capture or kill Abu el Taqha. We already have an agreement with el Taqha that they will release forty-six of the hostages in exchange for our on-board negotiating group.

"To achieve those objectives, we have three teams – one overt, two covert. The overt, visible, team – designated 'Red-One' – will be Ms Goody and her escort of five, which will be led by me. We have one covert team – Blue-One – already in place on the *Mastodon*. They 'chuted in early today and have established themselves, out of sight, on one of the stern towers. We are in touch with them via tactical radios and all is okay. The second covert team, Blue-Two, will insert at the bow of the ship, which will give access to the cabins and, we have to assume at this stage, the device. This will be achieved using a submersible, piloted by Shirley-Anne, plus a team of five, led by Jules, two of which, like Daz, are fluent in Arabic. And this is where our engineering friend can help us, by identifying a point of entry and directions for searching the cabins.

"The timing is important. We can't get Blue-Two on board until we get the input from Jens. Jules's team will need to gain entry before we land Red-One on the deck, or at the same time at the latest. The latter option might be better, in fact, as we will serve as a decoy, assuming attention will be focussed on us. Also, at that time, the forty-six hostages will be boarding the Chinook to take them off the vessel. So, much going on away from the bow.

"Once we have agreed a time with the terrorists, the six members of Red-One…" He paused and smiled at Grace. "Perhaps we should call it Green-One, Ms Goody. It goes better with your initials."

Grace laughed along with the rest. "Red's fine, Kade, I look terrible in green."

"Excuse me, ma'am," the silken French accent of Jules Cartier cut in, "but I find that impossible to believe."

The laughter continued, briefly relaxing the atmosphere. Grace smiled at the French Senegalese. "*Merci beaucoup, Jules, vous êtes très gentil.*"

"Okay, Red it is, then," Kade said. "As I was saying, once we have a time, we will transfer from here to HMS *Jura* for final equipping and monitoring. There, we will be wired with concealed radio receivers and transmitters. The team will, of course, be wearing protective gear including Grade-One bullet-proof armour. We will all be armed, including Ms Goody, who will carry a Glock 18. The escort team will each be carrying an automatic weapon along with the same handgun. El Taqha has been told, and had expected, that an armed escort would be present.

"As for timescale, from the moment the Chinook leaves with the released hostages, we are looking at completing the mission within one hour, two at the most."

Ruby gave a little gasp. "As quickly as that? I didn't realise..."

"Remember, ma'am, rescue not negotiation. It *has* to be as quick as that. We can't have Blue-One freezing their balls off on the tower for any longer than necessary, and once Blue-Two are on board and mobile, that well-known commodity hits the fan and we are all one team, in it together.

"However, in those first exchanges with el Taqha, it is critically important that we make him believe we may be willing to accede to their demands and we are there for the long haul if necessary. So, Red-One will show no trace of urgency, no anxiety or impatience, no looking like we're waiting for something to happen. Right, doctor?"

"Right," Lydia said. "And it won't be easy because they have heard many times that we – that's the UK, US, any western country – do not make deals with terrorists. So, Red-One's part of the plan is to create an atmosphere as close to trust as possible in these circumstances and convince them we are prepared to talk to them for as long as it takes."

"We have a couple of ideas as to how we can give that impression," Kade said. "We have insisted that the meeting will take place on deck. There is no way we will agree to meet below decks. That has been accepted but with it goes the challenge of how the meeting will be accommodated. In reality, it will not be a problem, because we won't be there long enough. But we will ask when we speak to them at nine o'clock what arrangements they have made. And we will resist if they seem anything less than perfect. This will help create the feeling that we are expecting to be there a long time." He smiled. "Bathroom arrangements, for example. One of the challenges of a mixed-sex mission.

"Secondly, MI6 are currently putting together a brief dossier on every person on el Taqha's list. This will include information on their current location and the process needed for their release. This last piece of data will be fake, by the way. Grace will take on board a single sheet for each of the eighty-seven names on the list, in a spine binder, along with a laptop, an iPad, a notebook and some other plastic folders. These Grace will set out on the meeting table, the objective being to add to the impression that we expect this to take some time. I am confident that we can create the impression within a short space of time."

Ruby raised a hand. "Excuse me, Colonel. That makes perfect sense and el Taqha may well go along with this, but what if he doesn't? What if it goes on long enough for him to become suspicious? I assume Grace will be stone-walling."

"On the contrary," Lydia put in. "Grace will be agreeing to everything, but emphasising the complexity of releasing all the people at once and in a way that is convenient for them to confirm it has happened. That is what they are expecting to negotiate."

Ruby nodded. "Of course. *Whether* we release them is not negotiable, only how and when. So, the very fact that we are sending a party onto the *Mastodon* is, in effect, an agreement to their release."

"That's it in a nutshell, Minister," Kade said. "We must all adopt the same mindset and be clear on what is happening here. I repeat, this is a *rescue*; Grace is a *decoy*. This will all be over very quickly. Okay?"

He looked round the table at the nodding heads.

"One way or another," he added.

★

"It was a Glock 17 with a silencer," David went on. "I picked up the table to cover my face and neck, to force him to shoot low. Not sure what ammo he was using, only it felt like he could probably have fired through the table, but I guess he thought he didn't need to. I don't know how many shots he fired. I went straight back over the chair and hit the wall. I must have been out for a while and when I came to my ribs felt like they were on fire and I couldn't move."

Marie had turned her head into David's chest. He put his arm around her and pulled her closer to him.

"It's a good job you *didn't* fully trust Weaver," Jo said. "When did you decide to put the body armour on?"

"Just before I went into the guest house." He smiled at Jo. "It was such a lovely leaving present and there are so few opportunities to wear it." He inhaled deeply and shook his head. "It was an afterthought as I was leaving home. I just threw it onto the back seat without really intending to use it. Then I thought, I'll be sitting there, unarmed, waiting for a murderer I put away for twenty years to walk into the room with a gun. What's to lose? So, I put it on in the car, put my jacket over it and..." He paused and swallowed. "Not a bad decision in hindsight."

His voice cracked a little as he spoke, and he squeezed Marie a little tighter. They were all silent for a while.

"Did you see Weaver when he entered the room?" Harry asked.

"I'm not sure, to be honest. It's a bit hazy. I was aware of some movement and then another crash. Then after a few moments, maybe longer, everything cleared for a few seconds and I saw the receptionist in the doorway. She was screaming and someone was comforting her. Then I must have passed out again." He turned to Marie and smiled. "What a lightweight, eh?"

"Hardly that, David," Harry said, "and it's a good job you didn't move so the second guy didn't realise you were still alive. But the original plan, of course, was blown to hell and everything was – *is* – more complicated. We had to explain Danny's presence to everyone, for a start. He shouldn't have been there at all as part of the so-called training exercise. In addition to that, I had to make a quick decision, and that was to go ahead as planned, go through the crime-scene protocol and let David stay dead until we had time to think what to do next. And now, having *had* time to think about it, I believe it may have been the wrong thing to do."

"What was the wrong thing to do?" Alice asked.

"To carry on with the pretence of David being dead."

"Why's that, sir?" Alice again.

"Well the *sole* objective of the plan was to catch the bad guys, right? The idea being that, if they thought David was dead, they'd turn up to pay off Danny, as arranged, then we'd grab them. We now know that that wasn't their intention, and Danny's involvement was only as fall-guy. So, the whole elaborate plan – the training exercise, the call to Jo – was a waste of time. So perhaps, with *hindsight*, just treating this as attempted murder without all the fakery might have been the best way forward."

They sat in silence for a time. Marie glanced at the wall clock.

"Now, I don't want to go all domestic in the midst of such excitement, but it's after seven-thirty and it seems this meeting has a way to go yet. Would you like me to make sandwiches, or cook something?"

The chorus of replies distilled into a collective "no, thank you", but David suggested maybe a take-away, perhaps Chinese if Marie didn't mind the residual odour. The group relaxed into discussing the possibilities and Alice assumed the job of writing out their list for pizza delivery, which Marie phoned through to their local supplier.

The natural break prompted a scattering of interests for a while, conversations criss-crossing the room with Alice, Natalie and Jo catching up on recent personal news. After a while, Seb lapsed into silence, frowning in concentration.

"Look," he said, cutting through the chatter, "I don't want to step on anyone's toes here, but..."

They all turned to him.

"That's good to hear, Seb," Harry said. "Mine certainly wouldn't take the weight."

Seb smiled and raised his right hand. "I promise. But, *if* these guys are involved with the surveillance, and that links with the disappearance of Tom Brown, then they could be, technically, on our side, by which I mean Special Branch or secret service, operating in some official capacity. They have access to sophisticated surveillance tools, knowledge of your secret meeting place and meetings schedule, most probably a means of intercepting calls to New Station and, if Weaver is tagged, that's probably how they could track him down. And if he *isn't* tagged, they'd need information relating to his release conditions so they could find him. It would also explain why Kemp felt he could take such a chance, because there'd be powerful forces at work to bail him out if things went wrong. Anything I've missed?"

They sat in silence, collecting their separate thoughts. Harry's phone trilled. He looked at the screen and pressed the answer key.

*

Grace had remained in her seat during a short recess – a "comfort break", as Kade had called it – hoping to have a private word with him. However, he had been deep in conversation with Daz, talking in soft voices in a corner of the room. The rest of the group started to drift back in.

"Ladies, gentlemen, it's 7.50; let's get back to work." Kade harnessed the group's attention as they all settled back into their seats. "But before we get to Blue-Two and their access to the vessel, Daz has a theory about the possible location of the bomb." He turned to the SBS man, a stocky Asian in his late twenties with a ruggedly handsome face. "Go ahead, Daz."

"Just a thought. If they do have a nuke on board, then it doesn't really matter where it is. If it goes up it will take the ship and the platform with it and we'll feel it here soon after. I should say, *they'll* feel it here – *we* won't feel a thing." The correction prompted some nervous laughter. "But if we're right and they have a conventional bomb on board, it would have to be huge to reach the accommodation on the platform. The deck of the ship would limit the impact by taking the immediate blast. Even if it was on the deck, or even somewhere on or in the superstructure, a bomb small enough to be sneaked onto the rig then man-handled onto the ship would hardly reach the height of the Alpha platform with a guaranteed destructive impact. With me so far?"

He looked round at the nodding heads and questioning looks.

"*Unless* the bomb was strategically placed, to bring the platform *down*. If we were doing something like this, we'd take out one or more of the columns. You could do that without blowing yourself up by attaching the bomb to a column, sailing away and using a remote detonation. But if you didn't mind feeding the seagulls over a wide area of the Atlantic, you just edge the vessel alongside the column and position the bomb – still on the ship – next to it, probably on deck with a channelled explosion sufficient to fracture the column.

"And the guys on Alpha, eight hundred of them, falling over three hundred feet whilst being thrown around against walls, furniture, fittings and whatever, crashing down onto the deck of the vessel and into the sea. They'd stand about as much chance of surviving as they would with a nuke, but this way would be a hell of a lot more painful."

He looked round at his hushed audience, who looked back, wide-eyed and silent, before turning to look at each other.

"A pretty graphic scenario, Daz," Kade said, "and it makes a lot of sense. We know from the fly-pasts and the drone that there is nothing attached to any of the columns – yet. If they did that, they would expose the device and we'd get a good idea of the type of bomb they had. It would certainly confirm that it wasn't a nuke. That's if it *isn't* a nuke."

"Just to check I'm getting this," Grace said. "If there's a nuke on board, we're not likely to see it because they can keep it out of sight. If it's not a nuke, which is what we believe, at some point they have to reposition it in order for it to pose a threat. And that would have to be when? Because once they do that, we'd know for certain what we were up against."

Jens raised his hand.

"They wouldn't need to reposition it, ma'am. The hull is completely sealed, of course, to enable the vessel to ballast down, and also reinforced. The deck is strong enough to take the weight of the largest production platform in the world and that, I am certain, is enough to withstand anything but an exceptionally large conventional explosion. And, as the gentleman said, this bomb has to be small enough to get it to where it is.

"However, just below the deck there is a sub-floor, which can be used for transporting cargo when the ship isn't being used as a heavy-lift. Close to the bow on both sides of the vessel, there are drop-down doors, which create a horizontal ramp for loading directly onto this floor rather than onto the deck. With the vessel de-ballasted, the lowered ramps are about four metres above the waterline and held in position by the drop-down mechanism and secured by chains. This lines them up with the servicing berth at its home anchorage in The Hague." He leaned forward and smiled down the table at Daz. "If you *were* planning on doing this, my advice to you would be to have the bomb inside the vessel close to one of the doors, ready to be detonated after lowering the ramp to rest against the column. But this would all need some careful planning based on inside knowledge. That's not to say they don't have this information but it's not something they could make up as they went along."

There was a pause as people looked around and nodded.

"Thank you, Jens and Daz," Kade said. "That gives us something to work with. When you take the call, ma'am, we should make it a condition that they move out from under the platform. I can't imagine they will agree to that and part of me hopes they won't. Because if they do, that will point to them having a very large bomb on board."

Ruby nodded and made a note.

"And they must drop anchor," Jens said. "They will currently be keeping the ship static using stabilisers to maintain their position. These are powerful, computer-controlled jets that kick in automatically, making minor adjustments to compensate for any movement in order to keep the vessel on a defined grid reference point. They're used to counter drift in ultra-deep water where anchorage isn't an option, but here the water is shallow enough to use an anchor. While they're in the current position under the platform, there is a risk of the anchors interfering with the pontoon but, once they're out from under it, they can be safely deployed. The vessel utilises four claw anchors which grab the seabed rather than catch on it: two each at the fore and aft, port and starboard and when they are raised, they are held tight against the hull, closing off the portal. When they are lowered, there is some space between the chain and the edge of the portal.

"One of them could give you your access."

*

Harry placed the phone on the low table.

"Hi, George. That was quick – I've got you on speaker, by the way."

"I'll try not to swear too much, then. Well, it was a good call, boss. Mrs Thornbury has no doubt that this was the man she saw. Does that solve something?"

"It certainly *adds* something. Many thanks, George. Good job. You can get back to your seven courses and give Sally my apologies if anything's spoiled."

"Will do, sir. I expect the candles will have burnt down by now and the champagne will be flat, but otherwise..."

"Same old George," Jo shouted across.

"Hey, is that DI Cottrell? Hi, Jo, great to hear your voice."

"Yours too, George."

"Thanks again," Harry said. "Cheers."

"Bye, all."

Harry looked round the group, eyes wide. "Well, then. That box is well and truly ticked."

David's phone treated them to the opening bars of Chopin's *Minute Waltz*.

"Is there a collective noun for Georges?" he asked, as he answered the call. "Mr Holland. What news?... I see... Absolutely sure?... But, you say, he's definite about it? Many thanks, George... I'll explain next time I see you, but that's really helpful... Bye."

He looked at the expectant faces and smiled. "Mr Dobson's friend in the north was the same man. He had, quote, 'designer stubble then but it's definitely him'."

"So," Jo said, "we have a man who..." she leaned forward to count on her fingers "... meets with Sammo Sampson in a place where he's shot dead a few days later, follows Tony Dobson to Shetland and bugs his phone, tracks down David to a meeting at Westmore Guest House, seeks out Danny Weaver and primes him for a hit on David, arranges a meeting at the same guest house so Danny can do the deed, then turns up to do it himself. Have *I* missed anything?"

They shook their heads.

"No, that's pretty comprehensive, Jo," Harry said. "And the common denominator in all those cases, as I see it, *is* Tom Brown."

"How come, Harry?" It was Marie who asked the question. "I'm not sure I get all the connections."

"Well, Sammo Sampson was one of the people Tom Brown was suspected of killing because of Sammo's involvement in the case against his son."

"His son? The boy who committed suicide? So tragic."

"It certainly was. Then, his bugging of Dobson's phone was straight after the journalist expressed some concern over the circumstances of Tom's death. And the other stuff, well – I'm guessing – but perhaps, with Jo and Dobson closely monitored, that only leaves David as a threat."

"And if they *do* see David as a threat," Jo said, "then it points towards the fact that there *was* something suspicious about Tom's death." She turned to David. "Or am I just conspiracy-theorising again?"

"You are, but I'm right with you this time."

CHAPTER THIRTY-THREE

8.00 p.m. BST

The screens around the room were now displaying three schematic diagrams of the vessel, a section from the port side, on the wall to Kade's left, from the starboard side on his right and, behind him, a plan from above.

"Okay," he said, "is everyone clear on the preferred means of entry? Let's not break with tradition; let's call it Plan A. Access via the opening for the anchor chain into one of the windlass rooms. Let's go through it again. Main issues, Holly?"

"Very narrow clearance between the chain and the bulkhead, made more difficult because even a slight movement of the ship could have a significant impact on the clearance with the danger of closing it enough to crush someone passing through."

"Action, Jules?"

"We take two telescopic braces to apply between chain and bulkhead to hold apart to allow safe entry. Suggest also, no-one on Blue-Two eat anything between now and go. Thin is good for this."

"*Bon idée, mon ami*. Daz, other issues?"

"Covert access to the chain egress point. The chain portal is eight metres above water, and the chain will be angled away from the vessel, making it – and any member of Blue on the chain – visible to someone looking down from the deck at the wrong time."

"Action… Sergei?"

"Create a diversion at same time, or they go with darkness."

"Problem with the darkness option… Shirley-Anne?"

"That commodity is in short supply, so very small window of opportunity. Also, problem with manoeuvring Cassie in the dark without our spotlight giving us away."

"And with diversion option, Robbie?"

"Nae guarantees. They could be mounting a continuous watch from the deck as we approach time zero."

"Alternatives, Rico?"

"Magnetic ladders to chain exit point. Curve of the hull means we are out of sight from deck *if* Cassie can get close enough to place ladders."

"And if not, what's the alternative? Go on, Rico?"

"We swim with ladders and all equipment and weapons. Worst option."

"Agreed. Tell us why."

"I can't swim." He raised his arms to stop the laughter. "Serious though, it means swimming without breathing tanks or to risk losing them when we climb ladders. No chance of access with the tanks."

"Unless you remove them *then* take them through," Kade said. "Or leave them attached to the ladders. Remember, that won't be your means of egress. We can afford to lose them, but we could collect them later, anyway. Even so, I agree, it is the worst option."

Kade spread his arms to include the whole group in his next question. "Catch-22?" He looked at Ruby. "Minister?"

"Plan A can only work if they agree to move the vessel from under the platform. The Catch-22 is that, if they refuse, that indicates that Jens's theory about the location of the bomb – and Daz's about how they intend to use it – may be correct, which is good because we have something to work with. But it means they cannot meet our demand to lower the anchor because of the risk of it snagging the pontoon."

"So, the alternative to Plan A? Jens?"

"Plan B would be access at the bow, onto the upper deck of the superstructure, which is a long, high climb and a long way back down to the below-deck area, where we think the bomb may be sited."

Jens took up the pointer and traced the route.

"Main challenge, Shirley-Anne?"

"Physical challenge of climbing that distance with the magnetic ladders. For a team of five personnel, it would need a minimum of six ladders, passing the lowest ladder up the chain an estimated ten or eleven times to reach the deck."

"Or, possibly…?"

"Two men using three ladders, getting to the deck much quicker and lowering a rope."

"Sounds better, don't you think, Sergei?"

"Except we don't know if there's anyone on the deck. No chance now to use drone to check without showing something happening at bow of ship. So, perhaps best for all five to arrive on deck at same time to deal with – how do you say – 'reception committee'. And me, I'd rather be on a ladder than a rope any time."

"Me, too," Kade said. He turned to Rico and Jules to his left. "You're the men we're talking about… decision, if it's Plan B?"

Jules gave a classic Gallic shrug. "We stay together, all five on the ladders."

Rico smiled and pointed with his left hand across his chest to the man on his right. "I go with him."

"We might be able to get you intel on anyone on the upper foredeck area with a fly-past," Sir Roger said. "Small charter – perhaps single-prop – with media livery, linked with tactical radio, swinging by as you reach deck level. The risk, as Sergei said, is drawing attention to the bow end of the ship. We'll be clearing the area of all air traffic, of course, before Red-One and Blue-Two go in, so they're not picked up on camera, but a one-off rogue reporter is unlikely to give you away. Your call, what do you think?"

Kade looked across at Jules, raising his eyebrows.

"That would be good," Jules said. "Less risk than not knowing."

"Okay, let's do that," Kade said. He checked his watch then turned to Ruby. "It's 8.38; next call with el Taqha is in twenty-two minutes and I'm guessing he'll be taking away our requests to consider. This might be a good time, Minister, to recap our conditions in preparation for that call."

"I was just about to suggest the same, and would you please call me Ruby? It makes me feel more like one of the gang."

Kade gave a little laugh. "Of course you're one of the gang, Ruby."

*

From the command centre on the second storey of the square tower with wrap-around windows in the administration building, the top of Platform Alpha and the blades of the fifty-five massive wind turbines surrounding it could be seen in the gathering twilight on the horizon.

Ruby was seated at the semicircular worktop in front of a variety of speakers, conference phones and recording machines. She was flanked on her left by Lydia, Kade and Grace, with Sir Roger, Mike Needham and Jules to her right. Lydia's fingers rested on the keyboard linked to the large wide-screen PC monitor in front of her and Ruby.

"Remember, Ruby," Lydia said. "No voice this time; everything through the screen. And, as before, in your own words just using the text as prompts."

Ruby nodded, drumming her fingers on the worktop surface.

The call came through at exactly 9.00 p.m.

"And who is my lucky contact this time?"

"It's Ruby again, Abu. Thank you for being prompt this time."

"Ah, Ruby, hello again. The time draws close. Do you have your team ready to meet me tomorrow?"

"They are ready and, assuming some assurances can be given, will meet you some time tomorrow."

"Some time? Your colleague Mr Latiffe said tomorrow morning. I hope you are not playing games with me, Ruby. Stalling for time."

"Not at all. We are as eager as you to get this started, and tomorrow morning is our intended time to meet. Whether that happens will depend on your meeting some minor requirements. Shall I proceed?"

"I thought we had met all your requirements."

"Not quite. Shall I proceed?"

"Please do."

"Firstly, we require you to move the vessel out from under the platform a minimum of one hundred metres clear of it and drop two anchors one fore and one aft. Do you wish to respond to that, or shall I continue?"

"Proceed with your other requests."

"Very well, but let me stress that these are *requirements*, not requests. None of which will adversely affect your negotiating position."

"Please continue."

"We need to ensure that accommodation is available on deck for rest periods and bathroom requirements. I understand that stored below there are a number of portacabins, which are used on deck when the vessel is open to the public for promotional events and exhibitions. We require a minimum of three of these on deck – two for our party and at least one for yours. Once the two sides begin negotiating, no-one should leave the deck.

"Thirdly, some form of shelter will be needed for the meeting itself, which will be in the open. Windbreaks at least, and also free-standing heaters. Again, there are enough of these available on board to ensure people are comfortable. The weather for the next few days is forecast to be good with a relatively gentle breeze and no rain, but this could change quickly, so a canopy should also be available if needed.

"Next, we wonder about food and drink. *You* have specified that we meet on the *Mastodon* and *you* have made demands which will take time to turn into actions, so we assume you must realise this and have plans for providing food and drink for our people. We would like to know what those plans are.

"Very importantly, we insist that the nuclear device be deactivated at least to the extent that the detonator is stable and the trigger is *not* manually restrained. If you agree to that, I would like to think I could accept your personal assurance that it has been done. However, in the interest of – as you said – not playing games, we will need you to explain the mechanism to one of the hostages, and demonstrate that you have complied, so that he can confirm it. After this call, we will be forwarding you the names of the forty-six people you are to release, and we will indicate which one you should speak to about the device. Should I continue?"

"You have *more*? Go on."

"We will be landing two helicopters on the ship close to the stern. The first, a Eurocopter X3, will deliver the six members of the negotiating group. The second, a Chinook, which will take off the forty-six hostages. We will need to see all forty-six people on deck before we land either aircraft. The Eurocopter will remain until the Chinook has left with all on board. I suggest you get them to stand in five groups of eight and one of six so we can easily account for them all. You may also want to consider the positioning of the screens and canopy, so they are not disturbed by the two helicopters landing and taking off.

"Those are *our* demands which must be addressed before we can start the process of meeting *your* demands. Our final requirement – for the time being, anyway – is an answer to the question, what happens *afterwards*? How will this end when we release your comrades and you have their freedom confirmed to your satisfaction? We should like to know that right now before you respond to our other requirements. My colleague who you spoke to you earlier tells me you have one objective – the release of the eighty-seven prisoners – and then you are going home. Just how will that work?"

"At this stage, I cannot share specific details with you, Ruby, but I can tell you that, when I leave, the bomb will be activated and on the MRTD. The person preventing the detonation will be one of the remaining crew. Perhaps even Ove, who is here with me now. It will then be up to you to get your brave bomb disposal boys here to take over. Take over from Ove. Quite poetic. Although this young man has done such admirable work already; perhaps someone else."

Lydia paused, then her fingers flew over the keys again.

"And how do we know you won't detonate this remotely after you leave?"

"You don't, Ruby, but I don't know if you won't shoot me as soon as I relinquish control of the trigger, do I? In fact, the device is not one which can be easily detonated remotely. It has a physical trigger, not an electronic one. Your experts will be able to explain to you what a zero-bomb is and how it works. But, at some point, trust must come into the equation, however uncomfortable it seems. In my second call to Scandoil, I made it clear to Mr Sundstrom that we did not want anyone to die. That is the truth. If we get what we want, no-one will. And, if so, it will mean we may be able to trade with the west again in the future. If I go back on my word, that will never happen. So, think of this as a test that I must pass."

"Very well. We will leave it for now. So, to our demands. Will you respond now or do we talk again later?"

"I can promise you that your party will be warm and dry and have access to the facilities you mention. Those plans have already been made. As for food, I cannot promise *a la carte*, but no-one will go hungry or thirsty. However, moving the ship to anchor away from the platform and disabling the bomb is certainly not part of our plans and you will need to explain why those steps are necessary before we talk. Those are the only cards we have to play."

"And you will have time to play them if we fail to reach agreement. But if I am to put a negotiating party on deck, I need to be certain the vessel is not capable of simply moving away with everyone on board. We require you to engage the starboard rear and port forward anchors to stabilise the ship.

"As far as the bomb is concerned, I do not want any risk of an accidental detonation through tiredness or carelessness if, for example, the talks go to a second or third day, which is quite possible, given the logistics involved in the demands you have made. We are not taking away your cards, Abu, we're simply asking that you put them to one side for now."

There was no response for over a minute, during which time they could here hushed and excited voices in the background. When the reply came, it was brief and terse.

"We cannot agree to that. We must think, and you must, also. We will talk in one hour, at 10.30."

He ended the call.

They sat back in their seats and all eyes turned to Sir Roger.

"A zero-bomb," Kade said. "That is a just about the last thing I expected. Are you familiar with them, sir?"

"I am. It's a device that..."

Kade held up his hands. "Best to tell the whole group. Let's go join them."

⋆

The conversation stopped as he came back into the room.

"We're going with the mugshots," Harry said. "The Super's cleared it all the way up to junior minister level... she *says*. Just how she's done that in half an hour I'm not sure – more important things going on at those lofty heights, I guess." He looked at Seb. "I mentioned your point about them possibly being part of some covert op, and she said in that case they can sort it out when we catch them. She was pretty keen that we *do* catch them, by the way, now that she's backed us. So, they'll make the screens and papers tomorrow. With what's going on in the Atlantic it'll probably be page eight of the dailies, but one of these guys is someone who gets noticed, so I feel pretty confident about this."

"That's great," Jo said. "I don't know Superintendent Hargreaves yet, but I'm surprised – and impressed – that she would *want* to move that quickly. Most people at her level would take time to make triple-sure their back was covered if it turns out they've stood on the wrong toes."

"She doesn't hang about, our Lynsey, I'll say that for her. Like she said, these guys tried to take out one of *our* guys, and, licensed to kill or not, that's not acceptable. Whoever they are, they're the enemy now."

"So, *exactly* when do the pictures go out?" Alice asked.

"The techies will want to play with the images a bit to get them sharp and clear – nice bit of overtime for someone. So, breakfast news tomorrow morning as early as possible, all channels, and, hopefully, the late editions of the dailies. We might miss a few of those but they'll be on their online pages at the same time as the news items. Obviously, this will be a long way below the hijacking, even if it's in second place. Oh, and she's going to put out a brief holding statement to the media tonight, just something bland so our anti-heroes don't start wondering why it's not been mentioned."

"So, what are we saying about them?" Alice again.

"At this stage, that the police are looking to interview them in connection with a shooting incident in the Westmore area of Guildford – and not to approach them, of course. No mention of the specific details or the victim." Harry smiled at David. "Sorry, but you'll have to wait a bit longer for your fifteen minutes of fame."

"If that's the price of fame, I'm happy to wait another thirty years."

*

The mood back in the main meeting room of the conference suite was much more subdued. During the past twenty-four hours each piece of new data they had received had increased the evidence against the likelihood of the terrorists having a nuclear device on board. All that evidence, however, had been circumstantial, just weighing the odds. For the first time, they had information about the actual device in question. A zero-bomb was a very real entity.

Sir Roger explained.

"Zero-bomb is a misnomer; almost a typo, you might say. This was a weapon developed in the fifties by British nuclear scientists whose original name for the device was O-bomb. The 'O' stood for 'Orange' – that's the fruit, not the colour – and describes the shape of the bomb. The name was changed when someone in the US mistook the letter 'O' for the number 'zero' and after that the name was generally adopted. Something to do with 'Orange' not being very scary and 'Zero' sounding more sinister and sexier. It's more commonly referred to by its initial – zee-bomb.

"If you think of the segments of an orange, ten separate slices, circled to form a globe. That's the exact structure of a zee-bomb. But before detonation, the segments – containing active uranium – which are spring-loaded to come together, are kept apart using a central cylinder to stabilise the device. So, the whole is still in the shape of a globe, flattened at the poles, but with space between the segments to allow neutrons to escape, harmlessly at this stage. Removing the cylinder will allow the segments to come together to form the compact, solid globe. Now there are no gaps in the structure. The surface from which the neutrons can escape is reduced to just the surface-area of the globe, a small fraction of the sum of the surfaces of the separate segments. Unable to escape – well, I guess you know what happens – they create a divergent chain reaction, a massive output of energy, a nuclear explosion.

"The safety cylinder itself is spring-loaded from below and held in place by a metal bar across the top. Remove the bar and the cylinder is ejected upwards and the segments slide together to fill the space it leaves. Easy to adapt for manual restraint. You just have a person holding the cylinder in place against the spring, instead of the bar."

"But surely the guy is being radiated while he's holding it, and someone has to be there to move the bar anyway, don't they?" Grace asked.

"You'd think so, but I'm not aware of any occasion when this device was used so I can't really answer the question. But the person would need protective clothing, or the device could be contained in, say, a leaded case with an extension to the cylinder outside to hold it in place. In so far as removing the bar is concerned, that could be easily done with a timing device, even a simple mechanical one. The bar could be hinged at one end and clipped at the other. You disturb the clip and the bar flips up vertically or swings horizontally."

"And what he says about remote detonation. Is correct?" Rico asked.

"It wouldn't be easy and probably not worth it, because he is right about one thing – although it is hypothetical and would never happen. If we did meet his demands and he escaped and *then* detonated, he could never expect to make another deal again."

"That makes sense if you conveniently forget about the hundreds of people he's already murdered, *thousands* if you do hold him accountable for 9/11," Ruby said. "He can't seriously think he'll be making any more deals in the future."

The room lapsed into silence, as they each collected their thoughts. Daz raised his hand.

"I'm just wondering why they would tell us what they've got. That is key information which I would have expected they would keep to themselves. I mean, they must be expecting us to try something other than just talk to them, and part of that 'something' has to be an attempt to disable the bomb. So, why provide us with the means to plan ahead?"

"Good question, Daz. Do you have an answer?"

"More of a theory than an answer, sir. We've all listened to the recording of Taqha's call to the Justice Minister. At one point, Mr Latiffe said something like 'the device which you claim to have' and Taqha got a bit uptight and said, 'don't you believe me?' or something. If it got him thinking we didn't believe he had a bomb on board, the best way to try and convince us would be to leak specific details about the device, or should I say *a* device which we would all recognise."

"So, your theory, Daz," Grace asked, "is that even if they *don't* have a nuclear device, by giving us specific details of one it's more likely that we'd believe they had."

"That's right, ma'am. A sort of double bluff – but only a theory."

"And why would they choose a zee-bomb to take on board," Grace continued, "or pretend to take on board?"

Holly leaned forward. She was of Caribbean ancestry, mid-thirties, medium height and tough-looking. "Some time ago, when we were training with some US Navy SEALs out in Afghanistan, these guys were telling us that back in the late fifties and sixties, during the Cold War, the Allies were working on portable nuclear weapons. Big problem, of course, apart from the radiation, was the weight. So, they considered a number of devices which could be assembled at or close to the target. The zero-bomb was one of these; the segments could be carried separately and easily fitted into a frame in situ. A team of, say, six men could carry one bomb – five with two segments each, separated – and one with the frame and central cylinder.

"If el Taqha was going to take a nuclear device on board, a zero-bomb would be easier than most other types, assuming he has enough men with him, which I think we can assume he has. And if he just wanted to make us *believe* he'd taken a nuke on board, then telling us it's a zero-bomb would be his best chance to convince us."

"Well I'm not sure he's convinced us," Kade said, "but he's sure as hell got us thinking. Thank you, Holly. Do you get chatted up a lot by Navy SEALs?"

"All the time, sir," Holly said, her hard expression morphing to angelic as she smiled. "But not *ex*-Navy SEALs."

"Not yet, anyway." Kade returned the smile and the laughter was a pleasant, if brief, distraction.

"Okay," he continued. "We're going to assume they do *not* have nuclear capability, so..."

"Assume?" Jules said. "*Eh, bien*, that makes me feel so much better."

"That's right, Jules, just like we have been doing so far. So, nothing's changed, and if, later tomorrow, we meet up in the great beyond, you can tell me I'm wrong. Okay?"

"You mean, you think we'll be going to the same place. Now I am *really* worried."

The laughter was louder and longer this time. Kade spread his arms and turned to Lydia with pleading, but smiling, eyes.

"It is good that we can laugh," Lydia said. "Like a valve. As the pressure builds, a release is necessary, just as long as we recognise it as just that, and not a relaxation of our concentration. And for the record, I am sure that Kade and Jules will end up in the same place, but it might not be the one they prefer or are expecting." She raised her hands to silence more laughter. "As Kade said, there is little point in wondering now about whether they have a nuke or not. Privately, of course, we will – we are not machines – but not in the context of this mission. The bomb must be stopped, no matter what it is."

*

"Understood. Out."

The Major switched off his radio and looked at the anxious faces around him. All five were sitting cross-legged in a circle under the makeshift canopy, their heads touching the low roof. The other four members of the team were similar in shape and build, shorter than the Major with more muscular upper bodies. Their craggy faces under the beanies also contrasted with their leader's sharp features, and the identical expressions of surprise and concern made them look even more like four figures from the same mould.

"I'm not sure what we are supposed to do with that information," the Major said, "but I guess Kade felt he had to tell us. If any of you can think of somewhere we can run to from here, please let me know and I'll start working on an escape plan right away." His wide grin was infectious and his four comrades relaxed into gentle laughter."

The group lapsed into silence for a while.

"Makes you think, though," Sam Hudson said, "when you look at what these guys have achieved so far – the *Mastodon*, the platform – you wouldn't put it past them having a nuke, would you?"

"We have to believe that the odds are still against it, but, as Kade said, it doesn't make any difference to what we have to do. It just makes failing a lot less attractive."

CHAPTER THIRTY-FOUR

10.05 p.m. BST

The Prime Minister leaned forward and picked up the receiver of his desk phone. He recognised the number on the display.

"Hello, Jackie."

"Hi, Andrew. Just checking, you should have a transcript of the call on your PC by now."

"Reading through it a second time. Difficult to pick up the dynamics without actually *hearing* what was said. What do you think? I take it you listened in on the call."

"Yes, and it's hard to predict how el Taqha will respond. It was clear he wasn't happy, particularly about moving from under the platform. And the trigger might be a sticking point, but... we'll see."

"Next call is in around twenty minutes, right?"

"That's right, but, look, Andrew, I need to get home. It's after ten and Lucy is in on her own this evening and under pain of death not to go out, but if I don't get back, she'll use that as an excuse to do just that. Round to her friend's or something and I'll end up having to track her down. Jonathan is at Thames House and is staying overnight. Lawrence is there to share the time with him, so..."

"You should go, Jackie. As long as you and I are on the end of a phone, at home or at Thames House makes no difference. Have you spoken to Grace at all?"

"No. She's with Ruby, so she will be her conduit to us from now. Ruby called me when they had a break earlier. She said Grace was okay and seems to have a lot of confidence in Kade. Quite honestly, I can't even begin to imagine what must be going through her mind."

"Me, neither. By the way, I'm meeting with the US ambassador tomorrow morning, as soon as it's confirmed Grace is on or heading for the *Mastodon*. I have asked Linus to stand by and keep his morning free, told him it's just to bring him up to date. But the main reason, of course, is to get the message through to Weston about Grace."

"Right. CNN are getting more and more vociferous with their demands for action."

"Any mention of the nuke in any of their reports?"

"No, I think we've managed to keep that off-limits so far. They are demanding – on behalf of the American people, of course – that they send in a team to take el Taqha off. Can you imagine that?"

"I'll try not to. I was hoping to catch a couple of hours' sleep myself, and I don't believe thinking about it would not be conducive to that end. I wonder if they'd be as keen to send their brave boys in if they did know about the nuclear threat. Anyway, I'm sure John wouldn't do anything without going through the proper channels. I know I tease Grace about him, but he's a good guy."

He heard Jackie give a little chuckle. "You'd best be careful, Andrew. You sound as though you might be turning into a human being. I, for one, wouldn't know how to deal with that."

"You're right. I *will* be careful."

"Good night, Prime Minister."

"Good night, Home Secretary."

⋆

Kade checked his watch. "Fifteen more minutes, then we should get up there again. Before that, Lydia, you had some thoughts about the MRTD?"

"It was around 3.30 p.m. yesterday afternoon – over thirty hours ago – when they said they'd activated the bomb with the trigger in place. There is no way that would be true. It's too great a risk. As the Home Secretary said, 'if the wrong person sneezes'. They will activate only when the time comes. We have to get there *before* the time comes, so to speak. That's if they've got an MRTD in the first place. This type of trigger is a great idea but, in our experience, it has never been used, except as a threat. I believe it's because people don't feel in control. It's not like throwing a switch, or pulling a chord when it's *your* movement that produces the outcome. This is almost a passive role, but in most cases an action which will end the person's life."

Grace was watching Lydia, rather than listening to her, and at last understood the reason for the discomfort she felt in her presence. It was her similarity to Maggie Tomlinson-Brown, the woman she had made a widow. And, in that moment, she knew exactly what Tom would have been thinking when he said those words to Lydia. The feeling of guilt and regret threatened to overwhelm her, just as her phone pinged with an incoming text.

She looked down at the phone, then up at the sea of faces turned in her direction.

"My apologies, it's some information I've been waiting for all day. Excuse me just for a few moments."

She stepped out of the room.

A text from Walcott.

Sorry for delay getting back. Busy making you safe. Sleep easy. J x

It had to be about Gerrard, then. He had done exactly what she'd asked him *not* to do. Except, he wouldn't necessarily have known she meant it. How many times had she said, "I'm telling you this officially… now go and do what has to be done", or similar? The games we play.

Grace wondered whether to reply, deciding against it. There was no way he could get there in time for the reason of her trying to contact him. Anyway, as the meeting progressed, she was growing more at ease and feeling more secure with the man who had smiled encouragingly at her just now as she left the room. In fact, she was beginning to feel uncomfortably close to him. Perhaps it was just an association with the American accent.

★

The M25 was still busy for that time of the evening but there was a level of sanity prevailing across the lanes which was absent during their earlier outward journey. It seemed to transmit itself to Alice, whose leisurely pace heading back to Guildford allowed her boss's eyes to close until his head lolled forward onto his chest. This latter movement jolted him awake. He checked the clock on the dash: 22.58.

"Let's listen to the news, Alice, find out how important we are."

Alice switched on the radio.

"The time is eleven o'clock; this is BBC 5 Live, the news headlines, I'm Matthew Barker.

"Our main story tonight: more on the hijacking by terrorists of the heavy-lift vessel *Mastodon*. Nearly forty-eight hours after the hijackers struck, details are now emerging about their demands. Our reporter in Stornoway is Marian Teesdale. Marian, what can you tell us about what the terrorists' objectives are?"

"Well, Matthew, we understand they are demanding the release of a number – a large number – of members of Islamic State whom they claim are victims of injustice. Of 'Western tyrannies' is the quote I heard. Now, it's a well-known fact that the UK, and all European countries along with the US, Canada and all parts of the western world, steadfastly insist they do not negotiate with terrorists. However, it seems that some sort of dialogue has been established with the hijackers, although we are not party to its nature or content."

"Thank you, Marian, no doubt we will hear from you later. Yesterday afternoon, the *Mastodon* ballasted down and re-floated the second platform, Beta, which was towed away to a sheltered part of The Minch, where it is now anchored close to Tarbert, Isle of Harris. We understand that the platform has been searched by UK coast guards to ensure there are no personnel or explosive devices on board. Earlier, at around 2.00 a.m. this morning, the heavy-lift vessel moved under the existing Alpha platform, where it is currently holding its position.

"And in a further development this afternoon, the American aircraft carrier USS *Ronald Reagan* arrived in the area from its anchorage off Iceland, seven hundred kilometres away. It is now stationary at a distance of four kilometres from Hotel St Kilda and the *Mastodon*. Our chief political reporter is Andrea Gomez. Andrea, can you tell us what you have found out about its mission?"

"The short answer to that question, Matthew, is nothing. No-one can tell us at this time the purpose of the carrier's presence, and that is because it appears there has been no official word from the US. The belief is that it comes down to who we now know is on board the *Mastodon*. Abu el Taqha was almost certainly the main architect of the terrorist attack on the Willis Tower in Chicago four weeks ago. Politicians here believe the Americans are keeping a watching brief as this unfolds as a sort of back-up to ensure the terrorist leader does not escape the scene. Which begs the question, does this tie the UK's hands when trying to reach a satisfactory conclusion to this incident?"

"Thank you, Andrea. And, of course, we will keep you informed of any developments as soon as they happen. And now the rest of the news.

"The proposed new one-stop rail link from London to Edinburgh, has been criticised..."

"Not yet, then," Harry said. "We're behind a rail link. How does that make you feel, Alice?"

"Well, certainly not surprised. It was only two hours ago that you spoke to the Super. I can't see it making the main news tonight. Maybe local TV news at midnight."

"I guess so but leave it on anyway." He turned the volume down and leaned back again. "You know what I find really frustrating about this whole business – Jack and Jason, Tom Brown, Mickey Kadawe, now Tony Dobson, Jo Cottrell, David Gerrard, the handsome would-be assassin...?"

"You do reckon they are all part of the same story, then, sir?"

"Yes, I think they are. Perhaps 'ironic' is a better word than frustrating. We do our work – statements, meetings, interviews, forensics, more interviews, more meetings – and the big breakthroughs come from private individuals deciding to help us out."

"Go on, sir. I'm sure you're right, but..."

"Well, firstly, Little Bo-Peep."

"Lily Bo-Peep."

"Right, the singer. She steps up with the revelation that Kadawe was in the Tomlinson-Browns' house with a sack full of drugs just a few days before we grabbed Jack. Okay, she didn't *know* he had the drugs with him at the time – we only found that out afterwards

– but it was enough to kick off the case against Kadawe. Then Dobson's girlfriend takes a holiday snap and proves – *conclusively* – that a piece of key information we had when we were searching for Tom Brown was faked. I wasn't convinced it was all that relevant when it was pointed out – possibly someone fooling around with Photo Manager or something. But I certainly feel differently now.

"Then – the biggest irony of all – a convicted killer steps in to help us catch some villains and sets a snowball rolling. How does *that* make you feel, Alice, because right now *I'm* feeling a bit superfluous to…?"

"Listen, sir," Alice interrupted, turning up the volume again.

"… do not yet know the motive behind a serious incident in the Westmore area of Guildford earlier today involving the shooting of an ex-policeman and an assault on a second man. Police are assuring local residents that this appears to be a targeted attack and there is no danger to the general public. However, the area is still cordoned off as a crime scene and some streets in the locality are closed to through-traffic. The police are not able to release full details of the incident yet until next of kin have been informed."

"Not bad," Harry said, turning the volume down again. "No address, no names, no motive and no details. Bland is right on the button, I reckon, but enough to assure our perps that they succeeded. Pretty clever, our Lynsey."

★

Grace walked alone towards the village street in the half-light of a moonlit Atlantic evening. She wrapped the collar of her coat around her lower face to keep out the chill. Behind her were the 1950s Ministry of Defence buildings and the Administrative Centre, where, two levels below ground, she had spent all but thirty minutes of the past six hours.

In front of her, the longest street in the Outer Hebrides looked both sinister and romantic. More than anything, it spoke of a bygone age when people existed on the very edge of survival, from centuries ago right up to relatively recent history. It was like walking into the past, something that, right now, Grace would have given anything to do. Twenty years past would be ideal, but she would settle for two years, even twelve months if she had to haggle.

She had never before felt so vulnerable. At a time when her mind should be focussed on one thing only – the single most important thing in her life so far – she was distracted by the implications of the news from the listeners, all but confirmed in the brief text from Walcott. That mindset did not bode well for the delicate operation tomorrow, but Grace's thoughts were on events beyond that; even if she survived that test, what would be awaiting her afterwards?

Walcott was good, she kept telling herself, better than good. But the niggling doubt was always there in her mind about his presence, his persona, his *looks*. People noticed him, *always*. It was his cover, he had told her, his way of defraying any hint of suspicion. Guys in his kind of work didn't thrust themselves into the spotlight, didn't project a glamorous image, didn't live their life in high profile. They skulked in the shadows and avoided being noticed.

"So, your cover is to be completely *uncovered*?" she'd asked him.

"I'll be as uncovered as you want me to be," he'd replied, with his usual smile.

She checked her watch: 23.22. Final briefing for today in twenty-three minutes, then the final, *final* briefing tomorrow at 7.00 a.m., an hour before they would leave for HMS *Jura*. Then on to the *Mastodon*. Then…

She heard a noise behind her and turned.

"Grace? Are you okay?"

The sound of the American's voice made her heart beat a little faster, and, for a second, she wondered again whether it was the accent or the person himself that was causing it. Kade stepped forward, his Hollywood looks taking form in the fading light as he stopped a couple of metres away from her.

"*Are* you okay, Grace?"

Grace turned to continue her walk, waiting a moment for Kade to take the few steps to bring him to her side.

"I'm fine," she said, her voice shaking just enough for him to notice.

"It's okay *not* to be fine, you know."

"No, really, I'm okay." She gave a little laugh. "I mean, why wouldn't I be, when you've promised to get me back safely?"

"That's good to hear. For a moment I thought you'd started to doubt me."

She sighed and walked on in silence. They had slowed to a gentle stroll, walking very close together.

"I really do feel okay about tomorrow, you know," she said. "Surprising, perhaps. I guess the only thing I find uncomfortable is the fact that I can't picture the scene. I don't have, in my mind, any idea of what it's going to be like out there. And perhaps, if that's what is making me feel okay, then it's a good thing."

"I'm not sure I have that picture either, Grace. Every time is different, and sometimes it's best not to anticipate too much, to predict the scene too closely. Being ready to adapt to anything is better than being over-prepared to deal with a specific scenario that you hold, in detail, in your mind. We've narrowed the possibilities by getting agreement on all the conditions. I wasn't expecting that, to be honest. In fact, that call with Ruby just now was a bit *too* easy."

"You think they've agreed but won't comply?"

"They'll have to comply with most of what we asked for, because it will be visible. The positioning of the vessel, the anchors deployed, the on-deck facilities, the readiness of the hostages. The big question is about the bomb. I think he'll change his mind about showing this to the hostage. And if he does, that won't necessarily be a bad thing."

Grace stopped and turned to face him, taking half a step back. "How does that work?"

"Think about it. The deal we asked for was for el Taqha to show one of the departing hostages that they had deactivated the bomb and *how* they had deactivated it. If they *have* got a zee-bomb like they say, they've got the perfect opportunity to *prove* it to us if he thinks we might not believe him. So, you'd expect him to go for it, to show the guy so he can confirm it when he gets off the ship. On the other hand, if it's a bluff – which we believe it is – then he *can't* show it to the hostage. I'm sure they'll have an explosive device of some kind on board, but the zee-bomb is such a unique design he'll know that when the guy describes whatever it is to us, it will kill the bluff. Anyway, that's the plan."

"Plan? That was part of a plan?"

"Lydia's idea, she was the one who..."

"Ah, the wonderful Lydia. The lady with brains *and* beauty."

"Hey, where did that come from? As a statement of fact, it can't be faulted, but I get the impression it wasn't just that."

Grace laughed. "Us girls. Tell me, did Tom and Lydia have a... *thing* together during their time on the mission?"

"Oh, now I see," Kade smiled. "And the answer is no. They were together for a total of five days, but all the time along with six other people."

Grace became serious again. "It was a job, you know, Kade. I didn't want it to be like that. I'd worked with Tom for nearly five years and we grew very close... personally... then..."

"Hey, Grace, if this is a sort of justification for what happened last year, then you have nothing to justify. I was the one out of order. I took on the assignment – nobody forced me – and I should have carried it through. I'm real sorry that I refused to shake your hand on that occasion. If I can shake it now, I'd regard it as a privilege."

He held out his hand and Grace reached to take it. Their eyes locked for a moment and then they moved together, embracing tightly. They made no move to kiss, but Grace held on to him for a long time. When they stepped apart, Kade held her eyes again, his hands resting gently on her shoulders.

"I guess we'd better get back, and don't worry, I won't tell the President."

Grace smiled as his face went into soft focus through her standing tears.

CHAPTER THIRTY-FIVE

Friday, 7 July

At 4.50 a.m. the cafeteria and conference suite were in complete darkness except for one room: the one they had occupied for almost seven hours the previous day. A schematic of the *Mastodon* was filling the screens along one of the long walls. An image projected onto the wall opposite the door, showed a hazy picture of the *Mastodon* under the platform.

The group around the table comprised Kade, the four other members of Grace's bodyguard, Lydia, Mike Needham, Jens Reinhardt and the full Blue-Two team. Shirley-Anne, Jules and Rico had been joined by their three colleagues.

"Let me introduce you three guys to our guest engineer," Kade said. "This is Jens Reinhardt, from Boskalis in the Netherlands. Expert on heavy-lift vessels, including the *Mastodon*, and ready to make sure you guys don't get lost on board. Jens has chosen to stay with us throughout the mission. He was initially due to fly home later this morning, so our sincere thanks, Jens, for staying the course.

"And this, Jens, is the other half of Blue-Two. Brig is the unit's latest recruit, ex-SBS with experience of hostage rescue at sea. Next to him, Joss, current-serving SBS and, one further along, Rom, also SBS." The two men looked similar enough to be twins, with the same muscular build and shaven heads. Rom just shaded it on looks with a schoolboy grin. "Short for Romeo, by the way. Don't ask how he got that name; it's too long a story."

"Too long a list, he means," Rom said.

The ripple of laughter was quick to subside.

"We have visual intel from the X3 which shows we have a problem," Kade said, "but also a possible opportunity… Yes, Brig?"

The man had raised his hand.

"Before we start, I just wondered, is our chief negotiator planning to join us?"

Kade gave him a wide smile. "No, I felt it was more important that she had her rest before tomorrow. Okay?"

"Good idea. And Sir Roger?"

"Same as Grace – catching up on his sleep. I'll brief them both, and Ruby, at seven."

"Good. Sorry for the interruption. You were saying, the intel?"

"First, the good news. They have set up the deck to our specification, with the cabins, heaters, windbreaks and canopy in place. However, although they *have* moved the vessel, it is not how we asked. Jens, would you like to show us?"

He turned to the engineer, who had picked up the laser pointer from the table and was shining the red dot on the side elevation diagram of the *Mastodon* on the wall opposite him.

"They have hardly moved the ship at all, in fact. It has been edged back about twenty or so metres and they have deployed both rear anchors, now comfortably clear of the pontoon That doesn't help Plan A because the blue men need to get in at the forward end, where we believe the bomb will be.

"However…" he moved the laser dot "… this is where the drop-down loading door is, shown here on the port side of the vessel; the other door is in the same place on the starboard side. And…" he turned to his left "… this is a video from the helicopter fly-past at first light." He touched the keypad in front of him and the hazy image on the end wall came into focus and began to move. "The important points to note are, one, the vessel is no longer central to the platform across its beam. The port side is very close, within a few metres, of one of the columns. And, two, the point on the vessel which is closest to the column is exactly where the drop-down door is."

"Which suggests Jens and Daz may have been correct with their theory yesterday," Kade said. "It seems they could be positioning the vessel to take out one of the columns. I think that gives our blue men of Blue-Two a clear destination, but no easy way to get there. So, insertion will be via Plan B, ladders, and no darkness. As we discussed before, we could use landing Red-One and collecting the hostages as a distraction. The Sikorskys will be around as well, monitoring the changeover, so there'll be a lot going on. That's one option.

"However, we are going to push back hard about them moving the vessel completely out from under the platform, which they agreed to do in our last call with them. I guess they will say they're meeting us half-way, in that they've lowered the anchors. While we are talking to them about this, there would be an opportunity to get you guys on board. Lydia…?"

"This is more gut feel than psychological analysis, by the way, but I think it would be natural for them to believe that, if we were being so insistent on getting the *Mastodon* completely clear, any action we might be considering would need that to happen beforehand."

"Or couldn't they see it as a delaying tactic to allow us to take action now?" Brig cut in again.

"If our insisting they clear the platform came as a new demand or a change of mind, then I'd say yes. But the fact that it was an existing conditions, then, no, I don't think they would think that. We keep pushing, they'll believe it's imperative for any plans we have. These guys are good – what they've achieved is amazing – so they won't be complacent. But there's a difference in the level of alertness between basic diligence and urgent anticipation." She smiled. "That's *not* gut feel; you can believe me on that point."

"So, that's the decision to be made," Kade said. "I know you guys are keen to make a start, I'm surprised we've managed to keep Jules in check for this long, but we need to think about timing once you are there. We don't know how many hijackers are on board, but we can assume that el Taqha will have enough men on deck with him to counter-balance Red-One once we are in position. So that's six, including himself. Then, say, one with the bomb or, if it *is* on an MRTD, two. That's eight. One with Ove in the radio room – nine. Two with the hostages, although they could be held in the same place as the bomb, so let's say still nine or up to eleven, and perhaps two for general surveillance, but perhaps not. So, any number between nine and thirteen.

"My guess, I'd say closer to nine, because he wouldn't have planned in advance to have that many – if *any* – on deck, and even nine is a lot of good men to lose on a potential suicide mission. I don't want to go all-American here, but the CIA and CNN could have done us a favour, because, for every man on deck, that's one less you have to take care of. So ideally, we need to get you moving through the ship, *after* they're on deck. I assume that will be just before or just after we land.

"With entry through the anchor portals, once inside you could have remained in the windlass room as long as necessary, out of sight until the time is right. But arriving on the upper deck of the superstructure is different. If I understand you right, Jens, there is no cover?"

"That's right."

"No hiding place, which points to you needing to be there for as short a time as possible before you start moving. We don't have to decide right now, but the sooner we get focussed on the endgame the better. Jules, you're leading the charge, what do you think?"

Jules remained silent with his thoughts for a long time before replying.

"I know what you mean, Lydia, about opportunity," he said, turning to the doctor, "but I think we must go at the same time as Red-One. That is the time when most happens, and people are looking away. And I think we decide *now*, not wait for more phone calls with the terrorists. Then we can focus as Kade says." He turned to look at each of his team. "*D'accord, mes amis*?"

Brig, Rom and Joss nodded in agreement.

"Any time is fine for me," Rico said, "just so I don't have to swim."

"Don't worry, Rico," Shirley-Anne said. "I'll keep you dry."

Kade nodded to Jens, who raised the pointer again, showing the stages of the descent. He placed the index finger of his other hand on the mousepad of the keyboard and moved the schematic as he traced the route, the image turning and tipping through three dimensions.

"There are four levels between where you will enter the superstructure down to deck level, then one further stage to the drop-down door level. Once you enter from the upper deck, a single staircase takes you down two levels, then splits: one to port, one to starboard through the accommodation areas. The ship has forty-two cabins, twenty-one on each side. A lot of opportunities for chance encounters. The stairs are metal, and I assume you will be moving quickly. It is not the quietest part of the ship."

"The noise won't be a problem, Jens – these guys are like ballerinas – but the chance encounters might be, especially as we have to assume that every one of these guys has a radio for them to cover all the ship effectively. Word will get out in seconds if they're discovered."

The group remained silent for a while as individuals focussed on their own thoughts.

"Right," Kade said. "Final briefing at seven o'clock. Just Shirley-Anne and Jules from Blue-Two to attend. So, that gives us ninety minutes to do whatever we want." He looked at the Blue-Two team. "Is there anything you need before you go that we can be getting ready?"

"A disguise would be good," Joss said, "but we've not seen enough of them to get a clear idea of what they're wearing, or if they're all wearing the same."

"We'll know soon enough when we take out the first one or two," Brig said. "Then we improvise."

"Good word, Brig, because we know that's what we have to do. Who was it who said, 'no military plan ever survived first contact with the enemy'?"

"You do, Kade," Jules said. "Every time, just before we go into action."

The others laughed and nodded in agreement.

"Well, it must be right then. So, let's stay loose and flexible, as we always do. Anything else for now?" He looked round the room, his eyes coming to rest on Mike Needham. "Mike, you look worried."

"I always look like this when I'm thinking. If we equip these guys with trackers, we could watch them through the vessel and guide them, if necessary, by radio. We've got the 3-D model of the *Mastodon*; we just need to fit the guys into it."

The people in the room looked around at each other, Brig speaking for them all.

"How the hell do we do that, Mike?"

"Okay, not *into* it, but *onto* it – superimposed, like the exiles on Alpha's digital lattice. It's just a matter of scale. Here's what we do..."

*

Lucy Hewlett pushed the remains of her breakfast cereal around the near-empty bowl, her eyes fixed on the screen of the iPhone propped against the sugar bowl on the breakfast bar in front of her. Her mother called from the hallway.

"Lucy, it's seven o'clock, please get a move on. I should be away from here by now. In fact, I should be *there* by now. Paul's been waiting outside for nearly half an hour already. You do know what's going on in the world, don't you? I shouldn't have been at home overnight really."

Lucy smiled sweetly to herself. "Oh, I know, Mum, and I'm *so* grateful. It's *such* an honour to be the daughter of the *Home Secretary*, and to have to get up at twenty past fucking six. I mean, all my friends get up at least an hour later than that."

Jackie appeared in the kitchen doorway. "Yes, but they don't have the *honour* of being the Home Secretary's daughter, do they? And I will not have you using language like that in this house. Or anywhere else, for that matter. Right?"

Lucy lifted her hands, limp-wristed, in front of her and shook them. "Oooo, how scary."

"I said, *right*?"

"Okay, okay." She looked up at the wall-mounted TV screen. "And, yes, I do know what's going on in the world, like we have to have the news channel on in every room. And where am I supposed to go after school today?"

"Carrie's mum will pick you up and take you home with them, then..."

"Do I have to be picked up from school? It's like I'm back at primary."

"You know why you have to be, Lucy."

"But that was years ago."

"Nevertheless, that's what's happening. Then Dad will pick you up afterwards and bring you home."

"Which dad? Number one or number two? I mean, you don't want me wandering off again with the wrong person."

Jackie glared at her. "For God's sake, Lucy, don't be such a... *teenager.*"

Lucy's eyes and mouth opened wide in her usual expression of shock, and Jackie burst out laughing. Lucy joined her in a rare moment of unity.

"Now come on," Jackie said, "let's go." She went through to the hallway.

"Okay."

Lucy dropped down from the barstool and reached for the TV remote as the news story changed from the hijacking.

"It is now seven minutes past seven, and time for the rest of the news."

Lucy's shocked expression returned as she stared at the screen.

"*Mum*, come here. *Quick*."

★

Milena Bakke answered the desk phone on its second ring. As was her habit, she did not speak, just waited for the caller to identify themselves.

"Good morning, Milena. *Early* morning. I wasn't expecting to get you at the first attempt."

Milena smiled to herself and spoke in perfect English. "Morning to you, Sir Roger. It's already after eight o'clock here; don't forget we're an hour ahead of you. And anyway, the Service never sleeps. I thought you knew that."

Sir Roger laughed. "Of course, and I'm very glad you don't, because we are a bit short of time to be asking a favour of you."

"Anything we can do. Go ahead."

"As you know, four hours from now – midday your time – we will be landing our negotiating party on the *Mastodon*, and, as you also know, the hijackers are claiming to have a zero-bomb on board."

"And the conclusion is that this is so unlikely to be true that we are assuming they are bluffing. Or perhaps that's an oversimplification."

"No, that's about right. Or *was*, anyway. But I've just had a conversation with Joe Kilby and he raises an interesting point. If a terrorist group claims to have a nuclear device, what would be implied is that they have gained access to materials which has enabled them to make one. Would you agree?"

"Yes, I would agree with that."

"But Joe's point is a zero-bomb is a single entity. The only way you can get a zero-bomb is to steal one. You can't *make* one. Its design is far too sophisticated and over-engineered for anyone to reproduce it from component parts. It's a really obvious point, but I think we've all been so much in denial about the possibility of a nuke that we perhaps haven't explored it thoroughly enough. Joe checked back through the transcripts of the conversations with el Taqha and he referred on one occasion to *acquiring* a nuclear device. Not the first reference to it, at which time we assumed they'd made one, but on a later call to our Justice Minister. Are you still with me, Milena?"

"More than just with you, Roger, I can see where you're going. Joe's point is: they are claiming to have a bomb they couldn't possibly make themselves? So, for their claim to be credible, there must be some zero-bombs still around somewhere and possibly – or at least *theoretically* – accessible."

"Exactly. There were relatively few in existence, but we believe those were deployed at bases around the border with Russia during the Cold War to deter local cross-border incursions. Then they slipped off the radar, but they could still have been in service until the Soviet dissolution in ninety-one. They were subsequently designated obsolete and decommissioned. Or so we assumed. The question is, were they *all* decommissioned or were some mothballed?"

"Mothballed?"

"Put into long-term storage, just in case. It would make sense to hold on to some, at least for a few years. But, if they did, you know what happens…?"

"Responsibility gets passed on, people inherit other people's records, things get lost or overlooked."

"Right. I have no idea how many of these were deployed or where, but along the Finnish border with Russia has got to be a possibility, although I know Finland's allegiance at the time was not clear-cut. One thing is certain: they won't feature in the IAEA database."

They were both silent for a few moments before Milena spoke.

"Well, *I* haven't got any, Roger, if that's why you're phoning me. But if there's any other way I can help?"

Roger chuckled. "I knew it couldn't be that easy. No, I'm thinking of our American friend, Horne. Elsa has been beating him up and keeping him in the dark about everything, particularly since the CNN leak, but now might a good time to bring him back into the light. I still believe they do *not* have a nuke on board, but I also feel I can't just ignore Joe's theory. The CIA should be in a position to settle our nerves."

"Or set us off worrying again," Milena added.

*

The main briefing room at Guildford New Station was occupied by all working members of the Major Incident Teams. The unprecedented early gathering reflected the reaction to an attempt on the life of one of their own – albeit retired and from another force. Present also were Jo and Seb, the latter commanding much of the attention from Jo's female colleagues – out of both curiosity and appreciation.

The room was large, light and airy, with tall windows along the length of the outside wall. In front of the windows the eighteen members of the three teams, plus Jo and Seb, sat or stood forming a shallow semicircle in front of a central table. On the table were a laptop, a telephone, several stacks of files and DI Harry Waters, who was perched on the edge closest to group. The wall behind him featured a seventy-two-inch monitor screen and several pin-boards holding details of current cases. Also in the room were eighteen modern workstations, arranged in three groups of six. To Harry's left was a line of four offices and to his right, in an adjoining room separated by a Perspex-panelled wall, a team of six uniformed officers were seated at a long table in front of a line of telephones. They had been there since 6.30 a.m., ten minutes before the appeal for information went out.

By 7.15 a.m., Detective Constable Greg Branwell had finished bringing the group up to date with the events of the previous day relating to the disappearance of the mum and her daughter. They had been in hiding at the same house where the elder daughter had been taken after school by her grandmother. So, while the police were scouring the area for the missing duo, the family had been together all the time, watching TV. The father, Greg informed them, was simply leaving London on a scheduled business trip shortly after he'd had a blazing argument with his wife, a frequent occurrence and a constant source of worry to their neighbours. Her faked disappearance was his wife's way of teaching him a lesson. Any relief the team had felt at mother and daughter being found safe and well had been more than offset by the sense of anger at the way they had been used.

"Not to worry," Harry said. "When we started the search for them, we would have welcomed this as an outcome stacked against some of the other possibilities.

"So, moving on, most of the people in this room were here a year or so ago and many of you worked with me on the case of Jack Tomlinson-Brown – son of the then-Home Secretary, Tom Brown – and Jason Midanda, At that time DI Jo Cottrell was based here and was also involved. You'll recall that, following Jack's tragic death, when he took his own life whilst in custody in the presence of, and – allegedly – assisted by, his father, we had a spate of killings. Five young males executed – each shot in the back of the head – and an explosion at a so-called 'safe house', which killed three more. It was Jo, in fact, who made the link between the eight people killed and in doing so very nearly got herself killed, along with DS Ramirez. You all remember that?"

"I do," Jo said, raising her hand.

"Me, too," Tina Ramirez spoke from the back of the group.

The laughter came easy, reflecting the team's memory of the feeling of relief at their colleagues' narrow escape.

"Every one of the victims was linked, in some way, to Jack and Jason and, more specifically, to their convictions. We didn't have many leads, but one involved a man who met Sammo Sampson, a licensed drug trader, at Middleton Green shortly before he was found dead there by DC Clancy. He was the last of the gun-shot victims. We were alerted to the location of the body by a Mrs Thornbury, who also gave us a detailed description of a man who had previously met with the victim. This was the e-fit that the techies came up with from her description."

He turned and reached behind him, clicking on an icon on the laptop. The monitor showed the image that had been circulated in the media at the time.

"And this…" a second click, and a photograph appeared next to the e-fit picture "… we now know, as of yesterday, is the real thing. I think we can congratulate Mrs Thornbury for a pretty good job with her description. Even so, you'll recall we had no success whatever tracking him down, let alone linking him to the murders. Mrs T had also described him as wearing 'leather gloves' and being 'expensively dressed', and we did find fibres from a very costly cashmere coat at the scene of Sammo's death, but that was all pretty tenuous and, looking back, probably clutching at straws.

"Then, not long after that, another theory – and another line of enquiry – emerged. Tom Brown himself had been seen and recorded on CCTV at or near some of the murder sites at the approximate times the killings took place. He was also heard by a number of people on several occasions saying he was going to get even with everyone who contributed to the conviction – and the death – of his son. You probably remember that I, for one, did not want to believe he could possibly be involved. However, an excellent and timely speech by DS Bradley put me in my place and kept us all focussed and objective."

He nodded towards Owen Bradley and the young detective smiled back.

"And, as you know, it seemed Owen was proved right, because Mr Brown disappeared and the gun that killed the five men was found among his belongings at his apartment in SW1; found by Jo, in fact, and Mr Brown's wife. Later, his car was recovered from Ullapool, on the west coast of Scotland, and, in the well behind the seats were materials consistent with the type of explosive used to construct the bomb which destroyed the property in Dorking. From that point, he became the sole focus of the investigation to the exclusion of all others.

"In early November last year, a small boat, which had been taken from a hamlet just north of Ullapool, was found grounded on an island in The Minch, a stretch of water between the Isle of Skye and the Outer Hebrides. In the boat was a holdall containing some of his clothes and personal effects. At the end of the year, after a thorough search of the area, Mr Brown was officially designated 'missing presumed drowned' and, there being no other suspects, the case was closed. Following the discovery of a body earlier this week on Skye, I think we can drop the 'presumed' from that designation. Most of you will know all that, plus a lot more of the details, but hopefully for those who have joined the team since then, that puts us all on the same page.

"So, that seemed to be that, until just over two weeks ago, when ex-Detective Chief Inspector David Gerrard contacted me to arrange a meeting."

*

All heads in the cafeteria turned to the door leading to the conference suite. The three people who entered and picked their way through the packed eating area wore expressions of fierce determination. Ruby Weller led the single file, followed by Lydia van Roden and Sir Roger Ashpole. Twenty-five minutes earlier, at just before 7.30 a.m., Jules and Shirley-Anne had trodden the same route on their way to join the other members of Blue-Two and prepare the submersible for their assault on the *Mastodon*.

When Ruby's group had left the cafeteria through the main doors, all attention switched back to the side entrance. An eerie and expectant silence prevailed for a full minute before the diners picked up their conversations again and continued eating, most of them watching the news channel on one of the four giant screens angled down from the corners of the room.

At exactly 8.00 a.m. the side door opened again. Kade and Grace led the members of Red-One through the cafeteria, smiling grimly to acknowledge the nodded and spoken greetings. Half-way through their short passage, a group at one of the tables closest to the main doors sprang to their feet and began to applaud. Within three seconds, every person in the room was standing: clapping and cheering and shouting. Grace felt a surge of emotion and turned to Kade who was smiling back at her. He leaned closer as they walked, more slowly now as people reached across to shake their hands.

"This is all for you, you know."

As they reached the door, she turned briefly to look at the TV screen to her left.

She felt her scalp and the back of her neck go cold. Her stomach churned and her eyes widened with shock. The warm feeling of confidence which had grown inside her through the fellowship of Kade and her close companions dissipated in a second. From the screen, the perfect features of Jamie Walcott stared out into the room, swamping her senses. His beautiful blue eyes seemed to bore straight into hers.

CHAPTER THIRTY-SIX

Harry described his and Natalie's meeting with David, the fake photograph, the boat and Tony and Rebecca's conversation with the man with the lobster creels; Tony's trip to Shetland and the discovery that his and, most probably, Jo's phones had been bugged, and Tony's computer hacked. He admitted that, at the time, he didn't necessarily share David's – and Natalie's – view that this cast doubt on the circumstances around Tom Brown's disappearance. Subsequent events, however, had caused him to think again.

He continued with the account of Danny Weaver's appearance on the scene, his meeting with the two men and his apparent change of spots in alerting David; the trap they had planned to catch them. When he described the telephone call to Jo, there were gasps from the group and all eyes turned to their colleague, who stared in obvious discomfort at the floor.

"Okay," Harry said, "if anyone at this stage wants to tell me what an insensitive bastard I am, then get it out of your system so we can move on together without being held back by an atmosphere charged with tension."

There was silence for several seconds until Owen Bradley spoke.

"Ready for another speech, sir? I think we know you well enough to believe any action concerning your colleagues would always be taken with the best motives and to cause the minimum pain. That's easy for me to say, of course, because I wasn't on the other end of the phone, and I can only speak for myself, but I'd be surprised if the rest of the people in this room didn't feel the same." He paused. "With the possible exception of Detective Inspector Cottrell."

The spontaneous laughter was followed by gentle applause and nodding heads. Jo smiled across at Owen and wagged a finger.

"Thank you, DC Bradley," Harry said, "for that vote of confidence. It makes a change from you telling me I've got something wrong. Anyway, we know the two men who approached Weaver were the two at the Westmore Guest House and we know they really did intend killing David Gerrard. The question is, why? And this is where I have my change of mind about what's behind the bugging of Jo's and Dobson's phones. Because every sighting involving Mr Perfect can be linked in some way to Tom Brown. DC Crusoe, do everyone a favour and let them listen to you for a change. Just summarise where our man fits in the story."

Harry moved to one side and Natalie stepped forward to take his place.

"In chronological order, then. As far as we know, his first involvement was his meeting in August last year with Sammo Sampson at Middleton Green, which, incidentally, is a surveillance blind spot as far as CCTV coverage is concerned. Don't know whether that's relevant. When he met with Sammo the man had a rucksack with him but Mrs Thornbury wasn't sure whether he gave it to Sammo. Sammo was a licensed street trader and one theory was that it contained drugs.

"His next appearance in our story was on the fifteenth of June – just three weeks ago – in Scalloway on Shetland, where Tony Dobson was meeting with a professor working for the university up there. This was shortly after Dobson had started wondering about Tom Brown's disappearance and where his body might turn up. I think we are now sure that this man bugged his phone." She turned to Harry, who nodded. "But before that he must have hacked into his computer for him to know Dobson was planning the trip.

"Next, on the twenty-second of June – one week later – he arrives at Westmore Guest House enquiring about the man who met me and the boss there a few days earlier. Evelyn, the receptionist, told him it was David Gerrard.

"Fourth time, he turns up at the Remington Arms in Clapham four days later with his friend and *just happens* to bump into the man that David Gerrard put away for twenty years. Quite a coincidence – we don't think."

"Sorry, Nat." The speaker was DC Greg Branwell. "The boss said all these linked to Tom Brown. Those last two sightings, what's the connection? Am I missing something here?"

"We believe – or let's say we think it's a strong possibility – that with Jo and Dobson wired for sound and restricted in any further enquiries into the circumstances surrounding Mr Brown's death, David Gerrard became their focus as someone who was free from surveillance and who could still keep digging if he wanted to. The last man standing, if you like."

"Pretty big step," Greg said, "from monitoring phone calls to cold-blooded, premeditated murder."

"And possibly reflecting a sense of desperation," Harry put in. "Or somebody sending a message, in which case they don't know our DI very well, do they? Telling her to stay away is like insisting that she carries on."

The group laughed again with knowing asides and nodding heads.

"I'll take that as a compliment, Harry."

"As it was intended. Carry on, Nat."

"Two days later – and we only know this from Danny Weaver, but it fits the story – he meets with Weaver to arrange the hit. Where do they meet? At Middleton Green again, where he hands over the first instalment of his payment for the job. And then, his sixth appearance, yesterday, back at the guest house, in Room 17 with a Glock 17. He shot David Gerrard six times in the chest. Thankfully, David was wearing body armour, as you know, and received only slight injuries and concussion when he was thrown back against the wall and hit his head."

Natalie looked across at Harry, who stepped forward and perched on the table again.

"So, our guy keeps cropping up all over the place and appears to have access to very sophisticated surveillance tools *and* our own internal systems and procedures. Our Corporate Time, for example, to find out about our meeting with David. Westmore Guest House – supposedly a secret meeting place. Not anymore, it seems. This might, as DS Carter suggested yesterday, point to our two friends acting in some official capacity. What makes that hard to believe and even harder to accept is the attempt on David's life. So, for now, we treat this as attempted murder, motive unknown. The Super is aware of the possible link to Special Branch or secret services, but to her credit has taken the view that the gloves are off when they start shooting our guys."

"Lynsey Hargreaves, I love you and want to have your babies," Owen said.

The group burst into laughter. Harry shook his head in dismay.

"I'll pass on your message, Bradley, and let you know what she says. But, please, no more comments like that. However, I would like your comments, thoughts and any questions on where we are and what we think should happen next." He spread his arms and looked round the room. "Who's going first?"

The phone rang on the table where Harry was sitting. He looked across to the room where they were taking the calls. A woman officer was standing facing him behind the Perspex screen, holding a receiver to her ear and pointing animatedly at the phone on the table. Harry scowled and picked it up.

"What, Ellie?"

"You need to take this, sir. It's the Home Secretary."

"Someone *claiming* to be the Home Secretary, you mean."

"No, sir. I mean the *Home Secretary*."

"You're sure?"

"Sure enough not to tell her to piss off and stop wasting our time. Please take it, sir. She's holding on and I reckon she must be quite busy right now."

She put the call through before Harry could speak again.

"Hello, this is Detective Inspector Harry Waters. Who's speaking, please?"

"Good morning, DI Waters. This is Jackie Hewlett, the Home Secretary."

"Yeees? How can I help you?"

He heard the caller laugh. "No, it really *is* me, DI Waters. I can't show you any ID at the moment, but I can tell you that your immediate boss is Detective Superintendent Lynsey Hargreaves, who took over from John Mackay in January, and she reports to Chief Constable Edwin Mills. Will that do for now?"

Harry gave a nervous little laugh. "Sorry, ma'am, but you can't imagine who we get helping us with our enquiries. A couple of weeks ago we had Wolverine from the X-Men phoning in. So, my apologies and how *can* I help you?"

"No apology necessary and I'm phoning to help *you*. One of the men you are looking for – in connection with the shooting – I have met him, and my daughter has met him twice."

"*Really?* Ma'am, we are recording all these calls. Are you okay with that?"

"Absolutely."

He looked through to Ellie in the comms room, who was still holding the receiver. She gave him a thumbs-up sign.

"And I'm in a briefing meeting with my major incident team right now. Would you mind if I put you on speaker?"

"Not at all, good idea."

"Thank you, ma'am. Please go ahead."

"Well, I'm not sure if you'll remember, or whether it even got as far as Guildford, but around four years ago, when I was Shadow Home Secretary and working on the structure of the New Justice Regime, my daughter, Lucy, who was then eleven years old, was abducted from school. She was released, completely unharmed, after about two hours, with a letter to me from the man who took her, warning me to stop work on the NJR or the next time… well, you get the gist. This morning, watching the news, Lucy identified the man who abducted her as the handsome half of the pair you are looking for."

"I *see*. Can you remember who led the investigation into the abduction?"

"No-one, actually. I decided that I would do what the person had asked in the letter. I resigned my position on the NJR project team and requested the police to take no action. Probably the wrong thing looking back, but Lucy's safety was paramount to me above all else and I didn't want a lot of publicity which might encourage similar – shall we say – persuasive tactics. Also, the NJR project was in the very capable hands of Tom Brown, of course."

"Right," Harry said, "I totally understand. But you say this happened four years ago?"

"Yes, and I know what you're thinking, Detective Inspector, that she was an impressionable young girl and how could she possibly be sure after all this time."

"Well, I suppose that *could* be the case, don't you think?"

"I *did* think exactly that when, last year, we – Lucy and I – met a man outside Tom Brown's apartment on the top floor of Balmaha on Vauxhall Bridge Road. Lucy and I had gone to visit Tom and this man was just leaving the other apartment on that floor. As soon as he saw us, he rushed off, but not before Lucy had recognised him as the man who'd taken her. He is, I have to say, extremely striking-looking, but at the time I thought the same as you: how could she possibly be sure? What I *am* sure about, however, is that he is definitely the man in your picture. And, okay, this doesn't *prove* it's the same man who took Lucy, but I'm inclined to believe her now."

"So am I, ma'am, and both incidents fit a picture of this man that is emerging. Can I ask how he managed to abduct Lucy? Was it after school? Was she lured into a car or something?"

"Nothing like that. The school received a call saying that Lucy was to be picked up early. The caller said she was from my office and described the man who would collect her and said he would have a letter of verification with him, on my official letterhead notepaper, signed by me. And he duly turned up at the pre-arranged time with the letter – signed, but certainly not by me – and took her away right under the noses of her teacher, the headmistress and the caretaker. He had balls, this guy, I'll say that for him. The staff were just about suicidal by the time I got there and then suddenly Lucy was on the phone telling me she'd had an amazing time with this really dishy guy. 'Dishy', for God's sake, I mean she was only eleven."

"They grow up quicker than we did, that's a fact. And when the staff were questioned, did they come up with anything unusual or different about him in retrospect?"

"Nothing at all, except they all said he was really good-looking. Oh, and he was wearing leather gloves, which seemed a bit out of place. It was November, but it was really mild."

"Leather gloves, eh? In which case, ma'am, I think you can be *absolutely* certain that Lucy is right about it being the same man. What did you do after you saw him outside Mr Brown's apartment?"

"I got in touch with Tom and he said that he'd noticed the man had been acting peculiar and he would look into it. In fact, that was the last time I spoke to Tom."

"So, you don't know if he found out anything about him?"

"No, I'm afraid not, and, look, Detective Inspector, I am going to have to leave now. I'm very late. Sorry to be rude."

"Not at all, ma'am, I'm so grateful that you rang. This has helped enormously. One very quick last question: did Mr Brown tell you the man's name?"

"Yes, it was Strange."

Harry waited. "Strange in what way, ma'am?"

He heard the same laugh again. "That was his name, Strange. I think he said Oliver – no, *Oscar* – Oscar Strange."

"Oscar Strange. Thank you so much for your time, ma'am."

"You're very welcome, Harry. Good hunting. Bye."

"Bye, ma'am. I'll keep you informed."

Harry replaced the receiver and looked across at Ellie, who gave him the same thumbs-up, then turned to the twenty people in front of him, who were all staring at him, wide-eyed. He shrugged.

"I've got the Home Secretary working on it," he said. "Should be a breeze from here."

The room erupted into a rabble of side-conversations.

"Okay," Harry said, raising his arms for quiet. "This adds to a consistently growing picture. It seems this guy is *everywhere*, and… yes, Beth?"

DC Elizabeth Gordon had her hand raised.

"Did I hear the Home Secretary right, sir? Did she say his name was Oscar Strange?"

"That's right, why?"

"Then I might be able to add a bit more to that consistently growing picture."

"Go on."

"About the time Mr Brown went missing, I picked up a call from the Super – Mr Mackay – asking us to find any information we could on a gentleman called Oscar Strange. He didn't say much more, except that the man had moved into the apartment next to the Home Secretary and it was just a routine security check on the gentleman. I thought that was a bit unusual anyway, because you'd expect Special Branch to do that sort of thing. Anyway, I found nothing at all about Mr Strange – no record of his existence, in fact. I even checked with the estate agent who was registered as having the property on the market for sale or let and they said they had no details of anyone living there. The property had certainly not been sold or let through them and they had the sole contract for disposal of the apartment. They believed it was still unoccupied.

"I fed this information back to the Super thinking we'd be picking up the job of finding this guy, but he appeared to be quite relaxed about it. I seem to remember he sort of implied that Mr Brown must have got it wrong, that he wasn't himself... well, we know what had gone on just before that. And, as that seemed to be the end of it, I just wrote it up for the file and didn't bother to flag it with you or the sarge." She opened her eyes wide and put her hand to her mouth. "I hope not telling anyone doesn't mean we've missed something important."

"If the boss didn't think it was important, Beth," Harry said, "no-one would have expected you to tell him otherwise. I seem to remember we had quite a bit on at the time. Okay, Beth and Nat, can you stay back, please? The rest of you take a quick break – fifteen minutes. Grab another coffee, then we'll add these latest couple of pieces to the ever-expanding profile of Mr Strange."

CHAPTER THIRTY-SEVEN

8.20 a.m. BST

The twelve-minute journey in the Eurocopter to the hospital ship served to deflect Grace from her current anxiety, but only by replacing it with the harrowing memory of her last time on board. The helipad of HMS *Jura* was where she had seen Tom Brown for the last time. Only it hadn't really been him by then, just a body on a stretcher in a thermal bag being loaded into a helicopter on his way to die in The Minch. Still breathing, but not for much longer.

It was not until she disembarked from the aircraft that she realised how distracted she had been, because she was suddenly aware of Kade standing next to her on the deck, looking anxious.

"Grace, I said, are you okay?"

Grace blinked herself out of her trance. "Sorry, what was that?"

"Just checking that you're okay. Can't have you anything but fully focussed." He said it lightly, then frowned. "It's not about last night, is it? When we were out walking? I mean..."

"Oh, no," Grace jumped in quickly, the memory easily edging aside other thoughts. She smiled. "Definitely not. That was... really nice. I guess it's just this, the *Jura*, some bad memories, that's all. I'm okay now – really. Just let me at 'em."

She could feel Kade's concern at her lack of attention, and for perhaps the first time in all of this she realised how much these people were relying on her. Any perceived lack of commitment or focus in front of el Taqha could be interpreted by the terrorists as a sign of betrayal, putting her bodyguard immediately at risk and the potential for a wider disaster.

Hearing voices behind her, she walked over to the rail. Below them on the port side of the *Jura,* out of sight of the *Mastodon*, was Archer-One, with its winch at the stern holding in place the flat, casserole-dish-shaped submersible they affectionately knew as *Cassie*. She recognised Jules and Rico and the sturdy, muscular figure of Shirley-Anne, whose round and pleasant face under a bob of short dark hair smiled up at her. They were preparing their craft for launching, and Grace assumed the three men with them were the other half of Blue-Two. One of the men glanced up from the Archer as she was turning away. He looked familiar, somehow, and she realised he was the one she had seen in the cafeteria, sitting alone near the entrance. She doubled back and looked down again. He had gone, as quickly as he had before. If he had been there at all, she thought.

She was aware of Kade's hand on her shoulder, steering her away from the rail and towards the door to below deck.

"Okay, let's go and see if they want to check us out yet. Ruby should be in touch with el Taqha at nine o'clock, in around forty minutes' time. She'll be asking him about the position of the ship – why haven't they pulled it clear – so, there's no need to get kitted out and tooled up yet while conversations are still taking place. That's almost academic now, anyway. Blue-Two are going in, top deck, with the ladders, whatever. But we'll go when we're good and ready, and by ready I mean mentally as well, not just dressed to kill. So, it's just the medical stuff for now unless they want to wait until just before we're due to go. Not sure if they're planning to weigh us but if they are, we'd best get in before Robbie and Sergei. I can't imagine the scales will still be working after they've been on them."

Grace stopped when they reached the bottom of the steps. She looked around to check they were alone then reached forward and took both his hands in hers. She looked into his eyes.

"Kade, if we get through this, I'm not sure what will be waiting for me when we get back. That will *not* affect how I am on this mission, but, while I have the chance, I just want to say thank you for looking after me. I was dreading seeing you again after the last time. Now I'm dreading *not* seeing you again after this."

Kade smiled and squeezed her hands. "*When* we get through this, we'll deal with whatever is waiting for you afterwards, *together*. That's a promise – *another* promise."

Grace could feel her eyes filling and forced back the tears.

"I don't suppose you have any vacancies right now in Team Kade. If you do, perhaps you could let me have an application form later."

*

The young woman picked up the desk phone on its second ring.

"Good morning, Home Secretary's office, Jenny Brittani speaking."

"Hi, Jen. It's Georgia." The voice of Grace Goody's personal assistant was barely audible.

"Hi, Gee. Sorry, didn't recognise the number. You don't normally call on your mobile. Why are you whispering?"

"I've just slipped out of the office for a few minutes; I'm in the stairwell. It's mad up here at the moment, as you can imagine, with Grace over on St Kilda. There are all sorts of rumours flying round. One is that she's going out to the ship herself. Can't believe that's true. God, I hope she's going to be okay." There was a slight break in her voice.

"I'm sure she'll be well looked after, Gee. Did you have a message for Mrs Hewlett?"

"No, well, that is, I'm not sure. I just wanted a word with you first – unofficial. Have you seen the news today? Silly question; I bet you've seen nothing else."

"It's on now right in front of me. Why?"

"I know most of it is about the hijacking, but have you seen the item about the shooting in Guildford, where they've put out two photos of the men they want to interview?"

"Yes, and I've already chosen the one I want – the one without the scar."

"I know, he's gorgeous, isn't he? And he's even better in real life."

"What? You mean you know him? How?"

"This is why I need your advice, Jen, because I don't know what to do. The man in the picture is called Walcott – James or Jamie, I think – and he's been here, in our building, at least twice for meetings with Grace. It's always just the two of them and always at a weekend. I know the police haven't said these men did the shooting, but it sounds like that's what they believe, don't you think?"

"Hold on."

Jenny clicked the BBC News icon on her PC and went to the story about the shooting. She read aloud from the report under the two photographs.

"'Police are looking for these men in connection with a shooting in the Westmore area of Guildford yesterday. They believe the men may have information that could help them with their enquiries. The one on the left is thought to be between five-foot-eleven and six-foot-one tall; the other man is of medium height and has a scar over his right eyebrow. Should any member of the public see either of the men, they are warned not to approach them but to contact the police immediately on one of the following numbers.' So, yes," Jenny said, "it does sound as if they believe they could be the shooters."

"I don't want to be disloyal to the boss, and there's no way I can contact her right now, but… what do you think?"

Jenny thought for a few moments. "I think you'll have to do one of two things, Gee. Either phone one of those numbers and tell the police what you've just told me, or leave me to tell the Home Secretary and let her decide what to do."

"Or I could just keep quiet about it, I suppose."

"That's not really an option, Gee. Not now you've told me. I'm sorry."

"No, you're right. But what if he's one of her undercover guys, doing official stuff. The shit will really hit the fan, and…"

"If that's the case, they'll all close ranks – you know how it is. Stuff will get hushed up; people will get moved on. And if he *is* one of Miss Goody's and he's gone rogue, then that's not going to reflect on her, anyway. I think the best option is for me to speak to Mrs Hewlett about it, because that sort of keeps it in-house for now. She'll know what to do, Gee, and I'm sure she'll look after you whatever happens. That's what she's like."

"I suppose, except there's no love lost between her and Grace, is there? I wouldn't want Mrs Hewlett using this against her in any way."

"I know they're not exactly good buddies, but they are on the same side and Mrs Hewlett is not the vindictive type. So, Miss Goody will only have to worry if she's involved in something dodgy."

There was silence for a while before Georgia spoke again.

"Okay, Jen. So, you'll speak to her… when?"

"As soon as she gets in, before she starts her meetings. I'm surprised she's not here already, unless she's gone straight to Thames House, but I think she would have let me know if she was planning to do that."

"Does it have to be right away? I mean…"

"Thing is, Gee, they're asking for information right now, aren't they? If there's something the police should know about these men, they need to know it before they taken any action. Right?"

"I guess so. Look I must get back in the office. What if Grace phones? Although I can't imagine she would. Shall I say anything? She's probably seen the news item herself."

"I suggest you say nothing unless, of course, she asks you about it or tells you not to say anything to anyone. Either way, just agree with what she says. I'm going to tell Mrs Hewlett, anyway."

Silence again. "Okay."

"Look, don't worry, Gee. I bet there's a simple explanation." Jenny felt like crossing her fingers as she spoke. There was no reply. "Gee, are you still there?"

Georgia had ended the call.

⋆

The group had reconvened in the MIT room with replenished coffee supplies, except for Natalie and Beth, who were speaking on the phone in one of the side offices.

"Okay," Harry said, from his perch on the table edge. "Here's my thinking on this, then I'll throw it open for Bradley to shoot me down. Just concentrating on the pretty one for now, each new piece of information adds to a picture of some sort of special ops. The use of state-of-the-art surveillance tools; access to police files, our Corporate Time *and*, apparently, the Shadow Home Secretary's office to get the letterhead stationery. Or he's well connected to a string of people to do this stuff for him.

"Add to that his managing to gain entry *and occupy* a prestigious apartment, *next door* to the Home Secretary, in a complex that's protected by one of the most sophisticated domestic security systems available. He's got to have high-level backing or cover to achieve all that. And it's ninety-five percent certain his occupying that apartment was *because* it was adjacent to Tom Brown's. The only thing that doesn't fit is his taking of Jackie Hewlett's daughter all those years ago. I mean, Mrs Hewlett was only a shadow minister then. It's also a long time before the other incidents, so I suppose it might not be anything to do with what's going on now."

"Not sure if this has any relevance, Harry," Jo said, "but during the break I checked back on the details of that incident. There wasn't much about the actual abduction because it was kept out of the news at Mum's request, but looking at what was happening around that time, it was just after the Opposition's proposals for dealing with street crime had been leaked. You remember the *London Evening Standard* got hold of an email from Jackie Hewlett's office, which set out what were *then* seen as really radical and controversial measures. Not now, of course, because pretty much all of them are included in the NJR.

"There was the inevitable media outcry and demand for heads to roll until the press realised how popular the proposals were with the general public. Hewlett went – excuse the cliché – from zero to hero overnight. But looking at some of the reporting prior to the leak, Hewlett had seemed to be less than enthusiastic about the proposed changes, and it had been Tom Brown who had been driving them forward. Then, *after* the leak, Hewlett stepped forward to *lead* the project – officially, anyway. However, the feeling was that Andrew Donald – then Leader of the Opposition – favoured Tom as the best person for getting it through. Then this happened with Hewlett's daughter, she stepped aside, and Tom took over. And made an excellent job of it, of course. It was the NJR proposal that was mainly responsible for getting his party elected. Not sure if that moves us on, but at least there's a link there between the abduction and Tom Brown, albeit a bit remote."

"And you got all that in ten minutes?" Harry said. "I'm impressed. The sooner we get you back from Leicester the better." He looked across at Seb. "Just kidding; we're all enjoying the break."

There were nods and smiles all round.

"I'd like to claim credit for pulling all that together, but most of it was from a leader article at the time by Tony Dobson, no less."

"Well, it certainly establishes a link, but if that was the desired outcome of the abduction, then you have to wonder at what level it was sanctioned. Not by Andrew Donald, surely, the leader of Hewlett's party. And also, that intervention resulted in the *promotion* of Tom Brown, in the context of the NJR leadership team, at least. All subsequent events seem to be linked in some way to his demise."

The side office door opened and Natalie and Beth entered the room. Harry pointed to two Styrofoam beakers on the table.

"Welcome back. Your coffees – probably cold by now – very sorry. Anything from Johnny Mac?"

"Essentially what we already know from Jackie Hewlett," Beth said, "but with a few more details. Tom Brown contacted Mr Mackay after the Home Secretary had phoned him about the man outside the apartment. Mr Brown told him that he – Oscar Strange – had been acting sort of…"

"Strange?" DC Bradley suggested.

"Suspicious. Said he always seemed to be around, out on the landing, whenever he was arriving or leaving. As if he was watching him, spying on him. So, when Mrs Hewlett contacted him and told him what her daughter had said, Mr Brown went across to see this Strange person. Apparently, he wasn't there, so Mr Brown somehow got into the apartment and found it was empty."

"The guy had left?" Harry asked.

"More than that. The apartment was, literally, empty. No furniture except for a couple of things just inside the entrance, which Mr Brown thought had been put there just to give the *impression* it was occupied when you looked in the front door."

They all shuffled on their feet or their chairs and a few minor conversations started up as they processed the latest information.

"I think your ninety-five-percent-certain that he was there to spy on Tom Brown has just moved up to a hundred, Harry," Jo said.

DS Belmont raised his hand.

"Yes, Craig."

"Might be going off at a tangent here, sir, but I don't think any of us *really* believed – at first – Tom Brown was responsible for sneaking around in dark alleys shooting people in the back of the head. Right?" He looked round at the nodding heads. "*Until* we found the gun. I know there was the circumstantial evidence of the

CCTV sightings, but if it had just been CCTV versus logic, logic would win. He didn't do it. But finding the gun in his apartment was a game-changer. The pendulum of doubt swung against him."

"Very picturesque, Craig," Harry said, "but where's this going?"

"Staying just across the landing from him, there's a guy who we now know is a killer and who kills with a gun. We also know that he can beat the security set-up at Balmaha and get into the apartments. As I recall, it's the same alarm system for all six apartments on the premises but with different key codes. So, it would be dead easy for him to get into Tom Brown's apartment and plant a gun in his sock drawer or wherever Jo found it?"

"There were no fingerprints on the gun, as I remember," Greg said.

"That's right," Craig went on, "and we explained that by concluding that for a trained soldier, ex-special forces, it would be normal for Tom Brown to keep any weapon in pristine condition through regular cleaning and servicing. But it could have been because our handsome anti-hero wiped the gun then handled it with his kid gloves afterwards before hiding it. I wonder if he ever takes them off."

There was more shuffling and murmurs of agreement.

"And if he did do that," Jo said, "I think we can assume that Mr Strange, himself, carried out the murders he was trying to frame Tom Brown for, or directed someone else to do them. Bearing in mind, of course, that he was already linked with Sammo's death before we turned our attention to Tom Brown."

There were a few moments of silence as the implications of the statement were pondered. Harry was looking across at Jo, who was staring, wide-eyed, back at him. Most of the group had focussed again on the two side-by-side images on the screen.

"This is... *beyond* Agatha Christie," Harry said.

"Well," Owen Bradley was shaking his head. "I guess we've just accidentally reopened the strange case of the Dorkford serial killer."

⋆

At 9.15 a.m., the six members of Red-One, plus Jules and Shirley-Anne occupied all the seats available round the rectangular table which almost filled the comms room of HMS *Jura*. Their attention was focussed on the propeller-shaped conference phone resting on its three blades in the centre. Ruby's voice broke the expectant silence.

"Ruby here. I'm with Sir Roger, Lydia, Mike and Jens. Who am I speaking to?"

Kade went through the names of those present. "That must have been a very short call with el-boy, Ruby. It doesn't sound like there can have been much in the way of discussion."

"Just under eight minutes. El Taqha made the point that he has complied with our request to drop two anchors so they can't quickly make a run for it. He's aware, of course, of the US carrier standing off, and he says coming out from under the platform makes them more vulnerable to a possible air attack. He might have a point there, in fact, because we have still had no official word from the US as to the purpose of its mission. I believe the PM has a meeting scheduled with the US ambassador this morning and is raising that with him. You can't enlighten us, can you, Kade, with your experience of US military tactics?"

"A bit out of touch, I'm afraid. And the chances are the ambassador won't know what they're doing there either. Did el Taqha mention anything about the bomb? Is he going to allow someone to check it has been deactivated?"

"He's changed his mind on that as well, although I think we were expecting him to, anyway, weren't we? He says that it gives away his only card, but he *has* confirmed that he'll deactivate it during the negotiations. I guess it's academic anyway, because he can *re*activate it in a moment if necessary."

There was silence for a few seconds before Sir Roger spoke.

"So, where are we right now in terms of readiness?"

"We need medical checks, body armour, weapons, wiring for radios. Just to recap on comms – we switch to tactical radios at 10.50 a.m. – that's both Blues, Red-One except Grace, and the command centre on Hirta. Team leaders to keep radios live at all times, others as directed by me, Jules and the Major. *Separately*, Lydia will have a direct link, different frequency, to Grace. That's still to be set up and tested, which will be done right after this call. Tracking chips are in place. Robbie has the one for Red-One and Jules, Rico and Brig one each for Blue-Two. So, when the decision to go is made, we are thirty minutes off ready. Okay?"

"Just for the benefit of us all, Robbie, take us again through your part of the tracker plan," Sir Roger said.

"When we land, I walk to the port side, as if to check the anchor is down. Then I walk directly across the deck to starboard, and do the same. From edge to edge it's exactly seventy-point-four metres. Mike will track me on the screen and superimpose the overhead elevation of the 3-D image of the *Mastodon* on the line I walk. He'll then adjust the size of the image so the width of the deck coincides with the length of my walk across it. Then we'll have the scale Jens needs to follow Blue-Two through the ship and advise on escape routes if necessary. Fucking brilliant! I'm amazed I didna think of that myself."

"I'm sure you would have done, Robbie, if Mike hadn't jumped in first."

"And once the big man's done his deck-walk," Mike said, "we'll be able to follow the three chips with Blue-Two just like we monitor movement of the exiles on Alpha on the digital lattice."

"Speaking of which," Grace said, "is anyone in touch with Lochshore? I guess in all the excitement it's easy to forget what those guys on Alpha are going through. They'll be following the news like everyone else."

"I've spoken to Lawrence Harding early today," Ruby said. "He's at Lochshore now. As you'd expect, there's not much movement to monitor because just about everyone on Alpha is round the observation deck. They'll get a great view of the comings and goings from up there. But health monitors are showing high levels of stress, as you'd expect."

"It wouldn't surprise me if they were enjoying this in a perverse sort of way," Lydia said. "Something different and exciting, and perhaps a feeling that they are still important."

They all remained silent with their thoughts for a few moments until Kade spoke again.

"So, if there's nothing else, we'll start getting ready. I think we draw a line under trying any more to get them to move the *Mastodon* further. Suggest we strike at eleven o'clock. We're at 9.32, so let's say 10.30 for final checklist. Okay?"

⋆

Ellie burst into the room.

"We have an address, sir!"

"For…?"

"Mr Smooth. No reported sightings yet for the scarred one, but we've had dozens of calls about the other one, including three independent calls from people who are convinced they know where he lives. Two people on the same road and a pizza delivery driver; no apparent connection between the three and all gave the same address. A Georgian terraced in Kennington, SE11, near the Oval. Twenty-three Cannon Road."

"Kennington? Shit. That means Metropolitan Police and London traffic. Craig, get that address to the CCTV Monitoring Centre that covers Kennington. That would be Lambeth, I guess. Should be plenty of coverage there close to the cricket ground. Make sure they have all the pictures of this guy that Weaver took and get them to check current feed around the property and locale plus all the footage from the time the appeal went out. Let's assume he saw it at the first showing. Everyone who left that building, similar height and build. I can't imagine he'll be flashing his perfect teeth at anyone today, so hoodies, caps, scarves. And tell them to look for gloves, just in case he *can't* take them off. Then get up there with a couple of the guys and link up with me from the Monitoring Centre. Need to contact the Met and get them on board. They'll have to provide uniforms and SFOs."

He called to Ellie. "You said nothing on Kemp, yet. Let Greg know if that changes." He turned back to the group as Craig made the call from his office and Owen and Tina gathered laptops and notebooks together as they prepared to leave with him. "Jo, can you hold the fort here and collate the info from the phones? I'll get the Super to clear it with your boss, if you like."

"Not necessary. He's not expecting us back until later today and this is my home patch, anyway, remember."

"Great. Alice, Nat, George – you'll come with me – two unmarked cars, lights and sirens until we get to Kennington. Although I can't imagine our man will still be there. My guess is he'll have been gone some time back, so the CCTV capture is critical. Greg, can you get on to Met CID and get someone on point for a person-to-person call from me? Try and get DI Hannah

Leasing if she's around. We've worked together a few times before. Tell whoever it is that I'll fill them in from the car on the way there and get back to me with their iPhone number."

The phone in Harry's office rang. He looked across at it then at Ellie, who was standing in the same place as before with the receiver to her ear. This time she was pointing animatedly to his office phone. He shrugged and went through to take the call.

"The Home Secretary again, sir. She said she needs to speak to you one-to-one and she doesn't want the call recorded. What shall I do?"

"Put her through, Ellie, and make *absolutely* sure we don't record it."

"Yes, of course, sir."

★

Jackie and Jenny sat across the huge desk from each other in the Home Secretary's office in Marsham Street.

"Harry?"

"Yes, Home Secretary?"

"Hello, again. I've got the phone on speaker and my colleague Jenny Brittani is with me to handle any follow-up from this call. Are you on your own and not recording?"

"Yes, ma'am."

"I have some more information, but this is rather delicate. In fact, I perhaps shouldn't be burdening you with this but I am due in a Cabinet meeting in less than ten minutes and I don't have the time to go elsewhere. What I mean is, this would normally be coming to you from higher in your own chain of command. I have further information about our Mr Strange, who appears to be connected in some way to Grace Goody, the Ministerial Director of Justice, under the name of James or Jamie Walcott. It seems he has regular meetings with her or, should I say, they have met in her office on more than one occasion. Just the two of them and at times when not many people are around."

"I see."

"This makes it awkward, as it seems the man may be part of some official operation and..."

"Sorry to interrupt, ma'am but what we are investigating is the shooting of a retired Detective Chief Inspector, six times at point blank range. It was premeditated – in fact, the perpetrator went to a lot of trouble to set up the hit. Mr Gerrard, the victim, who survived only because he was wearing a protective vest, is a lecturer at a college of further education. He has no links at all now to the police or security work, so..."

"I won't ask you right now why a college lecturer was wearing a protective vest, Detective Inspector," Jackie cut back in, "but the point is, I don't know what this man was – or *is* – working on, and until we find out we should suspend the investigation. I'm very pleased, of course, that the gentleman survived the attack..."

"With respect, ma'am, it's a little late now to suspend the investigation because we have his perfect features all over the media, as you know, *and* a probable address. We have to get this man off the street. Now that he knows we are looking for him, he might be a significant danger to the public. Remember, this is the person who abducted your daughter. We don't want him taking a hostage or anything."

Jackie looked across at Jenny, who nodded in agreement with Harry.

"Look, I'll do a deal with you, Harry," Jackie said. "Find him and detain him, then hold him until we get more information. But no guns. *Absolutely no guns*. So, no SFOs looking to be heroes, okay? Jenny will chase up any information on this man – both men – but you can imagine how difficult it is getting anything from the secret services, if that's who they're linked to. And I'm sure you realise that the very people we need on this have their eyes and minds elsewhere right now. I fully understand what you all must feel, someone attacking one of your colleagues, but I'm trusting you to handle this with kid gloves." She hesitated for a moment. "No pun intended," she added, with a little laugh.

"Understood, ma'am, and thank you."

"Jenny will get back to you immediately after this call with a number you can phone to keep her up to date and in case you have any questions. And now, I must get to that meeting or the PM will be locking *me* up. Good luck, Harry."

She ended the call and got up from her chair, grabbing her shoulder bag, laptop case and briefcase.

"Right, Jenny, your temporary promotion to Home Secretary starts now. Let DI Waters have that number, then I guess the best thing would be to get on to P-Ops direct. You've got a contact there, haven't you?"

"Yes, ma'am, Corporal Barrowclough. She's straight through to the Brigadier, so that could be helpful."

"Excellent. Ask the Brigadier if Mr Strange is one of theirs and, if he is, what the fuck is he doing gunning down ex-policemen?"

"And if he isn't one of theirs?"

"Then tell him the Home Secretary respectfully requests that he finds out who the hell he's attached to, other than Grace Goody. Metaphorically speaking, of course."

Jenny smiled. "Of course."

"I'll bring the Justice Minister up to speed. Jonathan will be at the meeting." She checked her watch. "*Already* at the meeting, I have no doubt. This could not have happened at a worse time."

"Certainly not for Grace Goody," Jenny said. "I'm sure she'll have seen the news feed, and this guy's mugshot and she'll be wondering what's happening at a time when she should be concentrating for her life."

CHAPTER THIRTY-EIGHT

9.30 a.m. BST (10.30 a.m. local time, Oslo)

Milena Bakke, the first woman Director of the Norwegian Police Security Service, was forty-one years old, tall, slim, and beautiful, with sparkling green eyes and dark-blonde hair pulled neatly into a bun at the back of her head. She wore a cream silk shirt under an immaculate grey suit with a short skirt. The venue for her meeting with her invited guest at the headquarters of the Oslo Police District was more like the drawing room of a stately home than part of a municipal building. Inside, to the left of the door, a large, light-oak bookcase occupied most of one side of the room with a long sideboard in the same wood against the wall to the right. Opposite the door was a single window, spanning the width of the room, reaching up to the ceiling from a low window-seat which ran along its full length. Heavy velvet curtains at either side were pulled back and held in place by gold-tasselled tiebacks. In the centre of the floor, arranged symmetrically on the thick-pile carpet, two long, soft-leather sofas faced each other across a low rectangular table with a matching armchair at each end.

Milena led her visitor into the room then turned to him and spread her arms, as if to invite his appreciation. It was spontaneous and sincere.

"Wow." Silas Horne's eyes opened wide with wonder. "This is not what I expected. I wasn't sure I hadn't been invited here to be arrested."

She smiled. "We'll come to that later. Please take a seat."

Silas sat at the end of one of the sofas and Milena took the armchair nearest to him. A tall, well-built young man in a dark suit and open-necked white shirt appeared in the doorway.

"Coffee and cookies?" Milena asked Silas.

"Coffee, sure, but nothing to eat, thanks."

Milena smiled at the young man. "Okay, Jorgen. Bring the cookies anyway."

"So, how can I help you, ma'am?"

"With some information, I hope, and please call me Milena. Thank you for coming right away. I hope it wasn't too inconvenient."

"Not at all, ma'am – Milena." He gave a little laugh. "Twenty minutes' notice to catch a plane is a luxury compared to some sprints I've had to make in the past."

"Well, it's very much appreciated. But what I'm going to tell you is extremely sensitive and I cannot risk this getting out into the public domain."

Silas sighed and spread his hands. "Like the ID of the terrorist leader, you mean. Elsa can hardly bring herself to speak to me right now."

"What I need, Silas, is an assurance that nothing we discuss in the next half hour or so will leave this room, except through me. Can you give me that guarantee?"

Silas sighed again. "That would kind of depend what it is, with all due respect. If, for example, it impacts on US lives, then I'd have no choice. And as I explained to Elsa, I have a responsibility... well, you know what I mean. I did make it very clear last time when I reported back that it must be kept secret for now, but someone over there decided..." His voice trailed off as the door opened and the young man came in with a small trolley, the contents of which – a tray with cups, sugar bowl, serviettes and cream jug, a silver coffee pot and a plate of cookies – he placed on the table.

"Will that be all for now, ma'am?"

"Yes, thank you, Jorgen."

Milena picked up the pot to pour. "So, you *can't* give me an assurance?" she asked.

"Not absolutely, but of course I'll do what I can."

"Very well, I'll take the risk," She gave him a wide friendly smile as she passed him his cup. "Just in the spirit of cooperation..." she removed her iPhone from her jacket pocket and placed it on the table "... let's make certain that no covert communication is happening right now. Your phone, please, Agent Horne." She gestured towards the table.

"Aw, come on, Milena." He sighed. "Okay, let's play games." He held up the phone to show the blank screen and placed it next to hers. "So, what's new?" He picked up his cup.

"Well, what's new to you, I think, is that the terrorists are claiming they have a zero-bomb – what I think you Americans call a 'zee-bomb' – on board the *Mastodon*."

Silas spluttered into his coffee and reached forward to put it carefully down on the table. He picked up a serviette and dabbed his mouth.

"*Sheesh*."

"Sheesh? Is that all?"

"I don't follow."

"Well, what I was hoping for was, 'sheesh, but that's impossible', or something similar."

"It's… it's certainly *unthinkable*."

"That's not the same, though, is it? A giant asteroid hitting the Earth is unthinkable – also very unlikely – but not impossible. Are you with me?"

"But that's just semantics."

"No, it isn't, Silas. What can you tell me about the zero-bomb?"

"Well, I guess the most significant thing about it is that it's obsolete. Extinct. No more. They were big news at one time. I mean, big news within the military."

"Not on CNN?"

"Very cute, Milena. No, of course they were top secret. They presented an option to use nuclear weapons tactically. One of a number of experimental weapons developed during the Cold War. They could be carried to a precise location, by a team of, say, six guys on the ground, assembled in situ…"

"And then blow up an area two miles radius with a shock wave of about five miles more and a creeping death beyond that. Yes, very precise and targeted."

"Yeah, well, it seemed like a good idea at a time when the future looked like it was going to be a lot shorter. Anyway, when the Cold War ended, they were decommissioned."

"Meaning what, exactly?"

"The component parts were separated and reused for domestic power and military propulsion. Submarines, mainly."

"So, *every* zee-bomb ceased to exist. You can guarantee that?"

"Jeez, Milena, I can't *personally*. I was about nine at the time, I don't remember them ever being mentioned on *Sesame Street*. It's just what we believe. I mean, what we're told."

"Are you making a distinction there, Silas, between what you're told and what you believe? Is that the crucial difference between impossible and unthinkable?"

Silas drew in a breath and looked down at his hands.

"Remember, this was way before my days in the service. But there was a rumour, which has been kind of passed down through time, that some were stashed on a just-in-case basis. Where, and how many? I have no idea. But, the story goes, after a while, a good number of years, somebody had the great idea that they should gather them all in and finish the job – the decommissioning, I mean. And, you know how it is?"

"Responsibility gets passed on, people inherit other people's records... things get lost or overlooked. That's the second time I've said those exact words in less than three hours."

"Yeah, well, you're right on. Because no-one knew how many were left out there, it was impossible to guarantee everyone had been reclaimed. That doesn't mean they *weren't* all reclaimed, of course. They could have been. But without an inventory..."

"You're not being very reassuring, here, Silas."

"Hey, but if *we* couldn't find them, and we knew what we were looking for and where to look, how the hell could anyone else? I mean they were stashed away, well hidden – *too* well hidden, as it turned out. The chances of someone just stumbling onto even one of these weapons are sub-zero. And, as I said, that's if there were any out there still to find."

"Is there any chance they might have been moved somewhere strategic like, say, Afghanistan? Iran? Syria? Iraq? Close to where new wars were taking place and where they might have been accessible to Islamic groups."

"I'm pretty sure none of those places, although I can't say for certain. I don't think they were ever moved from where they'd been deployed. Just hidden locally. And there weren't *that* many of them. When it came down to portable nukes, the Davy Crocket was the weapon of choice. That was one that could be fired from a launcher with a range of two miles or so. Still a bit close for comfort if the wind was wrong. The zee-bomb was regarded as a sort of novelty – a gimmick, to be truthful."

"Some gimmick. But they *were* deployed?"

"Yes, but..."

"And how were they hidden? I mean, you can't just put a nuclear bomb behind a tree and cover it with branches. There must have been a *method* to ensure they'd be safe."

"Sure, there must have been, I guess, but we're talking thirty-plus years ago, give or take. Look, I really don't think we need to worry. Like I said, I really believe it's... it's..."

"Unthinkable? But let's just *think* it through anyway, Silas. How would you go about storing a nuclear weapon safely? Where would it be safe?"

"I really don't..."

"What about in a place with other nuclear material, like a nuclear power station, for example. Does that make sense?"

"That would make sense if we could persuade the host country to take them. There'd have to be something in it for them, I'd have thought."

"What about Finland, do you think they would have been interested? They've got four nuclear reactors in two separate plants – all of which were operational before the end of the Cold War – *and* a twelve-hundred-kilometre border with Russia. Also – relevant to the current situation – they have a border with Norway."

"It's as likely a scenario as any, but it's still highly *un*likely." He pointed to his phone on the table. "Want me to check?"

"Do I want you to phone someone in the states, tell them there's a nuclear bomb on the *Mastodon* and ask if it might be one of yours? No, I don't want that, thank you. Not before I've spoken to someone. Wait here, please."

She got to her feet, picked up both phones from the table. and walked quickly from the room. The door was almost closed behind her before Silas realised what had happened.

"Hey, Milena, you can't..."

He heard the key turning in the lock.

*

Jackie was fifteen minutes late for the meeting at Number 10, but when she was shown through to the Cabinet Room, only Andrew was present. He was seated in his usual place with his back to the marble fireplace, at the centre of one of the long sides of the stretch-oval-shaped table. He was staring at his iPad, his expression drawn and anxious. The muscles in his jaw were tight.

"Sorry I'm late, Andrew." Jackie looked around the room as if she expected the rest of the group to suddenly materialise. "Or have I got something wrong. I thought we had a Cabinet meeting at..."

"Nine-thirty. We did. I sent them away." His words came out like tacks from a nail gun, sharp and deadly. "Have you seen this?"

He held up the iPad so Jackie could see the picture of Jamie Walcott on the screen.

"Yes, I have. Why?"

"Do you know who he is?"

Jackie sat down in the seat across the table from him.

"What's wrong, Andrew? What do you mean, you sent the Cabinet away? Not just because I was late, surely. I got delayed and..."

"Do you know who he is?" Andrew shouted the question this time.

"Well, yes, I do, as a matter of fact. His name is James – or Jamie – Walcott and..."

"How the hell...?"

"He's the person who abducted my daughter four years ago. And he's the reason I've been delayed, in fact."

Andrew's mouth fell open. He stared across the table, his eyes wide and unfocussed. Then he banged the table hard, several times, with the flat of his right hand.

"Andrew, what the hell...?

"He's got to be found. We have to get to him before they do."

"They? Who are *they*?"

"The police. Who do you think *they* are? Who else would put his picture out there – fucking Jehovah's Witnesses? You'd better get on to this right away and stop them looking. And get hold of Grace for me."

"Have you lost your mind, Andrew? Grace will be very shortly stepping onto the deck of a ship – which just *might* have a nuclear bomb on board – to try and save eight hundred of your citizens."

"Jackie, listen to me, you have to contact her right away."

"I will *not*. And I'm doing nothing, Prime Minister, until you tell me what is going on. What the hell is the matter with you? You have a meeting with the ambassador in about forty minutes. You'd better get yourself…"

"*Fuck* the ambassador."

"I hope that's not a direct order, Prime Minister, because I'd rather not." Jackie gave a thin smile in an attempt to defuse the tension.

"Don't you see?" Andrew's eyes were wild and menacing. "Walcott could bring everything crashing down. *He – has – got – to – be – found*." He banged the table again with each shouted word.

"Andrew, you are scaring me. *What* could he bring crashing down?"

"*Everything*. Me, the government, the country, every-fucking-thing."

"That's ridiculous." Jackie laughed out loud. "What would he have to do to achieve that?"

"Absolutely nothing."

"Nothing?"

"It will happen if he does nothing. He has to do *something* to prevent it. That's why they mustn't find him."

*

At a table on the terrace at Westminster, Jonathan Latiffe and Reggie Greyburn watched the news on Reggie's iPad with a growing sense of shock and incredulity.

"The time is ten o'clock, this is BBC News with Anna Macgregor and Rory Beaston. The main story: the hijacking in the Atlantic by Islamic State terrorists – and a significant new development. The following item from CNN Night-Time News aired just a few minutes ago."

The on-screen image showed a video of the *Mastodon* and the platform in the middle distance taken from a reporter plane, which panned across to the US carrier a few kilometres away, with a CNN presenter's voice-over.

"We are getting reports that the US military may be planning an air strike from the USS *Ronald Reagan* on the hijacked heavy-lift ship *Mastodon*, which is currently at anchor underneath the UK offshore prison facility known as Hotel St Kilda. The US supercarrier is at present lying off a few miles from the site of the hijacked vessel. These reports are unconfirmed, and we have no indication as to when such action might occur or whether British authorities are supportive of this possible development."

The report returned to the studio with two reporters, Helen Frost and Greg Winchester, seated behind their names displayed on the news desk. Helen Frost took up the story.

"It is known that the terrorist leader, Abu el Taqha, is on board the *Mastodon* and, we understand, is leading the dialogue with the British authorities. El Taqha is believed to have been the brains behind the recent attack on the Willis Tower in Chicago and a significant number of similar terrorist offences around the world, as well as playing a major part in the 9/11 atrocities in 2001.

"Pressure has been mounting on the President and his advisers over the past twenty-four hours to take decisive action in the stand-off, rather than risk an outcome which may lead to el Taqha's ongoing freedom. With the presidential elections coming up very soon and with President Weston hoping for a second term, it is not surprising he is seriously considering this option."

"*Supportive* of? We're not even officially *aware* of," Reggie said. "Perhaps that's what caused Andrew to tell us all to fuck off this morning. That was the expression he used, wasn't it?"

"That's right. I've seen him near-apoplectic before when he's been really wound up, but that was something else today. As much as anything, it was like stark panic. Just when I thought he'd been stabilising us all with his calm leadership. Too much to sustain for long, I guess."

"If this carrier thing *is* the reason for what happened this morning, I'd like to be a fly on the wall when he meets Linus."

★

The calm atmosphere in the medical suite on HMS *Jura* belied what lay ahead in less than an hour's time for the six people in the waiting area. The door leading to the treatment rooms opened and a woman in white trousers and shirt called through.

"Miss Goody."

Grace got to her feet and followed the woman through to a familiar place. It was as if every phase of the proceedings over the past twenty-four hours or so had been carefully designed to fill her mind with the worst memories and the maximum guilt. The room in which she was now standing was the scene of her last conversation with Tom Brown, which was *his* last conversation of all. The place where she had revealed everything to him: the level of betrayal and deceit which had brought him to this, his final conscious encounter with a human being. The room seemed uncommonly cold and she couldn't help feeling it was somehow a reflection – or even a statement – of what had happened there on that day.

"I'm Doctor Fenwick," she heard a voice at her side saying. "Please call me Trish. We've met before."

Grace turned; her attention drawn to the name badge on the doctor's waistband "DR P FENWICK".

"We have?"

"Yes, it was on a course a long time ago – probably ten or twelve years – when we were both training with Special Forces. You were with the glamorous lot, heading for the handguns, while I was heading for the Band-Aids. You were dispatching, I was just patching, we used to say."

Grace smiled. "I do remember. But you were Patty then, not Trish, right?"

"I am *so* impressed you should remember that, with all that's happened to you since then. I still meet up with people who were on that course with us and we *always* end up talking about you. You've always been a real hero to us, but now this. I know it's only the sort of thing the training was for, but… well, I think you're so brave, Ms Goody."

"Thank you, Trish, and, by the way, I haven't changed *my* name; I'm still Grace."

"Grace, then." Trish smiled and waved her towards a reclining chair covered in a white sheet. "Best get you checked out, then. Just slip your top off, sit down here, lean back and relax."

Grace pulled off her shirt, then lifted her legs onto the chair and stretched out. Trisha attached some monitors to Grace's arms and chest and wrapped a strap round her left upper arm, pressing the button on the console to inflate it and check her blood pressure.

"Are you feeling anxious, stressed – or perhaps angry at being asked stupid questions like those?"

Grace gave a little laugh. "I feel surprisingly calm about the mission, to be honest, Trish. I mean, I've got a great team around me."

Trish laid a hand on her shoulder. She frowned at the monitor screen at the side of the recliner, then at the pressure gauge again.

"So, if it's not the mission, what is it that's bothering you so much?"

Grace went rigid at the simple question, remaining silent for a long time. She felt tears form in her eyes and struggled to speak. When she did, it was in no more than a whisper.

"Something that would change your opinion of me being a hero."

⋆

Sir Roger re-entered the command centre on Hirta five minutes after excusing himself to take a call. Lydia watched him anxiously as he stared, unseeing, across the water towards the focus of their mission.

"Sir Roger? Do we have a problem?"

He shook his head to bring himself out of his trance.

"That was Milena Bakke, head of PST in Oslo. She's been talking to CIA Agent Horne about the likelihood of a zero-bomb still being in existence and falling into the wrong hands. You know, one of those conversations you have just to confirm that you have nothing to worry about. Except this one didn't quite go like that. Apparently, according to Mr Horne, there may be some zero-bombs out there somewhere. The US military are unable to confirm that they were all accounted for and decommissioned." He checked his watch and turned to Lydia. "Ten-fifteen; forty-five minutes to strike. Great timing. I guess I *have* to tell Kade, don't I?"

"Yes, you must tell him, but it doesn't make any difference.

Your Mr Kilby's theory certainly doesn't make it any more likely they've got a nuke."

"But if el Taqha knew that there might be some out there..."

"It would add credibility to his bluff that they had one, that's all. If the US military can't account for them, how is anyone else going to find one? You'd need intel to know where to look. I don't think this raises the stakes at all. The guys out there know there is a small risk of a nuke on board. As I said, nothing has changed."

Sir Roger was silent for a few moments, then leaned forward and pressed a button on one of the conference phones on the worktop.

"You're right." He nodded to Lydia, then spoke into the phone. "Hello, *Jura*, Roger Ashpole here. I need a person-to-person, five-minute call with Colonel Kade. Can you have him get back to me right away."

★

"Thank you for that, Sir Roger, but it changes nothing, of course. The objectives are the same, the tactics are clear in everyone's mind. And if we want the glass to look half-full, then if it *is* a zee-bomb, at least we know what we have to do to deactivate it."

"Understood. So, where are you in terms of readiness?"

"Good to go." Kade spoke his three favourite words with a cavalier relish. "Radios, armour and trackers in place. Lifting off at eleven as planned. Cassie will leave five minutes before then. Red-Two Chinook should leave Hirta at 10.45 and we'll wait until she's almost over us before we lift off, so we can arrive together at the target."

"Good. We've arranged a fly-past to check on-deck clearance for Blue-Two at the same time. A single-prop with an obscure news channel logo on the side. Do you still want us to go ahead with that as planned?"

"Yes, let's do it. Any sign of activity on the *Reagan*? We picked up the CNN report earlier. It would piss me greatly if we cleared the bomb then got blown up my own band of brothers."

Sir Roger snorted a little laugh. "There's a fair bit of activity on deck. Quite a number of fighters and a couple of choppers seeming to be readied for action, along with a lot of guys running around looking busy. But we've got six Typhoons now flying a loop and buzzing the deck making sure nothing is going to take off. So, a bit tense to say the least at the moment. It must be the first time the US and UK air forces have squared off against each other."

"Well you can tell the Typhoons they have my permission to kill the fucking Raptors if they do try to take off."

"I don't think you need to worry about that, Kade. The Prime Minister will be meeting with the US ambassador in London right now, after which I fully expect the *Mastodon* will be off-limits for US target-practice."

CHAPTER THIRTY-NINE

10.30 a.m. BST

Jackie rose from the wing chair as the door to the Study at Number 10 opened and Marcus Winshaw, the Prime Minister's chief aide, leaned into the room. Any surprise he felt at the absence of the country's leader was admirably suppressed, and he spoke in his usual professional timbre, without a trace of inflection or apparent interest.

"Ambassador Longhorne to see you, Home Secretary."

"Thank you, Marcus."

The substantial and flamboyant figure of Linus Longhorne almost brushed Marcus out of the way in his hurry to enter the room. The ambassador wore a dark lounge suit, over a white shirt and sported an emerald green bow tie and matching handkerchief in the top pocket of his jacket. He beamed at Jackie.

"Hello, Linus, I…"

"Hey, Jackie. Great to see you."

The door closed behind him and he all but lunged forward to grab her hands and kiss her on both cheeks.

"What a treat. And to think I could have spent this morning looking forward to this meeting instead of dreading it." He gave an exaggerated frown. "With all due respect to your leader, of course."

"Of course." Jackie mimicked his frown. "Andrew sends his sincere apologies, but he is feeling unwell and has asked me to stand in for him."

Linus frowned again, mischievously this time. "Sincere? Apologies? Are you sure?"

"Now, Ambassador, please behave yourself."

Linus roared with laughter, infecting Jackie.

"I'm sorry, Home Secretary, please tell the Prime Minister I hope he is soon feeling better, but any time he wants to dump me onto you, I'd be more than grateful. And now, to business, I guess."

"You guess right. Please take a seat." Linus settled his large frame into the offered chair, which creaked a little under his weight. Jackie picked up one of the china coffee pots from the tray on the low table between the chairs. "Black, strong, no sugar, right?"

"Dead right. Thank you."

She passed him the cup and saucer, then took a sip from her own drink.

"No prizes, Linus, for guessing the reason for the meeting. The situation around Hotel St Kilda is delicate to say the least and I think it's important that we understand the dynamics for both our countries."

"Quite agree, and I am aware that you were less than impressed by our leaking the news about el Taqha to CNN. I don't know how…"

"'Less than impressed' doesn't come anywhere close to describing how I felt about that." She held up her hand to stay a response. "But we are where we are and no harm done – *yet*. We just want to make sure we can drop the 'yet' from that statement with an assurance from you that there will be no interference in the process to bring this to a satisfactory conclusion. And, by satisfactory, I mean we save one hundred percent of the hostages without any casualties on our side *and* secure all the perpetrators, including el Taqha. So, my simple question is, can we rely on you to let us do our job?"

Linus sat up straight, rested his elbows on the arms of the chair and tapped his fingertips together.

"I assume that is a reference to the *Reagan*, languishing a couple of miles off the action. Well, I have to say…"

Jackie leaned forward and opened her eyes wide in mock astonishment. "You mean the USS *Ronald Reagan*, Linus, the *supercarrier*? Well, this *is* a surprise because we have had no word at all from our trans-Atlantic brothers that one of their warships has encroached, uninvited, into British territorial waters. Thank you for letting us know. Perhaps I should call the Minister of Defence and tell him not to attack it. What do you think?"

"Aw, come on, Jackie. I thought this was going to be an update on what progress was being made, not a Yank-bashing session."

"At least I'm still sitting down. Andrew would have been bouncing off the walls by now."

Linus drew in a deep breath. "That's true."

"So please do what you need to do, speak to whoever you need to speak to, to get the carrier moved away, preferably all the way back to Iceland. So we can get to grips with the devil we know."

"You rather flatter me, Jackie, if you think I have that level of influence."

"You have *access*, Linus. To the people *with* the influence. I suggest you start with your President, then you won't have to waste time working your way up."

"The President is in a difficult position, Jackie. Feelings are running pretty high over there, understandably, I think. It's not so much the Willis, although that was bad enough, it's 9/11. *Still* 9/11. They feel no-one has been made to pay for that, in twenty years. No-one who was hands-on, anyway. And there he is, the very man, negotiating with the Brits, for God's sake."

"Oh, come on, Linus, you don't believe..."

"No, that's what *they're* thinking, Jackie. And it's not just the voters. The security forces have taken a hammering from the press and they want to be let off the leash so they can put on a show for everyone. I can't sit here and give any guarantees that anything I say will make a difference or even be listened to. But I will feed back what you said, perhaps not direct to the President, but..."

"I really do think it *must* be the President, Linus."

"And why *must* it be him?" Linus sighed and spread his arms in exasperation.

"Well, he's the commander-in-chief, isn't he? No-one can over-rule his decision in what is effectively a potential military engagement. Oh, and I almost forgot, we are holding the negotiations on board the vessel..."

"Yes, I know that..."

"And the person leading them is the Ministerial Director of Justice, Grace Goody."

Linus spluttered a laugh. "Oh, come on, Jackie, that's a cheap trick. You don't expect me to believe that? You've just brought that out of left field. Something you had in reserve as a last resort. And I'm supposed to get on the phone now and tell the President. Is that what you expect?"

"Well, don't you think he'll want to know?"

"He'll want to know the truth so he can make an objective, balanced decision."

"The *truth*? Linus, we started this meeting like we were friends. Accusing me of being a liar is not the best way of sustaining that relationship."

The ambassador held up his hands. "Look, I'm sorry, but this sounds a bit like desperation. Can't persuade me to call off the troops so we'll tell him there's a lady on board."

"Not just *any* lady, though, is she, Linus? I think you just have to tell President Weston what I've told you. After all, if he's prepared to risk the lives of eight hundred or so British citizens in order to secure a second term, he really ought to know the identity of anyone special he might be murdering, don't you think?"

"I don't believe it will make a difference, so I'm not sure he needs to know. He is not the sort of man who would let personal feelings influence what he believes is right in the interest of national security."

"Well, bully for him. So, if it *won't* make a difference, I guess you might as well tell him anyway. Because if she *is* on the *Mastodon*, and if there *is* a US strike against it and Miss Goody is killed, and you haven't told him already, I promise you your President will find out you withheld that information almost before she's stopped breathing."

★

Harry checked his watch for the fourth time as they weaved their way at speed along the A3, lights flashing, siren whining. It told him it was 10.45 a.m.

"Sod's law," Harry said. "Second day of the final Ashes test. Kennington will be crawling with people." His iPhone sounded. "DI Waters speaking."

"Hi, Harry, it's Jo, on Seb's phone. We have a name for the address in Cannon Road. Max Mobsby. Investment Analyst, works for Danby Ashton Property Development, offices at Dreyfus House in Lambeth. And Seb has spoken to two of the three people who ID'd him and gave us the address. I'll put him on."

"Hi, Seb."

"Hi, sir. Neither of the people know Mr Mobsby, but they've seen him arriving and leaving the address a few times. Both women, relatively young, so perhaps not surprising they've noticed him. Jo is wagging her finger at me, by the way. I'm not supposed to make sexist remarks like that, but my point is that he's an exceptionally good-looking guy and people are likely to give him more than a passing glance. *Certain* people, that is."

"I know what you're saying, Seb, before you dig yourself in any deeper. But they're sure it's the same guy?"

"They both seem very sure. And, like Ellie said, they don't know each other. Not made contact yet with the pizza delivery person, who just happens to be female and the *only* female they employ. I've left a message with the pizzeria for her to phone me when she starts her shift this afternoon. Jo wants another word."

"I've checked with Danby Ashton," Jo said, "and though they can't release any personal details over the phone, of course, they did confirm that a person of that name is an employee of the company."

"Right, so we have three independent sightings, a home address, a work name and address, and confirmation of his work status. So, what do you think?"

He heard Jo sigh. "Honestly, Harry? We won't know until you get there, but it's starting to look a bit too easy."

"My thoughts exactly. Okay, Jo, I'll keep you updated. Thanks to Louise Hamilton here – a.k.a. DC Alice Grantham, who should seriously consider a career in Formula One – we are nearly at the address."

He ended the call and checked the time on his iPhone.

"Ten to eleven, Alice. Nat and George still with us?"

"Not far back." She smiled. "I've been going slow so we don't lose them."

"I hadn't noticed." Harry was making another call. "Hi, Harry Waters here. Is that DI Leasing?... Hi, Hannah. Long time no talk. I'll put you on speaker so my colleague can hear you."

"Hi, Harry." A woman's voice. "All ready for you. We're at a community centre just a few hundred metres from his road end, just off the A3. I think DC Grantham has it on satnav."

"Yes, I have, ma'am," Alice said. "We're just a few minutes away."

"Great. You'll see a marked police car on the road, just pull into the centre car park next to it. I've dismounted the cavalry, as requested. They're a few streets away. Oh, and we have a name for that address."

"So do we. Let's hope it's the same one. You go first."

"Max Mobsby."

"Check. That's a good start."

"I must say, though, Harry, I don't want the SFOs too far away if this guy gives us a problem. I think we need to discuss that before we go further."

"Agreed, Hannah. I need to bring you up to date with where we are on this. It is nowhere close to being straightforward."

"Is it ever thus?"

"I think that's the car," Alice said, pointing ahead. "We're here, ma'am."

Harry leaned back in his seat, wondering how much of his conversation with the Home Secretary he should divulge to his Met counterpart. He reached a decision. All of it, except the actual names – Walcott's, and that of the woman he had met on more than one occasion in Marsham Street.

*

Cassie swung slightly on her chains in the still air as she was lowered into the water from the winch at the stern of the Archer. The small patrol boat was on the blind side of HMS *Jura* from the *Mastodon*, so the launching would be unobserved. Shirley-Anne, already in her wet-suit, was on board the submersible, carrying out final checks before they headed for their target.

On board the Archer the five-man assault team prepared to join her, each storing his weapons and tactical radio into his waterproof bag before pulling on the hooded wet-suit over his combat gear and testing the seal on the facemask before letting it hang on the strap just below his chin. With *Cassie* fully checked and stable in the water, they climbed down the Archer's stern ladder into the passenger compartment behind the driver's seat. The craft was designed for a maximum of seven people – one driver and six passengers.

Once aboard, the men placed their bags in the watertight compartments next to their seats. They checked the magnetic ladders, fastened securely to the outside of the hull; three ladders each side, all two metres long with the vertical side-rails hinged at the mid-point to enable it to follow the contours of a curved surface, like the side of a ship. Each ladder's two powerful magnets could be attached and detached by locking levers – one at the top, one at the bottom of the ladder, connected by a rod, so that either lever engaged both magnets. Five people, six ladders, so there would always be five in place at any one time while the sixth was being taken from the bottom and passed up to add to the top as they ascended. Only one person to one ladder at any time.

Check complete, they tested the face masks and the breathing tubes attached to air tanks under their seats, each giving Shirley-Anne a nod to say they were ready to go. She pulled on her own facemask, attached the tube and waved to the winchman above her. The team uncoupled the lifting chains from the four anchor points on the submersible's hull and they were hoisted away to the deck of the Archer. Shirley-Anne reached for the controls, the reinforced Perspex dome closing slowly over them and sealing itself into position with a hiss of compressed air. Shirley-Anne checked the time on the console: 10.53 a.m. She pulled a lever to her right, flooding the passenger compartment with Atlantic water, its coldness offset by powerful heaters kicking in beneath their feet.

The image of the Archer above them rippled and distorted as *Cassie* descended to her cruising depth of ten metres, passed under the *Jura* and headed for the target, quickly building up to her top speed of eight knots.

*

The Eurocopter with Red-One on board circled the scene at a height level with Alpha's viewing deck, the continuous glass corridor which ran around all four sides of the platform at the base of the accommodation blocks. It seemed that every one of the nearly 800 exiles were lining the floor, pressed against the windows, watching their fly-past.

"Go round again," Grace shouted to the pilot, "closer in."

On the next circuit they were near enough to make out individual faces.

"Wave and smile," Grace said. "Let them know we're here for them."

They did as she asked, giving thumbs-up signs and getting similar signals in reply. No angry faces, no obscene gestures. Grace felt a sudden, gut-wrenching surge of sympathy for them.

Kade leaned across to her. "Eight months ago, that's where I was, on that same floor. It was never my intention to get this close ever again."

"And that's where you nearly left Tom?" Grace asked.

"How did you know that?"

"He told me. You left him your Glock, right?"

"That's right. It was the only reason I took it, the only weapon we had with live ammunition. He didn't need it, as it turned out, but it came in useful for screwing the transmitter."

He stepped forward to the cockpit, "Take her under the platform, length of the deck, nice and slow." Turning back to the team, he added, "All of you, count the hostages. There should be forty-six. Blue-One has already confirmed, but let's make sure. Ruby said to line them up in five rows of eight and one of six to make it easy for us to check. We don't land until we account for the full group on deck."

A vibrating in the pocket of Grace's jacket alerted her to an incoming text. She frowned. This was her second phone, and only one person had access to its number. She checked the screen.

Higher and further out, the Chinook was circling.

CHAPTER FORTY

10.58 a.m. BST

The two UK Coast Guard Sikorskys hovered at main deck level, each within twenty metres of the *Mastodon*, one off the bow and the other at the stern. Ruby had informed el Taqha that they would be there to observe during the landing and take-off of the X3 and Chinook, after which they would return to Hirta for the duration of the talks. In reality, the former was there to create a disturbance in the water to mask any sign of *Cassie*'s approach, the latter to dilute attention from the other.

Shirley-Anne brought *Cassie* to a stop against the forward underbelly of the vessel, backing up slowly until a view of the sky directly above them through the clear water indicated full clearance to the surface. She reversed the movement of the lever to purge the ballast tanks of water and the submersible rose vertically to the surface a metre away from the hull. The dome eased open.

The men pulled off their wet-suits as Ruby attached the fore and aft magnetic anchors to the side of the vessel, then wound in their steel chord to pull the submersible firmly against it. With the men's Glocks in under-arm holsters, MP-5s strapped tightly across their backs, and knives in their sheaves at their right thighs, the assault team again checked the tactical radios, testing contact with Red-One, Blue-One and the command centre.

All good, they unclipped the ladders, one-by-one, from *Cassie*'s sides. Jules positioned the first against the ship's hull, pressing down the lower locking lever to secure the magnets. He stepped onto it and leaned back to take the second one from Brig, reaching up to position it above the first. He climbed up onto the second ladder, vacating the first for Brig to start his ascent. The third ladder was passed up through Brig to Jules, and so on, until five were in place, with one man holding on to each. Shirley-Anne passed the sixth to Rico, who was the last to leave *Cassie*, and it found its way swiftly to Jules, who attached it to the hull above him. From checking radio contact to this point, the operation had taken just under three minutes.

Shirley-Anne closed the glass dome again and flooded the passenger compartment before taking *Cassie* down to begin her short journey back to Archer-One. Jules climbed up onto the top ladder, Brig waiting until he was clear before continuing his own ascent, and each below him did the same, waiting for the vacant ladder above him. The moving of a single ladder from the bottom to the top and each man moving up one stage, would take around thirty-five seconds. Blue-Two had carried out the process many times in the past to polish their performance and establish the timing. They had also done the calculation for this particular ascent. The rail of the top deck was thirty metres above sea level. The height of the initial five ladders was ten metres and moving the bottom ladder to the top added two metres each time. Meaning it had to be done ten times, which meant three hundred and fifty seconds – say, six minutes – added to the initial three minutes.

Red-One would be assuming a maximum of ten minutes for Blue-Two to gain access to the top deck from the time of the radio check.

*

At 11.04 a.m., three minutes after they had checked their tactical radio link with the other covert assault team, the five members of Blue-One noticed the sound of large rotors getting louder. It was twenty-one hours since they had established their position on the starboard tower in a space about the size of a single garage. They stretched their limbs and breathed a collective sigh of relief as they watched the huge personnel-carrier, which had been circling the platform at a radius of around one kilometre, heading directly towards them.

They had seen the hostages walk out onto the deck and arrange themselves into six lines, and had contacted Hirta to confirm that all forty-six were present. The Eurocopter X3 had completed two circuits of the platform plus one fly-through along the deck before coming to rest in its current position at the stern end.

They continued to watch as the six members of Red-One alighted and Kade and Grace walked over to the hostage group, who now broke formation to crowd round their rescuers in a scramble to shake their hands. The five men lay flat at the edge of the tower overlooking the deck, resting the barrels of their sniping rifles on the low rail which ran around its perimeter. There was no sign of any of the hijackers.

The Chinook touched down close to the Eurocopter and the twin rotors slowed and dipped and eventually came to a stop. The forty-six members of the ship's crew began to embark. They would shortly find themselves safe in Stornoway, where they would be checked by a medical team, interviewed and provided with a meal, before being flown to Oslo to meet with officials from PST and Delta, the Norwegian counter-terrorist unit; then on to Stavanger and other destinations to be reunited with their families and friends.

The five members of Grace's bodyguard formed a half-circle around the embarking operation, their backs to the Chinook, Heckler & Koch MP-5s at the ready, watching the doors leading onto the deck from the forward superstructure. They were currently closed, and there was no sign of movement in any of the windows facing the deck or on the bridge itself, towering high above them.

The men of Blue-One lowered the edge of the canopy, leaving just enough of a gap to observe the action, and settled down to wait.

*

Eight minutes after the rotors had stopped turning – during which time Robbie had performed his "deck-walk" – the hostages were all aboard and the doors of the Chinook closed. The six people remaining on deck braced themselves against the draught from the rotors as they started to turn again and, less than a minute later, lifted the huge helicopter from the deck.

"Watch!" Kade shouted.

They adjusted their positions, MP-5s raised to shoulders ready to respond to any action against the departing craft. The doors onto the deck remained closed, windows eerily devoid of any sign of life. Behind them, the Eurocopter X3 rose from the deck and followed the Chinook.

"Easy, stay on alert," Kade again.

None of the group moved for a full minute except for a slight relaxing of limbs and shoulders. They continued to maintain their positions as Grace and Kade took in their surroundings.

It was nearly 200 metres from where they stood to the gigantic bridge structure at the bow of the ship. Half that distance away, off-centre towards the starboard side of the deck, four portacabins were positioned as if across the corners of a square, in the centre of which were two large rectangular tables with their long sides across the deck and a metre gap between them. Two chairs had been placed facing each other across the tables and the gap, making them about three metres apart. The square was completely covered by a single canvas canopy, stretched between the portacabins, and protected by two-metre-high fabric panels acting as windbreaks, suspended by metal rings between horizontal, parallel bars attached to poles bolted to the deck. Ten deck heaters formed a circle around the tables and chairs. It looked like the set-up for some sort of exhibition or training session, which, as Jens had said, was what the equipment was normally used for.

"This is absolutely unreal," Grace shook her head. "Little wonder you can't picture what something's going to be like, when there's nothing in your life's experience to compare it with. It's totally bizarre holding any meeting under these conditions."

"Excuse the cliché, Grace, but this isn't just *any* meeting, and we've already saved forty-six people just by being here." He nodded towards the arrangement of the furniture. "What do you think about one chair each, are you okay with that? We'll be all round you, so it's not like you'll feel on your own, but we can insist on, say, Robbie and Sergei sitting with you."

"I think they'd have more of an impact standing up."

Kade gave a little chuckle. "I think you're right."

He turned to the team behind him. "Let's go."

They all set off walking towards the covered square as the door opened ahead of them and Abu el Taqha stepped through it onto the deck, followed by a group of five men. The leader's escort were all wearing camouflage combat gear and traditional Muslim skullcaps in a matching pattern. The lower half of their faces were covered by scarves wrapped loosely around. Each was carrying an automatic weapon. El Taqha himself was dressed more traditionally in a loose-fitting cream Muslim-style suit featuring a long tunic which buttoned down the front. He also wore a skullcap, the same colour as his suit.

"Welcome aboard, Miss Goody," he said, smiling. "May I call you Grace?"

"You may."

She walked up to the nearest table and placed her laptop bag, briefcase and shoulder bag on it, before sitting down. She was feeling amazingly calm, and wondered if it was because she had no expectation of coming out of this alive, and, after reading Andrew's text – *They have Walcott's address* – she had no wish to.

★

The final ladder had reached to within half a metre of the deck level, with the rail rising above that. Close enough to reach but an uncomfortable distance where half a second could be critical when clearing the rail. Jules looked down at the four pairs of anxious eyes below him and gave as full a version of his hallmark shrug as he dared without destabilising himself.

The first moment of real danger for Blue-Two.

The sound of a single-engine prop reached their ears and the plane swung past them a few moments later.

"Deck clear." The two words sounded in Jules's earpiece, audible only to him. He looked down again, this time pointing upwards and nodding.

Brig, second on the ascent, climbed higher to where his weight remained on his own ladder but he was able to lean against Jules's to hold it in place. Jules stepped up slowly until his torso was above the top of the ladder, his arms spread wide and upper body pressed against the hull until he could reach up to the bottom bar of the rail. At that point his arm would be visible to anyone on the deck.

The second moment of danger.

Jules pulled himself up, rolling over the top bar of the rail and taking in his surroundings in a couple of seconds. The foredeck was deserted. There was only one door leading off it, giving access to the inside of the superstructure, hinged to open outwards and currently slightly ajar. Jules signalled all-clear to Brig then raced over to the door, pressing himself against the wall next to the hinged side of it, so, if it opened, he would be screened from anyone coming through onto the deck.

As he watched Brig swing over the rail and reach back to help Rom, Jules heard a noise behind the door. Heavy boots on a metal staircase and voices arguing over something. The door was pushed fully open just as Rom cleared the rail. A man stepped out, followed by another. It took the first man less than three seconds to register the presence of the intruders, by which time his companion behind him was on the point of death, choking on his own blood from the deep slash across his throat from Jules's knife. The first man made the mistake of reaching first for the radio, instead of his firearm. Although it wouldn't have made any difference; Brig had covered half the distance between them and shot him in the head with his suppressed Glock before the radio had left its clip. He bent down to check the body.

"No bomb vest," he said.

"Not here, also," Jules said, as he pulled the scarf and the combat suit off the man he'd killed before it became too bloody.

"We have our disguises, *n'est-ce pas*?" he said.

★

"Blue-Two aboard, inside and on level four. Time check: 11.20 hours." The Major shared with his team the message he'd received from Jules. "They're now being tracked from *Jura*. Two terrorists down. Not good this early in the op. I'd expect them all to have radios, so a regular check-in will expose a covert insertion right away. They'll have to move really quickly now and rely on the device being where we think it is." He shook his head. "And we've really fucked up with covering the deck."

He looked down again towards where Grace, Abu el Taqha and their armed guards were clustered together, where the terrorists had done too good a job in protecting the square. The participants were invisible to his group from their elevated location. They would be unable to take out anyone when the time came unless they moved outside the screened area.

"We could do with getting a couple down to deck level."

He crawled across to the rear of the tower roof, still under the canopy, and looked over the edge at where the superstructure dropped vertically over sixty metres into the sea beyond the stern. The sergeant appeared at his side.

"How'd we do that, Major? Rope to deck level then swing round onto the stern? We'd give ourselves away for certain. They must have people watching the deck from the bow end. That's if Blue-Two haven't killed them all by now."

"Well if they have done that, it must include the trigger man, and I haven't heard a bang yet, so that would be good – as far as it goes. I just hope those guys on deck are not wearing vests, especially el Taqha. Things go bad and Grace won't stand a chance if he blows himself up. That would be a terrible waste."

"In more ways than one, a woman like that," his companion said.

The Major turned to look at him and frowned. "Not very professional, Sam." He smiled. "But true all the same."

*

The six detectives were seated around one end of a large table in a meeting room off the main activities area of the Centre. Harry had taken Hannah and her colleague, Detective Sergeant Will Denton, quickly through the facts of the case from the trap they had set for the two men up to the present time, filling in the gaps from his first conversation with Hannah an hour or so ago. Hannah was medium height, slim and attractive, with auburn hair cut very short. She wore skinny jeans and a tan leather jacket. The two Met officers had reacted to the account of the Home Secretary's involvement by leaning even further forward across the table.

"And so," Harry said, "our hands are tied to some extent given the very specific directive concerning firearms, which, like you, Hannah, gives me a problem, because our main concern in all of this is the safety of the public. If this is our man, we know he'll have a gun and we know he'll use it. What we don't know, of course, is whether we'll get near enough to him for that to be an issue." He checked his watch. "Eleven-thirty. It's four and a half hours since we put out the appeal with the photographs. I don't think we could have got to this point any sooner, but – if he is our man – I can't see him still being around."

His iPhone signalled an incoming call.

"Excuse me, this is my sergeant, from the CCTV Monitoring Centre. Hi, Craig. We're with DI Hannah Leasing and DS Will Denton. I'm putting you on speaker so don't say anything bad about the Metropolitan Police."

"I didn't realise there *was* anything bad to say about them."

"Well said, Craig." Hannah laughed. "You're ahead on my card."

"So, how are we doing?"

"Well, someone left the house at 7.25 a.m. A man with a daypack and a briefcase, which could have been a laptop case. Short dark hair, smartly dressed in a mid-blue suit and open-necked, light-coloured shirt, no gloves. Walked from the house to Oval Tube station. Captured him getting on a northbound on the Northern Line and picked him up two stations on at Elephant and Castle. Then tracked him on foot for about half a kilometre to Blenheim Street, where he entered a building – Dreyfus House. Ring any bells?"

"The address of Danby Ashton. So, he's just a guy going to work. And he hasn't emerged since then?"

"No, sir, and no activity around the house either, except the postman at around 10.30, who also called at all but one of the houses in the terrace."

Harry sighed. "Do you think he's our man, Craig?"

"Not sure, sir. He certainly attracted some attention, quite a few admiring glances from passing females, but… how tall is he supposed to be?"

"About six feet."

"Thought so, well I'd put this guy a good couple of inches shorter, possibly more. Having said that, camera angles can distort the image, of course. Seeing him always from above. So, might be, might not."

"Okay, let's stick with the 'might be' for now. And you say no-one else has entered or left the house since half-seven?"

"No, sir, at least not through the front. There's a rear gate to the property into an alley, which runs behind the terrace into side streets at either end, and there are no cameras in either street. But DI Leasing's team have that covered with on-the-ground surveillance. I'm in contact with them and they confirm no activity at the rear either since they got there. Could have been before that, I guess."

"That's right," Hannah said, "we've had ground cover on the house since I got your call, Harry, at around half nine. One car at front and another at one end of the alley where they can see all gates leading on to it."

"Right. Thanks, Craig. Keep us informed if anything changes at either location, and we'll let you know what we plan to do."

He ended the call and turned to Hannah.

"Well, we know where he is, whoever he is. We don't know whether he lives alone, so there may be someone still in the house. I have a slight sinking feeling that this is not our murderer – *attempted* murderer. And right this moment, I'm not clear on how to find out. I know it's my call, Hannah, but… any ideas?"

"We could check out the house, to see if there is anyone else living there. If it's a significant other we can legitimately question her – or him – about Mr Mobsby. Check if they know where he was yesterday. Given the Home Secretary's softly-softly approach, grabbing him at work might not be what she had in mind."

"Actually, sir," Natalie said, "this low-profile stuff could work for us. If there is no-one at the house, we could perhaps gain entry somehow and search the place. I know we should get a warrant – even with our liberation under NJR – but we could claim to be keeping paperwork and records to a minimum to preserve his anonymity. In fact, that's what we would be doing."

"That's an excellent point, detective," Hannah said. "It's got my vote. He's not going anywhere without your man spotting him, and the house is just down the road."

"Okay. How should we play this? If it *is* the guy, and if there *is* someone in the house, then whoever they are, they could be armed as well. In fact, it could be our man with the scar, wielding a table lamp or similar. Can we get a few of your uniform guys in the alley?

They're wearing vests, right? Nat and I will take the front door – 'just calling to eliminate people from the search' – that sort of thing. The rest of you in an unmarked car close by. You okay with that, Hannah?"

"Fine with me. Suggest we use one of your cars – new to the patch – just in case they've clocked ours previously. I'll let the guys in the surveillance vehicles know and they can contact Craig. And I'll tell the SFOs to move closer and stay ready. They can park up here in the centre car park. They're in unmarked vans, so they won't attract any attention if they stay out of sight."

As they stood to leave the room, Harry's phone sounded again.

"Hi, Craig."

"Our man has just left work two minutes ago. He's got his daypack with him but not his briefcase. He seems to be in a hurry, speaking into his phone, and heading for the Tube station, we think."

"Okay, thanks, Craig. Nat and I are just about to call at the house. Keep us posted through George as to where he is."

"Right, sir. Take care, all." He ended the call.

"Okay, let's get vested up."

CHAPTER FORTY-ONE

11.26 a.m. BST

"I still can't hear him, Grace. The directional microphone in the laptop isn't picking him up. Make sure it's exactly square-on to him. Don't reposition it right now; choose a moment when you're using it to check something. Your button-cam's working well and I can lip-read some of his words but not enough to make sense of what he's saying. Give a little cough if you copy."

It was the first time Grace had detected any hint of anxiety in Lydia's voice. She had been somewhat intimidated by the doctor's ice-coolness so far and welcomed the suggestion of a possible imperfection, before immediately dismissing the thought for its pettiness.

Grace cupped her clenched hand to her mouth and coughed as instructed. So far, they had been exchanging what, under the circumstances, passed for pleasantries, and, in spite of herself, she had been impressed by his manner and general demeanour, and certainly his articulation.

"It is my sincere wish that everyone on this magnificent vessel will leave safely in the very near future. We are not here to die for our beliefs but to liberate innocent fathers and sons of our people who are being detained simply because their dress, their language and their God are different from yours. Are we, as *you* say, on the same page, Grace?"

"Certainly, in that I am not here to die, either. I have here…" she lifted the laptop an inch from the table and put it down again "… the details of the people you wish to discuss. Also, here." She patted a thick folder of documents in front of her. "In spite of the short period of time we have been in possession of this list, we have worked hard to review each individual case. As you, yourself, said, they are not all in the one place and some are being held in countries other than the UK. Some of them are awaiting trial, but others have been through the due process of law and been found guilty of crimes, including murder, and are now serving sentences for those crimes. I'm sure you will understand it is not easy for me to agree that *those* people are innocent – as you describe them – and they are certainly not victims of discrimination as you suggest. We have people from every social, religious and ethnic background detained for such crimes. And it is worth pointing out that those who have been through the same due process of law and been found *not* guilty are now free to continue with their lives without further interference."

Abu el Taqha smiled and remained silent for a few moments. Lydia's voice came again, sounding more relaxed this time.

"I still can't hear him, Grace, but that line of dialogue is perfect. We'll carry on trying to clear…"

Grace was already listening to the terrorist's reply.

"I'm disappointed that we start with a misunderstanding, Grace. I think it was made clear that the agenda for this meeting was not *if* we release these people, but *how* and *when*. If that is not your understanding – and your purpose for being here – then we have a serious problem."

He shouted a single word over his shoulder and the five men standing in a line behind him raised their weapons and aimed them at Grace. At the same moment, her bodyguard responded in kind and in less than two seconds ten automatic weapons were trained on the two people at the tables. Grace's eyes never left el Taqha's. There was complete silence for half a minute before the terrorist leader spoke again.

"Whatever the outcome today, Grace Goody, you are a very brave woman. It would fill me with great sadness if something bad were to happen to you."

Grace paused before responding. "Thank you for your concern," Grace said. "Are you suggesting we cannot proceed with this meeting? There are eighty-seven people on this list. If – and I stress, *if* – we are unable to free them all, are you prepared to sacrifice the others?"

"I say again, the number was not negotiable."

"*Everything* is negotiable, el Taqha, for intelligent adults living in the real world. Perhaps to move things forward, we could start going through the names on this list so I can provide you with data on each of your countrymen. I assume you have a copy of the document you emailed to my colleague, the Home Secretary?"

"Yes, I do, but..."

"Then let me start the ball rolling."

Abu el Taqha spread his arms and sighed. He turned again to his men and nodded. They lowered their weapons. Kade signalled for his team to do likewise.

★

Jules continued down the metal stairwell, holding in front of him the small iPad showing his position on their route which would take them past the twenty-one port-side cabins, through numerous corridors and down four levels. The yellow dot on the screen was there courtesy of the tracker attached to his belt being followed on a three-dimensional digital image of the *Mastodon* on Hirta and transmitted back to his handheld monitor. The voice with just a trace of a Dutch accent in his earpiece gave constant directions guiding him and his team towards their target.

Immediately behind him were Brig and Rom, in their newly donned disguises of camouflage gear and skullcaps, the front of Brig's top and the scarf bloodied from the fatal wound inflicted by Jules's knife. Bringing up the rear, one flight of steps behind, Joss and Rico followed them, keeping a suitable distance between themselves and the first three to deal with anyone emerging to investigate their passing,

As they reached the main deck level, entering the corridor that led to the stairwell down to the storage floor, they heard the sound of voices coming from a cabin ahead of them on the left. They sounded agitated and one person was shouting, repeating the same few words.

Jules held up his hand and turned to stop them. He did the standard telephone mime with his thumb and little finger and mouthed the word "radio". They all understood; the man was trying to contact someone on the radio, and they knew it must be one – or both – of two people who were never going to answer.

Watching the open door, they backed up along the corridor until it turned a corner taking them out of sight of anyone leaving the room. They turned and moved quickly back the way they had come, until they found an unlocked cabin. Jules waved for Rico and Joss to join them and they slipped inside and closed the door.

"How many voices?" Jules whispered.

"Two, maybe three," Brig answered.

"We must assume three, then. So, we have six on deck, two dead, three here. Total eleven so far and maybe more. Ever know terrorist attack with more than ten before?"

The others looked at each other and shook their heads.

"That's a full operating cell," Brig said.

"As Kade says, they would not have counted needing so many on deck," Rico said. "Eleven is not so many when you think the size of ship. Not like holding hostages in one or two rooms of a building, or even plane. But take five away to guard negotiator, then too few."

"And there must be someone with the bomb, if they have a bomb," Joss said.

"Unless they can set it off remotely," Brig put in.

"And if it's on an MRTD, there'd have to be someone there," Joss again.

"If it *is* on MRTD, they would need two people with it," Jules said, "which could mean as many as thirteen, or the bomb is in that room with the three men and we are already here."

"So, I wonder: where are the hostages?" Rico asked. "My guess, then, locked in a room on their own somewhere to be brought out when needed to work the ship. Who knows?"

Jules lifted his hand to his ear at the sound of Jens's voice. He nodded to the others to switch on their radios.

"What has happened? Why have you gone back?"

Jules explained.

"The room where you say the voices are is the comms room. It's where Ove Fossen is likely to be unless, as you suggest, he is imprisoned somewhere with the others."

"Is there another route to the target?" Jules asked. "Do we *have* to go past the comms room? We don't believe there can be many terrorists below deck. We know where ten or eleven are. That must be most or all, so perhaps we are good to go more freely below."

"You would need to go back up to where the stairs divide and take the other stairwell down. The same route but a mirror image. Then once at the starboard drop-down door, cross the loading floor."

"*D'accord. Merci*, Jens. We will let you know in two minutes what we will do."

He switched off his radio and turned to the others.

"However many terrorists and where they are does not matter right now." Jules looked at each in turn. "The alarm is as good as raised. They know they have a problem with two men. We must act now and take the comms room."

They heard footsteps on the metal floor; someone heading towards them from the room where they had just heard the voices. One person's footsteps. He hurried past the cabin where they were hiding and began to climb the stairwell to the upper deck, they presumed to check why no-one was answering the radio call.

Jules nodded to Joss. The SBS man slung his MP-5 behind him and tightened the strap over his shoulder to hold it in place; he removed his knife, then slipped out of the cabin to follow the person as he ascended the stairs.

*

The noise of the terrorist's boots on the metal stairwell was more than enough to drown out Joss's own silent steps in his sound-suppressing foot gear one and a half flights behind him. The man ahead of him slowed as he approached the door to the upper foredeck, unslinging his automatic weapon and holding it one-handed, his finger on the trigger and the stock against his upper arm.

Joss stopped where he could see him from below and crouched down low to make himself as small as possible. The man gave a glance behind him, then pushed open the door, stepping back and flattening himself against the wall just inside the opening. He shouted a name which Joss could not hear clearly. Then another name – Hamid, or something – when he got no reply. Joss could sense the man's nervousness. He leaned for a long time against the bulkhead, breathing deeply. After nearly two minutes, he lifted the front of his jacket and unclipped his radio with his free hand. He seemed to reach a decision and rushed through the door onto the deck, swinging his weapon in a wide arc right and left.

It took Joss three seconds to race up the two flights to deck level. He peered round the door. The man was alone on the deck, his two comrades having been consigned to the Atlantic Ocean half an hour ago. He was kneeling where Jules had made the first kill, looking at the blood-stained floor of the deck. He got to his feet and raised the radio to his mouth.

Josh closed the distance between them in less than a second. He reached round with his right arm, grabbing the man's gun hand and forcing his own finger into the trigger guard behind the trigger, to prevent it being fired. In the same movement, his left arm plunged his knife into the side of the man's neck with a force which took the tip of the blade through to the other side, robbing him of his life in a few seconds. He lowered him to the deck, after removing the man's finger from the trigger to avoid any chance of a spasm in his death throes alerting the whole ship.

*

Lydia leaned back in her chair and shook her head. She checked the time on the screen.

"Eleven-thirty-six. They've been talking for twenty minutes."

"Still no joy?" Sir Roger asked, anxiously.

"Grace isn't doing anything wrong," she said. "That's the good news. You can more or less guess what el Taqha's saying from her side of the conversation, but body language tells me he's angry. And Grace must sense that as well, as close as she is to him. I don't understand why the mike isn't functioning. We checked it just before they got on the X3 and then while they were on the flight, just so we could test the noise filters."

"Perhaps that's why he separated the tables, anticipating we'd try to listen in, so he'd be further away and, with the wind and sea…"

"That doesn't help, but we should be okay up to, say, five metres at least. The only thing I can think is she's not aligned it properly.

If he was sitting to one side, it wouldn't be easy – she'd have to angle the laptop towards him and that would look suspicious. But he's sitting directly opposite her, so there's no reason it should be a problem. We should have had a back-up on Kade's MP-5, clipped to the barrel. He could have held the gun at his side, pointed at el Taqha, loose and relaxed, un-threatening."

"So why not?"

"Kade didn't want to do it. The mike would have been visible, though probably not recognisable, and he didn't want to send any wrong signals. I do understand, but... Well, that's hindsight. Totally worthless, unless you learn from it."

They lapsed into silence, leaving Lydia with her thoughts. About the tension between her and Grace, particularly in their conversation concerning Tom, and about one possibility she hadn't considered. Perhaps there wasn't a fault with the directional microphone. Perhaps Grace decided she didn't want any help from her and had deliberately left it switched off.

*

This time Brig and Rom led the way back to the cabin where they had heard the voices. Each in their combat outfits and skullcaps, with the other three waiting out of sight at the turning in the corridor. Outside the door, Brig stooped down low, bending his back. Josh held him under his armpits, one arm across his shoulders. Heads well down, faces concealed, they pushed open the door, Brig groaning loudly as if in severe pain.

There were three men in the room, two in the same combat gear, and one sitting at a worktop full of communication equipment, including monitor screens fed by CCTV cameras covering all areas of the ship. The man's face was ashen and partly covered by a piece of tape across his mouth; his arms were tied behind him, and a rope around his waist secured him to the back support of the tilt-and-swivel chair. Josh dumped Brig on the floor, kneeling beside him, head still lowered and shaking him as if to wake him from a sleep. He shouted in Arabic for the others to help him and, as they came across, he sprang to his feet, grabbing the front of the nearest man's jacket and pressing the barrel of his Glock hard against his forehead, backing him up against the wall.

It took the second man a moment too long to react, during which time Brig had rolled onto his back and shot him through the throat. The surviving terrorist tried to speak, but Josh pushed his gun hard into his mouth, the man choking as his tongue was forced back. Brig stepped back through the door, and waved for the others to join them. He went across to the man in the chair.

"Mr Fossen, I presume." He picked loose a corner of the tape. "This is going to hurt. Press your lips hard together as much as you can, okay?"

Ove nodded and Brig ripped away the gag. Tears sprang to the man's eyes, and a cry of pain escaped his injured lips. His head lolled forward for a few moments, but when he looked up he was smiling.

"Thank you." His voice was no more than a whisper.

Jules spoke into his radio. "Comms room taken at 11.42 hours. One more down, one captured. Will attempt interrogation of prisoner before proceeding." He looked at the comms officer. "Ove safe and smiling."

Ove got to his feet and stretched his legs and arms, rolling his head to ease the tension in his neck. "Who…?"

"Not important," Brig said. "Are you okay? Not injured?"

"Hungry, that's all. Look, whoever you are, I'm really grateful to you guys, but could you do something else for me? They've got some of their people watching my house in Egersund. They threatened to kill my family if I tried anything. Could you let the police in Norway know so they can get them? I only hope they're not in the house – you know, holding them as hostages."

"We'll get that moving right away," Brig replied. "The Delta guys over there will be thirsting for some action by now. Oh, and by the way, the bluff with the Chief Engineer – great stuff, Mr Fossen. If this all goes to plan, it'll be down to you as much as anybody."

"It worked, then?"

"We would not be here if you had not done that," Jules said, "but right now we need answers to questions."

*

Joss and Rico took Ove from the comms room heading for the kitchens close by, partly to address his hunger but more to remove him from the site of Rom's impending interrogation of their prisoner.

Brig contacted Scandoil on the ship's radio, to a joyous reception at the news of Ove's release, and told them of the watchers on his home in Egersund. Elsa Tongan took on the task of mobilising Delta.

Jules updated Kade, the Major and Sir Roger.

"*Monsieur* Fossen cannot tell us how many terrorists are on board. He has seen different people in and out of the comms room but all in same combat dress with faces half covered – except el Taqha, of course. He says at least eight including the leader, which is no help as we know definitely of eleven, and that there may be at least two more. He also knows nothing about a bomb. Not even if there *is* a bomb, so cannot say where one might be. He says they speak in Arabic most of the time, only occasionally in English. So, he doesn't know what they discuss."

"Any indication where the other hostages are?" Sir Roger asked.

"There are forty-two cabins as well as the group rooms and comms room, so they could be anywhere. My guess is they are with the bomb, or somewhere close to it where one or two men could watch both. But that is just a guess."

"Anything from the prisoner?" Sir Roger asked.

"Not yet. Rom is going to try something a bit persuasive. We'll end contact now so you don't hear the screams and tell you later of any progress."

He turned to where Brig and Rom had just finished strapping the prisoner to a dining-style chair, his hands tied together to the upright back and each leg secured at the ankle and top of the calf against one of the chair legs. Brig stood behind him and Rom in front, his gun pressed hard against the man's forehead.

He spoke to him in Arabic, Brig translating for Jules.

"Now, comrade." Rom's voice was soft, almost kind. "We are both soldiers. On different sides, but both believing in our own cause. You help us now, you live to fight another time for your cause. You refuse, you die in agony and there is one less soldier to help achieve your goals. It makes sense to help, yes?"

The man turned his head away, then back again to spit in Rom's face. Rom stepped across to the worktop where the radio and monitor screens were and took a tissue from an open box. He wiped the spittle from his face and placed the used tissue next to the box. Facing the prisoner again, he held the gun by his side.

"I tried to treat you with the respect I believed you deserve as a soldier, but that has just changed. We have no time to spare and the agony I promised must begin right away. *Unless* you answer me two questions."

The man sneered. "I will never lower myself to help a servant of western evil. You are beneath me, like the dog turd in the dust. I spit on you again."

Brig leaned forward, reaching over and sealing the man's mouth with the piece of tape he'd taken from Ove.

"I think you'll find it difficult to spit now," Rom said. "But worse than that: you won't be able to scream."

He placed the gun against the man's left kneecap. The terrorist's eyes widened and rolled in frightened anticipation.

"So, tell me. How many men do you have on board, and where is your bomb? Then you live to fight on. Otherwise, by the time you meet with your seventy-two virgins in the afterlife, there will be a separate piece of you for each of them. Nod your head if you will answer."

The man's eyes hardened with rage. Rom pulled the trigger.

An inhuman squeal came from somewhere in the depths of the man's soul and his pupils rolled up into his head, which jerked from side to side as if out of control. With the tape firmly in place, his silenced scream of agony seemed to be pushed down inside his body, causing it to shake and shudder violently. His leg changed shape inside the combat trousers, as the two halves of the patella shot apart in a chaos of splintered bone and severed ligaments. Blood soaked into the fabric.

Rom placed the gun against his right knee.

"I'll ask you again."

*

Harry and Natalie had walked the 200 or so metres from the community centre to the house. The three-storey brick property looked well-maintained, with unblemished white paintwork to the window frames, and a bright green front door with two patterned lights above a brass letter box. Full hanging baskets at each side of the door festooned with trailing lobelia, geraniums and two varieties of ivy. The gate in the low picket fence in front of the property opened immediately onto three stone steps up to the door. An old-fashioned brass knocker in the shape of a horse's head looked inviting, but Harry pressed the bell on the wall at the side. They could hear it ringing loudly inside.

After thirty seconds with no sound from within, Harry pressed it again. He looked round at the car, thirty metres away on the opposite side of the road. George, in the front passenger seat, held up his phone, pointing to it with his other hand. Harry nodded, and five seconds later his iPhone trilled.

"Yes, George?"

"Craig called to say target is on the tube heading south, presumably to Oval Underground. It's two stops, five minutes, then another five minutes' walk to here, if this is where he's heading."

"Okay, thanks, George." He ended the call and checked his watch. "Eight minutes to twelve. Hard to believe that just twenty-four hours ago we were carrying David Gerrard down a flight of stairs in a body bag."

"Did you say 'we', sir?" Natalie smiled.

"The royal we." He sighed. "Well, since then it hasn't been dull, has it?"

He leaned on the bell once more, this time for a long time. Then he took out his phone again and found Hannah's number.

"Hi, Hannah. When our man arrives – if he *is* heading this way – we'll intercept him before he has chance to get inside. I can't imagine he'd be walking the streets of London, going in and out of commercial buildings, packing a shooter, unless it's in his daypack and he leaves that hanging on the railings outside. But as we approach him, can you get one of your marked police cars full of uniforms to pull in behind you, just to send a message?"

"Will do. Hold on, George wants to speak to you again." She passed her phone over to him.

"More from Craig, sir. He did get off the Tube at Oval and he's definitely heading your way. And he's still in a hurry, apparently, so you should be seeing him in less than two minutes."

"Thanks, George."

"All set?" Harry turned to Natalie, who nodded. "Watch out for the daypack. If he suddenly starts to take it off, we need to grab him. Right?"

"Right." She sighed. "How is it I never get to grab a guy like that in the *right* circumstances?"

Harry snorted a laugh. "Here he comes."

★

Brig and Rom carried the prisoner, still secured to the chair, to the cabin where they had all hidden just prior to taking the comms room. The man had passed out after losing his second kneecap, but with his honour intact, having held out against answering any questions. Rom put his Glock against the man's temple.

"Shall I put the bastard out of his misery? What do you think?"

"No, let him come round and feel the pain," Brig said. "We keep him alive, he might share something useful with us later, even if not today. The virgins can wait."

"Blue-Two leaving comms room at 11.53 hours." Jules spoke into his radio. "Joss is staying behind with *Monsieur* Fossen to search the ship with the CCTV cameras. Some are down; he is checking why. If all are okay, even if we don't find the bomb where we think it is, we can eliminate a lot of areas. Heading to next stairwell, then down again to target area. Jens, please confirm."

"Jens here. Confirm. No obvious danger points along the route. The only cabins are singles for crew accommodation, so unlikely to be more than one person in any place. One point, though, that is the only pedestrian access to the storage deck from the levels above on that side of the ship and the narrowest point along the way is a standard single door's width. That's less than one metre, so easily guarded by one man on the storage deck side of the door."

"*Merci bien*, Jens. I make sure to send one of the others through first."

They set off, Jules and Brig leading, Rico and Rom staying back.

*

El Taqha shook his head and turned away in his chair.

"I'm not sure what this game is, Grace Goody, but I don't understand the rules. I believe you are playing for time and I suspect your role is not quite what it seems. I sincerely hope nothing is happening elsewhere right now except on the deck of this ship. If that is not the case, you will have about a millionth of a second to realise your error of judgement before we are turned into a cloud of ash."

"This is *your* game, el Taqha. *You* made the rules. I am here because *you* asked for me in person. Very flattering, I'm sure, but if I'm honest, I would rather be somewhere else."

"Perhaps on a plane to the US?"

"As an alternative to a heavy-lift ship in the Atlantic, yes, a plane to the US – or anywhere – would be preferable. So, I'm keen to progress this as quickly as possible, but 'quickly' is a relative word given what you have asked us to do."

"It is almost midday. So far, you have taken me through the files of eight of the people on the list. It has taken us about twenty minutes. At this rate the complete list of eighty-seven will take, by my calculation, about two hundred more minutes – over three hours. These are not the rules of *my* game. All I need to know about each person on the list is when and where he will be released. You say that you – your colleagues – have worked hard on this list since you received it. Doing what? Do you really think you have told me anything so far that I didn't already know?"

He reached inside his tunic and five automatic weapons behind her came up into firing positions. El Taqha raised his other hand and, very slowly, pulled out a small radio handset. He turned it so the keypad was facing Grace.

"This is pre-set to alert one of my brothers below, who at this moment is saving all our lives. If I press the zero button it tells him to release the trigger. Please don't make me do that, Grace Goody. You do not deserve to die."

"Again," Grace said, "we are in total agreement. Nor do I *intend* to die. It is, by *my* calculation, around forty-six hours since you informed us that you had hijacked this vessel. But less than *sixteen* hours since you provided us with the list, refusing to share your demands in the meantime. Given that you waited thirty hours before you felt it appropriate to tell us what you wanted, I hardly think you can accuse *us* of playing for time, when you have wasted so much of it."

El Taqha smiled. "Ah, Grace Goody. How I wish we could be on the same side. You know, we are not so different, you and I."

Grace hesitated. His words seemed to penetrate her concentration and shake her self-confidence. Could he be right? Someone prepared to take lives, innocent lives, for what they genuinely believed was the greater good. Just as she had done – almost innocent lives, anyway. And hers were targeted innocents, her own people, not just unlucky random victims of circumstances; collateral damage; wrong place, wrong time. *I might as well have been pulling the triggers myself for all the difference it makes.* The morality was the same, only the scale of killing was different. She looked at the laptop screen in front of her and tapped the additional key at the side of the keyboard.

"I can see that you are thinking about that, Grace Goody. And I believe we agree on that as well."

Lydia's voice sounded in her earpiece. "I can hear him now, Grace. Keep going, this is great. I'll just prompt when I think I can help."

Grace watched him place the radio, keypad upwards, on the table in front of him.

"This time, I'm *not* flattered," she said.

"Flattered or not, I can see you believe it could be true." He smiled. "So, Grace Goody, when do we end this dancing around each other and cut to the chase? It is now twelve o'clock, so we have half of today left. How many of my people can you release before midnight? That would really move us on, and we can look at the remainder once those arrangements are in place."

Grace nodded towards the radio on the table.

"I am not prepared to discuss anything while you have a live trigger six inches from your hand. Please put the radio away, after instructing your man to deactivate the device. That was the agreement, to deactivate the bomb while we talked, and now you're telling me you only need to press one button on that radio keypad and that will send a prompt to your trigger man to detonate. Or am I mistaken?"

"Well done, Grace, thanks for that." Lydia's voice again.

El Taqha didn't reply but frowned in concentration.

"And where *is* the bomb? Am I sitting right on top of it?"

He paused for just a moment with a look of surprise which he quickly suppressed before answering.

"It hardly matters, does it, with a zero-bomb? Anywhere close – or not even close – would do."

*

"Did you see that?" Lydia asked Sir Roger. "That look of surprise. The eyes wide, an unconscious reflex. Unless he's the world's greatest actor, Grace got it exactly right. She's sitting right over the bomb and, for a second, he was wondering how she knew. The bomb is over that side, ship's starboard. Which means Blue-Two are heading the wrong way."

"But that would mean the bomb wouldn't be up against a column," Sir Roger said, half to himself. He turned to Lydia. "But it *would* be right under the centre of the platform. Which would be the obvious place for a very big bomb."

They stared at each other, wide-eyed.

"Like a nuke," Lydia said.

They turned back to the screen at the sound of Grace's next words.

*

"So, the radio," Grace said. "Either put it away or press the button."

"You don't think I would?"

"I won't know about it if you do, will I? We'll all be dead in a millionth of a second, I think you said, and your eighty-seven people will still be held in custody. And more securely in future, because they were on your list, so must have some special importance to the cause. Am I right? Don't bother to answer – purely rhetorical."

No-one spoke for what seemed like a long time. Abu el Taqha

picked up the radio and made as if he was going to put it away. He stopped, and locked eyes with Grace across the tables.

"Let's do it," he said, and pressed the keypad.

CHAPTER FORTY-TWO

The man was striding towards them. When he was twenty metres or so past the police car on the road outside the community centre, it started moving, keeping pace with him. He was glancing right and left as he walked, as if he was looking for something. Harry and Natalie stepped through the gate onto the pavement. The man stopped when he saw them, his eyes widening in surprise. He walked on, confidently, stopping again a couple of metres away.

Harry put his height at around six feet, taller than Craig had suggested, with a well-developed upper body and narrow waist. He certainly could have been the man in the photograph. His hair was short and dark brown, with a side parting. His clothes looked expensive.

"Can I help you?" His voice was higher pitched than they expected.

"I hope so," Harry said. "Is this your property?"

"It's where I live, if that's what you mean. Who are you, and what do you want?"

"Detective Inspector Waters; this is Detective Constable Crusoe." They showed their badges. "We're investigating an incident which took place yesterday in Guildford and…"

The man started laughing. "I don't believe it. I've had about six people telling me at work today that I look like the guy on the TV – you know, the photo of the wanted man. Is that what this is about?"

"Could you tell us your name, sir?"

"Maxwell Timothy Mobsby, and it is, isn't? I'm a wanted man."

"And can you confirm where you work, please?"

"I can, but I doubt you'll have heard of it, Inspector. Danby Ashton, property developers. Northern firm; I work at its London office in Lambeth. But not today! Well, not *all* today, anyway." He gave them a wide smile showing perfect teeth. "I'm heading for the Oval."

"And what about yesterday, Mr Mobsby? What were you doing then?"

"Working all day. Had meetings from eight-thirty right through to mid-afternoon."

"And where did these meetings take place?"

"At the office in Lambeth, Dreyfus House."

"And someone can confirm that?"

"Eighteen people can confirm that, Inspector – or they're all lying." He laughed. "No, seriously, it was our mid-year financial review. Even the Test match must wait."

"But you're heading to the Oval now?" Natalie asked.

"That's right, and..."

"Which is in the opposite direction, I believe."

"Right again. I was planning to go there straight from work but one of my neighbours phoned me just after I'd left the building to tell me he'd seen two cars parked close by the house – one on this road and one on Manvers Street, down the side. He said they seemed to be checking out some of the properties. We've had a spate of break-ins recently – all daytime – so I came back here first to check. I guess that's your lot, eh? Stopping me watching the cricket." He smiled. "Just joking; only doing your job."

"That's right, Mr Mobsby," Harry said. "Good of you to recognise that. What have you got in the daypack, by the way?"

"Mmm... Not sure I should tell you."

"Why is that?"

"Well, how fond are you of tuna and sweetcorn sandwiches, and Irish whiskey cake? As I said, I was planning to go straight from work to the cricket ground. I don't want my lunch confiscated on the pretence of it being needed for forensic analysis."

He slipped the daypack off, Natalie stepping behind him and taking hold of it. She handed it to Harry, who unfastened the single strap and peered inside. He picked out the pre-packed sandwich and the cake, wrapped in clingfilm, plus two cans of Stella Artois.

"Very nutritious, Mr Mobsby. I envy you your afternoon." He handed the bag over. "And you can rest easy for now. The people in the cars *are* the police and I'll instruct them not to rob your property – I mean, the place where you live. We will need confirmation of your whereabouts yesterday, and for someone to ID you. It's just routine, but very necessary in order to eliminate you from our investigation. Sorry for the further inconvenience but, as you said yourself, we're just doing our job."

"Certainly." He reached into the top pocket of his jacket and pulled out a business card. "This is how to contact me during the day, and..." he gave them his smile again "... you know where I live. Oh, and the switchboard number is on there as well, when you want to confirm I was at work yesterday."

"You've just answered my next question, I'll do that right now, if you would wait, please."

"No problem. Is it okay if I pop in and get changed now I'm here?" He stepped up to the front door.

"We'd like you to wait here with us while we check, just in case we need you to give them permission to divulge the information. We won't keep you long. Excuse me."

Harry walked away a few metres and phoned Jo.

"Hi, Harry. What news?"

"Plenty, Jo, I'll bring you up to speed in a few minutes, but do you still have the contact number for Danby Ashton?"

"Sure, right here. Have you got a pen or should I text it to you?"

"Can you just tell me what it is?" Harry checked the number against the business card as Jo read it out. "Right," he said. "That's the number I've got here."

"Is that good?"

"No, it isn't. It's the contact number on a business card our man in Kennington has just handed me, inviting me to phone his employer to confirm he was in a meeting all day yesterday. I was hoping it would be a fake card and number and that there'd be an accomplice waiting to take the call. I think I'm turning into you, Jo."

"So, it isn't him?"

"It isn't him if his employer IDs him and confirms he was at the meeting yesterday. It seems we were right to conclude it was too easy. Any more sightings coming in from the appeal?"

"Four more for the incredible hunk, including one from the receptionist at the hotel in Shetland where he and Dobson stayed.

He's not exactly a shrinking violet, is he? The guy who took the call said he could almost hear her drooling while she spoke."

"And the other three, where and when were they?"

"One close to where you are now, the others obviously not him, forty miles apart in Merseyside and Cheshire. All three reported seen yesterday. Oh, and one woman called to ask when we catch him could she have him for an hour before we lock him up."

"And the other guy?"

"Just the one possible sighting. Interesting, though. Earlier today in the little boys' room at the Kendal services on the M6 in Cumbria. The caller said he was standing next to him at the washbasins. The guy was wearing a dark-grey hoodie, but pushed the hood back to splash water on his face, and he caught sight of a scar over the man's eye. He noted the scar because of the mugshot on the news, but thought it was on the left side of his face. It was only afterwards that he realised he'd seen it in the mirror, and that it was on the *right* side."

"Christ, more Agatha Christie. When exactly was the sighting?"

"Around 10.30 this morning, but he didn't call it in until an hour later, within the past half hour."

"Okay, so if he saw his mugshot on TV at seven o'clock and let's say he was still in or around Guildford then, would he be able to get that far by then?"

"He'd have to go some, but yes, he'd make it with half-decent traffic conditions."

"Thanks, Jo. I must make this call, then I'll get straight back to you. Seems like we'll be heading home, anyway. And I guess if that's our only lead for the second guy we need to follow it. Can you get them checking CCTV at all services heading north up to and beyond Kendal – M40, M1, M11, M6..."

"Beth's already on it, Harry, and checking at Kendal to see if we can capture him with a vehicle and get a registration. Then we can check ANPR as well. Speak soon."

"Great. See you, Jo."

He put the call through to Danby Ashton and spoke to the Finance Director, who, after some hesitation, confirmed Max Mobsby's attendance for the whole of yesterday's meeting. Harry ended the call and walked over to the four detectives in the car. The front and rear offside windows lowered as he approached.

"*Looks* like our guy, but almost certainly isn't," he said, holding up his phone. "He was at a meeting at work all day yesterday." He paused. "I guess we could close this off now by getting him ID'd properly. I'm going to ask him to come back with Alice and me to his office so they can confirm he is who he says he is. I'm quite sure a man called Max Mobsby was at a meeting there all day yesterday. Just want to be sure it's the one Nat is chatting up over there."

"I can't say I blame her," Hannah said, "but why don't Will and I check his ID for you so you can have a brew at the centre before you set off back. We'll take him to Danby Ashton and drop him at the Oval on our way back for the debrief. It's only a few minutes away by car if you know the way. Then Will can check that he really is heading for the cricket."

"If you're sure, that would be much appreciated."

"I'm sure. It would make me feel better, to be honest. I don't feel like I've done any work at all so far today."

Hannah got out of the car and they walked over to Nat and Max.

"Well, Mr Mobsby," Harry said, "I think we can clear everything up today. I'd like you to go with Detective Inspector Leasing here, and her sergeant, back to your place of work so they can identify you. Then the inspector will drop you off at the ground. It shouldn't take more than…" He looked at Hannah.

"Thirty minutes, I'd say." She smiled. "That's if you are who you say you are, of course. If not, it will take much, much longer."

"So, it will be thirty minutes," Max smiled back.

"Good. I hate all that paperwork."

Will Denton pulled up next to them in the Met's unmarked car.

"And then," Harry said, "it's time for you to get off to the cricket and enjoy your lunch. Thank you for your time, Mr Mobsby, and for your good humour."

"Bye, Inspector. Good luck with the manhunt."

⋆

The group in the Comms Tower on Hirta let out a collective shout and slumped back in their chairs. Jens sprang to his feet and stalked back and forth across the room in a frenzy of relief as the moment passed and the *Mastodon* continued to float majestically at anchor. Ruby was leaning forward, elbows on the tabletop and her head in her hands. Lydia and Sir Roger looked at each other, eyes wide and questioning. Mike sat rigid in his seat; eyes tightly closed.

"*Fuck*." That particular word coming from Lydia's lips was almost as big a shock as what had just gone before. "I thought she'd screwed up then – calling his bluff like that. God, poor Grace."

"What just happened?" The Head of MI5's voice was hoarse with tension.

The answer came through the speakers from el Taqha himself.

*

"Clumsy of me. I must have pressed the wrong button."

Grace had been starting to feel the cold in spite of the powerful deck heaters all around them, but it was nothing compared to the chill that hit her like the impact of a heavy blunt instrument in that millionth of a second. In the moments that followed she fought to regain control and composure. The fortress of unflappability she had carefully constructed was dramatically breached and she hated with a sudden passion the man in front of her who had destroyed it.

No words were reaching her from Lydia, but when Grace spoke her voice was calm again, and she was on the attack.

"I thought you didn't approve of playing games."

"I am *not* playing games, Grace Goody, I merely…"

"Then, I'm not sure what that just proved. That you have issues operating a simple keypad, or that you pressed the correct button but your man decided not to follow orders. Or you don't have a bomb at all and pressing any button would have had exactly the same result or, rather, *no* result."

"I see, then perhaps another demonstration would answer…"

"Or perhaps we could continue with the agenda for this meeting. To decide how we satisfy your demands and save the innocent people you are currently putting at risk."

"You mean the seven crew members below. Those are the only innocent people on this ship, Grace. I am sure your five companions behind you have killed many more people than my brothers here on deck with me. In the name of their country and its values, of course, just as we do in the name of ours, but they have clearly forfeited their innocence in doing so." He looked up at the underside of the vast platform and pointed with his finger. "And as for those young men, they have, to use your own words, 'been through the due process of law and been found guilty of crimes'. So not a lot of innocence up there either."

"Your point being what, el Taqha? If you are going to pick me up on single words in order to give me a lecture about them, we will be here long enough for everyone on board to starve to death. So how would you like to proceed? My purpose in going through the status of your brothers-in-arms individually was to point out the diversity of their circumstances and, hence, the complexity in securing a block release. If you feel that what I have shared with you is a large enough representative sample to demonstrate that point, then we can move on. And just to prepare you in advance, in spite of your commendable efforts in establishing the facilities for the meeting, I am feeling very cold and will need to take a break very shortly. So, let's try to make some steps – if not *strides* – forward before that is necessary. Okay?"

"Very well, Grace Goody."

"So, what next? Your call, given that *I* seem to have got it wrong so far."

"Perhaps *now* would be right for your time-out, so you can warm yourself and become comfortable again before we proceed." He indicated the portacabin behind her to her right. "I hope the accommodation meets your approval."

Grace got to her feet, gathering up her folder, bags and laptop. "In the interest of openness and co-operation, I will be making contact with my base and giving them an update of our discussion so far. They may also have more information regarding the release of your… brothers."

"Of course, although I'm sure they have been listening intently to our conversation so far by some hidden means."

"You flatter us, el Taqha, with your assessment of our efficiency and speed of response. Can I assume there are no listening devices in the portacabin?"

El Taqha gave her a wide smile. "Such luxuries are not part of standard hijacking equipment so you may rest assured. And while you are taking your break, I assume *your* brothers – and sister – will avail themselves of the facilities. And thirty minutes from now, at 12.50, we will resume talking, or I will press the *right* button."

Grace nodded to him, turned and walked across to the portacabin, followed by Holly.

*

The three team leaders were alerted to Sir Roger's incoming message by the buzz in their radio earpieces.

"*Un moment*, Sir Roger, *s'il vous plaît*," Jules interrupted. He nodded to the rest of his team and pointed to his earpiece. They all switched on their radios. "At this stage, I think we all hear this, *n'est-ce pas*?"

Sir Roger continued.

"We've just had a few minutes of high drama which might possibly help us. Kade, you witnessed it first-hand. I hope your nerves are back in place. El Taqha is claiming, as he always has, that the bomb is on a restraining trigger. He also claims that pressing the zero button on his radio keypad will send a signal to the trigger man to release it and detonate. The radio handset is on the table in front of him. If that is the only means of initiating the detonation, then it offers an opportunity, which I'm sure Kade has already assessed. But, of course, we don't know if there are other signals.

"That's the first thing.

"Secondly, without it being conclusive, we've been alerted to the possibility that the bomb is not where we thought, but may be on the starboard side directly below where you are negotiating. This is based on el Taqha's reaction to Grace's asking if she was sitting on top of the bomb. He seemed surprised by her question, as if he wondered how she knew. It was all over in a second but long enough even for me to notice and Lydia feels it was significant. Kade, you must have noted his reaction close up, and I know you have absolute faith in Lydia's judgement, so I feel we must assume this is a strong possibility. I guess you're unable to respond in words right now, but…"

Kade's voice took them by surprise. "I'm in the portacabin at the moment during the break. We've got three guns still on deck,

Holly is with Grace in the other cabin. And, yes, I have absolute faith in Lydia's judgement. Is she there with you?"

"Not at the moment; she's taking a break as well. So, it seems we *could* be wrong about the bomb's location, although it's by no means certain. In which case, Jules, it's over to you. Let us know when and what you decide, unless you can say now."

"We are so close – one minute – two at most – to our first target. Is that right, Jens?"

"That's right."

"So, we will go on to find the bomb or eliminate that location. Then we think again. Joss is with Ove searching with the CCTV cameras. No luck yet but they will keep trying."

"One other thing," Sir Roger added. "If the bomb *is* on the starboard side, it means it is positioned in the centre of the platform. If that is deliberate – and it does seem that this man knows exactly what he's doing – then, for the explosion to damage the platform from there, it would need to be a very large bomb. Dare I say it, possibly a nuke."

"That is most comforting, Sir Roger," Jules said. "And what was the high drama you mentioned?"

"Kade, you were there. You'd tell the story better."

After reliving his briefly anticipated end-of-life experience for the benefit of all, Kade said, "So, we're no further on. It doesn't prove whether they have an MRT or not, or a nuke or not. But he knows how to shake things up, I'll give him that."

There was silence for a few moments before Kade spoke again.

"*Allez*, Jules. Save us all."

*

It took Jules and Brig less than fifty seconds to reach the door to the storage deck that Jens had told them about. The door was closed and secured by a small hand-wheel, an excellent early-warning device for someone on the other side, assuming there was one there as well, connected to the same mechanism. They were all aware that, if the bomb was there and on a manual restraining trigger, opening the door was likely to be the last thing they ever did.

They fell back from the door a few metres as Rico and Rom joined them. Jules spoke softly into his mouthpiece. "Jens, can you confirm we are in the right place?"

"Confirmed. Take care."

"Joss, you there?"

"Receiving."

"We are about to enter the storage deck on the port side. Are there cameras in there, and if so, what do they tell us?"

"Listen to Ove, Jules. He has some news."

The comms officer spoke into Joss's radio.

"We have checked all the cameras now. The ones in the accommodation areas – the cabins, the communal rooms that people would occupy or where they would congregate – had almost all been switched off, but we have reactivated them remotely."

"Jens, are you hearing this?" Jules asked.

"Loud and clear."

"Go on, Ove."

"They were right to do this, because the images we see here can also be picked up in the monitoring centre in Stavanger. I've been forced to tell them that we have a systems failure which we are working on. I'm not sure how the terrorists would know to do that, but..."

Brig cut in. "Scandoil believe one or more of their employees have been involved in the hijack and may be part of the onboard group."

"That would explain it, so..."

"Please go on, Ove," Jules said. "The cameras?"

"Yes, most of the cameras in the storage and engine areas are working, including the one on the other side of the door where you are now. There is no sign of any person in there, but there is a lot of equipment and crates. Someone could be there and hidden, but..."

"But?"

"It wouldn't make sense. If they were going to put someone there, then surely they would disable that camera."

"Thank you, Ove. So, we can..."

"There's more. Four of the cameras on the storage deck *have* been disabled. One is near the drop-down door on the starboard side of the ship. One is in S24 and two are in the access aisle leading to it from the forward accommodation area."

"Jens, does that mean anything to you, and can you guide us there?" Jules asked.

"Yes, to both questions. S24 is starboard bay number twenty-four, almost exactly halfway between bow and stern. Right, Ove?"

"Right, and that one is the furthest disabled camera from the forward bulkhead. So, I'd guess, that's as far as they've gone towards the stern of the ship."

"And, it seems, to do one thing, *n'est-ce pas*?" He treated his three companions to the shrug. "*Merci*, Ove. I think we have a target and a plan, assuming no-one is waiting for us through this door."

CHAPTER FORTY-THREE

The four Guildford detectives prepared to leave the community centre at just after 12.40 following the debrief with DI Leasing. The one officer missing from the group was DS Will Denton. Hannah had dropped him off just after they'd delivered Max Mobsby close to the cricket ground after his immediate boss at Dreyfus House had confirmed his identity.

"Thanks for the help, Hannah. Great to see you again and only sorry it appears to have been a false alarm. Please pass my thanks to the uniforms and SFOs, and apologies as well."

"No problem." Her phone sounded. "Excuse me. Hi, Will… He has?… straight there… Okay, thanks… What?" She gave a little laugh. "No, you can't. Get yourself back here." She ended the call. "Well, our man has gone into the ground and has taken his seat. Will checked with the security CCTV ops room there and he's eating his lunch."

"Well, that's that, I suppose," Harry said.

"And what is it that Will can't do, ma'am?" Natalie asked.

"Oh, he asked should he stay there until close of play and keep an eye on him. You can't fault our Will for diligence. The lengths he's prepared to go."

They laughed and said their goodbyes.

"Right, let's get back to sunny Guildford," Harry said, "and see if Jo's got anything else. George, Nat, one of you bring Craig up to date and tell him to stay there and carry on watching the house. And get him to forward all the captured images of Mobsby from the CCTV feeds to New Station up to him returning to Cannon Road. I want to see them soon as. See you back at base."

"Does that mean I don't have to hold back this time?" Alice asked, as she pulled on her seatbelt.

"Just try to keep the wheels on the ground at all times. I will attempt to distract myself by means of a conversation with DI Cottrell."

After bringing Jo up to date with what had occurred in Kennington, Harry pressed himself beck in his seat for the remainder of his latest white-knuckle experience with DC Grantham. The sound of his phone, ten minutes later, was welcome as much to take his mind off the drive as for the new information imparted by Jo.

"We have a registration for the vehicle our alias Mr Kemp is driving. It's a black 300 series BMW Sport, registered to a Mr Curtis Rinder at an address in… guess where."

"Grimsby?"

"Lambeth. Why did you say Grimsby?"

"Just to get the guessing out of the way quickly. Anywhere near SE11?"

"If both addresses are in Lambeth they can't be far apart, but no, they're not that close in the context of the borough."

"Shit. It feels we should be heading into Lambeth rather than out of it."

"Well, let us check out the address first, and the driver."

"Okay. Do we know anything about Rinder?"

"Nothing yet, only just got the reg a few minutes ago. I've got my little friend here working on it. He likes to think he's helping, especially when he believes he's still in disgrace. Although I think he's passed the job on to Beth. Ops have just received the CCTV stuff from Craig. Shall I start checking through it? New pair of eyes, that sort of thing."

"Good idea. One interesting point was that Craig thought the guy was medium height from the CCTV, but he looked around the six-foot mark to me. See what you think."

He ended the call and turned to Alice.

"I have a gut feel there's something in those images."

"I'll get you there as soon as I can, sir. I can't go any faster."

"That's okay, I was just about to ask if it's possible to go any slower."

*

Brig and Rom, still in the borrowed combat gear, were first through the door on to the storage deck. Joss's voice came through from the comms room as Jules and Rico joined them.

"We're seeing you now on camera. Still no movement anywhere, including when you were opening the door. The drop-down ramp is about twelve metres ahead of you. Ove has got that camera working now, but no sign of any person or device. It seems Lydia was right. It ain't there."

They advanced the short distance to where the heavy hydraulics machinery defined the position of the huge door in the ship's side. The area of floor in front of it was clear of cargo or equipment. A little further past the door, a floor-to-ceiling wall stretched the full width of the ship, with two four-metre-square openings in it giving access to separate aisles running the length of the vessel between lines of storage bays down the centre, and the port and starboard sides.

Jules looked up at the camera angled down from above the door.

"Okay, confirm no-one and nothing here at target location," Jules reported. "So, we head for S24. Are the cameras back on there, too, Ove?"

"No, I think they've been damaged, so permanently out of action."

"Which suggests that's where *our* action is," Joss said. "Should I join you there?"

"No," Jules said. "Stay with Ove. Watch the screens and let us know anything. *D'accord*?"

"*D'accord.*"

"Jens, you have us on your graphic, yes? We are all radios-on, so take us to S24."

"It's very easy. Head along the wall towards the starboard drop-down ramp. To the right, the second opening takes you down the aisle to S24."

They set off across the beam of the ship, checking down the first aisle before moving swiftly past the opening. They stopped just before the second opening leading to the starboard bays.

Jens again. "The bay is about seventy metres down on the left. All the bays have wide openings with no doors, so any noise you make will be easily heard if anyone is in the bay."

The four men exchanged glances.

"I think we're already on borrowed time," Brig said. "Five men down means five radios out. They'll probably be waiting for us, noise or no noise.

*

Red-One took their positions again at exactly 12.50 p.m. Further along the deck towards the bow, el Taqha was in animated discussion with his group, who formed a tight circle around him. After several minutes, he walked over to the tables where Grace was waiting. His expression was angry and hostile. Kade stepped forward to stand closely at her side. El Taqha stood behind his chair, addressing Grace.

"We have a problem," he said.

Grace frowned. "When you say 'we'?"

"I mean all of us, because we are all affected by it. And I fear it may only be resolved in one way."

"And what is the problem?"

"I am unable to contact five of my men. They are not responding on their radios."

"Surely you're not suggesting that we are somehow jamming your radios," Grace said. "Why on Earth would we do that? To what end?"

For a moment el Taqha looked unsure. Then his expression hardened again.

"No, I do not suggest that. I believe they are not answering our attempts to contact them because they are incapable of doing so. Quite possibly dead." He turned to Kade. "I have no doubt that you have the facility to contact your superiors. I suggest you do so now and tell them to cease whatever is happening on this ship, to put an immediate end to this betrayal. If not, I will press the correct key this time and *you* will be responsible for hundreds, if not thousands, of deaths. And you should know that my brothers who are with the bomb are instructed to allow detonation at the first sign of an attempt to capture it."

"As far as I am aware," Kade replied, "the only thing that is happening on this ship right now is this conversation. I can't speak for the loyalty and commitment of your men, but perhaps they have grown tired of what you are putting them through. And if anyone dies, it will be one hundred percent *your* doing. Do not try to lay this at my door."

"The loyalty of my men is absolute; make no mistake. There can only be one explanation. You have betrayed us, and if you are not prepared to accept that your cover is blown and to call off your dogs, then *I* will end it for all of us now."

He reached inside his jacket.

⋆

Brig stumbled along towards their target, again playing the part of the wounded terrorist supported by Rom. The man watching their approach was already standing in the centre of the aisle looking in their direction when they had turned the corner, as if he was expecting them, or someone.

"Help me," Rom shouted in Arabic, making his voice sound as close as possible to that of the man he had interrogated, but relying on their bloodied appearance to carry a clearer message.

They had covered half the distance to Bay 24. Brig staggered against the wall, slipping to the floor. Rom bent to lift him, struggling to raise him to his feet then pressing unsteadily forward. As they approached, they noticed that the man was dressed differently from his comrades. He was wearing some form of protective clothing over his combat gear; a hooded, all-in-one body suit which gave him the appearance of a scene-of-crime officer, except the suit was of a heavier material which made it seem structured and inflexible. Its significance registered with both of them at the same time.

"Oh, *fuck*," Brig said, behind the folds of his wrap-around face covering. He sunk back down to the floor to give himself a few seconds more to click on his radio.

"Jules, maximum care. Nuclear."

⋆

El Taqha took out the radio with his left hand and looked deep into Grace's eyes.

"Just how brave *are* you, Grace Goody?"

Grace got up from the chair, turned to her right and walked towards the starboard edge of the deck, stepping through the narrow gap between the windbreaks and out from under the awning.

"Grace, stop," Kade called to her.

"Grace Goody, where are you going?"

She made no reply. El Taqha moved to follow her through the opening and to within a metre of the edge, where the deck ended with no protective rail. He was still clutching the radio in his left hand.

"And what exactly is this supposed to achieve?" he asked.

★

The Major dropped a little lower on the starboard tower and lined up the telescopic sight of his sniper rifle, something he had done on hundreds of occasions over two decades. In truth, he missed the mental challenge of those early days, computing all the factors – meteorological and positional – which contributed to a successful hit. These days, it was all done for him by the third-generation sniper system which calculated and displayed everything on the rifle's optic, and projected it onto the reticle.

He spoke into his radio.

"Clear shot at main target. Whenever."

The tone of his voice betrayed his excited anticipation.

★

The man in the protective suit had not spoken or moved, as Brig and Rom halved the remaining distance between them to less than twenty metres. He raised his automatic weapon to his shoulder into a firing position. Brig dropped to the floor again, this time lying still with Rom shaking him as if to revive him. After a few seconds, Rom got to his feet, his shoulders slumped as if in resignation and with his back turned to the terrorist. Brig twitched once on the floor, then lay still again.

The terrorist spoke to someone in the bay then walked towards them, letting his weapon hang by his side. They waited until he was within five metres before Rom turned and shot him in the throat with the silenced handgun. The man shot backwards onto the floor, his weapon flying sideways and crashing against the metal wall.

"Assad, what's happening?" a voice from Bay 24 called out in Arabic.

Brig was on his feet, pulling the protective suit from the dying man. They both looked towards the bay. No-one had stepped out into the aisle to investigate, but the shout came again from deep inside.

"Assad, are you alright?"

They looked at each other. Brig said what they were both thinking.

"The trigger man."

★

Kade broke his silence on the open deck for the first time, with el Taqha out of earshot.

"Jules, assume you copy the Major's message. You call the shot when ready. I hear Brig's warning. Nuclear – the nightmare scenario. Good luck."

The two groups on the deck of the *Mastodon* were now facing each other in an uncomfortable stand-off across the empty tables. The gap between the two windbreak panels through which Grace and el Taqha had passed was less than a metre wide. It was unthinkable that either group could rush the opening without sparking a firefight.

Robbie resolved the problem. He walked over to the panel on their side of the gap, which was held in place by rings on horizontal rails top and bottom of a tubular metal frame. The panel pulled aside like a heavy curtain, folding concertina-style to allow them sight of the two figures at the edge of the deck. Their counterparts followed suit on their side and all ten stepped through into the open and felt the cold Atlantic air.

Grace was standing closest to the edge, with el Taqha less than two metres away from her, almost within touching distance. He was still holding the radio, his hand stretched out towards her as if to make sure she was fully aware of it and of its significance.

★

Rom raced towards the bay as Jules and Rico hurried along the aisle to join them.

"Get the suit," Brig called to Jules, letting the man fall back to the floor. He set off after his comrade.

Rom turned into the bay without breaking stride, his handgun ready. Brig, a second behind him, heard the first shot and a cry before he reached the opening. Following Rom's lead, he went straight into the bay, running low, and took in the scene.

Rom was writhing on the floor, his hands covering his face and blood starting to leak through his fingers. In the centre of the bay, some distance away, another man in protective clothing was standing beside the bomb. It was exactly how Sir Roger had described it. The sphere was about seventy centimetres in diameter and consisted of ten separated segments, like those of a citrus fruit, but with gaps between. Across the top of the sphere was a metal bar holding in place the central, vertical cylinder which kept the segments apart. The terrorist's left hand was resting on the bar. In his right hand was the gun he had used to shoot Rom.

Not quite a manually restrained trigger, but only one swift movement away from it.

⋆

Grace had remained silent for over a minute, listening to Lydia's urgent words. When she spoke, it was with calm assurance.

"Before keeping your appointment with martyrdom, Abu, perhaps you'd like to hear how far we have got with your demands – what I discussed with my contacts during our recess. Then, when you reach your paradise, you'll be able to reflect on how successful you *could* have been and how much more you *might* have achieved if you hadn't been in such a hurry to get there."

"Do not mock me, Grace Goody. You have no idea…"

"Sixty-three so far. We have isolated sixty-three of the people on your list at the places where they are being held. That is an enormous achievement on our part to move forward that far so quickly, and on your part as well if we can go further to completion. There is still much to do and to discuss. You will want assurance that they are free and safe, and, of course, beyond recapture, but I would say this is progress, wouldn't you?"

El Taqha hesitated before replying, as if carefully weighing the truth of the statement. Then he smiled.

"I think we are past that, Grace Goody. You cannot be trusted. You will get what you deserve. This time, the zero key for the zero-bomb."

He pressed the keypad.

★

The man had already turned to release the bar when the single note sounded through his radio.

Brig was moving fast towards the bomb, but he was still ten metres away when he fired the shot, hitting the terrorist on the side of his head. The man, already leaning forward as the bar came away, slumped over the sphere, holding the cylinder in place for a couple of seconds before sliding down to the floor.

Brig hurled himself forward, diving across the sphere and preventing the cylinder's upward movement. The force of the spring mechanism caused him to cry out in pain as the end of the cylinder hit his sternum. He felt and heard the crack of at least one of his ribs as the cylinder descended beneath him. The terrorist, crying out in agony and bleeding from the headwound, managed to scramble to where he had let the gun drop when he went to release the bar. He twisted round, taking aim at Brig. A muted shot sounded and the man jerked sideways as two more bullets from Rico's Glock ended his resistance.

Jules, in the first man's protective suit, raced across to Brig, forcing his hands under his chest to hold down the cylinder and allow him to stand free. Brig pulled over the bar again to hold it in place and disable the bomb, before sinking to a sitting position against the bay wall, his features twisted in pain and his arms wrapped around his injured chest. The terrorist's radio sounded for the second time, momentarily distracting them, then they looked anxiously across to where Rico was kneeling beside Rom. Rico looked up at them and shook his head.

"Gone."

Jules spoke into the radio.
"Bomb secure. Free to take shot from now."
Sir Roger's voice. "Major, you copy that?"
"Copy that."
"And the bomb?" Sir Roger again.
"Nuke. Zero-bomb."
"Any casualties?"
A pause.
"Rom down."
"Down?"
"Dead."

CHAPTER FORTY-FOUR

1.05 p.m. BST

It seemed to Kade that, for the first time since he'd appeared on deck two hours earlier, el Taqha was confused and vulnerable. His two presses of the keypad had yielded nothing, although the terrorist had seemed unfazed by that. The change in his expression came as Kade heard the news from Jules about disabling the bomb, and he wondered if el Taqha had read some sign of relief in his own expression. An unintended change in his body language, which he had failed to suppress. Was that the moment he realised he had failed? If so, like any cornered animal, this was when he would be at his most dangerous.

Kade moved forward, raising his MP-5, but el Taqha was too quick for him. He stepped behind Grace, dropping his radio and forcing her away from the edge of the deck. He wrapped his left arm round her neck, pulling her to him and pressing hard against her throat. Before anyone could react, he swung her half to the side, still in his stranglehold, and pulled back the front of his tunic with his other hand to reveal the tubes, wires and packs of Semtex which made up his explosive vest. He gripped the length of cord close to his waist.

"Lower your weapons and move back," he said.

Kade turned away and spoke into his radio. "Listen, all. We have a situation."

*

"*Fuck*. Two seconds too late."

As the terrorist leader made his move, his head had been in

the crosshairs of the Major's rifle and his finger had already eased the trigger through the first part of its arc to where it was ready to engage. The shot would have been just about makeable. Perhaps not a clean one-shot kill on the gently swaying structure, but with easily enough margin of error to be sure of missing Grace and buying Red-One a moment or two advantage over their opponents on deck. Kade's team would have been waiting for his intervention as the signal to take the terrorists out before they had time to realise what was happening.

He'd missed his chance. Grace and el Taqha were now, as far as a possible hit was concerned, close enough to be a single entity.

There again, he thought, if he *had* made the shot and it *hadn't* been a straight kill, el Taqha might still have been able to activate his vest, with the result that, as of now, everyone on deck would be dead. Perhaps a fortuitous two-second delay after all, especially as the presence of the vest reduced his margin of error.

"No shot now," he spoke into his radio.

*

Kade turned to his team.

"Lower your weapons. Back away. Behind the cabins."

The four dropped back, MP-5s down at their sides. Kade lowered his weapon but stood his ground, close to the two at the edge of the deck. The five other terrorists held their positions, to their leader's right and facing Kade's team. They seemed relaxed and resigned to whatever fate he had in mind for them.

Grace turned her head sideways to relieve the pressure on her throat so she could speak.

"Get everyone off the deck, Kade, *now*. And I mean *you*, too. He's lost; we've beaten him. Let him blow himself to hell, or wherever fucking mass murderers like him go. Let the bastard..."

El Taqha squeezed harder, trapping her words.

"What an evil mouth, Grace Goody. And after all the compliments I've paid you today." He turned to Kade. "Let me tell you what is going to happen now."

*

The call came through on Jackie's iPhone at 1.20 p.m. as she sat in the private office at Thames House, which she had adopted as her base for the time being.

"Hi, Ruby. What have you got?"

"Good news, but with some unfinished business, it seems. But most importantly, they've found and disabled the bomb."

"Thank God for that. And the type of bomb?"

"A nuke. Exactly what el Taqha claimed: o-bomb, zero-bomb, zee-bomb, depending on where you live, it seems."

"*Fuck.* There I go again, Ruby. When did they disable it?"

"Just a few minutes ago. Sir Roger told me a minute after he got the news."

"Casualties?"

"Six terrorists dead, one injured, one of Blue-Two. Shot dead within metres of the bomb, trying to reach it."

"*Fuck* – again. And the unfinished business?"

"A stand-off on deck. El Taqha has Grace and an explosive vest. That's all I know. I'll keep you posted, of course."

"Oh, shit. Kade's with her?"

"As far as I know. Will you bring Andrew up to date?"

"I will if I can find him. He disappeared just before he was due to meet the US ambassador. In a panic about a person the police are looking for. It seemed to him like a bigger crisis than this one, can you believe?"

"So, he never got to speak to Linus?"

"I met with him instead. Is anything happening out there with the carrier? Last I heard we had the Typhoons buzzing the deck."

"A lot of activity on deck reported up to about an hour ago – planes and helicopters – looking like they were gearing up for something. But it's all gone quiet now."

"So, it could be Linus got the message through."

"Could be. And, if he did, it looks like our Ms Goody has saved the day twice already. Anyway, I'll leave you to find our errant leader."

"Okay. Thanks, Ruby. God, I hope Grace gets through this. She deserves to. She's an incredibly brave woman."

"And your new best friend, it seems."

Jackie chuckled. "Never that, but… I just hope she's okay."

"Me, too. Speak soon."

*

Andrew did not pick up the desk phone in his inner office at Number 10 but listened to Jackie's voice feeding into his voicemail.

"Andrew, just on the off chance that you're still interested in what's going on in the Atlantic, Ruby has informed me that they have located and disarmed the bomb; a nuke, in fact. So, we were all wrong in not believing what we were told by the only party to the dialogue who actually *knew* what it was. Anyway, I guess it doesn't make any difference now it's safe.

"It's not all good news, however. It seems Grace is being held by el Taqha, still on board the *Mastodon*, and he's wearing an explosive vest. So, it doesn't look particularly good for Goody right now. Sorry if that sounds flippant, but I don't know what the *fuck* you are playing at.

"Oh, almost forgot, the US ambassador asked me to say he hopes you're feeling well again soon."

*

Kade had dropped back to join his team, as if in response to Grace's insistence. He spoke into his radio.

"We wait until Taqha's transport arrives, then we can take that out as well. And the longer we all wait with nothing happening, the more relaxed he's going to be, and with his way out of here that close, my bet is he'll be less inclined to pull that cord. It might only give us a few more seconds, but that's all we should need. One thing I'm certain of is that Grace will *not* get onto that chopper. So, we need to be ready to react to anything she does. We won't get a second chance. Lydia, make sure Grace gets all that?"

Kade was standing with his team under the awning close to the nearest portacabin. They had been waiting there since el Taqha had explained that he, along with his men, would be picked up by helicopter within thirty minutes. That had been twenty-two minutes ago. Since then, the terrorist leader had moved a metre or so further away from the edge of the deck He was still holding Grace in the same position, except that his left arm was now round her waist, and, in his left hand he held the Browning pressed up between her breasts.

"Jules, hostages?" Kade asked.

"All accounted for and well. As well as can be, that is, when you have been tied and gagged ten metres away from a nuclear bomb. But they applaud our little rescue and mourn our lost colleague. They are now back on duty, ready for orders. I have left Rom's radio with Ove in the comms room so he can stay in contact with us, and he can reach the other hostages through internal ship's radio."

"Is Joss back with you?"

"Yes, he's here, along with Brig and Rico."

"And, where are you?"

"Just inside the door to the main deck on the starboard side."

"Okay, stay ready. Major, you okay?"

"You bet, Kade. This is way overdue."

Kade turned his attention back to the two figures near the deck's edge. He was in no doubt that Grace would make a move, but now with the vest *and* the gun, he was having difficulty working out what she could do.

★

Grace knew exactly what she was going to do. In fact, she had been doing it since her captor had informed them how he was going to leave the scene, taking her with him as security. Keeping herself in the same position, turned half-away from him and blindside of his guards; with her left hand she eased the handgun from the thigh pocket of her loose-fitting combat trousers. Desperately slowly, lifting it by walking her fingers, a millimetre at a time so there was no detectable movement, second-by-second, minute-by-minute.

It took her over ten minutes this way to clear the pocket. She shifted her position, as if to make herself more comfortable, shrugging her shoulders to let the long sleeve of her jacket drop over her hand, concealing the Glock.

Then she waited.

★

Kade watched Grace's slow-motion preparation with interest and appreciation, but with still no idea of her intentions. He thought back to their conversation on HMS *Jura – I'm not sure what will be waiting for me when we get back… I'm dreading not seeing you again after this*. He hoped she didn't have anything heroic and suicidal in mind.

Exactly twenty-eight minutes after el Taqha's announcement, the sound of a fast-approaching helicopter reached their ears. It was arriving from the south-west, the direction of the southern tip of the Outer Hebrides.

Kade spoke into his mouthpiece.

"Major, approaching chopper. Get out of sight again until it's close to landing on deck. Copy that?"

"Copy and done."

El Taqha had strengthened his grip on Grace and turned to watch it arrive. One of the terrorists spoke into his radio. The aircraft came in fast, dropping below the level of the forward superstructure and speeding along the deck under the platform and away again. It made a full circle before taking the same route back, this time more slowly, to hover just off the starboard edge, close to where el Taqha was holding Grace. El Taqha raised his right hand in acknowledgement, momentarily releasing the cord to his bomb vest.

As he reached down again for the cord, Grace twisted in his grip to bring her left hand round in a narrow upward arc, and shot him in his right arm just above the elbow. At the same time, she arched her back in an attempt to force el Taqha's gun away from her chest. El Taqha reeled away, his face contorted in agony, his right arm hanging by his side, and howling in pain. But as they separated, he pulled the trigger of the Browning, and blood fountained from Grace's neck. They fell away from each other, el Taqha dropping the gun and reaching across his body with his left hand. Then he was bounced backwards along the deck as the Major's first shot hit him high on the chest, a couple of centimetres above the bomb vest.

"Blue-Two on deck!" Kade shouted into his radio. He moved forward, but Robbie was already racing past him as the terrorist leader made another, much weaker, move to grab the bomb cord. El Taqha's head exploded in a gruesome spray of blood, brains and bone as the Major's second shot found its mark. Robbie threw himself on top of his twitching body to negate as much as possible any effect of the vest exploding.

The helicopter peeled away while the terrorist guards watched, frozen in shock, as their leader died in front of them. Jules's team had already burst onto the deck, taking in the scene in a second. Brig shouted in Arabic.

"Lay down your arms, my brothers, so we may fight another day to avenge our leader."

The five men turned as one, clearly confused by the language and the familiar clothing of the shouter, accompanied as he was by three of the enemy. By the time they had turned back, Kade, Holly, Sergei and Daz had moved to within a couple of metres of them.

Brig shouted again, still walking towards them.

"This is not the time to die for Allah. We must *live* for Allah. We must *fight* for Allah. We have shown them what we can do. Allah and Abu are proud of us."

The man who had called the helicopter dropped his radio and raised his machine pistol. Kade responded in a split second, shooting him in the head with his Glock. The man's body arched backwards and crashed onto the deck.

"*No!*" Brig bellowed this time, only a metre or so behind them. "This is not the way to die."

The four men dropped their weapons as Kade and Jules' groups converged to within touching distance of them, their MP-5s now pressed against them, front and back. Kade reached down and pulled open the radio man's combat jacket.

"No vest," he said. "Check them all. Brig, tell them they are our prisoners, but they are brave soldiers. They should feel no shame."

Brig nodded and spoke to them again in Arabic.

"Jules," Kade said, "get Ove to tell the crew to move us out and away from here."

⋆

On the top of the starboard tower at the stern, where the canopy had been pulled aside, the Major waited until the helicopter was well away from the ship. Then, dropping down onto one knee, he raised his second rifle and took aim at the shaft of the main rotor.

Steadying his left elbow on his raised knee, he squeezed the trigger and shot it down. The aircraft spiralled in the air before tilting to one side and dropping into the sea, the blades threshing against the water for a few moments. The same motion seemed to drive the body of the helicopter below the surface before a muffled explosion sent a powerful wash spreading out in a rapidly growing circle.

The Major held up his rifle and turned to the man at his side.

"A Barrett M82, Sam, the most powerful sniper rifle in the world, capable of bringing down a helicopter with a single shot. Remind me to tell you sometime why these last few minutes have meant so much to me."

"That look in your eye, Major, I reckon I won't need to remind you."

⋆

Kade raced across to where Robbie was leaning over Grace. She was clutching her throat and bleeding badly.

"You are some warrior, Grace Goody," Kade said. "Don't try to speak."

"Can't… anyway." Grace gave a little choking laugh and a small fountain of blood escaped her lips. Her eyes rolled as she fought for consciousness, twisting her head from side to side to mitigate the pain. Kade glanced at Robbie, who had knelt down beside her with standing tears in his eyes.

"You, too, big man. You would have saved us all."

Robbie swallowed. When he spoke, his voice was surprisingly small.

"Och, no. I knew he was dead. I'm nae fool."

Kade nodded and smiled. "Check the vest, Robbie. Make sure it's safe."

"Done that, sir," he said, getting to his feet, "but no harm in double-checking."

⋆

Grace looked up through what seemed like a swirling fog, one second dense enough to make her almost blind, then opening to reveal the ice-blue eyes in the anxious face above her. The pain, at first so intense and unbearable, now seemed to be receding, along with all her senses. She was aware that the man was holding her hand and stroking her face.

Just as the mist closed in again, another face materialised next to that of her comforter, disembodied in the haze. Her eyes opened wide, as if of their own accord, the features came clearly into focus and her mind made one final attempt at understanding. The ghost – the man in the cafeteria and on the Archer patrol boat – the man who appeared and disappeared. But how could it be him? Unless it had been a premonition, and now she had passed over, moved on to join him. The man spoke, and she knew for certain.

"Grace." Barely a whisper.

She felt herself slipping away and put all her remaining strength into her last two words, before the shifting, translucent mass morphed into solid black oblivion.

"Jason… doughnut."

CHAPTER FORTY-FIVE

Harry and Alice joined Jo, with Seb, in front of the multiple monitors of the CCTV operations room at Guildford New Station at just after 1.45 p.m.

"Anything?" Harry asked.

"Something, following up what you said about his height," Jo answered, "but whether it's relevant or not… Seb spotted it. Go on, Seb."

Seb leaned forward, picking up a remote control from the long narrow table in front of them, and pointed to one of the larger screens.

"This isn't real time," he said. "The guys have just strung some images together of Mobsby going to and from work."

The screen showed Max leaving the house, then jumped to his entering the Oval Tube station, boarding the northbound train, and more points along the way until he disappeared through the revolving doors of Dreyfus House. The whole edited sequence was less than two minutes.

"Let's go back and stop the action in a few places." Seb jabbed the remote and the sequence started again. He stopped it almost immediately, with Mobsby on the top step locking the front door of his house. "That door will be two metres high – six-six or thereabouts – and he looks some way short of that. Now watch him against other pedestrians on his way to the Tube station: he doesn't stand out at all in a crowd, not height-wise, anyway. This is at the station, him boarding the Tube. The doors are *less* than six-six high but there's quite a bit of clearance as he steps through them. You can see why Craig thinks he's no more than average height." He let it run up to Mobsby entering Dreyfus House. "Difficult to gauge anything here because we don't know how high the entrance is to the building, but – for future reference – just note his height against the column of plaques at the left side of the doors.

"Now, watch this. Around four hours later, this is him leaving work, and this is the key moment. Note his height alongside the same plaques this time. He's around half a plaque taller. I reckon that would be two inches at least, maybe three. Then he retraces his steps back to Cannon Road." He pointed to a line of four smaller screens under the one they had been watching. "These are stills from the feed, taken in the same place – as close as possible, anyway – on the outward and return journeys." Each of the screens showed two side-by-side images of Mobsby; walking in a crowd, boarding the Tube, at the entrance to Dreyfus House and back home. "What do you think?"

Harry and Alice leaned in towards the stills, screwing up their eyes in concentration. Alice was the first to speak.

"Different man?"

"Same man, different shoes. Look at this." Seb enlarged the images of Mobsby in the tube station, focussing on the man's feet. "On the way to work, he was wearing trainers, like many commuters do these days, then change into something more suitable at work; makes a lot of sense. On his return, smart, formal shoes. My guess is he keeps the smart ones at work. The daypack doesn't look big enough to take a pair of shoes."

Harry looked at Alice and then back at Seb.

"Well, that solves the mystery of the incredible shrinking man, or, should I say, stretching man. He wears built-up heels at work, presumably for the purpose of image. Other than that, I'm not sure what…"

"Neither are we," Jo said. "But you wonder why, with a pair of trainers at work, which we might assume he normally puts on for his home commute, he decides to spend six or seven hours watching the cricket in his high heels."

They sat in silence for a few moments before Alice spoke.

"Didn't he say that he'd received a call about someone hanging around his property? Couldn't that have sent him rushing straight home? Perhaps he just didn't think to change his shoes. I mean, he was certainly in a hurry when he arrived on the street."

"But he said he received the call *after* he left the building, didn't he?" Jo asked.

"That's right, he did. So… theories, Detective Inspector Cottrell?"

"Working on them."

The door behind them opened and Natalie and George entered, followed by DC Gordon, who was holding her open notebook.

"Any joy, Beth?" Seb asked.

"The address in Lambeth is an old-fashioned tobacconist and the manager has never heard of a Curtis Rinder. Also, I've not been able to find any reference at all to anyone of that name anywhere else."

"So, the only thing we know about him," Jo said, "is that, right now, he's somewhere north of Kendal."

"Well, he's certainly that, ma'am, because he was captured on CCTV again at Abington services on the M74 about an hour and a half ago. I've just been speaking with a guy called Brendan Moss, who's the security manager there. When he received the info we circulated about the car and the reg, he checked back over the past hour or so and picked it up on their CCTV. They've got a really good set-up: five cameras in the main services, plus three in the refuelling area. He said the car arrived at 12.33 and pulled into one of the spaces farthest from the building"

"And the driver?" Harry asked.

"Entered the building, picked up a chocolate bar in W H Smith's then went through to the toilets…" Beth checked her notes "… wearing a dark-grey top with the hood up and pulled forward, like at Kendal, this time carrying a daypack."

"And that was, you say," Harry checked his watch, "an hour and a half ago. So, what happened next?"

"Well, Brendan rolled the tape forward and at the time he phoned me, it *seemed* that he was still in there, because there was no sign of him leaving. That was an hour after he'd arrived, which Brendan agreed was a long time, but they have some showers in there, so he thought that might be why he was taking so long."

"I don't buy that," Harry said. "If he *is* our guy, then around thirty hours ago he was accessory to a very violent attack on an ex-policeman. I can't see him taking time out in a public place so soon afterwards just to freshen up."

"That's exactly what I thought, sir, so I asked Brendan to – *very carefully* – check whether he was still there. And, to cut a long story short, he wasn't. Brendan found the daypack hanging on the back of one of the shower-cubicle doors, but no sign of the owner. The hoodie was inside the bag along with a pair of cargo pants and a shaver. He must have got changed and shaved in the toilet."

"Shit." Harry shook his head. "Second dead end. Anything else?"

"I asked Brendan to check for any guy coming *out* of the toilets who didn't go *in*, if you see what I mean. And he found him, now wearing a light, safari-style jacket over a white tee shirt, faded blue jeans and the same black trainers. He had a plain, grey baseball cap angled low over his forehead. The cameras captured him walking out of the building towards the fuelling area – not back to the car – and then away from the services altogether."

"And when was that?"

"Twelve fifty-three, exactly twenty minutes after he arrived. So, just over an hour ago."

"And did your new friend have any theory as to where he might be walking?"

Beth checked her notes again.

"Gut feel, he thought he'd head north. South would take him along the main A702 trunk road, where there are cameras. North, there are no cameras and within half a mile the road forks and each way leads to a network of B and minor roads. And if he was still on foot, he wouldn't have to stick to the roads, anyway. It's popular walking country and he could strike out over one of the hills."

"So, vanished without a trace," Harry said.

"Well, not without a trace, sir. I've asked Brendan to cordon off the car so we can get it forensically reclaimed, and, for now, to put the daypack back where he found it in case someone comes to remove it. And if no-one does, it might yield some DNA."

"Great stuff, Beth. And seeing as you're so on-side with this, can you liaise with – would it be Borders? – and arrange for them to get the car. And they might want to have a presence there for a while in case someone does come for the daypack. Give them my number for follow-up. And thank Brendan from me, would you?"

Harry stood up, sighed and stretched.

"Right, MIT room, Nat; gather the troops."

*

Within five minutes of Jules's message to Ove, the anchors had been raised and the deck shuddered as the mighty vessel began to edge forward from beneath the platform. Even before it had fully cleared the structure, the Eurocopter X3 with two medical teams from HMS *Jura* had landed close to where Abu el Taqha and Grace Goody still lay near the edge of the deck on the starboard side.

With the terrorist leader being past needing assistance, all attention was focussed on Grace. She was "still alive, breathing shallow, pulse weak," Gus Walker, the chief paramedic informed them. "Fifty-fifty at best, next couple of hours critical." Kade and Brig, still kneeling beside her, had heard it all before many times. Today it was different.

Another team had attended the wounded terrorist where he was just about conscious in one of the forward cabins. He would live, they reported back, but walk again? Too early to tell.

"At least Rom won't have to face the travesty of an inquiry," Brig said. "You know the rules over here, Kade. Once everyone is safe again, the cretinous bastards seated comfortably behind their desks start dissecting how we behaved. We should take a few along with us next time, just to show them what it's really like. Rom is a fucking hero. He took that bullet in Bay 24 for all of us."

"Amen to that,"

Kade squeezed Brig's shoulder as he got to his feet and walked across to the edge of the deck. He looked up at the starboard tower as the *Mastodon* pulled away from the platform, heading due west into the Atlantic, following more or less the same course as the diminishing shape of the USS *Ronald Reagan*, now already halfway to the horizon. He could see the heads and shoulders of the five members of Blue-One, looking up at the platform and waving to those lining the observation deck. The exiles, packed tightly along the two sides of Hotel St Kilda that had sight of the vessel, were applauding, some with hands raised above their heads to ensure the Major's team would be sure to see.

"Would you look at that," Kade said.

Brig joined him and looked across.

"Would you just *look* at that," Kade repeated. He glanced at Brig, who was staring at the exiles, tears welling in his eyes.

They both turned back to where Grace was being lifted into the X3, accompanied by Holly. The chief paramedic walked across to them, shaking his head.

"We'll do our very best, of course, gentlemen, but no promises. She doesn't deserve to die, but she's in a very bad way. I'll keep Sir Roger informed."

"Thanks, Gus."

They watched the Eurocopter take off and remained focussed on it until it was out of sight, heading for Stornoway on the island of Lewis.

Brig turned to Kade.

"What did she mean, 'Jason doughnut'?"

*

Harry was about to step out of his office into the Major Incident Team room when Jo stopped him at the door.

"Craig's on the landline, Harry. Wants to know if he should get back. The Met guys will carry on covering the house."

"Okay, tell him yes."

"*And*, Nat tells me your boss – *and* mine – wants to see us both."

"Lynsey?"

"I think you mean Detective Superintendent Hargreaves? I wouldn't be so bold… But, yes, she'd like to see us both."

"Okay, just rein in Craig, then we'll go to see her."

They walked together in silence to the DS's office. Harry knocked on the door and stood aside to wave Jo through when Lynsey shouted for them to enter. The senior officer walked round from behind her desk to shake Jo's hand.

"So pleased to meet you at last, Jo, and I owe you an apology for not doing so sooner. I know you're still on assignment in Leicester as part of our FRT flying squad, but the least you should expect is for your new boss to say 'Hi'."

"That's quite alright, ma'am, no apology necessary, and thank you for not referring to me as a 'fart'."

Lynsey gave a brief laugh and went back behind her desk, but instead of sitting down she removed her jacket from the chairback and slipped it on.

"I will need a complete update from you, Harry, on what has happened and where we stand on the hunt for these two men, plus what you recommend we say – and when – to the press about the incident at Westmore. But, not now, you can tell me by phone in the car. You two are going for a little ride."

"With respect, ma'am," Jo said, as she and Harry followed Lynsey out of the office, "I should get back to Leicester with Detective Sergeant Carter. We've been away for nearly twenty-four hours, and..."

"Not yet, Jo. I'll speak to Seb and Superintendent Wallace, and I'll fully brief your team on the situation, Harry. But we're all seriously outranked for the time being."

They stepped outside into New Station Yard, the large rectangular courtyard of the Guildford Centre of Justice. The centre had been developed to reflect Guildford's status as one of the NJR's regional hubs. The site included a range of buildings, dominated by Guildford New Station, the police headquarters for the South Thames Division covering the area bounded by the Metropolitan Police District to the north, the M3 to the west and the English Channel to the south and east, and which housed the region's FRT – Flexible Response Team.

A gleaming black 700 series BMW with shaded rear passenger windows was quietly ticking over, awaiting their arrival. A large man with no neck, a shaven head and wrap-around sunglasses, and wearing a dark-blue suit which strained to contain his bulk, squeezed out of the front passenger seat and opened the nearside rear door. Jo and Harry both turned to Lynsey.

"In you go," she said. "Don't forget, Harry, call me in transit with an update. And behave yourselves."

The big man smiled and nodded to the senior officer, then closed the door after them and got back into his seat. From a few yards away, a motorcycle pulled past the car and stopped in front of it. The driver pipped the car horn and the outrider switched on his flashing blue lights and led the way out through the courtyard gates.

CHAPTER FORTY-SIX

During the hour since Grace and the injured terrorist had been lifted from the *Mastodon*, the vessel had travelled thirty kilometres due west from Hotel St Kilda, where it was now holding its position awaiting the arrival of a team from the British Army's Ordnance Explosive Disposal Group. The bomb was disarmed mechanically, but there was no guarantee that its few moments of rough treatment had not destabilised it. Jules and Rico, in their borrowed protective suits, had returned to Bay 24 to ensure the base of the device still adequately supported its deadly burden.

During the course of their west-bound journey, the Chinook had returned to take the four uninjured terrorists, escorted by the Blue-One team, along with Sergei, Robbie and Daz, to an improvised secure unit on Hirta to await onward transportation to London. They also took with them Rom's body and those of the eight dead terrorists.

Kade, Brig and Joss had remained on deck.

A second Eurocopter with the OED team had landed soon afterwards and Brig led them down to Bay 24, relieving Jules and Rico of their bomb-watching duties. Now, as the five men stood together looking out to sea past the forward superstructure at the dot on the horizon which was the largest supercarrier in the world, the door onto the deck opened and the commander of the small unit walked across to them. He gave them a cheery thumbs-up as he approached.

"Didn't stop to introduce myself properly before," he said. He reached out to shake Kade's hand. "Captain Andrew Marvell," he went on. "Neither a poet nor a superhero, I'm afraid, but I *can* tell you the bomb is safe. Thanks to this man here with the damaged ribs." He nodded to Brig.

Kade introduce the other members of his team.

"Thank you for that, Captain," he said. "I can't imagine you've had any experience of this type of bomb. I know it's never been used in anger before."

"Experience, no; knowledge, yes. Our theory training covers just about every type of bomb that's ever been produced, or even tested or suggested, just in case someone's taken up a prototype and gone into production for themselves. So, we knew about the zee-bomb, but – you're right – none of us had ever seen one. Even so, it wasn't a difficult ask, just secured all potentially moving parts with straps and tape." He turned to Brig and smiled. "So, there'll be no more demands on your body, you'll be pleased to hear."

"I *am* pleased to hear, thank you."

"I guess it's safe now to turn round and take this big guy back. We're still waiting to hear who will claim the device, and where and when. My guess is they'll lift it off the ship rather than dock with it. Then there'll be the high-level arm wrestling to decide who'll get the blame for letting it fall into terrorists' hands. I'd love a ringside seat for that."

*

Harry finished his call to Lynsey and put away his phone. He looked out through the darkened windows of the car.

"I don't believe it," he said. "God, if I pass Ripley Services once more today. This is the third time."

Jo laughed. "I think this love affair with the A3 has gone far enough, Harry, don't you?"

"It won't last, I can tell you that. This guy's nearly as fast as Alice. There's no respite."

"And our boss can't even tell us where we're going?"

"*Won't* tell us, I reckon. Knowing Lynsey, she wouldn't have let them take us if she didn't know. As long as it's not Cannon Road. I could do with a change of scenery."

"'Seriously outranked', she said. I wonder what that means."

They sat back in their seats, Harry with both hands holding the diagonal strap of his seat belt, as was his habit when DC Grantham was driving, and watched the miles unfold to *exactly* where he had been earlier. This time, however, they drove past the end of the road where they had turned off to park at the community centre, and on to Vauxhall Bridge. As they passed over the Thames, they looked at each other.

"Surely not Balmaha?" Jo said. That was the name of Tom Brown's London residence, on Vauxhall Bridge Road, where Jo had found the hidden gun which had started the hunt for the former Home Secretary eight months ago. The answer came quickly as the car turned right onto Millbank and, a few minutes later, left into Thorney Street, which brought them to the rear entrance of Thames House, home of the Security Service, also known as MI5. They were met on the steps by a young man in a smart grey suit, white shirt and blue tie, who took them in a lift to the second floor of the building. The only words he spoke were, "This way, please" on three separate occasions as he led them to the meeting room.

The office into which Harry and Jo were shown was formally set out but not unwelcoming. A huge antique desk bearing the marks of a century-or-so's usage occupied the centre of the room, with a large tilt-and-swivel from the same era behind it facing the door. On the chair sat a man of a later vintage who completely filled it. He sported a large walrus moustache which rose part-way up his ruddy cheeks. His cream shirt with yellow cravat were worn under a mustard-coloured waistcoat which was tight across a barrel chest.

Four captain's chairs were arranged around the other three sides of the desk, one at each end and two facing the man in the large chair. The walls to the left of the door and behind the man were covered by floor-to-ceiling bookshelves, and in front of the window in the wall to the right, stood a brass tripod supporting an old nautical telescope, which was pointing out through it.

The man behind the desk remained seated, but the occupants of the end chairs got to their feet, each with an easy smile. They stepped around the desk to shake hands with Jo and Harry.

"Good afternoon, Detective Inspectors, welcome to Thames House. I'm Captain Peter Drake." The Captain was slim, medium height, with sandy-hair and a short goatee beard which was barely visible against his skin colour. He wore a pale-blue linen suit over a white open-necked shirt. "This is my colleague, Corporal Vicky

Barrowclough, and your main host today is Brigadier Barrington Henshaw, Head of Section."

"Pleased to meet you all," Harry said, "I'm..."

"That's okay, DI Waters," the big man said, "we know who you are, *and* your colleague, the famous Detective Inspector Joannita Cottrell."

"Famous, sir?" Jo screwed up her face in a frown.

"Within the Section, that is, although that fame came when you were still a Detective Sergeant. Please, take a seat, both of you. We have tea and biscuits arriving any moment."

It was that precise moment, in fact, and the young man with the suit and the blue tie entered the room pushing a silver trolley, and immediately withdrew. Harry half expected him to say "this way, please" on his way out. The Brigadier himself poured the tea from a large teapot shaped like an old army tank, then passed round a landing-craft-shaped plate of biscuits from the same collection.

"The set was a retirement present," he said, smiling for the first time. "Only I didn't retire, so I keep it with me all the time in case they try to take it back." He turned to the corporal. "Vicky, over to you."

Vicky Barrowclough picked up the clutch of papers in front of her and stood to hand two A4 sheets, and a pen, to each of the detectives. The corporal was an inch or two shorter than the captain. Her round, attractive face was framed by curly dark-brown hair which hung loose onto her shoulders.

"Just a formality," she said. "We need you to sign one of these. Read through them if you wish, it's just an agreement under the Official Secrets Act."

"We've already signed..." Jo began.

"This applies specifically to this meeting," Vicky said. "It's for you to commit to not acting on any information you receive here today and to accept that you will be directed in your further investigation by this Section only."

Harry leaned forward. "I'm sorry, but we are investigating a very serious crime. I'm not sure at what level, but I assume that somewhere our respective chains of command come together, so I don't understand why people seem hell-bent on preventing us doing our job. I'm not sure we can sign this and agree anything."

The Brigadier leaned forward on his elbows with enough force to shake the desk and rattle the cups.

"It's not about *agreeing*, DI Waters, but *accepting*. What I am going to tell you now will mean my taking a big chance with your integrity. I believe you deserve that trust, but we have gone beyond the point of choice. You *will* sign those documents, and, in exchange, I will pay you both the compliment of sharing with you information to which very few people have access."

"And this is information relating to the premeditated, brutal attempt on the life of an ex-policeman?" Jo asked.

"No, it isn't, DI Cottrell. It relates to the perpetrators – *one* of the perpetrators – but *not* specifically to his part in this action."

"'Action' in this context meaning crime?"

"As you wish, DI Cottrell – look, may I call you Jo? It will save a few syllables each time I address you."

Jo found herself smiling. "Yes, of course."

"I understand why you are both eager to conclude this investigation with an arrest and a charge. It is important within the police that, if someone attacks one of their own, they must pay. 'Blue Justice', I've heard it called. This is your case, DI Waters…"

"It's Harry, sir."

"This is your case, Harry, but the victim was *your* long-time colleague, Jo. So, an extra incentive for you."

"My problem, sir, with respect," Harry said, "is that I am paid to do a job and I'm trying to imagine getting back to Guildford and telling my superior – and her having to tell *her* superior – that it's case closed because we signed a bit of paper. First thing that will happen is she'll pass the case to someone else."

"I think I've made your superintendent aware that this was outside the scope of your authority, and hers, for that matter."

Jo and Harry looked at each other.

Jo shrugged. "'Seriously outranked' the Super said. I guess we now know what that means."

They both reached forward and picked up the documents, reading through and signing them as requested.

"There now," the Brigadier beamed, "that wasn't too bad, was it? So now make yourself comfortable while I tell you what this is about. Oh, and help yourselves to biscuits. More tea? No? Then let me begin.

"This Section, of whom we three are part, offers a range of services to the government, the military, the police and, when appropriate, to friendly nations. And, on occasions – shame on us – to rebellious factions in *unfriendly* nations when we believe such assistance may be to our advantage. We are a one-stop shop for any, let's say, *extracurricular* mission requiring special expertise. My job, that is, *our* job…" he spread his arms to include the other two "… is to provide the resources, not to sanction the activities. That's the *official* position, but we do have a secondary role, which is to monitor those activities, which makes us – *unofficially* – a sort of passive conscience for all the secret missions that take place outside the normal remit of MI5, MI6, Special Forces and Special Branch. With me so far?"

"I'm not sure I am," Jo said.

"It doesn't matter. That's just recruitment talk anyway. But the reason we maintain an interest is because these secret missions – and missionaries – fall outside the scope of normal, and sometimes legal, behavioural restrictions."

Jo leaned forward in her chair.

"So, you're saying these people are encouraged to operate unlawfully?"

"Absolutely not. At least, not *encouraged*. Our motto is…" He half-turned and pointed to a framed plaque on the wall next to the window. It displayed just three Latin words *AD MAIUS BONUM*, which he read aloud for the benefit of his audience. "Do you know what that means?"

"For the greater good," Jo replied.

"Excellent, Jo." The Brigadier was clearly surprised and impressed. "You're the first one I've asked who's got it right. And really, it's just a nicer way of saying the end justifies the means. That's what we're about, and sometimes the things that are needed to achieve that end are not exactly within the rules. Here's an example of the greater good, Jo, which you can relate to and which is the source of your fame within the Section.

"John Deverall, a.k.a. James Lorimar, a.k.a. Alex Anderson, is one of ours. The man you and your colleague, DCI Gerrard, arrested and successfully charged with the murder of the Brady brothers, three of the worst human beings on the planet. I exaggerate, perhaps, to make the point. Deverall killed three people and liberated three thousand – the entire population of the Cullen Field estate. So how big a crime was that?"

"You're telling me he was doing that under orders from you, or somebody like you?"

"No, he certainly wasn't. It was pure vigilante. But the point is, with the possible exception of their own family and the toe-rags that followed them around, everyone in the country thought it was a great thing that he did. He didn't do it for that reason – to free the estate of evil. We know it was to avenge the death of his mother who had been terrorised by the gang. But the liberation of the whole community was the overwhelming effect, and will be his legacy, I've no doubt."

Jo was looking across at Vicky Barrowclough.

"That's where I've seen you before," she said. "At the memorial service for John Deverall's mother, Alma. Am I right? I seem to remember you were with a young man in a wheelchair."

"Yes, I was there. The young man is Mike Wilson, another one of our colleagues here in the Section."

Jo turned back to the Brigadier.

"You still haven't explained why I'm famous,"

"*Infamous* would be more literally correct, perhaps, but a little unfair. You see, Deverall is one of six people in the world forming a virtual group of – well, I guess you'd probably call them assassins, although executioners would be a better word. He is the best of the six, and you took him out of circulation for two years. You and Mr Gerrard did a great job, Jo, but in doing so, you did your country a great disservice. *That's* why you are a sort of legend here in the Section."

"But that's ridiculous." Harry stepped in. "Jo being demonised for catching a killer."

"No, no, no, Harry. Jo's reputation was unscathed; enhanced, in fact. No-one doubts that you are an excellent detective, DI Cottrell, but that is the irony of the motto 'for the greater good', which in the case of the killing of the Brady brothers would have been for the perpetrator to have got away with it. We were too late on that occasion to intervene. But not this time, which is why you are both here now."

"Just before you go on, sir," Jo turned to Vicky again. "I seem to remember Maggie Tomlinson-Brown mentioning that she'd seen a young woman and a man in a wheelchair at John Deverall's funeral last year. Was that you as well?"

"Yes, that was me and Mike. The Brigadier and Captain Drake were there, too."

"We go to all John Deverall's funerals, don't we, Corporal? Sort of collect them."

"John is one of our Phoenix operatives," Peter Drake said. "That's how he happened to be alive after having been blown up in Afghanistan. He rose from those particular ashes as James Lorimar, an investment analyst, the man you and David Gerrard arrested. He had a working double at the investment company where he was officially employed. A person who did John's work while John was used for... well, the greater good."

"A double, did you say?" Harry asked.

"Not a physical double in this case," Peter said, "just someone to cover John's role in the investment company, to create and maintain his new credentials. He jokes that the person was a sort of inverse stuntman. John did all the dangerous stuff himself but used a stand-in for the desk job."

"But we do provide doppelgangers as well," the Brigadier said. "Physical doubles for agents operating in the public arena."

"You said John Deverall was out of circulation for *two years*," Jo said. "And you keep referring to him in the present tense."

"John Deverall is very much alive, Jo. I assume you have both been following events in the Atlantic off St Kilda. What you don't know yet is that the hostages have been freed and an explosive device disabled. I am not at liberty to disclose *full* details of the mission's outcome and certainly not the tactics employed, but what I *can* tell you is that John Deverall was instrumental in bringing this to a satisfactory conclusion by taking out the man who is – *was* – arguably the world's most dangerous terrorist."

"Abu el Taqha?" Jo asked.

"The very same. A timely reminder of his worth in respect of the greater good, don't you agree?"

He picked up the teapot, reaching across to top up their cups.

"So, now to the current case, regarding Mr Jamie Walcott, a.k.a. Oscar Strange and a string of other names. Walcott is also one of ours but is currently out on loan at the request of a very high authority."

"The Ministerial Director of Justice," Harry said. "The Home Secretary told me earlier."

"Miss Goody is who Walcott was assigned to and who he has been working for, but she was not the person who requested the loan."

"And not the Home Secretary either."

"Why do you say that? Anyway, it doesn't matter, because you're right, it wasn't Jackie Hewlett, and I'll leave you to speculate at your leisure as to who made the request. Anyway, Walcott's been working *wholly* under the direction of Miss Goody, although his methods in carrying out that work spring from his own creative mind. His latest adventure, by the way, if indeed he is the person who shot Gerrard, was contrary to what he had been told to do. And, more to the point, it failed, which at this end of the business is almost a bigger crime in itself."

"I don't understand how failing to kill my ex-colleague can be regarded as a greater crime than succeeding. I'm not at all sure we're on the same side here, sir."

"Oh, we most definitely are, Jo, and I am genuinely pleased that DCI Gerrard survived. It's nothing personal, but failure leaves a trail, as proved in this case. So, our criteria for success will differ significantly at times. We're looking at the bigger picture; you're focussed on a few pixels in the corner. Nothing wrong with that, by the way; it's important we get the right balance. But it means we won't get a win–win every time, and when we don't, it's important that it's not a lose–lose."

Jo shrugged and shook her head.

"So, Jamie Walcott," the Brigadier continued, "is out there somewhere, and we think we know where. But the next contact with him must be managed very carefully, because he is in a position to cause significant damage if things go wrong."

He leaned forward on the desk and looked from one to the other of them, holding their eyes each time and remaining silent for several moments.

"What I've told you so far has, I trust, been new and interesting, but much of it you would probably have worked out for yourselves from your conversations with the Home Secretary, once you took a break from rushing around between London and Guildford. What I'm going to tell you next is the reason you have signed those bits of paper."

CHAPTER FORTY-SEVEN

The Western Isles Hospital in Stornoway is not well-equipped for dealing with the aftermath of offshore gunfights, but the town boasts an airport as well as the hospital, so its proximity to the action in the Atlantic was fortuitous as a first stopover for the injured.

Thirty minutes after taking off from the deck of the *Mastodon*, the Eurocopter, with Holly and the paramedic team of three from HMS *Jura* in attendance, touched down close to the hospital. Awaiting its arrival were two ambulances, one with a range of medical equipment, a doctor and three nursing staff. The wounded terrorist was taken to a secure private ward, leaving the medical team to attend Grace. After an initial examination, they decided to treat her and make her as comfortable as possible in the helicopter, to avoid moving her more than necessary ahead of the few minutes' flight to Stornoway airport and the onward journey. They spent the best part of an hour before the senior doctor was satisfied that they could do no more to give her the best chance of survival for her trip to the specialist unit in London.

"You did a great job getting her this far," the doctor said, addressing the paramedic team. "You've given her a fighting chance. The bullet missed the brain, the main blood vessels and the top of the spine, which is good. But it nicked the trachea and, with the internal as well as external bleeding, she'll have a lot of blood in her lungs. We've secured the trachea for now, but she needs more stitches and a lot of work under very controlled conditions. Stuff that we can't do here."

"Will she make it as far as London?" Holly asked. "Is there nowhere closer to save time?"

“Glasgow, Manchester perhaps, but London will be her best chance. Once she’s airborne the difference in the fight times will be less of a factor than the quality of specialist treatment she receives at her destination. We’ll alert medical staff at Glasgow and Manchester hospitals, so if she deteriorates en route, you can divert. But if I’m brutally honest with you, there is no room between her current condition and death to accommodate any deterioration.”

Twenty minutes later, at 4.10 p.m., with the doctor’s stark message still sounding in their minds, Holly and a medical team of six people, comprising a doctor, three nurses and two of the paramedics who had first attended Grace, boarded the Cessna Citation II air ambulance for the 850-kilometre flight to London City airport.

*

The Brigadier leaned forward again in his chair.

“Jamie Walcott is one of what we rather glamorously refer to as our ‘urban warriors’, or ‘street cleaners’ as others like to call them. Like Deverall, Walcott is the best we have at what he does, but whereas Deverall’s hunting ground is very much in the military and political arena, Walcott does his bit on the mean streets of… wherever. Ironic really, because the killing of the Bradys would have been right up one of Walcott’s mean streets. Not that something like that would have qualified for an official mission, just taking out part of a local street gang…” He paused and pursed his lips in thought, lifting his moustache almost level with his eyes. “Except, I suppose, in retrospect. I mean, thinking of the bigger picture, firing those three bullets was probably the catalyst for the New Justice Regime.”

“Four bullets, sir.”

“Sorry?”

“John Deverall fired four bullets. Three head shots and one to wound Jimmy Brady in the leg.”

“I stand corrected, Detective Inspector. Anyway, Walcott, like many such operatives in the domestic arena, has taken out an insurance policy. This is how it works.

“He keeps an up-to-date file of all his instructions from his handlers – handler, singular, in this case – and all the activities resulting therefrom. This, as you can imagine, is white-hot material, which can do a lot of damage to those who are directing him if it falls into the wrong hands. And, above a certain level in office, that damage can have a knock-on effect beyond the individual to threaten the very core of government and even national security. In this case, at the very least, the country would be rocked by an unprecedented political scandal."

"You're talking blackmail, sir?"

"It depends how you define blackmail. There's no intention to use this to exhort money or favours for personal gain. As I said, it's for insurance, for his personal protection, in case anyone feels that he knows too much and decides to get rid of him. This record, which we understand he updates each evening, is attached to an email in a draft folder, with a rolling twenty-four-hour delay in sending. When he updates it, a new twenty-four-hour period starts from then. So..."

Jo interrupted. "*So*, if he is denied access to his computer, laptop, whatever, for a period of more than twenty-four hours, the email gets sent and big names get dropped in it."

"Succinctly and accurately put. I'm glad you worked it out for yourself, Jo, because now I know you'll understand why we can't let you get to him first."

"And who's this email addressed to?"

"That, we don't know. It could be many people, it could be just one, or he could change the destination each time he updates the file."

Jo and Harry looked at each other with expressions of disbelief.

"So, do all your agents who undertake this sort of work hold the country to ransom like this?" Jo asked. "I have to say, it sounds like blackmail to me."

The Brigadier sighed, displaying just a hint of frustration. "It's like a game, Jo. They set these up, we knock them down. We have people at GCHQ in Cheltenham who can deal with it. Don't ask me how, because I've no idea, nor do I *want* to know. Vicky's more up to speed on this sort of stuff. Vicky?"

"The usual method of blocking them is to access the person's email and redirect the draft straight into the intended recipient's Spam folder, then change the timing of the dump from Spam to every few seconds. It will be the same email address, so the sender has no reason to believe anything had changed, but unless the recipient is actually looking in the Spam folder at the moment it arrives, they would never see it. So, in effect, the email goes nowhere."

"However," the Brigadier said, "Walcott is out on his own in this field. No-one has managed to access his files or email. Layer-upon-layer of firewalls and security tricks. I'm told that at GCHQ Miss Goody has a hacker working on this full-time, but we have no way of knowing whether he or she has been successful yet. So, we must assume *not*. The main concern with Walcott, then, is the status of his handler. Mostly we could deal with the fallout if an insurance claim was successfully made. People can be moved, even hidden for a while, but not our Grace Goody, and definitely not now."

"It doesn't sound much like a game to me. So, say we allow him to make the change today, what then?"

"Well, firstly, it's very important he *does* make that amendment. After that, now that his pretty face is a focus of national attention, I expect him to make contact with us. There are ways and places, how and where that can be achieved."

"And you'll just take him back on board, even though he's a suspect in an attempted murder? I use the word 'suspect' in the procedural sense, of course. In reality there's no doubt he did it."

"That would depend on *how* he came back to us. Whether we could manage the circumstances of his return, which I fully expect we will be able to do. He really is the best we have."

"But you as good as said he'd sort of gone rogue," Jo said. "Acting outside his remit."

"That is just this last incident, involving your ex-colleague. Up to then, he just followed orders to the letter. Look, we're big boys and girls here and used to handling accidents from the sort of activities Deverall and Walcott are involved in. No-one gets to know about these incidents, and no-one is any the worse off for their ignorance. If you lifted our carpet, you'd be amazed just how much dirt has been swept under there; all for the greater good, don't forget."

"So," Jo said, "Grace Goody hired this… assassin – sorry, *executioner* – to do some dirty work for the greater good, which, incidentally, if Harry and I are correct in what we now believe, may well have included two attempts on my life."

"Of that I know nothing," the Brigadier interrupted, "nor do I care – except, of course, I'm very pleased in your case that he failed."

"Well, thank you so much for that, sir. But I'd really like to know…"

The Brigadier slammed the palms of his hands down on the desk, making them all jump.

"Right," he boomed. "Let me be clear on this. The *only* interest I have in Jamie Walcott right now is to ensure he updates the timing of his email. That's all – *everything*. What he has done to date, and to whom, is of no consequence in the current circumstances. My reason for not wanting the email sent is because it could discredit Grace Goody, and at this moment that would be very unfortunate. Let me tell you why.

"It is Grace Goody and not Jamie Walcott who has been under our microscope in recent months, for her role in something much more significant than an attempt on the life of an ex-policeman. Just because she's one of the best in the business at what she does, it doesn't mean that no-one is watching *her*." He sighed, as if momentarily distracted, "It's surprising how often they forget that, you know." He shook his head.

"Anyway, I mentioned John Deverall's role in the saving of the hostages a few hours ago. Grace Goody played an even greater part in achieving that end. She was the person who negotiated face to face with el Taqha on board the *Mastodon* while a covert squad found and stabilised the bomb. After that she was taken hostage by the terrorist leader, who was wearing an explosive vest. She managed to disable him long enough for Deverall to take the fatal shot before he could activate the vest, but in doing so she was gravely wounded.

"Right now, she is in a coma, en route to Royal London Hospital, where a specialist team will try to save her life. Realistically, I'm told, the odds are against her surviving. What she did was heroic beyond what I can easily believe, and now is not the time to expose details of what she has done in the recent past which the general public will undoubtably fail to understand in the wider context."

Jo and Harry looked at each other wide-eyed. After a long silence, the Brigadier spoke again.

"And, just in case that wasn't exciting enough for you, the bomb was a WMD, a nuke, which would have vapourised the platform if it had exploded."

There was a further exchange of shocked expressions between the two detectives, accompanied this time by headshaking.

"I think I speak for both of us, Brigadier," Jo said, "when I say of course we understand the need to protect Miss Goody in the circumstances. Like you, I can't begin to imagine the level of courage you'd need to do what she did."

The Brigadier nodded and looked at Harry, raising his eyebrows with the unspoken question.

"Of course, I agree," Harry said. "If we need to give Walcott time to do what he has to do, then so be it. As to what happens next, I guess you're going to tell me, sir, because I haven't got a clue. I've got a highly motivated team of detectives focussed on finding this man. I'd be grateful for any ideas you have on how to soften their focus without pissing them off altogether."

"It's a fair point, Harry, and by now your boss will have sent them all home for the weekend with a message about the case being on hold until the Home Office has been contacted about certain issues, or something equally bland. They won't have experienced the thrill of signing something, like you have, but they will have been told not to discuss the case with anyone outside the room where the briefing took place. I trust they will respect that."

"I'm sure they will, sir. And what of Monday morning? What then?"

"I will be very surprised if our Jamie hasn't sorted something out by then. But, at the moment, I am more concerned about Miss Goody's chances of surviving. And now, you must excuse me. It's been a pleasure to meet you both."

He got to his feet, prompting the other four to do the same, and strode round the desk and out of the door, this time shaking hands with both Jo and Harry on the way.

Peter Drake smiled.

"You two must be hungry. I suggest we all adjourn to the cafeteria for a bite to eat, then we'll arrange to drive you back to Guildford. I thought that went really well."

⋆

Andrew came out of his trance at the unfamiliar chime of his iPhone. Unfamiliar, because only two people knew the number of this particular phone and he used it mainly to make, not receive, calls or texts, something he had been doing for most of the past six hours. As such, the sound was a welcome intrusion on his thoughts, and the accompanying text succinct and reassuring.

Sorry for delay replying, no need to worry, no claim forthcoming, JW

"Thank *fuck* for that." Andrew's voice exploded into the empty office, where he had been in hiding since aborting his meeting with the US ambassador, and only half-listening to the messages left by his Home Secretary. He leaned forward with his elbows on the desk and his head in his hands. He stayed like that for a long time until his anxiety fully receded. He checked the time on his iPhone – 5.35 p.m. – and pressed the key for Jackie's number at Marsham Street.

"I'm sorry, she's not here, Prime Minister. She's still at Thames House. You can get her on her iPhone. Such a shock about Miss Goody. I do hope she's okay, but it does look bad..."

"Thank you, Jenny."

He phoned Jackie, feeling the coldness in her voice when she answered.

"Jackie Hewlett here. Can I help you?"

"Look, I'm sorry, Jackie, but I..."

"Who is it speaking?"

"Jackie, for God's sake. How's Grace?"

"Oh, it's *you*, Prime Minister. Sorry I didn't recognise your voice. It's been so long that..."

"Yes *alright*, Jackie. Don't push it, I said I'm sorry. Something had to be sorted, but now I'm back and thank you for holding the fort. It seems I wasn't needed anyway. How is Grace? Is she at the hospital yet?"

"Just about, I think. They landed at London City ten minutes ago. With the lights and sirens, she should be at the Royal London within a few minutes. And as for how she is, pretty bad, I understand. Touch and go."

"Sssshiit." Andrew made the word last a long time. "She should never have been on that ship."

"I don't agree, Andrew. She did a brilliant job, by all accounts. *No-one* could have done better. And now I understand her background I can see why she was so good. Don't you think someone should have made the Home Secretary aware that the Ministerial Director of Justice was Special Forces-trained?"

"I'm not sure why. It wasn't that qualification that got her the job. She changed careers over ten years ago when I recruited her for the party. I could see she had the skills and qualities we needed."

"When we have time, I'd love to hear which of the *particular* skills you identified as useful to the cause as a result of watching her on a shooting range. And what jobs she has carried out for you using those skills."

"I don't know what you're implying, Jackie..."

"But that's not for now. I take it you've received all my updates. Bomb safe, one SBS killed, el Taqha dead along with seven other terrorists and one injured. USS *Ronald Reagan* heading back to Iceland – I assume – and the *Mastodon* returning to Stavanger. They're flying out a replacement crew and I believe the CIA are arranging to have the bomb airlifted off somewhere. It would have made sense for the carrier to make itself useful and take it with them, but I guess it will need specialist handling. I think that's all the trivia I have for you at the moment, Prime Minister."

"Just let it go, Jackie, okay?"

"I just hope Grace makes it through. She deserves to; she's a brave woman."

"Yes, she is. Where are Kade and his buddies, by the way?"

"Some still on board, others escorting the surviving terrorists. One with Grace, I believe. They've carried out a full search of the ship and are waiting to be lifted off back to Hirta. There are two Norwegian Coast Guard vessels escorting the *Mastodon* home."

"Right. Thank you again, Jackie, and can I ask you one more thing? Will you make a statement to the press about this? You'll be in a better position to answer questions. I'm going to the Royal London to see Grace. There's something I need to tell her about that issue I had earlier today. It involved her and I'd like to put her mind at rest."

"Yes, I'll speak to the press, Andrew, but I don't think you've been listening. Grace will not hear you, and it is more than likely that she will never hear anything ever again."

★

Max Mobsby pushed open his front door and stepped into the hallway, struggling to keep his balance. The man close behind him had wrapped his arms round his waste and almost tripped him up as their legs became intertwined. Max turned to face him and forced him against the wall, their bodies pressed together. They kissed with a furious passion, Max reaching down between the man's legs and feeling his eagerness. Their lips disengaged and they clung to each other panting and groaning. The man glanced to his right.

"Hadn't you better shut the door?"

Max broke away and put his hand to his mouth.

"Whoops."

They both giggled as Max closed the front door, and came together again to kiss gently and briefly this time.

"Go through, Jez. Make yourself at home. Pour us both a drink." Max waved him through a door on the right of the hallway. He hung his daypack on the hall stand and picked up two letters off the doormat. He followed Jez into the large living room, which stretched the full depth of the house to a floor-to-ceiling bay window on the end wall. The room was tastefully furnished with two antique-leather sofas facing each other across a low rectangular table. At the far end of the room in front of the bay was a dining table with two chairs at either side. A multi-fuel burner stood on a granite base near the wall facing the door, with a large television to its right and an old-fashioned cocktail cabinet to its left.

Jez was sprawled on one of the sofas. He squeezed up against the back and patted the space beside him.

"Care to join me?"

Max smiled and shook his head. "Don't be so eager, and where's my drink?" He nodded towards the cabinet. "I just need to deal with this *urgent* mail."

He sat down at a small console table to the right of the door and opened the letters.

"Ooh, look at this," he said, in mock amazement. "I can get sixty percent off a stairlift with free installation. *And*, according to this flyer, the vacuum-cleaner that this same company persuaded me to buy last year turns out to be a crock of shit in the light of the revolutionary technological advances they have made in the meantime. Nice of them to let me know, don't you think?"

"Do you want this drink, or not?"

"I'll have it if he doesn't."

They both turned to the man in the doorway, who looked exactly like the man opening the letters. Jez swung his legs down off the sofa, his eyes wide in surprise and fear. He looked from one to the other as his mouth sagged open.

"Hey," His voice was shaky. "What is this?"

"Don't be alarmed," said Jamie Walcott. "It's all done by mirrors."

"It's okay, Jez, this is…" Max began.

"I'm out of here." Jez placed his glass on the table with a shaking hand, spilling some of his drink. He made to leave, but Jamie held his ground in the doorway, moving to stop him squeezing past him. He moved again as Jez tried to pass him on the other side. Jez turned back into the room.

"Maxie, tell him to let me go."

"*Maxie*, is it?" Jamie said, stepping to one side. "Off you go, *Jezzie*. And don't talk to any strange men. Any *other* strange men, I mean."

Jez scurried past him and out of the front door.

"Well, thanks for fucking up my evening," Max said. "I thought you'd be long gone by now,"

"A lot safer to stay here than to try and leave. At least it was until your little friend came along and saw us both together."

"He's not my little friend; I met him at the cricket for the first time today. Anyway, why didn't you just stay out of sight. It took me a long time to convince him it wasn't *my* mugshot in the press this morning, but now he's seen the same one on somebody else. He's not the brightest button in the sewing basket, but when he realises he wasn't hallucinating, what's he going to think?"

"Yes, that's unfortunate. For everyone."

They were both silent for a few moments.

"Where's Renner?" Max asked.

"On his way north. Should be in deepest Scotland by now."

"Doing what, exactly?"

"Outside your need-to-know, Max."

"Of course, so I don't give away too much under torture."

Jamie placed a hand on his shoulder. "It's not like that, Max, and you know it. Listen, I'd like to show you something in the office. Just give me about thirty minutes."

*

The only access to Jamie Walcott's office and armoury in the attic of 23 Cannon Road was via a steep, narrow staircase in the chimney breast of his first-floor bedroom. Access to this staircase was through the ornate, but fake, Edwardian-style fireplace which included a large gilt-framed mirror above the mantlepiece. Or, more accurately, access was through where the fireplace normally was, prior to its being swung away from the wall like a heavy door, hinged at one side and supported by castors on the other.

He checked his watch as he booted up his computer. It was just after nine o'clock, leaving him well over an hour to update his file and change the timing of the email. He helped himself to a bottle of water from the fridge near the window, sat down at his desk and clicked on the Tor browser, then Sky News. There were no further updates on the aftermath of the hijacking, except for the promise of a statement from the Home Secretary at 9.30 p.m.

It had been a shock hearing about Grace. He was sorry now he hadn't made contact with her the previous day when she had tried so many times to reach him. The brief text he had finally sent now seemed totally inadequate if that was to be the last words that passed between them. Especially when their relationship seemed to be improving. She would live on in his fantasies, of course, but "what might have been" was nowhere near as satisfying as "what might happen".

He went through the six-password security system to access his personal data then to the word document he needed. There was nothing much to add to the record in terms of action or contact for today, other than his brief text to the Prime Minister and a note that he was now a national celebrity. Which was in stark contrast to the events of yesterday: the killing of David Gerrard and the framing of Danny Weaver for his murder. With any luck, the killing of Weaver as well, if he didn't pull through. That had gone to plan; the recording he had received of Waters's call to Cottrell had confirmed that. So, it had been a shock to discover he was being sought as a possible key witness. Also, he was confused as to where his picture had come from. The only possibility was that he had been right in believing Weaver had photographed them as they left the Remington Arms, and the police must have found the images on his phone.

He added a few lines of text then clicked on his email tab and pulled up the Drafts folder to delete the existing attachment and replace it with the new one.

The folder was empty.

Jamie's eyes and mouth opened wide.

"What the *fuck*?" He waited, wondering whether there was a delay in loading.

Fifteen seconds.

Twenty seconds.

Nothing appeared.

He clicked on the Sent folder, looking for the name of the person he had chosen to receive his story. He felt a wave of relief when he saw it wasn't there. Tony Dobson would have to wait a bit longer for the biggest scoop of his lifetime. He breathed in deeply and relaxed, leaning back on the chair and swivelling side to side, his mind racing.

What the hell had happened, then?

He went deeper into the system to check the activity log and for the first time in his life felt a wave of panic wash over him. An email with an attachment had been sent from his Draft folder at 4.30 p.m. Four and a half hours ago, eighteen hours after the timing had been reset for twenty-four. The name and address of the recipient had been deleted, but Jamie was in no doubt about its content.

The truth was out.

He'd made his claim.

CHAPTER FORTY-EIGHT

Saturday, 8 July

Kade rolled over on the narrow bunk at the sound of his name, whispered by someone close to his face. He felt under the pillow to check his handgun was there. It took him a few moments to take in his surroundings – a small room in one of the restored buildings from the 1950s' military establishment on Hirta. The whispering man had been occupying the bunk immediately above him.

"Brig? What's happened?"

"Nothing, but I've just thought of something."

"Nothing?" He checked his watch. "It's one o'clock. I'd just managed to get to sleep. What's wrong with you? Not tired at all?"

"Yes, but I *couldn't* get to sleep because of something that's been going round in my mind."

"Let me guess. 'Jason… doughnut'?"

"That's right. Why, have you got a theory about what she meant?"

"She was barely conscious, Brig. She just wasn't making any sense, that's all."

"I don't think so. She was talking to *me*, so it was something she felt *I* needed to know. About Jason."

"Okay, so what do you reckon, bearing in mind that Jason is dead? And why is it more important that I know this right now than it is for me to get some sleep?"

"I think, not only was she telling me Jason is alive, but also where I can find him. Sorry to wake you, it was just to let you know I'm getting ready to leave. Now you can go back to sleep."

⋆

Harry leaned back in the passenger seat of the unmarked police car and looked out of his window. He checked his watch.

"Eleven-twenty. I can't believe this is really happening, Nat. It's like bloody Groundhog Day."

"Except you've got me instead of fast Alice."

"That's true. Thanks for the early start with the short notice, by the way. God knows what's going on with our Mr Mobsby. Or is Mr Mobsby the reason you don't mind the early start?"

"No, he's not for me, sir, and I'm definitely not for him."

"Why do you say that?"

"I'm not the right shape: bulges in all the wrong places and one vital appendage missing."

"*Really?* I didn't pick up on that."

"Well, you weren't fluttering your eyelashes at him and getting nothing back in return."

They drove on in silence for a while, Harry counting off the now-familiar landmarks along the A3 between Guildford and Kennington.

"What happened to you and DI Cottrell yesterday, sir? We were all waiting in the MIT room and the Super came and sent us all home. She said there'd been a development and you were both heading for a meeting."

"And that's about all I can tell you at the moment, I'm afraid, Nat. I'll get everyone back on board on Monday. Is this the turning?"

"The one after."

They drove past the community centre where they had parked the previous day and stopped at the kerb opposite Max Mobsby's house on Cannon Road. Hannah Leasing and Will Denton were waiting for them at the front gate.

"Long time no see," Hannah said, with a wide smile.

Harry checked his watch. "About twenty-three hours," he said, "and you don't look a day older. So, remind us why we're back here in Kennington?"

"We got a call this morning at just before eight o'clock from Max Mobsby's boss at Danby Ashton to tell us that Mobsby has disappeared overnight."

"They work Saturdays?"

"Not normally, but Mr Chesterton – that's his boss – went in early today to finish a proposal for something-or-other which had to be ready for Monday morning. The night security guy hadn't gone off shift yet and told Chesterton that Mobsby had been in during the night and taken some stuff away from his workstation in the open office. When Chesterton got to his own office, he found a letter from Mobsby that had been pushed under his door. It said he had to leave the company for family reasons and had removed his personal effects during the night. Very apologetic, said he didn't expect any pay due to him because he'd breached the contract with the company in not giving the appropriate period of notice, but he had to go with immediate effect as it was an emergency. I'm paraphrasing, of course, but that's the gist."

"And this Chesterton felt we should know because we'd been making enquiries about him?"

"Exactly. Since just after half-eight we've had the same guys as yesterday watching the back of the house. They're delighted, as you'd expect. According to the cameras, no-one has entered or left the house through the front door since around 8.30 yesterday evening, when Mobsby and another man went in. About ten minutes later, the other man left, apparently in a bit of a hurry. So, as it's linked to your case, I thought you'd want to be the one to break the door down."

"Have you knocked yet?"

"No, waiting for you."

"Okay, let's go."

Harry climbed the three steps and pressed the bell while the others waited on the pavement. There was no reply. He pressed the button again and at the same time hammered with the heavy brass knocker. They waited for thirty seconds, then Harry turned the doorknob. The door was unlocked; he pushed it open and they all entered the hall.

"Mr Mobsby!" Harry shouted up the stairs while Hannah and Will checked the living room to their right. Further along the hall past the stairs and to their left, a door opened onto a large dining kitchen with units around three walls and a breakfast bar along the other, under a window looking out over a small rear garden. There was no sign of anyone. They headed upstairs.

There were three good-sized bedrooms, a bathroom and separate WC. Of the made-up beds in each room only one seemed to have been recently slept in. But the house, it appeared, was deserted.

"I thought these houses had second-floor loft accommodation?" Harry asked. They checked the ceilings in each room and on the landing but there was no sign of any access.

"But not this one, it seems," Hannah said. "Strange that someone would leave their home, even in a hurry, and not lock the front door. It's not as if he dropped everything and rushed off somewhere after hearing about the emergency. He had time to go to work, clear his desk, leave a note."

"Listen." Natalie held up her hands for quiet. "What's that noise?

They all looked up at the ceiling from where a low humming sound had suddenly started.

"Sounds like a fridge kicking in," Hannah said. The humming continued. "A bit unusual having a fridge in a place that there's no access to."

"I'll tell you what else is unusual," Will said. "That fireplace isn't square-on to the chimney breast. It's sticking out at the left-hand-side."

*

The face of the man slumped in the office chair looked surprisingly normal, but the back of his head had ceased to exist, at least as an attachment to his body. It was spread over a wide area of the attic behind him, including the desk, computer keyboard and screen, and most of the printer, where a single sheet of paper lay on the exit tray. The gun which they assumed was responsible for the damage was still in the corpse's hand, macabrely held in place by a finger hooked through the trigger guard.

Harry and Natalie, virtual spectators for the moment, were standing at the top of the stairs to avoid any unnecessary interference with the scene while Hannah and Will tiptoed around the attic making an initial assessment before calling in the troops. This death was the Met's problem now, given that Mobsby had been cleared of the crime in Guildford.

"Why would Max go to all that trouble to clear the decks, come up with an excuse for disappearing, and then kill himself?" Natalie asked. "And in a place where we were lucky to find him."

"I don't know," Harry said. "Perhaps they'll find a note. But I think he meant us to find him, leaving the access to the stairs open like he did. You'd think he would have closed it properly, if he was intending not to be found. Though he wouldn't have expected it to be as soon as this unless he knew his boss was working today."

Will called to Hannah. "Ma'am, you might want to see this."

Hannah went across to where the sergeant was standing at the desk.

"Just touched the mouse to refresh the screen. There's a message. Doesn't mean much to me, not with that name at the bottom, anyway."

They watched Hannah lean forward and read the words on the screen, then she turned and walked across to them, her brow furrowed in thought and confusion.

"It seems our suicide – if that's what he is – has an alias. The note on the screen is signed 'Jamie'."

Harry drew in a breath.

"I think I'd better be the one to make that call, Hannah. Don't speak to anyone yet. I'll explain as much as I can in a few minutes."

He took out his phone and scrolled through the contacts to the name he had added to the list less than twenty-four hours ago just before leaving Thames House. Excusing himself, he descended the steep stairs to the first-floor bedroom. The phone sounded just as he was about to press the call key.

"Hi, DI Waters here. Who's speaking?"

"It's Ellie, sir. We've been on the phones again this morning. DS Belmont said just in case we had some late callers. The mugshot's been pulled as requested, but someone's phoned in, anyway. A man who wouldn't give his name or contact details, but he said last night he was at the same address in Kennington where you were yesterday, and he saw two of them. Two *identical* people and – he said – they were definitely the one on TV. I asked him what he meant by *two* people being the one on TV, but he rang off. He seemed really agitated. Sorry to bother you, sir, but I thought it might mean something to you."

"It's no bother, Ellie. You might be interested to know that I'm back at the same house where I was yesterday and where your nervous informant thought he was seeing double. Thanks for the information."

He stood for a long time deep in thought.

"Doppelganger," he said out loud to himself. The ring tone sounded again and Jo's name appeared on his screen.

"Hi, Jo, you're a mind reader. I was going to phone you in a couple of..."

"Harry." Her voice sounded weak and strained. "Are you okay to talk?"

"Yes. You alright? You sound... different."

"I'm not sure if I'm alright or not, actually. Are you at work?"

"Working, yes, but not *at* work. In fact, I'm back in bloody Kennington at Mobsby's house. We've got a body here... but, tell me, why did you call me and why are you not sure if you're alright?"

"I'm at the station in Leicester. I came in to catch up on a few things, checked my inbox, and found I'd received an email at 4.30 yesterday afternoon. It was from Jamie Walcott."

Jo paused, but he knew what was coming.

"Harry, it's *the* email."

*

From the air, the "Doughnut" looks a little like a smaller-scale model of the Pentagon with the five angles smoothed round. Constructed mainly of steel and local stone, the distinctive GCHQ building at Cheltenham measures twenty-one metres in height and has an external diameter of one hundred and eighty metres. The building is surrounded by car and bicycle parking and guarded by a two-metre-high fence. A half-circle of conifers outside the fence partially screens the facility from the local residential area.

Brig stepped down from the Cessna onto the tarmac at Gloucester airport and spotted his lift. The man was standing next to a black Jaguar SUV at the edge of the airfield fifty or so metres away and walked forward to meet him halfway with a firm handshake. He was in his mid-thirties, tall and very upright. His smart grey suit and open-necked white shirt failed to disguise evidence in his posture of a military background. He introduced himself as Jordan White, supervisor of the department in the National Cyber Security Centre where the person Brig was seeking worked as an IT operative.

"And today, I am also your chauffeur and guide," he said. "I'm told you are known as Brig, is that right?"

"That is right."

"How do I address you? That doesn't give me much of a clue."

"Just Brig is fine," he replied, with a laugh. "And you?"

"Jordy. So, is that short for Brigadier? In which case I guess I should have saluted you, sir."

"It's a nickname – a code name, if you like – and it was given to me by a fellow soldier in the SBS. A young man from Glasgow who told me that my attempt at a Scottish accent was the worst he'd heard since the last time he watched *Brigadoon*. And the name came from that – and stuck."

Jordy laughed. "And you've flown down from Stornoway, so I assume you've been involved in the hijacking in some way."

Brig smiled. "Yes, in some way."

It took them less than five minutes to arrive at one of the three entrances to the building via the underground access road. Jordy parked in a reserved space and led Brig through a set of revolving doors to a long crescent of a reception desk, staffed by five people seated at two-metre intervals behind it. Jordy approached the middle receptionist, a fifty-something woman with a pretty face and a wide smile.

"Hi, Kirsty."

"Hi, Jordy. And you must be Mr Brig? Could you sign in for me, please?"

He signed the register with the single name and Kirsty handed him a clip-on plastic badge which he attached to the top pocket of his jacket.

"Thank you, Kirsty," he said.

It was a long walk to Jordy's department, along the glass-covered walkway known as "The Street" which runs around the whole of the building, and, as good as his word, his host was an excellent guide, pointing through doors and up staircases explaining the different areas and the workings of the building. It was something

Brig was very familiar with, and he could have corrected him once or twice on minor factual discrepancies, but he played the part of the fascinated tourist with suitable expressions of awe.

"We were surprised at receiving the picture of Joseph," Jordy said as they neared their destination, "especially with the thing about his other name. We're used to secrets and mysteries here, but they're usually related to the faceless agents we just hear about – Security Service, MI6. The IT guys are pretty anonymous. Most people don't know their names – as if they're just extensions of a qwerty keyboard – so for one of them to have *two* names. He must be special."

Brig didn't reply and Jordy went on.

"Tell the truth, he *is* special. Quite possibly the best we have, at least up there with the best. Only been with us six, eight months or so, but he's got the attention of some high-up people. He's even had a couple of one-to-ones with Grace Goody. God, it would be such a tragedy if she were to die after what she's just done." He turned to Brig. "Sorry, I guess you were close to it all."

"Yes, quite close," he replied. "Listen, I wonder if I could meet with Joseph in private, at least initially."

"No problem. In fact, that's what I assumed you'd want to do. If you'd like to wait in here, I'll get him and bring him to you."

Jordy opened the door to a small meeting room, set out to accommodate up to ten people, with a rectangular table in the centre, four chairs along each long side and one at each end. "It's a bit formal, I'm afraid, but it's reserved for you for as long as you need it."

"Thanks, Jordy."

"I'll be less than a minute; he's just next door."

It seemed like a long minute, as Brig wrestled with a raft of feelings from anxiety to joyous anticipation, and all points in between. When the door opened, Joseph was on his own.

Except it wasn't Joseph.

"Hi, Jason," Brig said, his voice hardly above a whisper, muted by emotion.

It took almost half a minute for the tall young Kenyan to identify his visitor. Then the eyes in his handsome face opened wide in astonishment. He opened his mouth to speak, but Brig placed his forefinger over his lips and shook his head.

"No names." This time a deliberate whisper.

Jason closed the door behind him and the two men faced each other for a long time. Then Brig opened his arms and they embraced for much longer, holding on tightly as if to ensure that neither would be lost to the other.

CHAPTER FORTY-NINE

Sunday, 9 July

Vicky Barrowclough's voice conveyed an element of surprise.

"It's Detective Inspector Cottrell on the phone for you, sir. Can you take the call or will you get back to her?"

"Put her through, Corporal. It's okay." He nodded to the person across the desk. "You might want to hear this." He pressed the speaker button on the base set.

"Good morning, Jo. This is a pleasant surprise."

"Good morning, Brigadier. I didn't expect to speak to you today, not at ten o'clock on a Sunday. I was planning on leaving a message."

"Ah, the Section never sleeps, y'know, Jo. How can I help you?"

"I'm not sure, Brigadier, because I don't know how much you already know of what I'm going to tell you.

"Well, you go ahead and I'll stop you if I do. Right?"

"Okay. Have you got me on speaker, sir?"

"Yes, I'm hands-free so I can enjoy my tea and biscuits without impersonating a circus juggler. Please carry on."

"Well, I received an email on Friday afternoon – it arrived at a time when I was with you at Millbank, but I only picked it up yesterday back at the station in Leicester. It was from Jamie Walcott and it's what you described as his 'insurance claim'. I haven't a clue as to why he should send it to me. It had an attached file containing three folders. One is a summary – a sort of index – listing his past four years' activities. Another is a detailed record of the past two years when it seems he was working solely for Miss Goody. The other is a record of the two years before that when he was also working for who I assume was the 'higher authority' you referred to on Friday. And it's interesting that for part of those two years, the person concerned was in Opposition to the government, not part of it."

"Tell me, Jo, at what point when you saw the email did you realise what it was? Was it not until you had read through all the attachments?"

"Well, no. The email itself made it clear what..."

"So, if you knew that, and in the light of what you signed in my office on Friday, what made you think it was alright to open and read the attachments?"

"Firstly, because your Mr Walcott *chose* to send his insurance claim to *me*, presumably as a representative of the police. And, secondly, because of what I *did* sign on Friday, sir, a copy of which I have in front of me right now."

"You have a copy?"

"Of course. Your colleague, Vicky, did seem a little reluctant to give us copies until I pointed out that, without a note of what we'd signed up for, how would we remember what we could and couldn't do under that specific section of the OSA?"

"Well, she shouldn't..."

"So, go back a year and Walcott's right in the middle of the serial killing in Guildford and Dorking, in which, incidentally, as I mentioned on Friday and is confirmed by his own account, a certain Jo Cottrell was a target on two separate occasions. And when Mickey Kadawe emerged as a suspect, he had to be removed so the investigation would focus on Tom Brown. Followed by the planting of the gun in his apartment and the explosive equipment in his car.

"Then, once the police started focussing on Mr Brown, it appears that for Walcott it was job done, because he seems fairly inactive after that, apart from arranging for my phone calls to be intercepted. Until, that is, a certain journalist and his photographer girlfriend unearthed some discrepancies in the evidence against him. At which point, Jamie's back on the job, hacking emails and bugging phones. And, you will note, I haven't mentioned in all that, the attempted murder of David Gerrard to remove the one person in the loop whose emails and phone were not covered by Walcott's surveillance, and which is the *only* part of the story covered by your piece of paper. Or should I have said Miss Goody's surveillance, because, as you were at pains to point out yesterday, Mr Walcott was only following orders in pursuit of an end which justified whatever means necessary."

"While we are baring our souls in the pursuit of the meaning of life, Jo, let me ask you a question. Let's assume the late Mr Walcott did cause those deaths. What is a worse fate, a quick death by a well-placed bullet which leaves no time for pain, or a slow demise in an offshore prison with no hope of a meaningful future? Because the latter of those is Tom Brown's contribution to the greater good. We deplore one and we applaud the other. Which one would you choose?"

"I think that, if I were innocent of any crime, I shouldn't have to make a choice. But going back to what you did and didn't know, were you aware that I was the recipient of the email?"

"No, I wasn't until now. We took over the crime scene when your colleague DI Waters called us and informed us of Walcott's death, and we confiscated all the contents of the attic which, without going into details, comprised a lot more than a computer and a printer. Walcott had wiped all his records before he killed himself, except for the note he left on the screen, which he had also printed out."

"So, you had no idea that the email had been sent?"

"Of course I did. It was covered in the note he left, but he didn't reveal to whom. So, I guess we'll never know why he had you as his preferred recipient."

"What else did the note say?"

"That he realised the game was up – I paraphrase – that the email had been sent accidentally, that he couldn't face the prospect of twenty years of getting butt-fucked in prison because of his classical good looks and bisexual appeal. And he figured this might be the last chance he'd have to take the quicker way out."

"I see. Are you surprised he did that, took his own life?"

"Absolutely astonished. But where do we go from here, Jo? Let's say I concede your point that earlier activities which fell outside the law were not covered by the document. We have Walcott dead, Goody – by all accounts – soon to be dead if not already. So, what next?

"The earlier stuff. Let's not piss about, Brigadier, we're talking Andrew Donald, our esteemed leader. But how the hell did he manage to arrange for Walcott to take Jackie Hewlett's daughter when he was the Leader of the Opposition?"

"He put it to us through Grace, who had links to us in a previous role. And the New Justice Regime seemed such a great idea, with the potential for releasing large numbers of police officers for more serious crime fighting. It was felt that Tom Brown had a better chance of getting it through. So, it was like supporting rebels in an unfriendly country." He paused. "Well, perhaps not a *lot* like that, but you know what I mean."

There were a few moments silence before he spoke again.

"Have you shared the information you received with anyone else?"

"Not exactly."

"Meaning?"

"They have hard copies of the email and attachments in a sealed envelope with instructions not to open it unless directed by me or in the event of my – let's say – meeting with an accident. That's what I mean by 'not exactly'."

"When you say 'they', does that mean more than one person?"

"It could do or it might just be a way of not divulging the sex of just one person. Look, Brigadier, I buy into your motto – *ad maius bonum* – and I support the NJR with its seemingly harsh treatment of a minority of individuals for the benefit of the large majority, all that stuff. I do realise sacrifices have to be made for the greater good. But there is a difference between legality and morality. So, with Walcott and Goody unable to be held accountable, I have to warn you that I will *not* ignore what is attached to that email unless I hear that some action will be taken against Andrew Donald.

"Oh, and by the way, just to save Vicky the bother of checking afterwards, I'm calling from a payphone in Highcross shopping centre in Leicester. But if I need to call again, I'll use my own iPhone. So, in the meantime, you might want to think about how many people, and who, you'd like to be listening in to that conversation. You might even decide to take me off surveillance altogether."

Neither spoke for a long time. The Brigadier broke the silence.

"In which case, DI Cottrell, I would ask you to do nothing or speak to anyone about this call, but to wait for further developments. And in the meantime, let me assure you that, following a meeting attended by the Home Secretary yesterday afternoon, what you desire regarding our 'esteemed leader', as you call him, is *exactly* what is going to happen."

"Thank you, sir, I…"

"Don't thank me, because it is *not* as a result of your call today or our meeting on Friday. We do not respond to threats, no more than we negotiate with terrorists. Wheels are already turning. I'll be in touch. Goodbye, Detective Inspector."

He ended the call before Jo could respond and sat for a full minute in silence, staring at the telephone. He looked up and across the desk at the person in front of him.

"Don't get any ideas about getting rid of DI Cottrell, Mr Walcott. When the time is right, I believe she could be an excellent addition to the Section. And if you screw up again, who's to say it might not be as your replacement?

★

The small private room in the Royal London Hospital was already filled with life-support apparatus and monitoring screens even before the team of technicians arrived soon after midday with their audio-visual equipment to set up the trans-Atlantic link. By the time they had completed the task, the room looked more like a hi-tech hardware store than a leading-edge medical facility. The presence of Special Branch police outside and MI5 agents inside the room added considerably to what appeared to be an escalating state of chaos.

At the appointed hour, however – 1.30 p.m. in London, 8.30 a.m. in Washington DC – all was calm and hushed in readiness. Grace was again the sole occupant of the hospital room, except for the seated figure of President Weston on the TV monitor screen at the foot of the bed. Beside the monitor was a camera, relaying Grace's image to a similar screen on the President's desk in the Oval Office.

John Weston's expression was a mask of concern and sadness.

"Hi, Grace. I have it on good authority that this is a private call, although that is a little hard to believe given the amount of hi-tech activity and the number of people invading this office over the past hour or so. I am told that you will probably be unable to hear me, but I hope the strength of the admiration and affection I feel for you will help the words find a way through the mist of your suffering and reach your mind and your heart. I was advised to wait before speaking to you until your prognosis became clearer, but I dare not risk losing the opportunity should things not turn out well for you.

"It seems, my lovely Grace, we will not be able to have the future together which I so desired and which I believe you wanted, too. My understanding is that, if you survive this terrible trauma, which I pray to God you will, your life is likely to change significantly. This I understand from a telephone communication I had late yesterday with a gentleman in a branch of your secret service. A brigadier who I have known by reputation for some time but have never previously spoken to.

"My situation has also changed as a result of the events of the past few days. I have decided I will not be running for a second term. You and I talked recently about a conflict of interest which might be problematic for us in pursuing both our personal and professional ambitions. I experienced an example of that on Friday following a call I received from my ambassador in London. The call was to tell me you were on board the *Mastodon* and came at a time when I was discussing with my naval commander the possibility of taking action against the vessel. An action, I am ashamed to admit, that was in part driven by the weight of public opinion, against a backdrop of the run-up to the forthcoming election. I immediately called off the action and directed the US Navy to leave the area. It was the right thing to do, but from a presidential point of view, for the wrong reason, my concern for your safety instantly over-riding my obligation to my country.

"I do not regret either the decision or the reason for it, but it focussed my mind on what is important to me. You, Grace, above everything, I now realise. And if we cannot be together, that doesn't change my feelings, my priorities. So, I have decided I am unfit to lead my country. E. M. Forster, one of your great novelists, once said, 'If I had to choose between betraying my country and betraying a friend, I hope I should have the guts to betray my country.' He would applaud me, then, but perhaps my third-of-a-billion subjects across these fifty states would not.

"I sincerely hope that fate will find a way to provide us with a chance sometime in the future to take forward our mutual affection into the tenderness of love. But if that is not to be, I will never *ever* forget you, my brave and beautiful Grace Goody."

The tears welled in his eyes before his head slumped forward. His hands, resting on the desk in front of him, clenched into tight fists. He remained like that for a long time before sitting upright, switching off both the screen and the camera and pressing a button to signal the end of the call to the waiting technicians outside.

Six thousand kilometres away, after a few moments of silence, the door to Grace Goody's hospital room opened and AV technicians and medical staff poured through from the corridor. The former dismantled the video link while the latter checked the screens for any variation in output of the patient's vital life indicators. If they had first looked at her face, they would have noticed the lines of two tears leaving her eyes to roll behind the mask holding the respirator in place.

*

The two women peered up at the skyline high above and behind the cottage.

"How did you manage to see something that far away?"

Maggie Tomlinson-Brown was dressed in a loose-fitting shirt tucked into calf-length walking trousers. Her golden-blonde hair was pulled back into a ponytail, which hung below the Tilly hat she was wearing.

"I was watching a group of red deer through the bins just below the ridge, and they suddenly scattered, shot off in all directions." Her daughter, Katey, was the same height and slim build with hair that was white-blonde and straight, hanging loose behind to the middle of her back. She wore shorts and a tight-fitting tee shirt, and trainers with no socks. "When I looked where they'd been without the bins, I just spotted two heads – silhouettes – right on the skyline, sort of bobbing up and down as they dropped out of sight."

"So, they were walking away from us, that's why they dropped out of sight. Right?"

"But where would they be walking *from*? This is the only place for miles. We'd have seen them climbing the hillside. They must be on this side of the ridge heading towards us." She raised the binoculars again. "We just can't see them against the rocks and heather."

"So, who…?"

"Hold it," Katey interrupted. "I've got them. Dropping down along the edge of the burn."

She passed the binoculars to Mags, pointing to where a rough track ran parallel to the course of the waterway.

"Yes, I see them. Two people, can't make out any detail. Could just be walkers, of course."

"Unlikely. There are no trails around here that I know of. Do you?"

"Well, no, but freedom of access and all that… And they're as likely to be walkers as anything else." She lowered the glasses and frowned. "Aren't they? I mean, who else could they be?"

"I don't know," Katey said, "but I don't feel good about this at all after what's happened. Perhaps we're next – someone's come to finish the job."

Mags gave a little shiver. "Don't even joke about that."

"What have we got, a shotgun and a hunting rifle, right? Are they loaded?"

"What exactly do you have in mind?" Mags said, wide-eyed with horror.

"We're not going to make this easy for them if I'm right."

A baby cried and they looked towards the cottage. A voice from inside shouted, "I'll go."

Katey handed Mags the binoculars. "Keep watching them. I'll get the guns." She ran towards the cottage.

"Katey, wait…" But her daughter had disappeared inside.

Mags steadied the bins and watched the two figures descending at the side of the burn. She gasped, lowering the glasses for a moment, then raising them again to watch their approach. They were now leaving the side of the burn to head directly towards them.

Katey appeared again at the door. She looked across at the intruders, who were now within two hundred metres of the cottage.

"Where are the keys to the gun cupboard? It's locked." She looked again. "Mum, *quick*."

Mags lowered the binoculars and turned to Katey, whose expression changed to shock at her mother's wide smile and tearful eyes.

"I don't think we'll be needing the guns, darling," Mags said.

*

Tom and Jason missed their footing several times as they drew close to the cottage, unable to take their eyes off the two women looking back up at them. They saw one of them run inside, reappearing less than a minute later. Then they moved together, clinging to each other and the men knew they had been recognised. They moved forward more quickly, as close to running as was possible on the uneven ground strewn with loose rocks.

By the time they came to a stop, a few metres way from the women they loved, tears were running down all four of their faces. Katey crumpled to her knees, her whole body shaking as she sobbed out of control. Jason threw off his rucksack and rushed forward, dropping down beside her, strong arms pulling her into a protective embrace from which he would never want to let her go.

Tom and Mags continued to stare at each other, as if rooted to the ground, their expressions frozen in something close to ecstasy. Then they flew together, clinging tightly to each other in breathless disbelief, Tom relishing the pain as he crushed his wife against his injured chest.

"Where the hell have you been?" Mags's voice trembled as she spoke.

"Did you get my message? I assumed Will would contact you."

"Three weeks ago. Did you walk all the way up here?"

Tom began to laugh, his body shaking against her and soon they were both giggling like naughty children. A scream made them turn to the cottage. Leila Midanda was rushing across to Jason and Katey, her eyes wide in astonishment.

"Jay, Jay, Jay, Jay!"

She wrapped her arms around her son, who had helped Katey to her feet, but continued to hold her to him. The three huddled together, swaying, for a long time, then all five came together in a joyous scrummage. They were jerked back to reality by the sound of a baby crying.

Tom and Jason looked at each other, eyes wide and questioning. Mags looked from one to the other and began to laugh, Katey picking up on her amusement, then Leila. Soon all three women were crying with laughter, Mags struggling to speak.

"God, your faces," she said. "You should see your faces. Wait here."

She went into the cottage and the crying stopped. She appeared a few moments later carrying a baby boy.

"Do you remember those two wonderful days we spent here in April last year?" she said. "Jack, meet your daddy. Daddy, meet Jack." She handed the baby to Tom, who held him at arm's length for a few seconds as if making sure he understood what he was being presented with, before pulling him to his chest.

"Jack?" he said, his voice tiny and hoarse with emotion.

"Yes, just Jack," Mags said.

CHAPTER FIFTY

Monday, 10 July

Following the excitement of Friday, with the chasing-up of the two leads half the country apart, the mood at the morning briefing in the Major Incident Team room at Guildford New Station had been one of frustrating anti-climax. Afterwards, Harry sat pensively in his office, looking from one to the other of two A4 sheets of paper on the desk in front of him.

He picked up the statement which had just been read out to the teams by Detective Superintendent Lynsey Hargreaves. He went through it again, aloud but to himself.

"Following a shooting in the Westmore area of Guildford on Thursday, 6 July, police had been searching for two men in connection with the incident. Thanks to an excellent response from the public following the publishing of their photographs in the press and on television, the police tracked down one of the men to an address in Kennington, SE11, where he was later discovered to have taken his own life. And, whereas the search continues for the second man, police believe he was not party to the killing but may have been a witness to the perpetrator's leaving the scene. They are appealing for the man to come forward to provide a statement for their records. The victim of the shooting and another man who was at the scene are both recovering from injuries received at the time."

Lynsey had explained that the piece would appear on inside pages in the local press and that the abrupt closure of the case and low-key reporting had been directed by Special Branch, who were looking into the activities of the two men, though not in relation to their involvement with this particular case. It was not a new experience for most of those present at the briefing to have cases snatched away from them in such a way, but when it concerned an attack on a police colleague it was a disappointment to say the least.

The only new information to come to light was a piece of the puzzle relating to the second man. A policeman's jacket and cap had been found in the boot of the BMW at Abington services before the vehicle had been taken away by Border Police. It pointed to his means of escape from Westmore Guest House. They concluded that he must have hidden them somewhere in the yard behind the building and put them on when he went outside, supposedly for the cigarette. They would go well with his navy trousers and white shirt, and, with the numbers of police around the site at the time, it would be relatively easy for an unfamiliar officer to walk from the scene without arousing suspicion.

Harry sighed and placed the copy of the statement back on his desk, picking up the second sheet. It was the document he had signed on Friday at the MI5 headquarters on Millbank. He read it through again, wondering how far-reaching its influence was and whether he should make his next phone call. If for no other reason, curiosity demanded that he did. He scrolled through the Recents list on his iPhone and touched the name. It was answered within three seconds.

"DI Leasing."

"Hi, Hannah, Harry Waters here."

"Hi, Harry. This is getting a regular thing. Are you coming to see us again?"

Harry laughed.

"Not yet, but who knows? I just wondered if you had access to the autopsy report on Walcott's death yet, or if not, when you might expect to. I know the case was snatched away from you, but I assume they will provide you with something to complete your record."

"If you're wondering about the cause of death, I can tell you that without the report."

Harry laughed again. "Have you got it?"

"Hold on, I'll check the case file and see if it's been posted yet."

Harry could hear the faint tapping of keys and the sound of Hannah humming a tune as she searched.

"Got it," she said. "Good timing, Harry. Posted just twenty minutes ago. It's short and sweet, as you'd expect. Any particular part of interest? And I was right about the cause of death, by the way – bullet to the head."

"You're wasted in that job, you know. First page, probably, what was the recorded height of the victim?"

"Say that again."

"His height. Heel to top of his head, or where the top of his head used to be."

"I know what height means, Harry, but it's just about the last question I expected. Why?"

"It's just to settle a silly argument between me and Nat."

"Okay, let's see… one-seven-five."

"What's that in old money?"

"Hold on… a tad under five-nine."

"Is that a full tad or just part of one?"

"Given the head had to be reconstructed to measure him, I think you can call it five-nine."

"Thanks, Hannah. Look, it was good working with you again, even though we didn't achieve anything."

"Yes, it was nice to catch up. Good hunting, Harry."

"You, too, Hannah."

Harry leaned back in his chair. "Five-nine," he said. "Not six feet."

He read through the signed document again, then looked for a long time at his iPhone. He put it away in his pocket.

"For the greater good. Something I'll live with."

*

Mags and Tom climbed up to the ridge behind the cottage and looked across to the four Munros forming a semicircle to the east which marked the rough boundary of the Knoydart peninsula, recognised as the remotest part of the whole United Kingdom. On a clear day such as this, it was difficult to argue against that classification. Tom pointed out the route he and Jason had walked the previous day from the side of Loch Hourn.

"Just tell me again why you decided to walk and not fly in like normal people."

Tom smiled. "Just guys bonding," he said. "Girls wouldn't understand."

"Do you want a poke in what's left of your ribs?"

"It's not far from the truth, actually. I thought it was important we took time out to share what had happened to us before we got here and there hadn't been a chance to do that since we met up the previous day. I think it was time well spent, even though it was only three hours or so."

"So not *only* to make a dramatic entrance, then?"

"Well, there was that as well."

They laughed and turned to look over to the west, where they picked out the jagged rocky teeth of the Cuillin Hills on Skye, the ridge which had lent its name to the Farcuillin Lodge where they were now.

They had all stayed up until the early hours of the morning. Tom had told them the bare minimum he could get away with, deflecting wave after wave of Katey's questions with the promise that all would be revealed tomorrow – later today – with the arrival of the two men who had saved his life. Jason had been even less forthcoming, hiding behind the same promise. The fact that they were there – back from the dead – seemed enough to satisfy the three women for the time being. Any other time, Tom thought, they wouldn't have got away so painlessly with Katey's demand for explanations.

They heard the sound of the helicopter before they spotted it in the clear blue sky heading towards them from the north. Tom checked his watch.

"Eleven-thirty. They're early."

Scrambling down the same track Tom and Jason had used yesterday; they reached the lodge as the chopper touched down on the helipad close by. Two men descended as the rotors slowed to a halt, dipping as they did so. The tallest of the two checked his watch then called something up to the pilot. After a few seconds, the props began to turn again, waiting for the two visitors to get clear before lifting off.

Tom led Mags by the hand to greet them, introducing her first, then the two arrivals.

"Mags, meet Marty Kade and Mike Needham, the two guys

who saved my life." They each stretched out a hand, but Mags stepped closer and embraced them both.

"Thank you," she said, her voice full of genuine gratitude.

"You are very welcome, ma'am," Kade said with a wide smile. "He's proved pretty useful since then."

"Well, he's not been much use here since he arrived. He has told us virtually *nothing* about what happened to him, but has promised you will tell us *everything*. So, I hope you've got your script ready."

Kade laughed. "I'll do my very best to make him look really good."

Katey, Jason and Leila were standing in the doorway. Kade looked across and walked over. He held out his hand.

"Hi, Jason. We were never properly introduced."

★

"I'm not sure at which point during the mission I decided not to go through with it. It might have been as early as our first meeting in the cabin on Ardnamurchan, before we even left the mainland."

Kade was seated in one of the three armchairs which, along with a four-seater sofa, were positioned around a long, low table in front of the inglenook fireplace at one end of the huge open-plan area which comprised the whole of the Lodge's ground floor. All the seats were occupied, with Mags and Tom, Katey and Jason squeezed together on the sofa, and Leila and Mike in the other chairs. Just outside the circle, Jack slept peacefully in his cot, moving just often enough to suppress the volume of the conversation.

"The main objective of the mission was to get this young man…" he nodded at Jason "… off Hotel St Kilda. He'd been showing off his IT skills – building a transmitter/receiver, contacting God knows who offshore, messing with systems on the platform. A liability, in fact, and posing a risk to the security of the platform by possibly attracting attention from forces who might want to exploit this outpost of the United Kingdom. Which is ironic, I guess, given what's just happened, eight months later.

"Mr Needham here, who designed the platform, knew of a means of access which we could use to reach the exiles. We took a team of six on a patrol boat, piloted by Mike, to within a few miles of Alpha, then the insertion force of five in a submersible to the structure itself. Leaving one as driver, four of the team – including me and Tom – climbed the inside of one of the columns and gained access to the viewing corridor of the platform. I should point out that Tom believed that the sole purpose of the raid was to rescue Jason so he could reunite him with you, Katey – and with Leila, of course. He had no idea it was an official op and believed we were working for him alone. He agreed to pay for our services himself and was included on the team ostensibly in case Jason needed convincing to leave, rather than relying on him trusting four complete strangers dressed in black and carrying automatic weapons. But in reality, Tom was there because we planned to leave him behind.

"We also had another patrol boat, which we used as a diversion to draw most of the exiles away from the radio room, where we managed to hold Jason's attention with some mysterious messages from our Russian comrade on the second boat. You can be proud of him, Katey," he smiled. "The diversionary tactic we used was a beautiful lady doing a pole dance around the mast of the second vessel. So, while around ninety-nine percent of the exiles were watching Lydia van Roden, Jason remained steadfastly at his post listening to Sergei reciting Russian nursery rhymes."

Katey turned to Jason, pulling slightly away from him.

"*Really*? Is that true?"

"That she was beautiful? *Definitely*. But I hardly noticed. My standards are so high."

They all laughed and Katey leaned back into him.

"Well, we achieved the first part of the mission. Disabled the transmitter, rescued Jason and I even got to leave Tom behind – for about thirty seconds. Closed the hatch with him still on the observation corridor with the exiles. Left him my Glock with live ammo to use on whoever he wanted – I figured, probably himself. I even thought that, once he was out of sight, I just might change my mind back, and refocus on the mission. Not to be; he was with us again within a minute and we were on our way down.

"Tom, at this stage, still believed he and Jason would be brought here to this lodge by chopper where they would hide out until they decided what to do next. The rationale for this location was that, because of its remoteness, it was out of range of the national tracking system for the surgical implants. Jason still had his implant, although Mike had disabled it long enough for us to get him away. But the *real* plan was that, by now, Tom wouldn't be there at all and Jason would be taken off and away for debriefing. As it turned out, they lifted both of them onto HMS *Jura*, and we joined them there later where they lay at anchor off South Uist in the Outer Hebrides.

"My boss was real pissed at me for not leaving Tom behind. Our hostage rescue company is a private concern. We are not paid a salary out of a defence budget funded by taxes like the Special Forces or the main military. We agree a contract price for a job of work with a sliding scale of success criteria. And not a linear scale, either. Doing only half the job was going to rob my team of around eighty percent of their fee. *Unless*… I finished what I'd started.

"So, the new plan was that Tom would be put into a coma with a tracker implant, like Jason's, attached to his chest just below the skin, where it would quickly become detached as the corpse decomposed or was eaten away. These devices are powered by the host – the human body – through a heartbeat or pulse. He would then be dropped into the sea close to the Shiant Islands, where he would drown. The drug he'd be given would be strong enough to prevent him being revived by the shock of the water. A post-mortem, should his body be found, would say natural causes. *Legally*, it would be murder."

"*Christ*! That's *barbaric*." Katey could not stay quiet any longer. "I can't believe all this."

"It does get better, Katey; just stay with me. So, we carried out the plan to the letter – almost. Tom was drugged and loaded into a chopper along with me and Rico, who was one of the four-man Alpha insertion team. We took off and flew to the Shiants, joined on the way by a second chopper from Benbecula. We hovered over the designated drop point and the body was rolled out of the aircraft into The Minch off the north tip of one of the islands. In the IT suite on *Jura*, Mike watched with the boss as the signals from the implant flatlined then ceased altogether. The escort chopper confirmed the co-ordinates of the drop, which were cross-checked with the ones on their screen. A week or so later, a boat was grounded on that same island with Tom's holdall in it, containing clothes and other personal stuff. *Fait accompli*, as Jules would say. We all got paid, and Tom was presumed drowned while trying to do God knows what."

Kade paused and reached for his glass of water on the table in front of him. He took a long drink then looked round at the faces of his audience with a wide smile.

"Any questions?"

After a long silence, Katey said, "I just can't help thinking that there might be more to it than that."

Kade laughed. "You're right, I did miss out a couple of details." He placed the glass back on the table.

"While we were waiting to leave, Mike fitted me with the implant they'd removed from Jason. It wasn't stitched under the skin, like Tom's, but inserted into a shallow cut on my chest and secured by tape. Close and tight enough, though, to power the chip."

He paused and looked across at the engineer.

"All the exiles on Alpha are fitted with surgical implants," Mike said, "which relay data on a number of health indicators and are also used to check the location of the person on the platform using a computerised schematic model of the structure, something we call a digital lattice. At this point, just minutes before take-off, I had readings on two separate screens and was monitoring both Kade *and* Tom. Once Tom was on board the chopper, and while I was still alone in the IT room, I switched off Tom's screen. So, when the boss joined me it was just Kade we were watching, but, because the signal was clearly from inside the aircraft, there was no reason to doubt that it was Tom."

"Halfway to the drop zone," Kade took up the story again, "we were joined by the second chopper from Benbecula. On board with the pilot was a sniper, who had instructions to shoot us down if I fouled up again and didn't make the drop. Well, we did make the drop, only it was me who went into The Minch, not Tom. Because the second detail I missed out was the fact that there was a fourth man in the aircraft. Jules – the other member of the insertion team – was already hidden in the toilet cubicle before Rico and I boarded with Tom. On the flight to the Shiants, I put on Tom's clothes. Jules was already wearing the same gear as me, including a beanie.

When the door of the chopper opened, Jules rolled me out into the sea, and slid the door closed again.

"It was good that we did this in half-light, because although Jules is about my height and build, he is Senegalese, his colour is about the same as Jason's, so he wouldn't have passed a close inspection. But as the only person watching the action closely through binoculars was the sniper on the escort chopper – and he was a guy called John Deverall – we probably didn't need to worry. Anyway, after bobbing about for a minute or so in the water, I stripped the chip from my chest and let it float away. Mike tells me it gave off some unusual patterns of data for the half minute or so after I released it, but, as Tom's situation was unprecedented, there was no suggestion of any malfunction or such. And with nothing powering it the signal died very quickly, as you'd expect if the host expired.

"Rico, with Tom and Jules, carried on north to refuel in Stornoway, then on to Mingulay, which had been the start point for the mission. I was picked out of the sea when both choppers had left the scene by a dinghy crewed by our Russian poet. Sergei rowed us back to the dinghy's mother ship – Archer-Two – anchored off Harris in a remote inlet, where Lydia was waiting for us. Before first light we were through the Sound of Harris on a course heading south down the west side of the Long Island to avoid any chance of meeting up with *Jura*. We linked up with the other guys on Mingulay early afternoon.

"Tom stayed unconscious for around twelve hours, but his breathing was deep and steady, and he eventually came round demanding to be fed. So, we figured he was okay."

He smiled and looked across at Katey.

"*Now* are there any questions?"

"Only about five hundred," she said.

"Fire away, Katey."

"In no particular order," she said, leaning forward. "That was really exciting, Kade – I mean, *really* – but it was eight months ago. Why has it taken this long for us to find out what happened to two people who mean so much to us and who we thought we'd lost forever? Didn't anyone stop to think we ought to know they were still around?" She turned to her father. "I guess that's one for you."

Tom sighed. "Jason can tell you his own story. *I* didn't know he was alive until a couple of days ago. As for me, I'm sorry, but it had to be managed carefully. It had to be thought through. For one thing, there was no guarantee there wouldn't be a second attempt. In fact, it was almost certain there would have to be, because the people who wanted to get rid of me couldn't allow me back. So, they had to be made to believe they'd succeeded until it was decided what to do."

"Who are '*they*'?" Katey asked. "Kade keeps referring to 'the boss'. Who is this guy?"

"*I* can't tell you that, Katey," Kade said, "because of an unwritten protocol which binds us to secrecy. And for that same reason, because he's part of my team, neither can your dad. But you'll have to know to be able to make any sense of all this, and there is someone in this room who *can* enlighten you."

Mags, Katey and Leila looked across at Mike, but it was Jason who spoke.

"I guess that's me." He looked at Kade, who nodded.

*

It took a few minutes for the shock of hearing the name to dispel, Mags in silent, angry disbelief and Katey in a torrent of expletive-laden abuse, for which she apologised as she regained her composure.

"Before we vilify Grace Goody," Tom said, "let's not forget what she has achieved over the past few days and the price she has paid for it. She risked her life to save nearly eight hundred people on Alpha, a couple of hundred on St Kilda, over fifty hostages on the *Mastodon*, and, as it turned out, given the device they had on board, possibly tens of thousands more on the Outer Hebrides. That is Grace Goody's most recent contribution to this country, and what she should be remembered for. Yes, she took a step beyond what was acceptable, but remember, she has a boss, too, and, without going into detail, a boss who had a very persuasive hold over her. I am not saying Grace was an innocent in all that happened, but she was under a lot of pressure from above."

"*Above?*" Katey said. "*Who* above?"

"I think you can probably work that out, Katey, but for now, I'll ask you to be patient until I can share that part of the story with you. I promise it will be very soon."

"Okay, then, but why? *Why* did you have to die? The police were looking for you in connection with the killings, so why didn't she just hand you over? I thought the Ministerial Director of Justice was on the same side as the police, for Christ's sake."

Mags had so far been listening in silence with a look of disbelief. When she spoke, it was softly and with hesitation, as if she feared the answer. "Tell me, Jason, did Grace have a hand in what happened to you and Jack? Was she involved in framing you?"

"No." Tom and Jason answered together. "In fact," Tom went on, "she believed very strongly in their innocence, and was worried that their convictions could be overturned if the key witnesses changed their stories or let something slip."

"Which would have looked really bad for the NJR," Mags put in, "and, by association, the government, Jack and Jay having already been irretrievably removed in different ways, and so..." She hesitated, choking on her words.

"And so, the witnesses had to be silenced." Tom continued for her. "Grace was responsible for the murders in Guildford and Dorking – not hands-on, of course, but she sanctioned them. I just happened to be in the wrong places at all the *right* times for her to be able to link me to the killings. It didn't help that I'd been reeling around these places telling people I was going to get even with everyone who had a part in fixing up Jack and Jay." He turned to Katey. "And I was also telling people that we should reverse some of the provisions of the NJR and we'd made a big mistake with the offshore prison. Grace figured there were still enough people around who would listen to me. So, to answer your question, Princess, getting rid of me made perfect sense. No-one to shake up the new system, and case closed on the serial killings."

Kade leaned forward. "For what it's worth, I know for a fact that Grace bitterly regretted what she did regarding Tom. Just before she lost consciousness on the *Mastodon*, she recognised him, and I'd like to think she died knowing he was still alive and that she *didn't* kill him. I believe she deserves to rest in peace on that count, at least."

There was silence for a long time. Tom checked his watch.

"I'm going to be out of here with Kade and Mike in thirty minutes, when the chopper returns." He turned to Jason. "I think it's about time they heard from you."

*

Jason sighed. "That's the first time I've heard the whole story. I knew about Mr Brown being wanted by the police, of course, and how, after he'd got me off Alpha, he'd gone missing. But other than that, this is all new to me. And while I've been listening, one thing I've tried not to lose sight of is that Grace Goody saved my life – twice. She gave me a new ID when I went on to Alpha, so no-one would link me to Mr Brown through Katey. She figured I wouldn't survive very long if they knew who I was. And if you'd seen the reactions of the guys on there when Kade did tell them who I was... well, you'd know she was right. Then, when they took me off, she saved me again. The deal was, I get a new ID – *another* new ID – and work at the Cyber Security Centre at GCHQ in Cheltenham. I'd be just one of the team there, but she'd have a direct line in to me if and when she had a special job to do.

"She made it clear that I couldn't return to life as Jason Midanda. There was no way of explaining how that could have happened. The incentive she offered me was that, sometime in the future, when all parties had been properly briefed and fully understood, it might be possible for Joseph Kimani – that's me – to meet Katey Tomlinson-Brown at some function or other. Sort of accidentally bump into each other, in a club or at a concert. Total strangers, instantly falling for each other." He smiled at Katey and pulled her closer to him. "I don't know if she really meant it, but it was something for me to cling on to.

"She took a hell of a risk, even with me under threat of death if I tried to contact any of you before she said it was okay. And that's where I've been the last eight months; just waiting, hoping. She came to see me a couple of times – and each time I thought 'this is it, I'm out of here'... or something. But it was just to check if I was okay." Jason paused and swallowed. "And then, with just about her dying breath, she told Mr Brown I was alive and where to find me. I know what she did was terribly wrong, but she's the reason I'm here today, and that the friends I made on Hotel St Kilda are still alive."

They sat in silence for a long time.

"You mentioned Uncle Jad." Katey said.

"John Deverall," Tom said, "now into his third life, was one of the observers on the chopper from Benbecula that escorted us to the drop zone. Soon after the incident, he checked with his boss – a brigadier, and Section Head in a branch of the secret service – which person or persons had sanctioned the action against me. He didn't say I was still alive, because he thought the Brigadier would have been party to the action. But it turned out that he believed my disappearance was due to some sort of accident which had occurred while the police were looking for me. The same as you and everyone else were meant to believe, in fact."

"He was pretty pissed about it," Kade said. "He felt the dispatching of a national hero fell well outside their motto, 'For the greater good'. He put Grace under close surveillance, only to discover that *her* boss was part of the conspiracy and, as you know, he's as high as they go. And the fact that the body had not turned up was making him very nervous."

"So, the Brigadier decided that it would settle their nerves if my body *did* turn up," Tom went on, "and put them off their guard, perhaps. So, at the end of last year, he dispatched a couple of guys to the NAFC centre on Shetland – part of a university, with a specialist on ocean currents and such. They found out from this professor where a body was likely to turn up if it went into the sea where I did."

"He means, where *I* did," Kade put in.

"Yes, of course, where *Kade* did." Tom laughed. "The following week, in early January this year, the Brigadier and Jad selected a body the same height, weight, blood group as me – a recent military death-in-service, I assume. They even had it tattooed with the SBS insignia." He pulled up the right sleeve of his polo shirt to show the sword and banner design on his upper arm. "A bit of an unnecessary detail, if you ask me. Then – and this gets a bit gruesome – to be passed off as me, it had to deteriorate beyond recognition. It was submerged in a steel cage just off the Shiant Islands and left to feed the fishes.

"Then, six weeks or so ago, a certain Tony Dobson started raising questions about a couple of pieces of evidence in the police case against me. I won't go into details, but the issue reached these two high-powered conspirators and the Brigadier decided it would be a good time for my remains to be discovered. The body – what was left of it – was put on some rocks on the south coast of Skye near Bonnie Prince Charlie's cave, which is a popular walkers' spot. A member of the Section was dispatched to Skye to join, then lead, a group of walkers to the cave where they… accidentally… discovered the remains. As expected, there wasn't much of me left to ID, but before they put it in the cage, they'd attached to the body a waterproof money belt with my driving licence, bank cards, keys…"

"In fact," Mags interrupted, "everything except your Visa Debit card for the third account and Granny Brown's locket."

They all turned to see her smiling broadly.

"How…? What…?" Katey began.

"You remember three weeks or so ago, when I went to London."

"To sign some papers?" Katey said.

"Well, it *wasn't* to sign any papers, it was to visit the bank. I got a call from Will Parks, the manager, to tell me someone had used your dad's debit card and advising me *again* that I should cancel it. I met him at the bank and he showed me a CCTV still of the person who had used the card. It was impossible to see the person's face, but what was quite clear was that he was wearing Granny Brown's locket, round his neck but outside his jacket."

"The bank account was a sort of signal we set up when I was in the SBS," Tom said. "Sometimes it was necessary for me to go missing as part of an operation. We kept this third account with a few hundred pounds in it so if I wasn't able to contact your mum direct, but I could access a cashpoint somewhere, I'd make a withdrawal and your mum would know I was okay by checking the account. In fact, this is the only time we've ever used it."

"But it worked – along with the locket," Mags said. "And I think I owe it to Will to buy him lunch and explain why I didn't take his advice."

"So, you knew Dad was alive three weeks ago but didn't think to tell me?" Katey turned to Mags.

"Believed, hoped, *prayed,* of course, but I didn't *know*. Not one hundred percent, not after so long. I just couldn't risk telling you; couldn't risk another crushing blow if it turned out not to be true. So, I decided to wait. I mean, it's not like you were grieving every day, in constant, abject despair or anything."

Katey looked at Tom. "Oh, don't believe her, Dad. I never stopped crying, not for a moment. Mum, how could you *say* that?"

"The way I see it," Tom said, frowning as the others laughed, "your mum has nothing to gain by lying, whereas..."

"Anyway," Katey went on, back on the offensive. "You've told us about the first couple of days of your disappearance. What about the next eight months? Who's going first?" She looked from Tom to Kade and back. "Well?"

"Your dad's been part of our HRU for the whole of that time – that's hostage rescue unit, by the way. During that period, we've been on three missions together, all successful. He's been an invaluable addition to the team, although I guess I'm resigned to losing him now. But his legendary status within the group was guaranteed three days ago, when he personally prevented the detonation of that massive bomb on the *Mastodon*, which would have killed everybody on Hotel St Kilda – along with me and Tom and about twenty others on the vessel. If you want my objective opinion, Katey, he's a bit special."

There was silence for a few moments. Katey looked across at Tom and smiled.

"That's what he's always told us," she said.

The laughter roused Jack from his sleep and his joyful gurgling from the cot sounded as though he was joining in the joke, prompting more laughter.

"He'll need changing," Mags said, getting up from the sofa and pulling Tom to his feet. "Come on, Katey will watch to make sure you do it right before you leave. I'll just finish packing and see you in a few minutes."

"Packing?"

"Yes, packing. You don't seriously expect me to let you out of my sight again so soon?"

CHAPTER FIFTY-ONE

Katey, Jason and Leila, with Jack snuggling in his sister's arms, watched and waved as the helicopter lifted off and headed south towards Glasgow to pick up the flight to Heathrow. The two women turned to go inside, leaving Jason still with his eyes fixed on the diminishing dot in the clear sky.

"You coming in?" Katey asked.

"Just give me a minute."

"*One* minute," she said, screwing up her eyes into a frown. "No more."

Jason grinned. "I doubt if I'll last that long, to be honest."

Katey went inside and Jason looked across at the faint, dark line on the horizon, the islands of the Outer Hebrides, remembering for a moment what lay far beyond, before his mind settled on the meeting with Kade and Mike which had just ended, and his decision to withhold the most important part of his story.

Grace Goody had visited him twice at the Doughnut in Cheltenham – that bit was true. The first occasion, soon after New Year, was nothing much more than a social call, to check how he was settling in. Her second visit was five months later on the morning of the tenth of June. He remembered the date because it was exactly one year to the day since Jason had said goodbye to Katey with a desperate promise that they would be together again sometime in the future. In fact, when Jordy, his supervisor, had told him he had a visitor, his mind was so full of Katey he thought for a moment that somehow it might be her, or Grace telling him they would soon be reunited. Instead, she did not even smile or speak his name; she seemed agitated, almost afraid, and without actually threatening him, she had made it clear that any possibility of ever seeing Katey again was dependant on his completing a task, and very quickly.

The task was to gain access to a person's email and redirect a message in his Draft folder which was on a twenty-four-hour digital fuse. This person, she explained, had some information, which could be damaging to the government. He was an active agent, but one who was in a position to threaten national security if he chose. The person updated an attachment to the email each day and reset the delay to send.

It was not something new to his department – he was aware that several of his colleagues had been involved in similar work, although it was a first for him. The person in question – a Mr Jamie Walcott – proved a more-than-worthy adversary; his security system was more complex than any Jason had hacked before and he struggled for a long time to make any progress.

The breakthrough had come after four weeks when he breached the final firewall. Grace had made it very clear that he should not have sight of the attachment, reminding him of his legal undertaking under the Official Secrets Act. However, Jason's curiosity, fuelled by Grace's demeanour at their last meeting, had got the better of him and he opened the attached file.

What he found in the attachment's three sub-files had horrified him. A catalogue of murder, with his benefactor removing everyone who posed any threat – either real or simply perceived – to her achieving her goals, including the man who had rescued him from Alpha. It made him realise that, once he had informed Grace that the problem of the email had been resolved, he was much more likely to die than to be reunited with Katey.

He remembered Detective Inspector Jo Cottrell from his and Jack's trial. How, even though she had been appearing as a witness for the prosecution, she had tried her hardest to mitigate her evidence to Jack's advantage. It had not proved popular with the prosecuting counsel. She was someone, he had always felt, who would intuitively put justice ahead of all other considerations, including her own professional safety in the face of senior authority.

He changed the addressee's name on Walcott's email and sent it to her. Then he deleted the record from the Sent box.

The great irony, of course, was that at the time he was sending the email, Grace was arriving at London Royal Hospital, where doctors had failed, it seemed, in an attempt to save her life, as she succumbed to injuries received saving hundreds of people who until eight months ago comprised his friends and co-residents. Perhaps a heroic death was better than a public scandal, and a more fitting legacy.

It was hearing that from Tom and Kade that had decided him to withhold the information about the email. And it occurred to him that, without his telling that part of the story, no-one would ever know how that message got to DI Cottrell.

"Three minutes, fifty seconds and counting."

He came out of his trance at the sounding of Katey's voice from the doorway. She was frowning at her watch.

"Four minutes."

He turned and ran towards her.

*

Their hands were clasped together on the central arm rest and Mags's head was on his shoulder. They had been like that ever since they had taken off from Glasgow and neither had the slightest inclination to move.

"So, what about Andrew? Or can't you tell *me* either?"

Tom placed his other hand on top of hers.

"That's what we discussed at my meeting with Jackie and the Brigadier on Saturday. Jackie, as First Minister, will be taking over from Andrew as he recedes from public life due to health problems, a cross which he has bravely borne in recent months and in particular in leading us through the hijacking crisis. His stock, I understand, has never been higher with his counterparts in Norway and the Netherlands for the safe return of their nationals from the *Mastodon*.

"Then, following a period of recuperation at a safe, undisclosed and *guarded* location, and when everything is back to normal, he will be taken, to quote the Brigadier, 'from there to a place where he will be – if not hung by the neck until dead – hung out to dry in disgrace. In short, the bastard will get what he deserves'. Unquote. He's got a wonderful turn of phrase for someone more used to barking out monosyllabic commands. He had a conversation recently, by the way, with your good friend Jo Cottrell, who apparently lectured him on the difference between legality and morality. I think he rather liked the distinction. It wouldn't surprise me if it appeared in a frame on the wall of his office very shortly."

"And Beta – what happens to the new wing of the hotel?"

"It will go ahead as planned, but they're reviewing the facilities' role for the future. It could become a sort of reform centre with on-site monitoring rather than a one-way ticket. Release would be based on individual assessment rather than an end-date. That was my recommendation, anyway."

"And why the change of mind?"

Tom took his time answering, as if he wasn't too sure himself.

"I don't know what I expected to find when we went onto Alpha last year. I had no idea at all, no picture in my mind. And we only had contact with the guys there for a few minutes, but what I found was a real community, although, of course, unlike any I've experienced before. They looked sort of... *together*. Like they belonged *somewhere*, and had made the most of what they had. And then on Friday, when it was over and the *Mastodon* was pulling away from the Hotel, they waved to us and applauded..." Tom's voice cracked a little and he swallowed. Mags squeezed his hand. "As if they still felt part of us. I guess, if they can co-exist in those circumstances, they deserve a second chance back in the real world. But only a *second* chance – not a third and fourth. So, Hotel St Kilda should still be there, ready and waiting." He turned to her and smiled. "Anyway, *they* will need to decide that."

"It's ironic, don't you think, that the two people who did most to put those eight hundred lost souls lost on Alpha were the same two who did most to save their lives. But you keep saying 'they'. Are you not planning to be part of that decision? Are you not going to be – how did Kade say you put it – 'one of those cretinous bastards sitting comfortably behind a desk'?"

Tom laughed. "No, thank you. I've served my time."

"So, what *is* next for you? Kade sort of implied you'd resigned from Thunderbirds."

"That's what I'll be discussing with Jackie tomorrow while you're dining out with Will Parks. *However*," he said, squeezing as close to Mags as the seating would allow, "I think I'll stick around Farcuillin for a while. I was thinking how nice it would be if Jack had someone to play with."

Mags smiled and squeezed his hand harder. "I'm getting a bit old for that sort of thing, you know. It might not happen right away. But I suppose, as they say, 'if at first you don't succeed, try, try again'."

"It was the 'try, try again' that I was looking forward to."

CHAPTER FIFTY-TWO

Saturday, 15 July

The initial whiteness morphed slowly into pale indistinct shapes which shimmered and swayed as if they were underwater. The woman's face in the midst of all this twisted and flexed hideously until it finally steadied to a blurred image on which the initial anxiety changed to shock as the eyes widened and the mouth smiled. The woman leaned forward, peering at something at the side of the bed, then gently massaging the pillows. Her lips moved, her eyes still smiling, but the voice she heard seemed to be inside her own head.

"Welcome back."

The face was gone, to be replaced by another; a man; a man she recognised. She tried to say his name but seemed to have lost the ability to speak. The man was smiling, too; he held her hand; she smiled back, then closed her eyes again.

The next time she opened them, everything was much clearer. The room, the woman – checking screens, securing tubes to her arms and adjusting a Velcro strap round her head – and the man, seated on a chair next to her bed, either still holding her hand or holding it again. He turned to the nurse and nodded. She gave the patient a wide smile and left the room.

"John Deverall, what are you doing here?" Her voice was small but clear.

"It's visiting time."

"Just remind me, are you alive or dead at the moment? It will give me a clue as to where I am." She gave a little sniffed laugh and grimaced with the discomfort.

"I'm between deaths at the moment, so we're *both* alive. How do you feel, Jess? Or perhaps the question should be, can you feel anything at all yet?"

"I'm not sure how I feel… *what* did you call me? You could at least get my name right. It's Grace."

"You're wrong, Jess. Grace Goody is dead. She finally succumbed to the injuries she sustained in heroically foiling a plot to detonate a nuclear bomb and, later, an explosive vest. Can you remember?"

Grace tried to force herself up on her elbows but dropped back onto the pillow. She lay still for a full minute, breathless with the effort.

"I remember standing at the edge of the deck for a long time with el Taqha, and him ready to activate his suicide vest. I don't remember dying. What the hell's going on?"

"You're in a Ministry of Defence Hospital Unit in deepest Surrey. You were moved from London Royal three days ago, when it was officially confirmed that you would not survive. Incidentally, at the time that is what they believed. But Grace Goody's demise had been decided before that. Your actual death will be announced very soon, but, as you were showing signs of recovery, it seemed only right that you should hear about it first."

John Deverall was smiling broadly now. Grace remained silent, feeling too weak to try and understand.

"Walcott's insurance claim went through, accidentally, as it happens. Someone hacked his files and sent it to the police. 'The truth is out there', to quote *The X Files*. If Grace dies, nothing about her in that claim will come to light and it will be as a hero. If she lives, it will be impossible to protect her from the shit that will hit the fan. You've been under surveillance since Tom's disappearance. The Brigadier was not well pleased that you chose to get rid of a national hero like Mr Brown, and neither was I, for that matter. But the hijacking changed everything. After what you did, saving so many people, it seemed appropriate that you deserved saving as well. As a person, but *not* as Grace Goody.

"They'll probably give Grace a state funeral, which you will not be required to attend, of course. So, from this moment, you are Jessica Grainger, a member of Phoenix Ops, working for the Brigadier. We haven't fully established your CV yet but it's well on the way. You will have to move away from London for a while, possibly overseas, and they'll change your appearance – hopefully not *too* much – and you'll be assigned the sort of work that you were initially trained to do. And I for one, will be delighted to see you on board."

John stood up.

"Listen, I'm going to leave you to rest for a while. I'm not going far so I'll be around when you wake again."

"John." She gripped his hand, which was still holding hers. "Don't *I* get to decide this?"

He sat down again.

"Decide what? Whether to die a hero then live on to fulfil your destiny, or probably spend most of the rest of your life in prison, convicted of murder."

"Whose murder, John? That was Tom on the *Mastodon*, wasn't it? He's not dead?"

"No, he's not." He smiled. "Kade again. Just can't follow orders. Should be court-martialled and shot, if you ask me."

Grace closed her eyes, and tears escaped from under her lashes. "Thank God for that, at least."

John stood up again.

"I must go. But talking about Kade, he told me to give you a message. You asked him while you were on the *Jura* whether he had any vacancies on his team. Well, he said to tell you one has just come up. Apparently, Brig will be leaving to sort out a few things with his family and the Home Secretary. Kade said if you're still interested, let him know, and you're as good as in. What shall I tell him?"

Grace opened her eyes and smiled.

"Tell him Jessica says, 'Yes'."

EPILOGUE

The scene in the main bar of the Dog and Duck on the late afternoon of Saturday, 12 August, was one of joy and celebration. The room was a riot of laughter, with people moving continuously, forming and reforming into small groups as the guests mingled with each other, manoeuvring for position in their attempts to engage with Mr and Mrs David Gerrard.

Much of the laughter had centred around the incident on the steps of Cullen Field Registry Office as the couple emerged after the short ceremony to meet their friends waiting outside. David wore a three-piece navy lounge suit, white shirt and red tie, the colour of which matched the rose pinned to his lapel. Marie's summer dress was of the palest pink, ending just above her knees and fitting closely enough to show off her trim, youthful figure. Her wide-brimmed hat featured a red rose like David's; the neat bouquet was made up of white and pink carnations. Her four-inch heels made little impression on their sixteen-inch difference in height.

After the photographs and the cheers and congratulations, someone had reminded Marie that she must throw her flowers into the crowd to identify the next candidate for marriage. Marie had turned her back, glancing over her shoulder, as if preparing to make the throw. Then she had turned back, walked down the steps and handed the bouquet to Jo.

"I'm no good at throwing," she said. "I might have missed you."

The assembled guests in the bar included George Holland, as David's best man, Marie's two sisters – the younger of whom was her maid of honour – and their spouses, David's daughter, Linny, and her husband Caz, Jo and Seb, Harry Waters and Natalie Crusoe, Tony Dobson and Rebecca, along with a host of Marie's neighbours, and residents of Meadow Village. Eventually, they all gravitated to the seats around the room, awaiting Jed's invitation to attack the buffet set out for them in the restaurant. David, Marie and George had taken their usual seats in the bay window along with the other five people who traditionally occupied that particular table.

The noise level had fallen, and the laughter was already muted when the stranger entered, bringing a hush to the room. In fact, to some of those present he wasn't altogether a stranger. Without looking around he walked over to the bar and surveyed the selection of beers and lagers on draught. The man was smartly dressed in a well-tailored sports jacket, neatly pressed trousers, shirt and tie. What drew the attention and stalled the conversations of many of the wedding guests, however, was the familiarity of the hard face, the shaven head, the scarred features.

"Pint of San Miguel, please." The man turned and leaned with his back against the bar as he surveyed the room, picking out David before turning back again as Jed placed the glass in front of him.

"Three pound twenty, right?" the newcomer said, reaching into the inside pocket of his jacket.

Jed shook his head. "On the house, mate."

The man smiled and nodded then turned back to the room. David had left his seat and was walking towards him, meeting him halfway. He reached out his hand and the man shook it. David moved to the man's side, towering over him, and placed an arm round his shoulders.

"Ladies and gentlemen, I'd like to introduce you to Mr Danny Weaver, the man who saved my life."

*

The lone figure in the small churchyard had remained perfectly still for several minutes as the darkness gathered around him. The man walking towards him from behind stopped a couple of metres away and gave a little cough, so as not to startle him too much. The first man turned at the sound, his face a complete contradiction as he recognised the newcomer, tears of sadness above a smile of unbridled pleasure.

"Tom," he said, his voice hoarse. "I wasn't going to believe it until I actually saw you."

"Hello, George. I am *so* glad to see you again, my friend."

They stepped together, missing with a handshake as they went straight into a close embrace. When they stood back from each other, George looked into Tom's eyes as if he still couldn't quite believe his own.

"Have you been to the pub?" George asked.

"No, I came to see you. Didn't realise there was a function on. I asked someone outside if you were in there and he told me you'd left and might be here."

"I come every day."

They both turned to read the inscription on the stone plaque screwed to the low wall in front of them.

Irene Wendy Holland
Loving Mum and Nana
Beautiful Wife
Rest in Peace and Wait for Me

They remained silent for a long time, before Tom spoke.

"We've both had to live through the ultimate nightmare, George. Holding someone in your arms who means more than the world to you, feeling them slip away, knowing you can do nothing to stop it happening. I think that somehow makes you and me even closer as friends. I'd like to think so."

"I would, too."

They lapsed into silence for a while, then George turned to him, smiling again.

"Fancy a short walk to a nice little cottage, wherein lies refreshment?" he said.

"Are you not going back in the Dog?"

"No, I've said goodnight to the happy couple."

"In which case, yes, to the walk *and* the refreshment. I guess it'll be the Grouse again?"

George laughed. "Well, you never know. Life's full of little surprises, don't you think?"

ACKNOWLEDGEMENTS

Once again thanks are due to the many people who contributed in different ways to the production of this book.

To Mike Welton, a close friend for sixty years, who cheerfully provided me with the plans and workings of a morgue for the opening scene of the book. To Victor Groundwater, for the information regarding the hardware and operational details relating to oil exploration in the North Sea, and, along with my thanks, apologies to Vic for any variances which appear in the book for the benefit of the story. To Roger Ashpole, fellow student half a century ago, for kindly lending me his name to use for the head of the Security Service.

To Mark Fullerton of the NAFC Marine Centre in Scalloway, Shetland, for directing me to the source of information regarding tidal systems in The Minch, and to Paul Swain of the UK Hydrographic Office for allowing me to use their chart as part of the manuscript.

To all the people whose generous feedback and requests for a sequel to the trilogy have been a major force in motivating me to write *The Blue Men*. To my publisher, Matador, for making the whole experience of creating these books such an enjoyable one, and, as always and especially, to my editor, Gary Smailes of Bubblecow, for his detailed critique and invaluable advice following on from this.

To my family for their continuing encouragement, and especially to my wife, Carol, for her support and her patience in converting my vague – and frequently changing – ideas on the cover design into such an excellent final image.

Thank you all.

MICHAEL KNAGGS was born in Hull in 1944. He moved to Thurso, Caithness, in 1966 to work as an Experimental Officer for two years at Dounreay Atomic Power Station, before attaining a degree in chemistry at the University of Salford.

From 1970 up to his retirement in 2005, Michael worked for the Kellogg Company – the global breakfast cereal manufacturer – latterly as Human Resources Director with responsibility for pay and benefit policy across the company's European organisation.

The Blue Men is his fourth novel in the *Hotel St Kilda* series, and a sequel to the original trilogy.

He lives in Prestwich, Manchester, with his wife, Carol. Their passion is hill-walking, and over the past ten years they have completed many of the long-distance national trails, including the West Highland Way, twice. They have two children and two grandchildren.

Matador